'TIL DICE DO US PART

This Large Print Book carries the
Seal of Approval of N.A.V.H.

A BUNCO BABES MYSTERY

'TIL DICE DO US PART

GAIL OUST

KENNEBEC LARGE PRINT
A part of Gale, Cengage Learning

GALE
CENGAGE Learning

Detroit • New York • San Francisco • New Haven, Conn • Waterville, Maine • London

GALE
CENGAGE Learning

LIBRARY OF CONGRESS CATALOGING-IN-PUBLICATION DATA

Oust, Gail, 1943–
  'Til dice do us part : a Bunco Babes mystery / by Gail Oust.
    p. cm. — (Kennebec large print superior collection)
  ISBN-13: 978-1-4104-2676-5 (large print : softcover)
  ISBN-10: 1-4104-2676-9 (large print : softcover)
    1. Retirees—Fiction. 2. Murder—Investigation—Fiction. 3. Retirement communities—South Carolina—Fiction. 4. Large type books. I. Title. II. Title: Until dice do us part.
PS3620.U7645T555 2010
813'.6—dc22   2010013849

Published in 2010 by arrangement with NAL Signet, a member of Penguin Group (USA) Inc.

Printed in the United States of America
1 2 3 4 5   14 13 12 11 10

ED191

*To Beth and Greg, Brianna and Caitlin,
and my sweet Caden.
You make my world go round.*

ACKNOWLEDGMENTS

In a production of any sort, there are always people behind the scenes who help make it a success. I'd like to take a moment to thank those who so generously shared their expertise during the writing of *'Til Dice Do Us Part.* Sometimes it really does take a village.

First on my list is Suzanne Burnes, professional photographer, neighbor, and friend. You truly are kindness and talent personified. Next comes Jim Montgomery, lieutenant, Detroit Police Department, retired. Who else would have arrived on my doorstep armed and dangerous and ready to prove the big bang theory? Any errors are mine alone. Then there's Fran McClain, my all-time favorite steel magnolia. Your wit and wisdom of how things work in a community theater helped me pull this off. I can't mention community theater without thanking the cast and crew of the Mighty Arts Players of Savannah Lakes Village. In the same vein, thanks to Bess Park, artistic director, Greenwood Community Theatre. Both of these groups graciously allowed me to be a mouse in the corner during rehearsals. Thankfully, no one broke a leg — at least not while I was around. Bob Stockton, I appreciate your PR help. I'm happy you can be easily bribed with food. And not to be left out, John and Ann McNab for sharing the exploits of "that darn cat." Sorry I had to turn him orange, but we all know why. Angela Koski, you rode to my rescue with your timely list of abbreviations. No one knows texting better than a teenager. Thanks, everyone!

I can't forget to give special mention to the Babes' very own fairy godmother, my wonderful agent, Jessica Faust at BookEnds, LLC.

And last but by no means least, my hubby, Bob, who never minds late dinners and will even eat burnt offerings. Thanks for patiently listening to the trials and tribulations of imaginary characters in return for hearing about your great drives, mind-boggling chips, and missed putts. It's a fair exchange.

CHAPTER 1

"Yoo-hoo, everyone! I'm baaack!" Claudia Connors Ledeaux burst into the room, looking larger than life in a black leather mini, matching waist-length jacket, four-inch stilettos, and flaming red hair.

The Bunco Babes and I were momentarily rendered speechless. No mean task, let me tell you. The Babes like to talk even more than we like to play bunco, our favorite dice game. We excel at both.

Tonight we were gathered at Pam Warner's for our bimonthly get-together. Granted, some may think bunco a silly, mindless game, but it's right up our alley. No skill, no finesse, no strategy. Dice just make it look serious. Shake, rattle, and toss. No previous experience required. The game couldn't be simpler.

"Claudia, honey, welcome home," I told her as my addled brain began to function again. I jumped from the sofa and ran to give her a hug. "We missed you."

"Kate McCall!" Claudia exclaimed, returning my hug. "Missed you, too."

Claudia is the twelfth member of our little band of bunco players. Several months back, she ran off with a man she met on the Internet. But she couldn't get away from the Babes. We pride ourselves on being well informed. If cell phones were an Olympic event, we'd be medalists. According to all accounts, this guy, Lance Ledeaux, was unemployed, light on money, and heavy on charm. When he and Claudia first hooked up, he'd been residing in Atlanta, a mere one hundred fifty miles to the west as the crow flies. The pair took off in a rented RV ostensibly to visit the Grand Canyon. Somewhere along the way, their plans took a detour. The pair got hitched in Vegas by an Elvis impersonator in a little chapel off the Strip. Vegas, I heard, was the closest they ever got to a natural wonder. To each his own, I suppose. The lovebirds have just returned to take up residence here in Serenity Cove Estates, a retirement community for "active" adults.

I stepped aside to let the others have a turn. I used the opportunity to study Claudia more closely. There were other changes besides the hair color. Her style of dress had undergone a transformation as well. Instead of the usual trendy but classy fashion she had favored in the past, she now opted for flamboyant bordering on flashy. And flashy, as we all know, rhymes with trashy. Of course, bless her heart, I'd never say anything to hurt her feelings.

"Your hair . . . ," squeaked Polly, our septuagenarian. "It's so . . ."

"Red," Claudia supplied with a grin. "Like it?"

"Yeah, red. That's the word I was looking for." Polly turned to Gloria, her daughter, and asked, "Do you think I'd look hot with red hair?"

"Mother, really," Gloria said with a weary shake of her salt-and-pepper bob that set her hoop earrings swaying. "Isn't it enough to be blond at your age?"

Polly fluffed her curls. "Can't blame a gal for wanting to maintain a youthful image. Maybe I need a new man in my life."

Connie Sue, the Babes' perennial Southern belle and former Miss Peach Princess, peered back toward the foyer. "Speakin' of men, where's that bridegroom of yours, honey chile? We're all just dyin' to meet the man who swept you off your feet."

Claudia shrugged out of her leather jacket and tossed it over the back of a nearby chair, revealing a shape-hugging emerald green sweater that showed considerable cleavage. "Lance is dying to meet all of you, too. He'll be along later."

"What made you decide to return home this soon?" I asked.

Diane, a fortysomething brunette and the local librarian, helped herself to a small handful of cashews from a dish on the coffee table. "Last I heard, you were planning to stay in Vegas until spring."

"What can I say?" Claudia shrugged diffidently. "Plans changed."

Bunco temporarily forgotten, Pam patted the sofa cushion next to her. "Sit down. Tell us all about this new husband of yours."

Claudia didn't need a second invitation. "Better yet, I'll show you." She plunked herself down next to Pam while the rest of us crowded around, eager to get the skinny. After giving her mini a tug or two to keep it from riding up her thighs, she dug through a handbag large enough to be considered carry-on luggage. "Here's my honey," she said, extracting a five-by-seven-inch glossy in a gold-embossed leather folder.

Worming my way to a better vantage spot, I craned my neck for a peek. It wasn't a simple snapshot, but rather a professionally posed photo — the sort I'd guess that went into the portfolio of an actor or model. Not that I'm an expert, mind you, but if I were an actor or model, it's the kind of photo I'd stick into my portfolio. Personally, I like to keep things simple when it comes to pictures of loved ones. I thank the good Lord on a regular basis for the invention of the digital camera. No more headless bodies of friends and relatives for me. No, sirree. Not since the kids gave me one of those cute little ones hardly bigger than a credit card on my last birthday.

"He's certainly handsome," Pam murmured before passing the photo to Rita.

Rita, big and buxom, fanned her face with her hand. "He's gorgeous. I feel a power surge coming on."

A bevy of *ooh*s and *aah*s and *isn't he handsome*s followed the picture from one set of hands to another. Claudia beamed, basking in Lance's reflected glory. "He's something, all right. My own personal hunka-hunka burnin' love."

"Not bad for an older guy," Megan Warner concurred.

"Watch your tongue, child." Claudia gave Megan's arm a playful swat. "Didn't your mama teach you to respect your elders?"

Pam rushed to her daughter's defense. "When you're only twenty, Claudia, even

Justin Timberlake is getting a little long in the tooth."

Perky, blond, blue-eyed Megan happens to be the darling of the Warner family. She's currently taking online classes and working part-time as a receptionist for the new dentist in town while trying to decide what to do with the rest of her life.

Finally it was my turn to worship at the Altar of Lance. "You gals are right. Lance Ledeaux is one hot dude." That is if one's taste ran to the superficial. Not mine. Personally, I'll take Bill Lewis, my handyman charmer in a tool belt, any day of the week over movie-star handsome. I passed the glossy to Janine, the Babes' very own Jamie Lee Curtis look-alike with her slender build and cap of short-cropped silver hair. A registered nurse, Janine is our go-to person for all things medical.

Janine's brows puckered in a frown. "His face looks familiar. I swear I've seen him before, but I can't place him."

Tara, the other youngster of the group at thirty-one, scooted closer for another look. Tara is Rita's daughter-in-law. She's staying with her in-laws while her husband, Mark, is deployed to Iraq. "Now that you mention it, he does look familiar."

"Of course he does, sweetie," Claudia

cooed. "He's an actor. A well-known actor, I might add."

"An actor?" we exclaimed in perfect eleven-part harmony.

"That's right. Did I forget to mention I married an actor?"

Claudia's expression was guileless as a cherub's. But I wasn't buying the innocent act. She had deliberately withheld this little tidbit, going for shock value instead. And judging from the awed looks on our faces, her ploy had worked.

"Lance has appeared in dozens of TV shows and had bit parts in a score of movies. He's what they call a 'character actor.' The play he was in in Atlanta had just ended its run when we happened to meet."

"Let me see." Polly snatched the picture from Janine and, bringing it closer to her nose, squinted at it. "Yeah, sure, now I recognize him. Didn't he do one of those commercials for men who can't get it up?"

Claudia's face reddened as she retrieved the photo and stuffed it back into her handbag.

"You know the kind I mean," Polly continued, unfazed. "In the commercial, the guy takes a pill of some sort. Next thing you know, he's leading a woman off to the bedroom."

15

"Lance has done all sorts of work," Claudia replied stiffly. "He's quite talented but never got his big break. He plans to drop by after bunco. He's got a proposition for you. . . ." She paused for effect, then smiled a cat-with-a-canary smile before continuing. "It's a very important proposition."

"One more question," Polly chirped. "Lance Ledeaux? That his real name?"

I poured Claudia a glass of wine. She looked like she needed one.

CHAPTER 2

No amount of prying, coaxing, or bribing could loosen Claudia's tongue about this so-called "proposition."

"It's classified information," Claudia insisted. "Lance swore me to secrecy."

After a brief discussion, we'd agreed to shorten the night's bunco in favor of meeting Lance Ledeaux. We'd play only three sets of six rounds instead of our usual six sets.

"OK, ladies, let's play bunco!" Pam announced.

Fortified with glasses of wine, we scrambled to find places. There were three tables of four for a total of twelve players. Each table was outfitted with three dice, score sheets, pencils, and the mandatory dishes of snacks. A bell Pam had found once at a garage sale occupied center stage on the head table, which for tonight was in the living room.

Glass in hand, I migrated to the head table and sat down opposite Claudia. Pam and Connie Sue joined us.

"Who has the tiara?" Monica demanded from the adjacent dining room.

"Got it," Gloria called from her spot in the den.

Gloria may favor serviceable polyester when it comes to clothing, but bling is her thing. She fairly sparkles in gold chains and bangle bracelets. The tiara literally was the icing atop her salt-and-pepper do.

The tiara had been Connie Sue's idea — go figure — a relic from her days as beauty queen. Each time we meet, the night's high roller is awarded the tiara. It's that person's to keep until the next time we play. Then, after scores are tallied, the reigning diva relinquishes the tiara to the new winner. It's childish, I know, like little girls playing dress-up, but we love the silly ritual — especially Monica, even though she'd die rather than admit it. Monica's determined to bring home the tiara at the end of each and every bunco night. But then Monica tends to be a bit on the competitive side.

Pam rang the bell and play commenced. I picked up the dice and, miracle of miracles, rolled a succession of ones. When my string of luck — my very short string — ran out, I passed the dice to Connie Sue on my left.

Now, rules of bunco vary somewhat from group to group. Your grandmother may have played the game one way, and your mother another. Allow me to explain the Bunco Babes' way. We decided early on that we'd play six complete sets before calling it a night. In each round, players try to roll the same number as the round. For instance, in round one, players attempt to roll ones; in round two players attempt to roll twos, and so on and so forth. One point is awarded for each target number rolled successfully. Bunco occurs when a player rolls three of a kind of the target number, for which she scores the grand total of twenty-one points. A player continues to roll as long as she's racking up points. The round ends when someone at the head table — which controls play — reaches a total of twenty-one, rings the bell, and hollers, "Bunco!"

Connie Sue didn't fare much better than I. Disgusted with her lack of success, she shoved the dice toward Claudia. Scooping up the dice, Claudia rattled them as though trying to shake the spots loose. Then with a flourish she let them fly. Instantly three ones appeared. "Bunco!"

Pam rang the bell, signaling the end of the round. Claudia's cry of triumph was met with moans and groans of despair. Since everyone gets at least one roll, Pam tossed the dice, but, failing to roll a one, tallied the score.

"That's not fair," Monica whined. "I only have six points."

Amidst good-natured grumbling, we totaled points — most of which were in the single digits thanks to Claudia's instant bunco. The winners advanced tables, except for Claudia and me, who remained at the head table.

I half stood to swap partners, but Claudia motioned me back to my seat. "Stay where you are. I'll change places. I just want to refill my wineglass."

A little red flag popped up at hearing this — or at least a tiny pink flag. Claudia wasn't much of a drinker. She rarely had more than one glass of wine, and if she did, it was certainly much later than in the first round. Had Vegas corrupted her? Or was something else afoot?

"There ought to be a rule against getting a bunco on your first throw," Monica groused.

"It's all a game of chance, sugar," Connie Sue reminded her as she helped herself to veggies and dip on the way to table three in the den.

"Yeah, yeah, I know, but I still don't think it's fair."

Monica, as I said, tends to be competitive. Anyone who think she's a bad sport at bunco should see her on the golf course.

When play resumed, I found myself watching Claudia more closely. I could see that when it came to tossing dice, she had spent some time in Vegas honing her technique. Her style definitely had more pizzazz than before. The dice fairly danced across the table each time they tumbled out of her hand. Once or twice, one of the little buggers skittered right off the table and onto the floor.

"You've certainly improved your know-how when it comes to dice," I told her, admiring the dramatic little wrist-flip she had acquired.

"And it seems to be paying off," she said with a grin as she rolled two — not one, but two — baby buncos in a row. Monica watched with undisguised envy as Claudia added ten more points to her score sheet, five points apiece for each baby. Baby buncos, by the way, occur when a player rolls three of any number except for the target number, which, as I already mentioned, is a whopping twenty-one points. I didn't need to be clairvoyant to know that

Monica was wishing Claudia, not I, were her partner.

"Bunco!" Claudia called out, then clanged the bell. The big smile she wore showed she was obviously enjoying her winning streak. "I spent a fair amount of time at the craps table," she confessed to a disgruntled Monica. "Picked up a few pointers."

"Were you this lucky in Vegas?" Megan asked, all perky innocence.

"Honey lamb, I broke the bank. Just wait 'til you see the prize I brought home." She imitated Rita's gesture, fanning a hand back and forth as if she needed to cool down.

Claudia's luck held for the remainder of the evening. Gloria no sooner finished placing the coveted tiara atop Claudia's flaming locks than the door chimes sounded.

"That must be Lance! Right on cue." Claudia sprinted for the door as fast as a miniskirt and stilettos would allow.

"Suppose Lance Ledeaux is his real name?" Polly asked for the second time. For once, there were no reproving looks from her daughter.

We flocked together into the living room, a covey of peahens eager to catch our first glimpse of the peacock who'd just flown in from Vegas. From the foyer, we heard a giggle followed by a loud smooching sound.

Polly craned her scrawny neck for a better look, almost falling off the sofa in the process.

After what seemed like an hour but was more likely only a minute, Claudia led her bridegroom across the foyer and into the living room. It was easy to see how this man could turn heads — and make sensible women do foolish things. He was tall, close to six feet, with sandy brown hair expertly styled and blow-dried and with just enough gray at the temples to give him a distinguished look. His tan screamed serious time spent in the sun. I placed him in his early fifties, younger than Claudia — no surprise.

Claudia smiled brightly and squeezed his hand. "Ladies, it gives me great pleasure to introduce my husband, Lance Ledeaux. Lance, these are the Bunco Babes, my best friends in the whole wide world."

"Claudia, my dove, your description failed to do these fair ladies justice."

Dove? Fair ladies? I wanted to stick my finger down my throat and make gagging noises.

Claudia proceeded to introduce each of us in turn. While I waited for the privilege, I gave myself a little pep talk. If Claudia had fallen head over heels for the guy, there had to be more to him than met the eye. I had to give Lance Ledeaux credit. He worked the room so well, he might've been running for public office. He greeted each of the Babes effusively, dispensing charm like candy on Halloween. I watched as the Babes seemed to succumb to his spell. Even Rita, the most levelheaded woman I know, was turning into a simpering female right before my very eyes. Was I the only one immune to polished good looks and smarmy charm?

Begrudgingly I gave the man points for his sense of style. He was a walking fashion plate in a three-button navy wool blazer over a blue and white striped oxford shirt, open at the throat, and tan pleated chinos. Expensive-looking aviator sunglasses were hooked onto his breast pocket. Why, I had no idea. No one in their right mind needed sunglasses at this time of night. Yes, indeedy, Claudia's jackpot could have posed for *GQ*. Not that my late husband, Jim, subscribed to that particular magazine, mind you. He was more the *Sports Illustrated* type.

"So," Polly was saying in a conversational tone, "you ever meet Brad Pitt?"

Here I half expected her to ask him whether Lance Ledeaux was his real name, and instead she was grilling the dude about the celebrities he knew. I should have guessed Polly would go straight for the jugular.

After assuring Polly that Brad was every bit as handsome in person as he was on-screen and twice as nice, Lance turned toward me. "And you must be Kate, the brave detective. Claudia's told me so much about you."

Detective? Had the man actually called me a detective? Hmm . . . Maybe I was being hasty in my rush to judgment.

He took my hand and held it — a little too long.

Up close, his face was smooth and unlined, making me wonder just how much younger he was than Claudia. "Welcome to Serenity Cove Estates," I said, gently extracting my hand from his grip. "I hope you'll be happy here."

"I'm certain I will be. In spite of being a small community, Serenity Cove Estates seems to have a lot to offer."

He beamed down at me. His choppers were the dazzling white of toothpaste ads. In that instant, he did look vaguely familiar. Was he the actor I'd seen in denture commercials? Darn these senior moments!

"Someday soon," he said, continuing to bestow upon me his mega-kilowatt smile, "maybe we can sit down, and you can tell me all about your, ah, let's say, your close encounter with a diabolical villain. It's got the makings of a great screenplay."

"A screenplay? Really?" I grimaced inwardly at hearing myself ask this in a breathy voice. Now who was simpering? My brain was turning into pudding.

"It's got all the right elements, my dear Kate. Mystery, adventure, danger, and, of course, a lovely damsel in distress who saves the day."

I nodded furiously in agreement. I was beginning to like Lance more and more each minute. No wonder Claudia was smitten.

Pam, in her role as hostess, brought Lance a glass of wine, which he accepted with alacrity. "Ladies, if you will, please have a seat. I have something I'd like to discuss with you."

Obediently as parochial school second graders, we arranged ourselves on sofas and chairs about the living room. Lance remained standing.

He set his wineglass down on a nearby end table and rubbed his hands together. "I suspect Claudia mentioned I have a proposition for you."

We nodded, twelve bobblehead dolls in the rear window of an old Chevy.

He let his smile slowly revolve around the room. "I've been working on a certain project for quite some time, and I think you ladies, the Babes, might be just the ones to help me pull it off."

"Who? Us?"

The Bunco Babe chorus was worthy of *American Idol.* Are you listening, Simon Cowell?

Pull it off? I'm not quite sure I liked the way that sounded. Lance made it seem as if he were planning a bank heist and wanted our help in the caper. If so, I hoped Pam wouldn't be assigned to drive the getaway car — unless the getaway car happened to be a golf cart. The dings and dents on her PT Cruiser speak for themselves. I, on the other hand, have been known to put the pedal to the metal and burn rubber. I'd be a much better choice for the driver of a getaway car. Not that I intended to rob a bank, of course, but I'm always up for an escapade.

I cleared my throat and asked tentatively, "Exactly what is it you have in mind?"

"I've written a play, a murder mystery, and plan to produce it right here in Serenity Cove Estates. From everything Claudia's told me about all of you, you're just what I've been looking for. I see 'star quality' written across your faces. With your able assistance, my dear ladies, we can make this into a production residents here will never forget."

Before we knew it, Lance was whipping out copies of his script, *Forever, My Darling.* "Let's give this a quick run-through, shall we?" he said, smiling broadly.

By the time the evening ended, I think we were all suffering from shell shock. Claudia and, of course, Lance had the starring roles. Megan would play the ingénue. I was going to be Myrna, the housekeeper. Gloria had displayed a surprising knack for the theater and, to Monica's chagrin, won the part of Lance's secretary. The rest of the Babes had offered their services as well. Connie Sue would be responsible for hair and makeup — no big stretch for a former beauty queen and cosmetics rep. Polly practically foamed at the mouth for the chance to be in charge of costumes. Diane volunteered her expertise on publicity, and Tara said she'd work on programs. It was agreed that a couple minor parts could be cast later.

What next? I wondered as I left Pam's that evening. Broadway?

CHAPTER 3

Great — first I was late, and now I was early. I staked out a corner table at the Cove Café and prepared to wait.

Vera MacGillicudy, the Babes' all-time favorite waitress, came over and poured me a cup of coffee. "You alone this morning?"

"No," I said sourly. "I overslept. Pam is meeting me here after Tai Chi. Connie Sue and Monica will be along after land aerobics."

Vera, being a wise woman, obviously sensed I needed caffeine more than conversation and wandered off. I took my first sip of Colombian dark and sighed in bliss. I could feel my mood begin to lighten already. Almost, that is . . .

It had been a week since Lance dropped his bombshell, aka proposition. For the life of me, I didn't know why I'd agreed to go along with his outlandish idea. I didn't know beans about acting, yet I'd volunteered to play the part of the housekeeper, Myrna. What was I thinking? Had the time finally come to get my head examined?

I drank more coffee, then signaled for Vera to top off my cup. I happened to glance toward the door, half expecting to see my friends appear, but I saw someone even better — Bill Lewis.

As usual, my heart did a little tap dance inside my chest at the sight of my favorite handyman. He'd had that effect on me ever since the day he came to repair a broken ceiling fan. Maybe it was the tool belt; maybe it was the Paul Newman baby blues, but whatever it was sent my no-longer-dormant hormones into overdrive.

Bill spotted me at the same time and gave me that hesitant, shy smile of his.

I held my breath, hoping he'd join me. At one time this would have been a given; these days I wasn't so sure. Pam used to insist Bill was sweet on me. But he'd changed. He'd recently returned to Serenity Cove Estates after nursing his brother, Bob, through a triple bypass and then staying on to see Bob through cardiac rehab. We hadn't seen much of each other since he'd come home — at any rate, not nearly as much as I would've liked. Our friendship/relationship seemed to have cooled during his absence

— not on my part, but his. If I were a microwave, I would've set the dial to reheat.

I let out a pent-up sigh as he ambled toward my table. "Hey, Bill," I said, smiling in spite of my misgivings. He had that kind of effect on me.

"Hey, yourself." He tucked his hands into the pockets of his Windbreaker. "You managing to keep warm during this cold spell we're having?"

It was hard to find a more neutral topic than the weather. OK, I thought, two could play this game. We'd keep it light, keep it simple. "After all my years in Toledo," I told him, "I can handle this kind of 'cold.' It's hard to believe it's actually winter with planters of flowers everywhere."

Bill nodded. "My camellias are blooming like crazy."

"The deer ate mine."

"Those buggers eat anything and everything this time of year," he commiserated. "Did you spray them with deer repellant like I suggested?"

"Oh, yeah." I nodded. "Problem was, it was windy. I ended up with more spray on me than on the bushes. It took two showers before I could get rid of the smell. That stuff reeks to high heaven."

"That's why the deer stay away from the

camellias."

For the first time, I noticed a man dressed in rumpled khakis and a faded brown sweatshirt hovering near the entrance. When he saw me look his way, he ducked his head. Bill followed the direction of my glance and motioned the man over.

"A friend of yours?"

Bill made the introductions. "Kate, this is Gus Smith. He's new to Serenity Cove Estates."

"How do you do," Gus mumbled, extending his hand but avoiding eye contact.

Knowing the Babes would want a full report on any newcomer, I gave Gus the once-over. He was average height and a little lumpy around the middle like many men his age, which I took to be sixtysomething. His hair was mostly gray and mostly gone, also like many his age. Except for a prominent nose, his features were unremarkable. He would blend perfectly into the male population of any retirement community in the country.

"Nice to meet you, Gus." Odd guy, I thought, but any friend of Bill's was a friend of mine. "What brings you to Serenity Cove?"

He shrugged. "I, ah, moved down here from a small town in northern Michigan.

Got tired of all the snow."

"Gus owned a place up near where I used to hunt," Bill explained.

Bill's originally from Michigan, too — Battle Creek, to be precise, cereal capital of the world. I remember his pinpointing the exact spot using the palm of his hand, a neat trick if you're from a state shaped like a mitten. Not so easy for those of us from Ohio, much less for those who happen to hail from New Jersey. But whether from Michigan or Ohio, Bill and I were both transplanted Midwesterners. After my husband, Jim, died of a massive coronary, I decided to remain in the "active" adult retirement community we had fallen in love with. I've never regretted the decision.

"He's temporarily leasing a small house with an option to buy," Bill continued since Gus was apparently a man of few words. "It's just down the street from me. The owners moved back to Pennsylvania to be closer to their kids. The place comes fully furnished but could use some updating."

"I heard about the woodworking club, the Woodchucks," Gus volunteered reluctantly. "Thought I could pick up a few pointers." He dipped his head toward Bill. "That's where we met. Bill offered to show me around. Introduce me to some folks."

"Gus fits right in." Bill slapped his new friend on the shoulder. "Soon as I told him about this play we're putting on, he offered to take charge of lighting and sound. Didn't even have to twist his arm."

Another falls prey to Lance's grandiose scheme. The more the merrier? Or should it be, "Misery loves company"?

"Well, we gotta run," Bill said. "I'm giving Gus the grand tour. Next stop, the rec center."

"I hope you'll be happy here, Gus," I said, infusing my voice with Welcome Wagon sincerity. "Serenity Cove's a great place to live."

"Yeah, thanks." Gus smiled for the first time, revealing a pronounced gap between yellowing front teeth. "It's exactly what I've been looking for."

Gee, where had I heard words to that effect? Lance maybe?

After breakfast with the girls, I ran into town to stock up on groceries. Since I was there already, I asked the store manager if he had any empty boxes to spare. It turned out I was in luck. The manager instructed me to drive around back and help myself.

All week long, when I wasn't memorizing my lines, I'd been cleaning out closets. I wanted to give myself a pat on the back. It was a New Year's resolution I'd actually kept. Every year, it seems, I make the same three resolutions: lose weight, exercise more, and clean out the closets. This year I was determined to make good on at least one of them. Closets looked the most promising. Now the clothes needed to be packed up and donated to Goodwill

In spite of the hundreds of times I'd shopped at the Piggly Wiggly, I'd never had reason to visit the loading dock. Produce department, frozen foods, canned goods aisle, yes, but not the loading dock. I drove around the rear of the store and spied a bonanza of boxes practically calling my name.

The sight of all those empty boxes set my pulse thrumming. Lofty plans to revamp every single closet in my home danced in my head. Every useless object, every trace of clutter, would somehow magically disappear. A little elbow grease and I'd be able to find everything I owned without the aid of a GPS. Voilà! I'd be organized.

I backed the Buick alongside the loading dock, jumped out of the car, and proceeded to fill my trunk. I confess I may have gotten a little carried away at the prospect of all those cardboard boxes; I could barely fit them into the trunk. I was about to drive off with my newly acquired bounty, when I spotted something unusual.

There, partially concealed behind a giant green Dumpster, was Lance Ledeaux's '69 Camaro. Normally I can't tell one car from another; four tires and a steering wheel, and they all start to look alike. Once I even lost my Buick at the mall, but that's another story. Lance's Camaro, however, was an exception. Only a blind person could miss his car. I may wear trifocals, but I'm not blind, I assure you.

I'd commented only a few days ago that it was the same red-orange as in a box of Crayola crayons. Lance quickly informed me the correct term for the car's original paint color was Hugger Orange. Lance then proceeded to get a little hot under his Brooks Brothers collar when he heard me refer to his car as "old." He wasted no time setting me straight. It wasn't "old," he said. It was a "classic." *Well, la-di-da!* I'd said, but not out loud. Old orange cars seemed a touchy subject.

But I digress. The question of the day was why his Hugger Orange Camaro was parked next to a Dumpster behind the Piggly Wiggly.

I sat there, hands on the wheel, and

pondered my next move. What was the harm in waiting awhile? I wasn't exactly spying on Lance; I was only admiring the lines of his "classic" car. Lance should thank me for guarding his prized possession against the off chance a band of vandals was roaming the loading dock in search of empty boxes.

I didn't have long to wait before a silver gray sedan whipped into the lot and squealed to a halt next to the Dumpster. Lance climbed out of the passenger side and exchanged what appeared to be angry words with whoever was driving. He then slammed the car door shut and stalked toward his Camaro. The driver of the sedan stomped on the accelerator and roared off. I caught only a quick glimpse of a dark-haired woman as she zoomed past.

Lance was in an equal hurry to make his getaway. He slammed into reverse, backed out of his hiding place, and peeled off. Curious to see what he was up to, I shifted into gear and followed, hoping he wouldn't happen to glance into his rearview mirror and spot me. Both cars cleared the Piggly Wiggly lot at opposite ends and turned onto the highway. The dark-haired woman headed east; Lance took off in the direction of Serenity Cove.

What was all that about? I wondered as I headed home. Who was the dark-haired woman? And why the secrecy?

I wished I had gotten a better look at the driver of the sedan. It really was time for new glasses. I'd been procrastinating for months, but the time had come to make an appointment with the optometrist. However, even at a distance, and even needing new specs, I could tell from the body language that Lance had been furious. Bill had recently made the observation that Lance had a way of ticking people off. Now someone had turned the tables.

Paybacks are hell.

CHAPTER 4

As agreed upon the day before, Connie Sue, Pam, Monica, and I formed a committee in search of the perfect gift for the newlyweds. Our task was complicated by the fact that Claudia, if she wanted something, bought it. Bing, bang, boom, she'd whip out her credit card. The Babes had given the four of us a price range and charged us with finding something "appropriate" for a woman who had everything, including a shiny new husband.

"I could have driven," Pam said for the third time.

"I know, sugar, but we can fit more into my Lexus than that little PT Cruiser of yours," Connie Sue told her as she made a beeline for Macy's. The rest of us tried to match her pace.

All of us were aware of the importance of having enough room to accommodate purchases after a shopping spree. Augusta,

Georgia, is home to the nearest mall of any size. It's only a hop, skip, and a jump down the road from Serenity Cove, but a big hop, a big skip, and a very long jump. When we go, we take a list and make it into an outing. And no outing is complete without show-and-tell afterward.

"Let's find a wedding gift first," Pam suggested. "Afterward we can separate."

"Sounds like a plan," I said. "Where do we start?"

Monica studied the store directory. "How about cookware?"

I wasn't fooled by Monica's sly suggestion. She was Martha Stewart with dark hair and a fetish for tiaras. "What about home décor?" I asked innocently. "Lance can never have enough frames to hold all his photos."

"Kate, shame on you," Pam said with a shake of her head. "We could check out bed and bath. Maybe get a nice set of towels."

"Sugar, there's a time to be practical and a time to be extravagant." Connie Sue tapped a French-manicured nail on the directory. "I was thinkin' of somethin' more along the lines of kitchen electronics."

Soon the four of us were in a heated debate over espresso machines — which to the best of my knowledge, Claudia *didn't*

40

own. My head was starting to spin. Who would have guessed there would be so much to consider? Things like programmable, a one-year versus three-year warranty, and adjustable cup heights. After much discussion, we finally agreed on a particular model that boasted a three-in-one capability: coffee, espresso, and cappuccino. *If* I ever remarry — and that's a pretty big if — I'm going to run straight for the nearest bridal registry and request one of these wonders. Imagine — cappuccino at my fingertips. I would think I'd died and gone to heaven.

Mission accomplished, we sent the three-in-one wonder to package pickup and headed for the four corners of the mall. In keeping with the coffee theme, we arranged to meet at Starbucks to load up on beans and caffeine before heading home.

"Are you single-handedly committed to reviving the economy?" Monica asked upon seeing Connie Sue's amazing collection of shopping bags.

"Everythin' was on sale. What's a girl supposed to do?" Connie Sue retorted, nonplussed.

"I bought new towels," Pam offered.

Pam, in sharp contrast to Connie Sue, is frugal to a fault, but it's these idiosyncrasies that make life interesting. When left to my own devices, I'd done a little shopping of my own, both the practical and the extravagant sort. I have a froufrou bag filled with freebie cosmetics, all sorts of tiny bottles filled with such things as moisturizer and exfoliator, along with a sample of a new designer fragrance. That goes to show my practical side. Problem was, I liked the new designer perfume so much, I bought one. I tried not to dwell on the price. And what's more, I rationalized, I didn't really buy it for myself; I bought it for Bill. The saleswoman claimed men found the scent irresistible. I could hardly wait to take it out for a test drive.

"I need a smoothie," Connie Sue announced, piling her bags on a nearby vacant chair. "Be right back."

While waiting for her to return, we huddled around a small table that gave us a view of the mall traffic. As it often did these days, talk centered on Lance Ledeaux.

"I can't believe we let him talk us into this," I complained for the umpteenth time.

Pam sipped her grande nonfat latte. "Remember this all sounded like a great idea at the time. No one held a gun to our heads and made us agree to go along with this play of his."

"Not simply a play, sugar," Connie Sue said, returning with smoothie in hand, in time to overhear Pam's comment. "A theatrical production."

Monica nodded grimly. "A theatrical production he's written himself."

"And plans to star in," Pam added. "As well as produce and direct."

I frowned, not caring if I might need Botox down the road. "Don't know much about the theater, but even to an amateur such as myself, it sounds overly ambitious."

Monica blew on her herbal tea to cool it. "Since we're all involved, maybe the marquee should read 'Babes on Broadway.' "

"Great idea, sugar, but I'm afraid it's already been done." Connie Sue took a long pull on the straw of her pink smoothie.

We stared at her.

"What's wrong?" she asked, finding us looking at her strangely. "Most everyone knows *Babes on Broadway* was a musical, back in the forties I think, with Judy Garland and Mickey Rooney."

I shook my head in wonderment. "Connie Sue Brody, sometimes you amaze me. When did you turn into the trivia queen?"

She shrugged prettily. "I declare, sweetie, growin' older is gettin' harder and harder. Some nights I can't catch a wink, so I end up watchin' old movies on one of those cable networks."

"Getting back to the matter at hand," I said, stirring my cinnamon-laced cappuccino, "the deal breaker came when Lance promised opening night proceeds would benefit Janine's favorite cause, Pets in Need."

"Especially since she's the newly elected president." Pam nodded her agreement. "You know how she's always talking about a new animal shelter."

Monica absently tucked a brunet strand behind one ear. "I have to admit Lance is a phenomenon to behold. He certainly didn't let any grass grow under his feet getting the ball rolling."

"He's a silver-tongued devil all right," Connie Sue chuckled.

I agreed with both Monica and Connie Sue. Seeing Lance in action had made me a believer. In the blink of an eye, he'd turned bunco night into a casting call. By the time we left Pam's, none of us knew what had hit us. One by one, we had voluntarily and of our own free will consented to participate in one manner or other in what he referred to as his *proposition*.

Monica's dark eyes snapped with irritation. "Imagine me — of all people — the prop princess!"

"That's mistress — not princess," I corrected.

None of us wanted to remind her she'd tried out for Gloria's part and failed miserably. Not even Janine, the casting director, could ignore that Monica didn't have a theatrical gene in her entire body. Instead, Lance had diplomatically convinced Monica that with her attention to detail, she'd be the right person to collect and organize props. Rita, by the way, had been awarded the plum job of stage manager.

"Enough doom and gloom," Pam scolded. "Just think, this play could be a lot of fun."

That's Pam, my BFF — "best friend forever" in texting jargon, which I'm learning to impress my granddaughters. Pam tends to look on the bright side of things, though sometimes her Pollyanna attitude can be downright annoying.

Batting her eyelashes, Connie Sue placed her hand over her heart. "*Forever, My Darling,*" she drawled in her best Scarlett O'Hara imitation. "Really, girls, do you think Lance could have found a cheesier title? Sounds like one of those trashy romance novels."

Now it was my turn to scold. "Connie Sue Brody, bite your tongue. You know you're addicted to romance novels, and there's nothing trashy about them."

"Well, sugar, I have to admit they're a heap better 'n watchin' all those dreadful crime shows you're so fond of."

"I'll have you know, my crime shows aren't dreadful. They're educational."

"They're also interesting and informative." Pam jumped to my defense. I was well aware that her addiction to *Law & Order* and *CSI* was nearly as bad as mine. If we got any worse, the Babes would need to stage an intervention.

"Those 'dreadful' shows, as you call them, helped hone my skills when we were trying to find out who murdered Rosalie," I pointed out.

"And almost got you killed in the process." Connie Sue slurped up the last of her smoothie and started gathering her packages. "Now we'd better get a move on if I want to have a hot meal on the table for Thacker."

We did likewise.

I heard Monica grumble under her breath about being the prop princess.

"It's not that bad, Monica," I told her as we hustled toward the escalator. "You'll do a terrific job."

"Wish I could be as sure as you are, Kate.

I don't have a clue what I'm supposed to do. Especially since one of the props happens to be a handgun."

CHAPTER 5

Rehearsal was scheduled for seven o'clock sharp Monday evening. I arrived early, hoping to spend some "quality time" with Bill. There were names for women like me, brazen hussy being one of the nicer ones.

I pushed open the doors of the auditorium and stepped inside. Only the stage was illuminated, leaving the rest of the cavernous space in relative darkness. Lance had flashed his charm and charisma at Serenity Cove Management and secured the rec center's auditorium for our use — or should I say *his* use. Cast and crew were merely the means to an end. Lest we forget, he was quick to remind us this was a Lance Ledeaux Production.

Lance and Claudia, unaware of my presence, occupied center stage.

"I don't know why you're making such a big deal over this," Lance complained.

"Maybe it's because thirty thousand dollars happens to *be* a big deal. Especially when it's a cash advance against *my* credit card," Claudia fired back.

"Claudia, dove, no need to get all upset. You're not exactly in the poorhouse."

Lance reached out to draw Claudia closer, but she jerked away. "That's exactly where I will be if this spending of yours keeps up. I've overlooked the new wardrobe, the laptop with every bell and whistle known to mankind, the fancy iPhone, but this . . ." Her voice trailed off.

I stepped back until I felt the door handle jab me between the shoulder blades. I hoped they were rehearsing a new scene from Lance's masterpiece. But I knew better. This argument was the real McCoy.

Claudia presented her back to Lance, then whirled to face him. "When were you going to tell me?" Her voice rose. "Did you think I wasn't going to find out?"

"Claudia, my pet, you need to trust me." He pressed his hands together and held them to his chest. The expression on his handsome puss was a page straight from Sincerity 101 — so saccharine in its sweetness, I wanted to barf. "This is a sure thing, darling. I know what I'm doing. I promise I'll pay back every cent — with interest — since money is such a big deal with you."

She advanced on him. In her tight black pants and animal print top, she looked like a lioness moving in for the kill. Only the pointy-toed ankle boots with three-inch heels spoiled the effect. I clutched my shoulder bag tighter, scarcely daring to breath. I don't know how Lance felt, but this was scary serious. I'd never seen Claudia this angry.

"While we're on the subject of money" — she poked him in the ribs with a fingertip lacquered bloodred — "I happened to get a call from the Jaguar dealer in Augusta just as I was leaving the house. The salesman claimed you placed an order for a new car — a seventy-five-thousand-dollar new car."

I smothered a gasp at hearing the amount. So much for Lance's pretending to love his "classic" Hugger Orange Camaro.

"Seventy-five thousand?" Lance waved his hand dismissively, but even from a distance I could see perspiration sheen his brow. "That's a drop in the bucket, sweetheart, compared to what my Super Bowl winnings are going to be."

I felt a sharp stab in the region of my heart. I never hear "Super Bowl" mentioned without being reminded of my late husband. Two years ago, Jim, the poor dear, landed facedown in the guacamole dip after suffering a fatal coronary during halftime. He never knew he'd won fifty bucks in the football pool.

"And if there are no Super Bowl winnings?" Claudia continued her tirade. "What then? Write another check out of my money market account to pay for it? Drain my account down to nothing? Lance, this has to stop!"

Lance adopted a new approach, his tone faintly mocking. "After watching you at the roulette table in Vegas, I never took you for such a tightwad. I'm seeing a whole new side of you, sweetheart — a very unattractive side."

In her fury, Claudia's face was turning as red as her hair. "I'm seeing a new side of you as well. I won't stand for this kind of behavior, Lance. This has to end — and I'm prepared to do *whatever* it takes to see that it does."

"Is that a threat?" he asked, feigning outrage.

I wasn't overly impressed with Lance's theatrical ability. At this point if I were a casting director, I'd have yelled, Cut!

"No, Lance." Claudia's voice dropped so low I had to lean forward to better hear her response. "It's not a threat; it's a promise."

"You're my meal ticket, babe. It's going to

51

cost you a pretty penny if you want to get rid of me." At last the kid gloves were off. Lance was showing his true colors; black with a white stripe down the center of his back.

"Over my dead body, you two-bit actor," Claudia snarled. "I'll find a way to get you out of my life — one way or another."

From the hallway outside came the sound of people talking and laughing. I nearly fell into Bill's arms when he opened the auditorium door.

"Whoa," he said, steadying me.

Unsettled by the argument I'd overheard, I blurted, "You're late."

"Looks like you're early," he countered. This time not even Bill's smile was able to cheer me.

I stood aside while Bill flicked the light switch next to the door. Monica and Rita entered, too engrossed in their conversation about props to give me the time of day. Gus, Bill's brand-new buddy, gave me a friendly nod as he shuffled by. The only one who hadn't made an appearance yet was Bernie Mason, who was to play the part of the villain in Lance's magnificent production.

Bill matched his pace to mine as I trailed the others toward the stage. "Gus and I spent all afternoon taking measurements and making lists of materials we need before starting on the set. We didn't realize the time and thought we'd better duck out for a quick bite before rehearsal. Besides," he added, "I need to ask Lance a couple questions."

"Questions?" I mumbled, trying to collect my wits after overhearing the fight between Claudia and Lance. Now, I'm no relationship guru like Dr. Phil, but I'd bet my last bag of M&M's this marriage was in trouble — big trouble. Lance Ledeaux seemed hellbent on sucking Claudia's nest egg dry. And Claudia wasn't about to take the nest egg–sucking lying down.

"Hey, everyone." Claudia turned and greeted us with a smile — a smile as phony as the creep she married. He was nothing more than a scam artist. I almost said "cheap" scam artist, but there was nothing cheap about someone set to rob you blind.

Lance looked spiffy in his fitted black jeans and yellow oxford cloth shirt with a black cashmere cable knit sweater artfully draped over his shoulders. The sweater alone probably cost a week's worth of groceries for a family of four. He didn't bother with a welcome but looked pointedly at his watch. Knowing his proclivity for the expensive, I wondered if the Rolex was real or a clever knockoff.

"As soon as everyone's here, we're going to run through act three, scene one," he announced, doing his best commander-in-chief imitation. "No one leaves until we get it right."

The announcement was met by a chorus of groans. The only good thing about that night's rehearsal was that all the cast members didn't have to subject themselves to Lance's edicts. This meant that of the cast, only Claudia, Lance, Bernie Mason, and I needed to be present, in addition to a crew that included Monica, Rita, Bill, and his ever-present shadow, Gus. The remainder of the cast, Gloria, Megan, and Eric Olsen, a nice young man and a member of the Brookdale police force, had the night off. Lucky them. What a shame I wasn't a tad younger; I would have tried out for Megan's part — the role of ingénue.

All of us trooped up the steps to the stage.

Bill approached Lance, who was inspecting an array of props spread out on a table. "Ah, Lance, do you have a minute?"

Lance looked up with a scowl. If one didn't know better, one would have thought he'd never laid eyes on Bill before. "Bill, isn't it?"

For crying out loud, Bill was an easy

name. Nothing complicated about it. How hard was it to remember the man who'd stepped up to the plate and graciously offered to build whatever set he wanted?

"Now?" Lance's scowl darkened even more.

"Yes, now."

I had to give Bill credit. He didn't cave beneath Lance's attempt at intimidation. Here was Lance all decked out in Ralph Lauren and Rolex. And then there was Bill in Levi's and Timex. Do I have to come right out and say who won my vote?

"There's a matter we need to discuss," Bill said, all business.

"Can't it wait?"

"Not if you want a set for opening night."

Lance assumed a put-upon look. "Very well."

"Gus and I spent all afternoon going over the diagram you gave us for the set."

Lance rocked back on the heels of his polished loafers. "So what's the problem? Too complicated?"

Bill's color deepened at the implied insult. The rest of us eavesdropped shamelessly while pretending not to. Some leafed through the script; others developed a sudden interest in the display of props.

"I can build your damn set with my eyes

closed. That's not the trouble."

"So, Bill, suppose you tell me just what the 'trouble' is so we can get on with rehearsal."

"It all boils down to the matter of money. Who's going to pay for materials? Lowe's isn't about to hand them over out of the goodness of their heart."

Now it was Lance's turn to redden as he seemed to sense all eyes fixed on him. Everyone ceased what they were doing in order to watch and listen to the minidrama being enacted right under their noses.

It was Claudia who broke the awkward silence and came to her bridegroom's rescue. "I'll give you my credit card, Bill. Lance can repay me from the proceeds."

Lance rubbed his hands together. "Good. It's settled, then."

At that precise moment, the auditorium door swung open and Bernie Mason sidled through. If pressed to describe the man, I'd call him a string bean with a bad comb-over. He always put me in mind of Bert, the character from *Sesame Street*. Kind of tall, gawky, and slow on the uptake. Like Gloria, however, Bernie showed an uncanny knack for the dramatic. He made a perfect villain in Lance's little drama.

"Good of you to grace us with your pres-

56

ence, Mr. Mason." Lance's voice dripped sarcasm.

Bernie ambled over, a hangdog expression on his face. "Sorry," he mumbled. "Car trouble."

Monica nudged me in the ribs. "Likely story. Guy probably can't tell time."

"Be nice," Rita whispered.

"Places, everyone," Lance barked. "Get ready to run through act three, scene one."

This was the part where all the action took place — the part where Claudia's character, Roxanne, confronts the villain who brags he just killed her lover and tells her she'll be his next victim unless she goes along with his blackmail scheme. She does what any red-blooded woman would do — she shoots him. At least that's what happens in Lance's version of what a red-blooded woman caught up in those circumstances would do.

"Let's go through the scene first without props, then a second time with them."

Claudia, Bernie, and I took our places.

As I mentioned, I played the part of Myrna, the housekeeper. Putting on what I imagined to be my best housekeeper countenance, I entered the pretend living room and announced that the lady of the house had a visitor. Out of the corner of my eye, I saw Bill give me the thumbs-up as I exited stage right.

Claudia ran through her lines, but her heart clearly wasn't in her performance. Bernie Mason was even worse. He kept flubbing his dialogue. When Lance berated him, Bernie admitted he'd been spending most of his time on the golf course instead of memorizing lines.

Lance, obviously frustrated, ran his fingers through his hair. No amount of spray could help a hairstyle withstand that amount of torture. If Lance happened to glance in a mirror, he'd scare himself. His usually smooth blow-dried style stood up in spikes. "How hard can it be, people, to inject a little emotion? Didn't anyone believe me when I said we're going to stay until we get this right — even if it takes all night?"

Rita and Monica exchanged looks. Neither looked happy at Lance's decree. Bill and Gus kept their heads bent over a set of blueprints. There was no telling what they were thinking — probably calling Lance a big fat jerk like the rest of us.

"Let's take five, everyone. Then we'll run through the scene again. Bernie, you stand aside and watch while I show a bunch of amateurs how it's supposed to be done. Maybe using the props will inject some life into this scene."

"Take five" always sounds so . . . so . . . theatrical. But I quickly learned that in reality the five invariably turns into ten — and occasionally fifteen. We milled about, chit-chatted, took bathroom breaks, and complained about Lance. No one seemed to like the guy.

"The man's an idiot," Bill said in a low voice. "A complete and total idiot."

"Let's hope Claudia comes to her senses before it's too late," I said, remembering the argument I'd overheard.

Bill's look sharpened. "What do you mean?"

I glanced over my shoulder and saw Lance look at his probably fake Rolex. The take-five break was over. I needed to confide in someone, but this was not the time or place. "Later," I told Bill. "Why don't you stop over for coffee and lemon bars?" Do I know how to play the seductress, or not?

He thought about it for a second, then nodded. "OK."

We resumed our places onstage.

"Claudia" — Lance pointed a finger at her — "I want to see you put some fire into your lines."

Tightlipped, Claudia gestured at the table holding the props. "Is the gun real?"

"Of course," Lance snarled. "What did

you think we were going to use — a cap pistol?"

"I didn't know . . ." Her voice trailed off.

"Don't be such a wuss. Just remember what I told you earlier, and you'll be fine."

Monica jumped to perform her duty as prop princess. Oops! I meant prop mistress. She gingerly placed the gun on a small table temporarily substituting as a desk, then retreated to the sidelines.

Claudia assumed her place center stage. "One more time, Lance. Then I'm calling it quits."

"That's for the director to decide, and, in case you've forgotten, that happens to be me."

"Will you two stop bickering?" Rita folded her arms across her impressive bosom, a disgusted look on her face. "Can we please get on with rehearsal?"

Lance huffed out a breath. "Remember, people, this is the scene where Roxanne, Claudia's character, confronts the man who brags he murdered her soul mate. I don't want puppets. I want action. I want drama. I want emotion!"

I cleared my throat, then nodded to Monica, who pressed a buzzer serving as a doorbell. Our esteemed producer-director-writer-star wanted drama? Wanted emotion?

Would my character, Myrna, be more interesting as a bipolar housekeeper — one who forgot to take her meds? Would Lance applaud my portrayal and nominate me for best actress in a supporting role? Or should I play it straight? Knowing the limitations of my acting ability, I played it straight. I entered, recited my lines, and exited, leaving Lance, subbing for Bernie, and Claudia-Roxanne to their big scene.

Claudia looked decidedly more animated this run-through. Lance read Bernie's lines, in which he brags to Roxanne that he killed her lover and now intends to blackmail her.

I watched from the wings along with the others while she opened a pretend desk drawer and pulled out a gun.

She took aim at the villain's chest. "Take that! And that and that!" she cried as she fired three rounds.

Lance fell to the floor. A single red blossom stained the front of his yellow oxford cloth shirt.

CHAPTER 6

"He's not moving."

Claudia dismissed Rita's concern with a wave of her hand. "Of course not, silly. He's a pro, bent on showing us mere *amateurs* a thing or two about acting."

And then it dawned on me.

Suddenly my brain cells fired on all cylinders. "Was Lance ever on *CSI*?" I asked.

Claudia shrugged. "Yeah, he had a bit part a couple years ago."

A distant image floated across my memory bank and crystallized. "I think I remember the episode. Did he once play a corpse?"

Memory is a strange thing. At times I can recall the smallest, most insignificant details. Other times I suffer senior moments — those irritating lapses when you remember a face but not the name; times you hope your children never know about. They'd send you packing to Assisted Living 'R Us in a New York minute.

"Yes, he did." Claudia let loose a harsh bark of laughter. "Let me tell you, I'm sick and tired of hearing about sexy Marg Helgenberger, who plays Catherine Willows on the show. Marg's the reason I dyed my hair this color."

Respect for Lance inched up a notch. I might not like the guy personally, but he had talent. Real talent. Anyone who can lie on a stainless steel table, a Y incision plainly visible on his torso, while a camera hovers overhead wins my sincere admiration. Not a single twitch. Not a blink. No slight rise and fall of the chest. Yes, sirree, someone who could play a corpse on *CSI* was truly gifted.

Rita edged closer. "You mean Lance is just pretending he's dead?"

Monica's dark brows drew together in a frown. "If he's faking, why's there blood on his shirt?"

Hmm. Monica posed a good question — a very good question.

Claudia's mouth twisted into a humorless smile. "Because it's not blood. It's dye."

"Dye?" Monica repeated, obviously in need of convincing. "Why would Lance ruin a perfectly good shirt?"

"He wouldn't." Claudia huffed out a breath. "Especially if it's Ralph Lauren.

Lance claimed the dye is biodegradable. Guaranteed not to stain."

I studied Lance's supine figure, sprawled across the floorboards. He still hadn't moved a muscle or fluttered an eyelid. Let me be the first to say this: Lance Ledeaux could have won an Emmy for his portrayal of a dead guy.

"So what's the deal with the dye?" Bill asked.

"It's a Hollywood thing. I'll show you."

Rita took the gun from Claudia and returned it to the table that held the props.

"Are you sure we should just leave him here?" I wondered out loud.

"Don't worry about Lance, he's fine. He's just showing off."

We took our cue from Claudia and followed her, eager to make our acquaintance with a bonafide piece of Hollywood trivia. She picked up what appeared to be a miniature plastic pillow and held it between her thumb and forefinger for our inspection. "These are dye packs. He got them from a guy he knew in special effects at one of the studios."

"Interesting," I murmured. "They remind me of the things I use in my dishwasher."

"That's exactly what I thought," Rita ventured. "The all-in-one kind. They're so much more convenient than those messy powders."

"I like them, too," Monica chimed. "I switched after I heard Janine mention them."

Bill picked up one of the dye packs and turned it over in his fingers. Gus peered over his shoulder. "How are these things supposed to work?"

"Lance taped three of them to his chest," Claudia explained. "He rigged them in such a way they'd activate with a handheld remote."

I glanced over my shoulder at Lance sprawled inert on center stage. "He hasn't budged."

We deserted the prop table and trooped over to study the still form.

Bill nudged him with the toe of his shoe. "OK, Ledeaux, you can get up now. You've had your fun."

Rita folded her arms over her ample bosom and scolded, "All that talk, Ledeaux, and now you're the one holding up rehearsal."

A nervous sound halfway between a laugh and a bray came from deep within Bernie's throat. "What did you do, Claudia? Kill the guy?"

Claudia knelt down and jiggled his shoulder. "All right, Lance, stop pretending. Everyone's impressed."

"He don't look so hot." Gus tugged on an earlobe. A hairy earlobe. Eeuww!

But earlobes aside, I had to agree with Gus. Lance didn't look so hot. Under his Vegas tan, his skin seemed a bit grayish; a bit waxy. This playacting of his had gone on way too long — even for an experienced corpse. Not even Michael Phelps could hold his breath that long.

Lance couldn't really be hurt, could he?

Of course not, I promptly answered my inner demon. Serenity Cove Estates had already had its one random act of violence. And only one was allowed. Surely all the residents would agree with me on that score. I've always said that denial is a wonderful thing — one of the best defense mechanisms God ever invented. But denial was quickly deserting me as reality took its place.

Lance looked . . . dead.

Apparently the same thought crossed Bill's mind. He crouched down next to Lance's inert figure. "If Lance taped three dye packs to his chest, why did only one go off?"

"Who knows?" Claudia swallowed, her eyes huge in her pale face. "Maybe he didn't do it right. He said it was the job of the special effects people. That's why he said he needed practice."

As all of us looked on, scarcely daring to breathe, Bill placed his fingers along Lance's neck, palpating for a pulse. I bit my lower lip to keep it from quivering, but I already knew the truth.

Lance was dead.

I knew it for a fact even before Bill said the words.

Everything after that seemed to happened all at once. In spite of dropping my cell phone, not once but twice, I managed to dial 911 and summon the sheriff. Monica became hysterical and threatened to barf. Someone, Bernie, I think, but it could have been Gus or even Rita, found a blanket and covered the body. I heard the scrape of the prop table being shoved aside to make room for EMTs, law enforcement, and the coroner. Bill dragged an overstuffed chair from the phony living room and gently eased Claudia into it. Claudia's face was the color of kindergarten paste. One glance at it had me racing for the nearby ladies' room to fill a cup with water. Out of the corner of my eye, I glimpsed something shiny on the floor near my feet. An earring? Stooping down, I picked up a gold hoop and slipped it into the pocket of my cardigan before rushing to Claudia's side.

I knelt on the floor and handed her the cup, but her hands were shaking so violently that water sloshed over the rim. She managed a small sip, then absently wiped her wet hands on her slacks to dry them. Wanting to comfort her, but not knowing how, I set the cup down and took both her hands in mine. They were like chunks of ice. I rubbed them absently to restore circulation.

None of us said much while waiting for the sheriff and his men to arrive.

Climbing to my feet, I stood next to Claudia's chair. I was worried about her. She still hadn't uttered a word. Clearly in shock, she resembled an escapee from Madame Tussauds Wax Museum. Her eyes were glassy as a mannequin's. Her red hair and lips contrasted garishly against her pale skin. Poor Claudia; I felt so sorry for her. What does one say to a woman who's accidentally killed her husband?

Accidentally?

Surely it was an accident. Horrible and tragic, but nothing more. Then I recalled the argument I'd overheard — and wished I hadn't. Claudia had told Lance she'd take the necessary steps to end his spending spree. She'd used phrases such as *whatever it takes* and *one way or another.* My mind struggled to make sense of what had just occurred. One thing was clear, however. No way would Claudia have pointed a loaded gun at her husband and pulled the trigger — no way at all. She was my friend, and my friends didn't shoot people. It was that simple.

My musings were interrupted by sirens wailing in the distance. The sound grew louder with each passing second. A pregnant pause followed; then all hell broke loose.

The double doors of the auditorium crashed open. Sheriff Sumter Wiggins swept into the room like a tornado mowing down a cornfield. He stood for a moment, hands on hips, surveying the scene, all six feet two inches of muscle and attitude. His skin was the color of pricey Colombian coffee, his eyes hard and shiny as black onyx.

His gaze drifted over the small gathering before settling on me. "Miz McCall," he drawled in a rich-as-molasses baritone, "might've known I'd find you here."

"Sheriff." I bobbed my head in acknowledgment.

The sheriff and I are old pals. We joined forces a few months back to find the murderer of Rosalie Brubaker, my friend and neighbor. At least I'd assumed we'd formed a partnership of sorts, 'til he informed me in no uncertain terms to butt out of police business. Apparently the sheriff liked to work alone. I suspect the man might've been an only child and wasn't used to sharing.

Close on the sheriff's heels was Deputy Preston. I never did learn the man's Christian name. The deputy and I are acquainted, too. We first met during the investigation into Rosalie's death. Unbeknownst to the sheriff, who probably eats raw meat for breakfast, Deputy Preston owned up to a fondness for my chocolate-chip cookies. I caught his eye and waggled my fingers at him. He started to wave back, but a stern look from his boss had him clearing his throat instead. So much for my friendship with law enforcement.

Sheriff and deputy moved aside to allow a flood of EMTs to pour into the room. One of the EMTs, a wiry, brown-haired man with the tanned leathery skin of an outdoorsman, knelt down alongside Lance. He placed his hand along Lance's neck just as Bill had done earlier and shook his head.

"The guy's a goner."

No kidding! I wanted to blurt. What gave it away? Lack of a pulse? The fact that the man wasn't breathing? Or the bullet hole smack dab in the middle of his chest? I swallowed down the hysterical giggle that sometimes tries to escape during times of stress. I find the reflex irritating and often downright embarrassing, especially at funerals.

The sheriff focused his attention on the case at hand. "Seal off the crime scene," he instructed. "Notify the coroner." He turned to his deputy. "Preston, get these people out of heah. Find a place for them to wait until I take their statements."

Heah? Is that Southern-speak for *here?* I pondered. Exactly how does one spell such a word? In Toledo, where I hail from, *here* has only one syllable. South of the Mason-Dixon Line, it acquires a second.

Then came the moment I'd been dreading. The sheriff turned his attention to the cast and crew of Lance's extravaganza. "Before my deputy ushers y'all out, anyone care to tell me jus' what happened heah?"

Apparently none of us were eager to fill in the blanks or connect the dots. We glanced furtively from one to another, shuffled our feet, and avoided the sheriff's piercing gaze. A lengthy silence ensued.

"I'm waitin'. Y'all care to enlighten me?"

Bernie raised a bony finger and pointed straight at Claudia. "She did it! She shot her husband deader 'n a doornail."

71

CHAPTER 7

Deputy Preston herded us into a meeting room, one in a series that lined the hallway leading from the auditorium. He then took up a position just outside the door, guarding it lest one of us wanted to make a break and run for the border.

Faux leather chairs rimmed a faux mahogany conference table. A Monet print hung on one wall in a feeble attempt at ambiance. Placing my arm around Claudia's shoulders, I guided her to a chair. "Here, honey, have a seat," I told her, urging her down. "Anything I can get you?"

She didn't answer. I'm not sure she even heard me. I was worried about her. She still hadn't uttered a word; hadn't shed a tear. Her complexion looked deathly pale. Oops. Poor choice of words. Guess I'd better reserve that expression for Lance, who literally was deathly pale. Claudia's eyes had lost their usual sparkle and were glazed, unfocused. Guess I'd be unfocused and pasty, too, if I'd just shot and killed my husband.

"How could this have happened?" Rita paced the length of the room, wringing her hands.

Gus slumped down in one of the chairs at the conference table. "A freakin' accident is how."

"I checked the chamber just like you showed me, Bill," Monica said, her voice high and thready. Her face was the moldy-olive green I associated with her weak stomach. She was definitely learning self-control. I had to hand it to her for not barfing all over the crime scene. Sheriff Wiggins would not have been a happy camper.

"I checked the gun, too." Bill shoved his fingers through his hair. He, too, looked shaken by what had happened. "I saw the blank cartridges."

"Why did I let myself get talked into this?" Monica whined. "I never should have gotten involved in this stupid play in the first place."

"I'm cold," Claudia whispered, her voice barely audible.

I shrugged out of my cardigan and draped it around her. "Here, this'll help."

She pulled my sweater tighter, but shivered

in spite of its warmth. "I want to go home."

"Soon, honey." I patted her shoulder in an attempt to comfort her. "The sheriff wants to ask us a few questions first."

She lapsed back into silence.

A minute later, Deputy Preston entered the meeting room and approached Claudia. "Sorry, ma'am, but I need to check your hands for gunshot residue."

She stared at him blankly.

The young man glanced around, the expression on his dark face almost apologetic. "Actually, I'll need to check all of you for GSR."

"This is an outrage!" Bernie Mason fumed, jumping to his feet. "Why are you treating us like criminals? Everyone saw her shoot the guy."

I saw Claudia flinch as Bernie's harsh accusation pierced the brittle shell under which she'd retreated. I gave her shoulder another reassuring pat. "Never mind Bernie, honey. He failed Sensitivity for Dummies and needs a refresher course."

"Won't hurt a bit, ma'am," Deputy Preston told her. I liked the man, a liking that had nothing to do with his fondness for my cookies. He had a gentle way about him. His mama ought to be proud.

Claudia started at the sound of the gunshot residue kit being ripped open.

"It's OK. The nice deputy is only following protocol." I was making it up as I went along; ad-libbing like crazy. Actually, aside from Rosalie, the closest I'd ever come to any murder/homicide investigation was on television. Not that one can't learn a lot watching classics like *Law & Order* and *CSI*. I'd picked up tons of useful information along the way.

Claudia watched dully as the deputy went about the task of collecting his sample. I watched, too, fascinated in spite of the gravity of the situation. All the while my mind echoed Rita's question, How could this have happened? We were simply rehearsing a scene from the play. No one was supposed to get hurt.

No one was supposed to die.

Having finished with Claudia, Deputy Preston straightened. "Who wants to be next?"

Bill stepped forward and held out his hands. "You can do me."

If Bill could be brave, so could I. "After him, you can test mine."

Satisfied with the samples he'd collected from all of us, the deputy still had more tricks up his sleeve. "Now I need to ask all you good folk to be patient a bit longer while I do the fingerprinting."

"Fingerprinting!" Bernie exploded. "What the hell you goin' to ask for next — a kidney?"

"No, sir," the deputy replied. "Already got two good ones."

Gunshot residue. Fingerprints. Wait 'til I tell my daughter, Jennifer, about this. But then again, maybe not. The wisest course of action would probably be to keep my mouth shut. Jen tends to overreact. She's finally getting back to normal after my last escapade into murder and mayhem. Knowing her, I'd be shanghaied and sent to LA, where I'd be relegated to a life babysitting my two adorable granddaughters. Granted, I love both Juliette and Jillian to pieces, but I don't want to spend my golden years a captive audience at a continuous round of dance recitals and soccer games. I may be a doting grandmother, but I'm a liberated one.

I worriedly cast another glance in Claudia's direction. Except for saying she was cold and wanting to go home, there was not a peep out of her; probably a good tactic under these circumstances. Perhaps I should advise her that it was her right to remain silent? Remind her that anything she said could and would be used against her in a court of law?

Bill, his Paul Newman baby blues full of concern, sidled up next to me and squeezed my hand. "How you holding up?"

I squeezed back. "Do you think we should call an attorney on Claudia's behalf?"

"Good thinking," he said in a voice low enough for my ears alone. "An attorney sounds like an excellent plan."

"Problem is, I don't know whom to call. She needs someone good — real good. Someone familiar with the South Carolina court system."

Bill rubbed his jaw. I racked my brain. Both of us were lost in thought. Whom could I ask for a recommendation? Who'd know the name of a good defense attorney? One ideally born and bred in the South. Ninety-nine percent of the folks in Serenity Cove Estates came from elsewhere — Michigan, Ohio, Indiana, Pennsylvania, New York; some from even as far away as California and Alaska. Not even Connie Sue, the Bunco Babes' very own dyed-in-the-wool Southern belle, could claim South Carolina as her home. She hailed from Georgia.

"I don't want that messy stuff all over my hands," I heard Monica complain to the deputy. "What if I get it on my clothes?"

"Don't worry," soothed calm, sensible Rita. "If you do, I've got just the stuff for getting out stains."

I noticed Bill's new buddy didn't seem the least bit perturbed by the proceedings. Gus had taken up a position at the end of the conference table where he played solitaire with a well-worn deck of cards. Bernie sat in an adjacent chair, watching the game, arms folded. I could hear the low rumble of the sheriff's voice issuing orders just outside the door. I could feel the sand slip through the hourglass. Soon now, Sheriff Sumter Wiggins would grill us like ribs at a Fourth of July barbecue.

Chilled after giving Claudia my sweater, I rubbed my hands up and down my arms to warm myself. "The sheriff isn't going to go easy on Claudia. She needs a lawyer and she needs one fast."

"Someone experienced in handling criminal cases."

I winced at hearing the word *criminal* used in conjunction with Claudia. She wasn't a criminal, unless that was the new term for falling for a low-down, no-good scumbag like Lance Ledeaux. Pardon me for speaking ill of the dead, but if the shoe fits, as my daddy used to say.

Suddenly Bill snapped his fingers. "I think

I know just the person who might help us."

"Who?" I asked, already digging for my cell phone.

"Eric Olsen. Being a Brookdale cop, he probably knows the name of the best defense attorney in the entire county."

"Bill, you're brilliant!" I could have given my favorite handyman a great big hug right then and there — and planted a big, fat, noisy kiss on his cheek. But I did neither. I was already busy punching in Eric's number. At one time I could have hugged and dialed at the same time, but I'm losing my ability to multitask.

CHAPTER 8

"I know just the person," Eric told me.

I disconnected, reassured Eric was on the case. He'd promised to find Claudia the best darn defense attorney east of the Mississippi and south of the Mason-Dixon Line. I made a mental note to bake him a double batch of chocolate-chip cookies as my way of saying thanks.

I settled down in a chair between Claudia and Bill to await Sheriff Sumter Wiggins. It wasn't long before he stormed into the meeting room. The scowl on his dark face resembled a rain cloud about to burst and drown its hapless victims. His presence seemed to suck all the air from the room. I now knew how it felt to be vacuum sealed.

He didn't waste any time. "I gather you're all in agreement that Miz Ledeaux is the shooter."

I flinched. *Shooter* put me in mind of street gangs. And street gangs reminded me of the Jets and the Sharks. I particularly loved that finger-snapping scene from *West Side Story,* one of my all-time favorite musicals. Lots of leather jackets, lots of swagger; thinking of Broadway musicals was a welcome distraction from thinking of Lance lying dead onstage.

"Well . . . ," he prompted.

Reluctantly we nodded.

"In the interest of bein' thorough, I had my deputy check everyone for fingerprints and GSR."

I knew GSR was police-speak for gunshot residue. I'd done my homework and was up to date on my acronyms: CSI, CIA, DOA, DNA, TOD, and GSW. I could rattle them off in the same way a kindergarten class did the alphabet. I prided myself on being savvy enough to know COD meant cause of death, not cash on delivery. I could work my favorite acronyms into a dinner party conversation with ease. I'd never had cause to use any of these terms in an official capacity, mind you, but I like to keep current. It holds dementia at bay.

Sheriff Wiggins took out a pen and flipped open a black spiral notebook. "Will one of you nice folks kindly describe what happened back in the auditorium?"

See no evil, hear no evil, speak no evil.

That about summed us up.

The sheriff was rapidly growing weary of our lack of response. "I'm goin' to get to the bottom of this if it takes all night. Now" — he glowered; we cringed — "first off, I need someone to give me a general idea what was goin' on prior to the shootin'. Afterward, I'll take your individual statements. Who wants to go first?"

My hand shot up. "I will."

He stared at me long and hard, then turned away. "Any *other* volunteers?"

Hmph! Guess I can tell when I'm not wanted. You'd think after my valuable contributions in the past, he'd be begging for my help. But no. He liked to think he could solve a case without the able assistance of a concerned citizen such as I.

"You." The sheriff singled out Bill with a pointed look. "Give me the *Reader's Digest* version of events that prompted the incident."

Bill shifted in his seat, looking uncomfortable. "We were rehearsing a play that Lance, Mr. Ledeaux, is producing, directing, and starring in. Gus and I," he said, motioning toward his newfound friend, "were there to take some measurements. I also needed to ask him a few questions. I'm responsible for the set," he added as an afterthought. "Gus agreed to be in charge of lighting and sound."

"We were rehearsing act three, scene one," I spoke up, wanting to participate and not wanting to be left out.

One pained look from the sheriff, and I lapsed into silence. It wasn't easy, let me tell you, when I desperately yearned to contribute.

"What about the rest of you folks? Y'all actors in the play?"

Rita cleared her throat. "I'm the stage manager."

"I, um, I'm in charge of props," Monica mumbled, her voice barely audible. She sat hunched, her arms around her waist, and stared at the floor.

The sheriff gave her a long, considering look that I'd wager made repeat offenders sweat bullets. "So you're the one in charge of the gun that killed Mr. Ledeaux." It was a statement, not a question.

Monica gave a jerky nod, her attention still focused on the nubby carpet.

Sheriff Wiggins jotted this down in his little black book. "I'll get your statement right after talkin' with Miz Ledeaux."

"I think I'm going to be sick." Clutching her stomach, Monica made a dash for the ladies' room. Seeing her olive green complexion, no one tried to stop her.

Bill continued his narrative. "Lance wasn't pleased with the way rehearsal was going. He insisted on running through the lines over and over until the cast got it right."

"It was his idea to use the props," Rita muttered.

Another notation in *the* book.

"Ledeaux didn't like the way I did my lines. Said he'd show me how a real actor would do it." Bernie shoved away from the table and rose abruptly. "This whole thing is Mort Thorndike's fault."

Pen hovered over paper. "Who's Mort Thorndike?"

Had I suffered a transient loss of consciousness while onstage? I could have sworn Mort Thorndike had been nowhere in the vicinity. And he was a hard person to miss, seeing how he irritated the heck out of me.

"Mort's my golfing buddy," Bernie replied in a tone that implied the sheriff should know this. "Weren't for him, I'da been learning my lines instead of out on the course."

So much for the *Reader's Digest* version. It was soon apparent that if Sheriff Wiggins wanted to hear what happened, it was all or nothing. Knowing he was outnumbered, he surrendered grudgingly and listened to us ramble. When our comments drew to a halt, he asked, "Who owns the gun?"

That brought me up straighter in my chair. I have to admit I hadn't thought about that part of the accident — at least not yet. Guess I'd assumed the gun belonged to Lance.

"It's mine," Bill admitted.

I swung around to face him. "Yours?"

Bill kept a steady gaze fixed on the sheriff. I needed to add "intrepid" to Bill's list of attributes. "Ledeaux heard I was a hunter, probably from Claudia, and asked if I'd loan him a handgun for the course of the play. But before I did, I made sure there were no bullets in it. I checked and double-checked — even tonight. Only blanks were in the cartridge."

The sheriff raised one eyebrow. "What happened next?"

The sheriff might as well have been speaking Swahili at this point. Bernie picked at a hangnail. Bill scuffed the toe of his shoe on the carpet. Monica returned just then, looking teary eyed and weepy. Upon seeing her, Rita started digging through her pockets for a tissue.

I shot a nervous glance at Claudia who remained ghostly pale and unmoving. Was she in a catatonic state? I didn't have the foggiest notion of what a catatonic state was, but I bet my diagnosis wasn't far off the mark. I made a mental note to Google this when I got home — if I ever got home. Right now my house on Loblolly Court seemed as far away as the moon.

At last it was Rita who rose to the challenge. Rita's like that. She's a take-charge kind of gal. That was the reason Lance had appointed her stage manager. If anyone could make a production and rehearsal run smoothly, it was Rita. She was organized, efficient, and . . . courageous.

"Claudia came to the part in the scene that called for her to shoot the man who killed her lover and was threatening to blackmail her." Rita absently smoothed a hand over her slacks. "She said her lines and pulled the trigger."

"Just like in the script," I added, trying to justify the whole terrible chain of events.

Claudia began rocking back and forth. "Oh my God," she wailed. "I killed him."

I put my arm around her. "Honey, it's not your fault. It was just a horrible accident. All of us know you never meant to hurt Lance."

Monica was next to burst into tears. "I never should have gotten involved in any of this. I don't know the first thing about being a prop princess."

I didn't have the heart to correct her. If she wanted to be a princess, it was fine by me.

"Was it at this point one of you placed a nine-one-one call?"

We looked at each other rather sheepishly. No one was eager to relate what occurred next.

"Ah, not exactly," I muttered when no one else seemed ready to cough up the information.

Now it was my turn to be the recipient of the sheriff's one-eyebrow lift — a gesture cultivated to intimidate; a gesture reminiscent of a Sister Mary Magdalene when she spotted one of her students chewing gum during algebra.

"Kindly define 'not exactly.' "

I stared down at my hands while the seconds ticked away. In the far reaches of my mind, I noticed I could use a manicure. Clearing my throat, I forged ahead. "Claudia told us Lance was only pretending to be dead."

"Pretendin'?" the sheriff thundered. "Who in their right mind 'pretends' to be dead?"

"All of us thought he was pretending," Bill responded, quick to back me up. "We thought Ledeaux was trying to impress us with what a great actor he's cracked up to be."

I patted Claudia's shoulder. "He was experimenting with dye packs."

"Dye packs?" The sheriff's eyes narrowed to slits. "What the hell are dye packs?"

"They're used in the movies for special effects — like bullet holes," Rita explained.

"Except the red on his shirt turned out to be real blood, not some Hollywood food colorin'," the sheriff concluded.

Claudia's wails had lapsed into sobs. Tears streamed down her face, leaving dark tracks of mascara. I searched the pockets of my slacks for more tissues but without success. Bill, seeing my dilemma, reached into his back pocket and produced a handkerchief, which I gratefully accepted and passed to Claudia.

"Back to the matter of the gun." The sheriff widened his stance as if hunkering down for the duration. "Other than Miz Ledeaux, who handled it?"

"He did." Bernie pointed at Bill.

Bill pointed at Bernie. "He did."

The sheriff sighed and duly made a note of this. "Anyone else?"

Monica seemed to shrink back into her seat. "I, ah, think I did, too."

"Me, too," Gus admitted sheepishly.

Rita cleared her throat. "I might've picked it up and returned it to the prop table."

"Think? Might have?"

The sheriff rolled his eyes. If I could've read his mind, I'd have said he was praying for forbearance.

"So six of you admit to handlin' the murder weapon?" I detected a cutting edge to his usually smooth baritone. He pinned me with a look. "How come you're not on the list, Miz McCall? You afraid of guns?"

"No need to get testy, Sheriff. You have plenty on your list already without adding my name," I reminded him acerbically.

"Can't argue with you on that point, ma'am."

Out of the corner of my eye, I noticed Gus Smith mechanically shuffling and reshuffling his worn deck of cards, seemingly impervious to the drama around him. He was so quiet, I'd nearly forgotten he was present. He probably wished he'd never heard of Serenity Cove Estates.

The sheriff addressed the group at large. "Hope all of you had the good sense not to disturb the crime scene."

"Of course," Rita said indignantly.

"What do you take us for? Morons?" So spoke Bernie, king of the morons.

Bill leaned forward in his chair, hands interlaced on the table, and asked quietly, "How is it possible for one to knowingly disturb a crime scene when one doesn't know a crime's been committed?"

Sheriff Sumter Wiggins heaved a sigh. I wondered whether he was weighing the merits of running for reelection. "Suppose y'all tell me what happened when y'all first realized Mr. Ledeaux wasn't playactin'."

Not bothering to check how deep the water was, Bernie dove in headfirst. "Gus helped me shove the prop table out of the way so you guys had room to work. There's not a lot of space backstage. Tends to get crowded."

The sheriff, an aggrieved expression on his face, jotted this down.

"I found a blanket and covered the body," Rita offered. "If I didn't, Monica threatened to throw up. Believe me, you don't want that to happen to your crime scene."

Bill drummed his fingertips restlessly on the faux mahogany table. "I dragged a chair from the set for Claudia to sit in. Didn't want her passing out."

"I went into the ladies' room and got her a glass of water," I recounted. "Claudia, the poor dear, was shaking so badly, she spilled it all over her hands."

Bernie's narrow face broke into a smile, the smile of the self-righteous. "Instead of standing around wringing our hands, we all pitched in to help. Like I said, we're not a bunch of morons."

"Let's see if I got this straight." The sheriff made a production of scanning his notes. "Six of y'all admit to handlin' the murder weapon." He paused. "And y'all, in one way or another, admit to contaminatin' my crime scene."

I nodded. "Yup, that about sums it up."

Just then the door opened with a bang, and a gentleman who looked like he knew his way around a buffet table entered the room. A mane of snow-white hair was combed straight back from a wide brow. In spite of his age, which I guestimated to be mid-sixties, his face was as pink and unlined as a baby's bottom. He wore dark pants, a navy blazer, and a pale blue shirt with a red and white polka-dot bow tie. I thought I heard the sheriff suppress a groan at the sight of him, but I could have been mistaken.

Ignoring the sheriff, the man addressed the group in general. "I'm Badgeley Jack Davenport the Fourth, attorney-at-law. Sheriff Wiggins, heah, likes to refer to me as 'Bad Jack' 'cause I'm a real badass, pardon the expression, in court. Friends call me BJ." He turned shrewd gray eyes on Claudia, who stared up at him dumbfounded. "Don't say another word, darlin', without the advice of your attorney, who in this instance happens to be me."

CHAPTER 9

Float like a butterfly. Sting like a bee.

Watching Badgeley Jack, aka Bad Jack, aka BJ Davenport, brought to mind boxing champ Muhammad Ali's oft-quoted line. Bad Jack was poetry in motion; a force to be reckoned with. I'd love to see him pitted against my favorite TV lawyer, Jack McCoy, played by actor Sam Waterston on *Law & Order.* Jack can filet opponents before they even know they're bleeding. I bet ol' Badgeley Jack Davenport IV can perform the same neat piece of surgery.

I've never confided this to anyone before, but my secret fantasy is to appear on an episode of *Law & Order.* Oh, I don't want a big part — certainly not anything that requires lines. No, I'd be satisfied to play one of the jurors. How hard could that possibly be? All one had to do was assume a thoughtful, intelligent expression. Maybe I'd nod my head to indicate I was paying rapt attention to the proceedings. A piece of cake, right? Of course, I'd need the right outfit to wear. I'd designate Polly my fashion consultant — then again, maybe not. Polly'd have me looking like a teenage hooker — or a grandmother on acid.

"Was this poor bereaved woman the only one with access to the gun?"

At Bad Jack's question, I snapped out of my woolgathering.

The sheriff wasn't happy, and it showed in his deepening frown. "No," he replied gruffly. "From what I understand, everyone in the room had access. We'll know more after we get test results back from the lab."

"I'm assumin' we're talkin' fingerprints and GSR." Bad Jack's pale, almost colorless, gray eyes skewered the sheriff. "You recall what they say about those who assume? I trust, Sheriff, you tested everyone heah in this room and not just my client?"

The sheriff gave a curt nod. "Of course."

"Unless you're ready to file charges, I suggest you let the unfortunate widow get medical attention. She needs to be sedated, comforted, not subjected to cruel and heartless interrogation — which won't stand up under my cross-examination."

Cruel and heartless? Bad Jack made it sound as if the sheriff were about to drive bamboo shoots under Claudia's fingernails — or subject her to the old standby, Chinese water torture.

"I agree with Mr. Davenport," I heard myself pipe, and earned a dirty look from the sheriff. "Claudia's still in shock. Can't further questioning wait until tomorrow?"

"It's my understandin' the widow and the deceased were newlyweds. Unless you can establish motive, Sheriff, we can only conclude this was nothin' more than an unfortunate, albeit tragic, accident."

Uh-oh. Motive was one of the Big Three, right up there next to means and opportunity. Did a new husband running up charge cards to the max qualify as motive? If not, what about withdrawing a thirty-thousand-dollar cash advance? And then the real kicker: Lance had placed an order for a seventy-five-thousand-dollar Jaguar? Three strikes and you're out.

I should have left the auditorium the instant I'd heard them arguing. I should have stuck my fingers in my ears and turned tail. But no, not I. I stayed, shamelessly eavesdropping on a very private conversation. Was it too late to make a New Year's resolution to mind my own business?

"Can we go? Please," Monica begged piteously. "I'm afraid I'm going to be sick again."

Sheriff Wiggins pinched the bridge of his nose between thumb and forefinger. "Anythin' else anyone wants to add before I send y'all home for a good night's sleep?"

Apparently not, because a lengthy silence ensued.

He tucked his little black book away. "This isn't over, folks, not by a long shot. Expect to hear from me in the near future. After I get the reports back from Columbia, we'll have ourselves a nice chat."

Turning on his heel, he marched out. We filed out of the meeting room, a solemn, subdued little group of thespians, just as the coroner and his assistant were wheeling Lance out in a body bag.

"Oh my God," Claudia moaned. "I can't believe I killed him."

"Hush, Miz Ledeaux," Bad Jack admonished. "No more talk like that while the sheriff's within earshot."

She shuddered violently, but I think she heard him because she said no more.

"It's going to be OK, honey." I wrapped my arm around her and led her toward the exit.

Rita came up alongside us. "Kate," she said in a low voice, "Claudia shouldn't be alone tonight. Can you stay with her? I'll see that Monica gets home safely."

"No problem. That's what friends are for." Claudia had no family close by. One son, whom she teasingly called Bubba, was a surgeon in Chicago. Her other son, Butch, was an engineer in Seattle. When the chips were down, the Babes took care of their own.

I felt Bill's hand at the small of my back. I looked up at him, and he summoned a smile — not a happy smile but a smile all the same. "If you give me your car keys, I'll drive you and Claudia home. Gus can follow in my pickup. Tomorrow someone can arrange to get Claudia's car to her."

"Thanks, Bill," I said with a nod. His was a good plan. So much for coffee and lemon bars. They'd have to wait for another time — a time without bright red bloodstains on a yellow oxford cloth shirt.

In Claudia's house I gave her a sleeping pill from a bottle I found in her medicine cabinet. Then I tucked her into bed as I used to do with my children and pulled the covers up to her chin. Minutes later she was sound asleep. I tiptoed out, leaving the bedroom door open a crack.

I stood for a moment, debating where to

spend the night. The guest room beckoned with its fluffy duvet and mounds of pillows, but I opted for the living room sofa. I wanted to be close in case Claudia woke during the night. I burrowed down on the sofa under a wooly throw but couldn't fall asleep.

Though my body was weary, my brain was wide-awake, replaying Lance's fatal shooting over and over again. Motive, means, and opportunity whirled like a merry-go-round inside my head. The means had been Bill's handgun. Lines that read, *Take that! And that and that!* provided the opportunity. And motive? Well, I'd overheard enough motive for several murders.

But in this instance, motive, means, and opportunity didn't add up to Claudia's being a cold-blooded killer. I said it before, and I'll say it again. She's my friend, and my friends don't kill people.

Rolling onto my side, I punched the cushion. How did a real bullet get into the gun's chamber? Could Bill have been careless? No, that wasn't the answer either. Bill wasn't the careless type. Not only was he a seasoned hunter but he was also the most safety-conscious person I knew. Most likely the cause would turn out to be a malfunction of some sort, and Claudia would be fully exonerated.

I shifted onto my back and stared at the ceiling. A wide-bladed fan hovered above me like the Goodyear blimp. An ugly question reared its head. What if money matters weren't the only reason for marital discord in the Ledeaux household? What if Lance was seeing another woman? Namely a dark-haired woman who drove an expensive automobile. Their clandestine rendezvous had taken place behind a Dumpster at the Piggly Wiggly. And if I was any judge of body language, they had appeared to be arguing.

Darn, darn, darn. There it was again, that nasty *M* word — motive. Not only was Lance robbing Claudia blind, but maybe, just maybe, he was seeing another woman on the side. What would the sheriff make of all this? I wondered. He'd have motive galore for murder. Claudia would be arrested and never again see the light of day. I had to do something. But what? I couldn't sit by and let my friend rot in prison.

In case my malfunction theory didn't pan out, perhaps I could conduct an investigation of my own. It couldn't hurt. *Always be prepared.* The Girl Scout motto still rang in my head even after all these years. Problem was I didn't know diddly-squat about detective work. But I wouldn't let that stop me — not with Claudia's life on the line.

Tossing aside the throw, I hopped off the sofa and padded down the hall to the home office at the front of the house. I knew where Claudia kept her laptop, and my computer skills were growing by leaps and bounds since I had joined Geeks and Nerds, Serenity Cove's computer club. As soon as the laptop booted up, I clicked Internet Explorer and was *surfin', surfin' USA.*

It didn't take long to find exactly what I was looking for. I typed in *private investigating* on my favorite book site and up popped hundreds of titles. The first one caught my eye. *The Complete Idiot's Guide to Private Investigating.* Just what I had in mind; it seemed perfect. Not that I'm a *complete* idiot, mind you, but at times I'm dangerously close. With a twitch of the finger, the book was on its way. Feeling much better now that I'd taken action, I switched off the computer and returned to the sofa.

And slept like a baby.

CHAPTER 10

The phone rang at precisely nine o'clock the next morning. I stumbled to answer it before it woke Claudia. Tammy Lynn Snow, Sheriff Wiggins's girl Friday, informed me her mean ol' boss wanted to see Claudia in his office and take her statement. I reminded Tammy Lynn that my friend had been advised not to speak without her attorney present during questioning. I felt proud of myself for remembering this. My brain's usually a bit fuzzy until my second cup of coffee kicks in.

I heard Tammy Lynn sigh all the way from Brookdale. "I'll call Mr. Davenport's office and set up a time."

She called back minutes later. We agreed that I'd drop Claudia off at the sheriff's office at noon. After finishing up in court, "Bad Jack" Davenport would meet her there. That settled, I refilled my coffee cup, sat down at the kitchen table, and pondered my next move.

Claudia was in one heck of a fix. Lance was dead, and she'd pulled the trigger. There was no way to pretty up the facts. It was time to rally the Babes and see whether we could put our heads together to come up with some sort of plan. I reached for the phone. As I always say, twelve heads are better than one.

Pam, my true blue best friend, was first on my list. Thanks to the grapevine, which thrives better than kudzu, she already knew the gory details. Kudzu, as I discovered upon my move from Toledo, is also nicknamed the "foot-a-night vine," the "mile-a-minute vine," and the "vine that ate the South." Compare our grapevine to run-of-the-mill kudzu, and you get an idea of how fast gossip travels here in Serenity Cove. Pam insisted I need worry only about getting Claudia up and running. She'd man the phone lines and round up as many of the Babes as she could on short notice. Armed and dangerous, we'd meet for a showdown at noon at the Koffee Kup, the local diner and coffee shop.

Getting Claudia moving took prodding, cajoling, and a gallon of high octane French roast. Her moods shifted between morose and manic. One minute she'd be sobbing and sad, then shift into defiant and angry. The sobbing and sad I could understand. I wasn't too sure about the defiant and angry. In some obtuse way, she seemed to blame Lance for what had happened. But I knew that beneath the crying, beneath the ranting, she was terrified — terrified she'd spend her golden years locked in a jail cell because of some freak accident.

I managed to get her ready with enough time left to swing by my home for a quick shower and change of clothes. I delivered Claudia into Tammy Lynn's capable hands minutes before her lawyer arrived, briefcase in hand.

He gave us both a broad smile. "Don't y'all worry about a thing. They don't call me Bad Jack for nothin'. I earned that title. And I'm damn, pardon the expression, proud of it."

I gave Claudia's shoulders a pat before Bad Jack hustled her down the hall toward the sheriff's office to meet her doom. Doom? A slip of the tongue. I meant meet her fate.

My BFF, Pam, was waiting when I arrived at the Koffee Kup, where she had secured the large corner booth at the back of the diner. "Claudia OK?" she asked by way of a greeting.

I slid in next to her. "As OK as anyone can be after shooting her husband 'deader 'n a doornail,' to quote ferret-faced Bernie."

"Ferret-faced? Kate, cut the poor guy some slack," Pam admonished. "Please tell me the man didn't really say that."

I solemnly drew a giant X across my chest. "Cross my heart and hope to die. Stick a needle in my eye."

"Figures. He can be such a jerk at times."

"At times? You mean all the time, don't you?"

Glancing around, I noted the diner was filled to capacity. The owner had taken its cue from the popular Cracker Barrel restaurant chain when it came to décor. Antique kitchen utensils, farm tools, and photos of long-lost relatives in ornate frames hung on the walls. Tables covered in red-checkered cloths held small vases of plastic flowers. The diner featured old-fashioned home cooking, reminiscent of Sunday dinner at grandma's, with classic offerings such as meat loaf, mac and cheese — a staple here in the South — catfish, and, of course, finger-lickin'-good Southern-fried chicken. And pies. Pies here at the Kup were phenomenal — pecan, key lime. My hands-down favorite was the lemon meringue with its meringue mounded mile high. But I'm wandering off course. We weren't here to talk food, but how to save Claudia's butt.

"Where's everyone?" I asked. "Did you stress that this is a matter of life and death?"

"Connie Sue's having her mammogram. Said she'd call later to see what she could do."

"What about Monica?"

"Monica's a nervous wreck worrying about meeting the sheriff later today. She said the mere mention of food nauseates her."

I picked up a menu but didn't open it. "Did you call Rita?"

Pam nodded. "Rita said the sheriff instructed her not to discuss the case until he talked with her."

The sheriff, it seemed, was a busy man. I wondered if I was on his hit list. I wasn't sure if I should feel relieved or disappointed not to have heard from him. But on the bright side, since I hadn't heard from him, I was free to talk about the case with whomever I chose.

Pam spread her napkin on her lap. "All I could muster on short notice were Janine and Gloria."

"If Gloria comes, so will Polly. No way she'll miss the excitement."

No sooner were the words out of my

mouth than the bell over the front entrance jangled. I looked up to see Janine trailed closely by Gloria and Polly. Janine's pretty face wore a worried frown. Gloria looked somber in a gray turtleneck and a gray and burgundy plaid polyester pantsuit with a flotilla of gold chains around her neck. Polly's face crinkled into a smile when she spied us. She'd dressed for the occasion in a marigold yellow knit top emblazoned with the purple-sequined question, AT WHAT AGE AM I OLD ENOUGH TO KNOW BETTER?

We made a production of jamming five people into a booth designed for four. A waitress, a slender brunette I hadn't seen before, approached our booth. She wore a HELLO, MY NAME IS name tag with *Krystal* scrawled in the blank space provided. She handed us menus, then departed to fill our drink orders.

"Claudia been arrested?" Polly wanted to know.

I shook my head. "Not as of ten minutes ago. I stayed at the sheriff's office until Bad Jack arrived."

"Who's Bad Jack?" Polly demanded. "Sounds like a bounty hunter."

I had to remind myself the others hadn't been present the night before. They had received all their information second or

106

third hand. "Bad Jack, called BJ by his friends, is Badgeley Jack Davenport the Fourth, Claudia's attorney."

"Quite a moniker," Gloria murmured.

"Actually, it suits him. He's quite a guy."

"Bad Jack, hmm?" Behind her trifocals, a wicked gleam lit Polly's eyes. "Sounds like a man after my own heart. I could go for one of those 'bad boy' types. I like a man a little on the naughty side. He good-looking?"

"Mother!" Gloria sounded exasperated to the nth degree. "I swear I don't know what I'm going to do with you."

"How'd she find him?" Janine asked, interrupting the mother-daughter exchange.

"I called Eric Olsen and asked whom he'd recommend. Apparently Eric's watched Bad Jack's performance in the courtroom a time or two and been impressed."

Polly gave Pam a broad wink. "Eric's a nice young man. He seems to be taking quite a shine to your Megan."

I had to agree. I'd noticed the byplay between the pair as well. Megan and Eric were cast as sweethearts in *Forever, My Darling* — Megan the ingénue; Eric the rooky detective. They were both unattached and made a cute couple.

Pam shrugged diffidently. "Megan likes him, too, but claims they're only friends.

We'll see how the friendship holds up once the play is over."

The waitress returned with drinks and took our orders. We rattled off our usuals — tuna and chicken salad sandwiches, respectively, for Pam and me, a chef's salad for Janine, BLTs for mother and daughter, who for once were on the same page.

"How's Claudia holding up under the strain?" Janine inquired.

"Not very well, I'm afraid, though she hasn't said much. And as we all know, that's not like Claudia."

"What do you suppose will happen next?" Pam posed the question on everyone's minds.

Was I the only one who'd realized the honeymoon was over for the newlyweds? "Don't have a clue," I said when no one else ventured an opinion. "Claudia's guilty as sin of firing the shot that killed Lance. We all saw her pull the trigger. That's why she needs the best defense attorney money can buy."

Janine tore open a packet of sweetener and added it to her iced tea. "What do you think will happen to the play now that Lance is dead?"

"Who knows?" I took a sip of coffee. I'd lost count of how many cups I'd consumed already and was surprised I didn't have a bad case of the shakes after all the caffeine. But drastic times called for drastic measures. "I really haven't given the matter any thought. Why?"

Janine's brows knit as she frowned. "Lance volunteered to donate the proceeds from ticket sales from opening night to Pets in Need."

Pets in Need, the local chapter of the Humane Society, was overflowing with abandoned cats and dogs and in dire need of funds. I knew canceling the play would be a devastating blow to her plans for a new shelter. No play meant no money.

"I announced Lance's offer at our last meeting." She swirled her iced tea with a straw. "The group was really counting on the money we'd receive. We've been talking about a new shelter for years. With the proceeds from the play, it could become a reality. Everyone's going to be so disappointed."

I thought of the cat I'd semi-adopted, a half-wild creature I'd been feeding canned tuna in the hope of taming. The color of orange marmalade, it was a scrawny, bedraggled feline I'd named Tang. Bill thought it might even be a feral cat — an animal abandoned and left to fend for itself. Whatever it was, the cat had the lungs and vocal cords of a feisty newborn and was as generous as Santa with gifts of mice and bits of fur and bone. An animal shelter was sorely needed to harbor poor creatures such as Tang until permanent homes could be found.

"I was hoping we'd come up with a way to help Claudia through this," I said.

"What about her sons?" Pam asked. "They should be told what's going on with their mother."

"I'll give them a call," Gloria volunteered. "I'll get their numbers from Diane. I think she might still have them."

"I don't like the idea of Claudia's being alone right now," Janine said.

"I'll move in with her for a couple days," Polly offered quickly. "Answer the phone, see that she eats, keep the reporters at bay."

I stifled a groan. Polly meant well, but I could see her granting interviews rather than keeping reporters at arm's length. In no time at all, she'd become a familiar face on the nightly news.

We exchanged nervous glances.

"Shame on you." Polly wagged an arthritic finger at us. "I know what you're thinking, but you don't have to worry. Claudia's my friend, too. I know when to keep my trap shut."

"Getting back to the play, Janine," I said, relieved immediate problems were solved, "I don't know how the play can continue without Lance in the picture."

Krystal, our waitress, returned just then, carrying a tray loaded with sandwiches. "Lance?" she asked. "That wouldn't be Lance Ledeaux, the actor, you're talking about?"

"Yep, that's him." Polly reached for her BLT. "He got shot and killed deader 'n a doornail last night."

"Ohh," Krystal mewed. Her eyes rolled back in her head as she keeled over in a dead faint. Tuna salad merged with chicken salad and BLTs. Pickles collided with chips, all to form a messy heap on the shiny red linoleum floor.

CHAPTER 11

At the sound of the crashing tray, silence thicker than bread pudding spread over the Koffee Kup. Patrons and staff alike craned their necks for a better view.

In a flash, Janine was on her knees beside the young woman, feeling for a pulse as we hovered over them.

"Should I dial nine-one-one?" I asked, digging for my cell phone, which had settled in the recesses of my purse.

"I think she just fainted," Janine said at last. "She'll be OK."

To my immense relief, the woman's eyelids flickered, and she stirred. I'm never quite sure what to do in a medical emergency. I take that back. I've developed my own protocol of sorts that I fondly refer to as the Trinity. No reference to the Holy Trinity, mind you, but a trinity all the same when it comes to medical emergencies. First step: Reach for the cell phone. Second step:

Reach for a glass of water. Step three: Pray Janine's nearby.

"W-what happened?" the young woman asked, dazed by the sea of unfamiliar faces peering down at her.

A stout, red-faced woman in a T-shirt and jeans rushed out of the kitchen to see what all the fuss was about. Since her apron proclaimed her Queen of the Kitchen, I assumed she must be May Randolph, owner and head chef. May neatly sidestepped the mess on the floor and bent over the waitress lying sprawled on a bed of bread and gooey mayo. "Krystal, you all right? What the hell happened?" she demanded in a throaty smoker's voice.

While Pam and Janine eased Krystal into a sitting position, I held a glass of water to her lips. The young woman shoved a dark strand of hair out of her face, then took a tentative sip. "I'm fine. Don't know what came over me."

"Is there someone we can call?" Gloria asked. "You still don't look well enough to drive."

Krystal shook her head weakly. "No," she said. "I'm new in town."

"This is the kid's first day," May explained, wiping large, work-roughened hands on her grease-stained apron. "I only hired her yesterday. Said she was on her way to Myrtle Beach to look for work when her car broke down. Claims they're always looking for all sorts of help with the big hotels and whatnot."

"Tough luck," Polly commiserated.

"Felt sorry for the girl after hearing she was flat broke. From the looks of her scrawny ass, I'd say she hasn't had a square meal in days."

I studied the young woman closer and was relieved to see color seep into her fair skin. She had a pretty face with even features, a full mouth, not the Hollywood, puffy fish lips type currently in vogue but full in a natural sort of way, and large hazel eyes. While her lips may not have been enhanced, I couldn't say the same about her boobs. Even though I'm not an expert in that sort of thing, they seemed a little too generous for someone with her slender build.

Reaching out, I plucked a slice of tomato from her hair. "Honey, do you know anyone here in Brookdale?"

"No." Tears sprang to the young woman's eyes. "My family's back in Iowa. But I can't go home. I've burned my bridges. Been on my own since I was nineteen."

Janine and Pam helped her to her feet. I could see she was a bit unsteady, so I pulled over a chair from an adjacent table. "Here, sit. You still seem shaky."

She gave me a tremulous smile.

May sent an anxious glance over her shoulder. The restaurant had assumed its normal hustle and bustle. "Gotta get back to work. Orders are piling up." She turned back to Krystal. "Take the rest of the day off, but if you want this job, you'd better show up bright and early tomorrow morning. I'm puttin' you on first shift. Good tips, but you earn every dime."

Krystal let out an uneven sigh and made a visible attempt to pull herself together. "Thanks, May. I'll be there; you'll see."

"I'll send a boy out to clean up this mess." With a brusque nod, May lumbered back toward the kitchen.

"Is there someplace you can lie down for a while?" Gloria asked.

Krystal burst into tears. In between sobs, she stammered, "N-no. I-I-I've been sleeping in my car."

Sleeping in her car? Dear Lord, I couldn't help but feel sorry for the poor thing. No money, no working vehicle, no place to stay. My heart went out to her. Before my head had a chance to engage, I blurted, "I've got lots of room. You can stay at my place until you get back on your feet."

Krystal's eyes widened. "Really? You mean it?"

Pam shot a warning dart in my direction. *Are you out of your frickin' mind?* I didn't need telepathic powers to guess what she was thinking. Had the situation been reversed, I'd have posed the same question myself.

"Sure — it'll be fun having a houseguest."

And it would. I had plenty of room and enjoyed company now and then. My kids were always too busy to pay their poor, lonely, widowed mother a visit. I was lucky to get an occasional phone call and a card on my birthday. Perhaps I'm being a bit facetious. Truth to tell, I confess I'm neither poor nor lonely. Thanks to planning and hard work, Jim had left me comfortably well-off. And I was rarely lonely. I'd made lots of friends here in Serenity Cove Estates, and there were tons of activities to occupy my time. Golf, Tai Chi, ceramics, book club, line dancing, and last but not least, bunco. Life was good; I had no complaints.

"Well then, it's settled," Janine said with a smile that seemed a bit forced. I could tell she wasn't happy with my decision, but what choice did I have? I wouldn't sleep a wink knowing this poor young woman was homeless, broke, and going hungry.

I felt a tug on my sleeve. Glancing down, I found Polly's scrawny fingers clutching my sweater. "Psst," she hissed.

"What's up?"

"Gotta tell you something. Meet me in the ladies' room." She scooted off before I had a chance to ask why.

I'm a sucker for cloak-and-dagger stuff. Seeing Krystal was in the capable hands of Gloria, Pam, and Janine, I mumbled an excuse and scooted after her.

"Lock the door," Polly instructed the moment I slipped inside the restroom.

"Curiouser and curiouser!" cried Alice. The words played in my head as I locked the door. "Why the need for secrecy?" I asked.

Polly regarded me, her eyes solemn behind shiny trifocals. "You know how I hate to gossip," she began.

I simply couldn't help myself. I laughed out loud.

Polly folded her arms over her modest bosom and glared at me. "What's so funny?"

"Hate to gossip?" I asked once my chuckles had subsided. "Out with it, girlfriend. Who are you, and what have you done with the real Polly?"

My veiled attempt at humor zipped right over Polly's head. She cast an anxious glance at the door as if expecting someone to crash through any second. "I saw something yesterday."

All mirth vanished in the blink of an eye. My pulse quickened a tad, the way it does sometimes when I sense bad news. "Polly, for crying out loud, just tell me what's going on."

She inched closer. "I happened to be in town having my hair done when I spotted Lance in that flashy orange car of his parked on a side street. Thought I'd surprise him, say hello. Maybe give him an update on how things are coming along in the costume department. You know, just trying to be friendly, his being new in town."

"And . . . ?"

"Well," Polly said, moistening her lips with the tip of her tongue, "I was about to tap on the driver's-side window when I realized he wasn't alone. He was with someone — a woman."

I frowned at hearing this. "A woman? You mean a woman other than Claudia?"

"Try to keep up with me, Kate. You're falling behind."

Mea culpa! Mea culpa! Shame on me for being a little slow on the uptake. "Sorry, Polly. I'll try harder."

"No need to get flip with your elders, young lady. I'm trying to tell you Lance had

his arm around a dark-haired woman —
and I think that woman was Krystal. Want
my opinion, they were acting pretty
chummy. Pretty chummy, indeed."

CHAPTER 12

What had I done? How old did I have to be in order to think first and speak later? Would I ever learn? Instead, I'd gone and invited a perfect stranger into my home — or, in this case, maybe a not-so-perfect stranger. But it was too late now for second thoughts. With the Babes' help, we'd transferred Krystal's belongings from her Honda Civic to my Buick. At the moment, Krystal was napping in my guest room.

After a stressful afternoon, I was in need of comfort food — and comfort food for me often took the form of tuna noodle casserole. I opened the pantry door and stood there — thinking. Could Polly have been mistaken about the woman she'd seen with Lance? What possible connection did Krystal have with Lance Ledeaux? Was Krystal the same woman I'd seen Lance with behind the Piggly Wiggly? I absently reached for the cream of mushroom soup, and realized belatedly I'd grabbed a jar of salsa.

I kept trying to make sense of things. The woman I'd seen with Lance had been driving an expensive-looking automobile, not a Civic on its last cylinder. Granted, I didn't get more than a glimpse, but I had the impression the driver was older than Krystal. Puzzling.

And I loved nothing better than a good puzzle.

I'd been relieved at Polly's offer to move in with Claudia temporarily. I agreed Claudia shouldn't be alone right now. We didn't need her going off the deep end. Surely when all the facts came to light, she'd be absolved of any malice in Lance's death. Facts would prove the shooting was just a malfunction of some sort; an accident in the worst degree.

Feeling somewhat better after my pep talk, I took out soup, a package of egg noodles, and my last can of tuna. I made a mental note to add tuna to my grocery list. Can't think of tuna casserole and not think of Bill. This happens to be one of his favorite dishes. When it comes to food, he's certainly an easy man to please. We seem to like many of the same things: chocolate-chip cookies, lemon bars, tuna casserole, and pizza. We even take our coffee the same way — black.

Aren't we a pair? At least, I used to think we were. Wish I knew what happened while he was in Michigan. Since his return, the temperature between us could stand some reheating. He might've gotten cold feet, but mine were still warm and toasty. Suddenly I had an idea. I reached for the phone before I could change my mind.

The phone rang and rang. I was about to hang up when Bill answered, sounding slightly out of breath.

"Bill? Hope I'm not interrupting anything important."

"Kate!" he exclaimed. "I almost didn't hear the phone over the whine of the table saw."

Bill has converted part of his garage into a woodworking shop that would rival those on HGTV. He owns nearly every power tool on the planet and knows how to use them. No small wonder he was elected president of the Woodchucks, our local woodworking club here in Serenity, two years running.

"Were you working on the set for the play?" I asked.

"Naw, after last night, that's at a standstill." Bill paused, then cleared his throat. "How're you holding up? It's not every day we see a man shot and killed right before our eyes."

I felt touched by his concern. "I'm fine. What about you? You were there, too."

"Have to admit I'm still a little shaken by what happened. Keep asking myself if I could've accidentally left a bullet in the chamber."

Now I was the one who paused while digesting this tidbit. "You think that's possible?" I asked when I rediscovered my voice.

"I've gone over this a thousand times. I've handled guns since I was a kid. The first lesson my dad taught me was to always make sure the chamber was empty before handing it over to anyone else. I pride myself on being safety conscious. Don't know how I could have missed a live round."

I stared out the kitchen window as we talked. I watched a sedan pull into the drive of the empty Brubaker house catty-corner from me and two women climb out. One I recognized as a local real estate agent; the other woman was a stranger. The house had stood empty for months. Last I heard, Earl Brubaker was undecided whether to sell or rent. For the time being, he was staying near his daughter in Poughkeepsie, New York.

Nice to see movement in the real estate market, first with Bill's new friend, Gus Smith, and now at Brubaker's. Maybe the economy was starting to perk up in spite of dire predictions from the media.

"Kate, you still there?" Bill asked.

"Sorry, I got distracted." I leaned forward for a better view, but the women had disappeared inside. "Looks like someone might be interested in the Brubaker house."

"Good to know. It's not healthy for a house to stand empty any length of time."

"You're right, of course." The sound of Krystal stirring in the guest room reminded me of the reason for my call. "Bill, ah, I need a favor."

"Sure. All you have to do is ask."

Had Bill been transformed into a genie about to grant me three magic wishes? What if I were asking for a million dollars? A trip around the world? A lifetime supply of chocolate? I reined in my imagination and got down to the business at hand.

"As of this afternoon, I have a houseguest. She could use some help." I proceeded to tell him what I knew about Krystal — which I had to admit wasn't very much. It dawned on me I didn't even know her last name. My information was sparse at best. She could be a fugitive on the lam. A drug dealer. A serial killer. Maybe Pam was right. Maybe I really was out of my frickin' mind. I don't remember who said it, but a mind is a terrible thing to lose.

My kids would have a conniption fit if they knew I'd invited a stranger to share my home. Jennifer would book me on the next flight out to LA, where I'd be sentenced to spend my retirement as a live-in, unpaid nanny. Mind you, I love my granddaughters dearly, but . . . as for my son, Steven . . . Well, he'd drop everything to enroll me in an assisted living center and feel smug he'd fulfilled his filial duty.

"Thing is, Bill," I said, continuing my explanation, "Krystal's car is out of commission. She'll need it repaired in order to get back and forth to work. I know nothing about cars. I thought maybe you'd be the person to turn to for advice."

I cringed hearing the helpless, wimpy note that had crept into my voice. So much for being a liberated woman. I might as well have simpered, *Nothing like a big strong man to help little ol' me.* Bottom line, I'd have simpered; I'd have whimpered, if that's what it took. I don't know a blame thing when it comes to cars. That used to be Jim's department. He took care of everything automotive, and that was fine by me. He's been gone nearly two years, and automobiles are still a mystery. I treat them the same way I treat my teeth. Off they both go every six months for a regular checkup whether they need it or not.

"I'm not much of a mechanic, but I know someone who is. As soon as we hang up, I'll give him a call. We can arrange to have it towed to his place. I'll drop by later to pick up the keys."

"Thanks, Bill. I owe you." No sooner were the words out of my mouth than a giant lightbulb went off in my head, a stroke of pure genius that deserved a pat on the back. I would have done just that, but it's a little hard to pat oneself on the back while at the same time holding the phone and talking. I'm not as good at multitasking as I used to be. "I was just putting a tuna casserole together," I said, all spur-of-the-moment innocence. "Why not drop by around dinnertime?"

Was there a slight hesitation on the other end of the line, or did I only imagine one? There never used to be a moment's doubt when I dangled the lure of a home-cooked meal.

"Sure," he agreed at last. "Sounds good."

"Great. See you around six."

I reached into my culinary bag of tricks and up popped lemon bars. Bill loved them. If food was the way to a man's heart, where

Bill was concerned, lemon bars were better than a GPS. A glance at the clock told me I had plenty of time to whip up a batch.

I had just finished assembling the ingredients when the phone rang. I was almost afraid to pick it up. I thought it might be Bill having second thoughts about my invitation to dinner. But it wasn't Bill; it was Tammy Lynn from the sheriff's office, calling to inform me the sheriff wanted to see me ASAP.

"Today? This afternoon?" What about my casserole? What about dessert? What about the *Oprah Winfrey Show*? I didn't bother asking. It would be a waste of breath. Sheriff Wiggins simply didn't care about my priorities.

"Yes, ma'am," Tammy Lynn replied in her unfailingly polite Southern drawl. "I've been tryin' to reach you all day. I must've left six messages on your answerin' machine."

Oh yes, the darn answering machine. I hadn't thought to check it. That wasn't exactly true. I'll confess I'd purposely avoided it for just this reason. Like it or not, I should have known the sheriff would track me down. Still, I deserved extra points for trying to avoid the inevitable.

"Sorry, Tammy Lynn. I've been out most of the day. You sure the sheriff said today?

127

He must have more important things to do than spend time with me."

"No need to worry, Miz McCall. Standard procedure, is all. Sheriff Wiggins said he wants you in his office at four."

"Fine." I sighed, resigned to my fate if not happy with it. "See you at four."

If I hurried, there was still time to whip up those lemon bars. I could practically make them in my sleep. While I waited for the crust to brown, I whisked eggs, sugar, flour, and lemon juice for the filling. My mind hopscotched back and forth between manslaughter and smoking guns. It shied away from landing on either square.

The whole truth and nothing but the truth, so help me God. The words sang through my brain like a refrain from *Les Misérables.* Should I mention the argument I'd overheard between Lance and Claudia, or keep it to myself? If I told the sheriff, he was likely to read something sinister into it. He didn't know Claudia like I did and was liable to suspect the worst. It might plant weird notions in his head — notions about motive with a capital *M.*

If I kept their argument to myself, would I be guilty of a crime? Obstruction of justice, aiding and abetting, and withholding information topped the list. I love Claudia, but not enough to be her cell mate at the state penitentiary.

Finally the dreaded hour was at hand. I dressed with care in slacks, a teal blue sweater, and a jewel-toned tweed blazer. Before leaving the house, I peeked in on Krystal, who was sound asleep. The poor girl; judging from the pile of soggy Kleenex on the bedside table, she must have cried herself to sleep. Had those tears been for Lance Ledeaux? I couldn't help wondering. She'd fainted at the news he'd been killed. God only knew what kind of relationship she'd had with the cad. Polly thought they'd looked chummy. I reasoned that there would be time enough to delve into that later. I spread an afghan over her and left a note saying I'd be home in time for dinner.

CHAPTER 13

"Hey, Miz McCall." Tammy Lynn Snow looked up from her computer monitor as I entered the Brookdale Sheriff's Department. "Sheriff had a few calls to make. He said for you to have a seat, and he'll be with you shortly."

"Thank you, dear," I told the young woman. I wondered if her wary expression was reserved only for me or for anyone who happened through the front door. She always made me feel the harbinger of bad news. Tammy Lynn tended to be overprotective of her boss. Quite often she led me to believe I upset him, though for the life of me, I can't imagine why that would have been so.

I put the plate of lemon bars I'd brought on one of the empty chairs. My mother always drilled into us children not to visit empty-handed. She insisted we bring our host or hostess a small token of esteem and

130

appreciation. It was a nicety I tried to instill into my own two, but with limited success. Oh, they liked the receiving part OK, but they were often neglectful on the giving end. I settled into a molded plastic chair and prepared to wait. I glanced around the room. Nothing had changed in the few months since my last visit — same drab office; same drab Tammy Lynn. Her style of dress gave vintage clothing a bad rep. I'd love to sic Connie Sue Beauty Queen on the girl. Gone would be the lank brown hair and the oversized glasses too large for her small face. After some tweaking in the hair and makeup department, I'd turn her over to Polly for help with wardrobe. No more serviceable brown cardigans and plaid skirts — no way, no how. With a sprinkling of makeover magic, the girl could be a raving beauty.

Restless, I got up and wandered to the bulletin board displaying Most Wanted posters. A couple new felons had been added to the assortment since my previous perusal. Beards, cornrows, and dreadlocks seemed to be the common denominators. These were the same unsmiling faces I'd seen at the post office, but I committed their sorry mugs to memory — just in case. It pays to be careful.

"Terrible thing about Mr. Ledeaux getting shot, isn't it?" I said, tossing out a gambit.

Tammy Lynn stopped pecking at her keyboard. "Yes, ma'am. It surely is."

"Did you plan on attending a performance of our play, *Forever, My Darling*? That nice young officer, Eric Olsen, had a part. He's quite a good actor."

At the mention of Eric's name, Tammy Lynn's cheeks turned rosy. "I, ah, yes. I was fixin' to buy a ticket. That is, I *planned* to buy a ticket until . . ."

Hmm. Interesting. Seeing her blush, I suspected the young woman had more than a casual interest in the handsome policeman. I recalled her once telling me that Eric was a few years older than she and a friend of her brother's. I decided to file the information away. Of late, I'd noticed Eric and Megan seemed to be hitting it off, as the saying goes. I'd noticed them laughing and talking together as they rehearsed their lines. I squelched the urge to play matchmaker. Jim always got so upset with me when I attempted to pair people up. Granted, the results had been just shy of disastrous, but as my daddy used to say, even a blind squirrel finds an acorn sometimes.

Just then the intercom buzzed.

Tammy Lynn gave me an encouraging smile. "Sheriff Wiggins will see you now."

I picked up the lemon bars, hoping I wouldn't be trading them for jail bars, and slowly proceeded down the hallway. *Dead man walking* was the expression that came to mind.

Tammy Lynn had directed me to the second room on the left. The instant I opened the door I recognized it for what it was — an interrogation room; sterile, austere, institutional. I'd seen the same gray metal table and uncomfortable-looking chairs countless times on TV. In fact, week after week, I watched hardened criminals break down and bawl like babies in such a room before being carted off in handcuffs. Fade out. Roll credits.

I straightened my shoulders and squared my jaw. I'd loudly proclaim my innocence for all it was worth. If that failed, I had Badgeley Jack Davenport IV's number programmed into my cell.

"Afternoon, Miz McCall."

I turned at the sound of the sheriff's voice behind me. His velvety baritone seemed better suited for a Christmas cantata at the Baptist church than an interrogation room. "Afternoon, Sheriff," I replied, recovering a degree of equanimity. I pasted on a valiant smile. It wouldn't work on my behalf to let nervousness show. I'd be a mouse; he'd be the hungry tomcat.

I'd be dinner.

"Brought you a little something." I placed the lemon bars in the center of the battered table. He eyed them with the same suspicion reserved for packages that went ticktock.

"What're those?"

Really! The man needed to learn that all gifts weren't bombs or bribes. "Lemon bars," I said, plunking myself down in one of the chairs and folding my hands primly. "I recall you don't have a sweet tooth, but lemon bars are more tart than sweet, don't you agree?"

"Can't say I've given the matter much thought."

The remaining chair scraped the worn linoleum as he pulled it out, then squeaked in protest as he lowered his two-hundred-pound-plus frame. He offered a smile as phony as the one I'd given him. I recognized the ploy instantly. The detectives on *Law & Order* use this technique all the time. It's the part where the investigating officer tries to establish rapport with the hapless interviewee; I, however, wasn't buying into Sumter Wiggins's act as Mr. Nice Guy.

"I trust Tammy Lynn explained this is just a formality. I'm taking statements from everyone who was in the auditorium last night."

I nodded. I couldn't get into trouble if I didn't open my mouth, could I?

He took out his little black book and flipped it open. I wondered if he slept with it. "Just relate to the best of your ability everythin' that happened yesterday evenin' from the time you entered the buildin' until the fatal shootin' of Mr. Ledeaux."

"All right," I said. "I arrived at the rec center. We rehearsed act three, scene one, and then Lance was shot."

His one eyebrow shot up. I've always admired his ability to do that. The overall effect can be quite formidable — if one had a guilty conscience. "That it?" he asked.

"That's it. Are we finished?" I half rose to leave. Leave? *Escape* would have been a more accurate description.

"If you don't mind, ma'am, I'd like a little more detail."

I sank back down. *Sank* also described my spirits. I was terrified I'd say the wrong thing and incriminate Claudia. It was bad enough to accidentally kill your husband without everyone thinking you'd done it on purpose. "There's really not much more to add."

Crossing his arms over a chest roughly the size of a football field, the sheriff rocked back in his chair. The nuts and bolts fastening it together shrieked in protest. I expected the chair to collapse any second. "My guess, Miz McCall, is you weren't raised Baptist."

"No," I said, startled by the question.

"Didn't think so. My guess would be Catholic, maybe Lutheran. Had myself a talk once with the priest over at Our Lady Queen of Angels. Catholics, I'm told, have somethin' called sins of omission."

Uh-oh. I didn't like the direction this conversation was heading. I squirmed. I actually squirmed. Years of catechism classes and parochial school flashed before my eyes. Hell-fire and damnation loomed like a gaping maw.

"I see I struck a nerve." He had the audacity to smile — a blinding flash of perfect white teeth — at my discomfort. "To refresh your memory, a sin of omission is failure to do somethin' one can and ought to do. In this instance, Miz McCall, instinct tells me you're leavin' out information. Makes me wonder why."

"I was under the impression statements were supposed to be concise," I muttered.

"I simply gave you the condensed version. No sense wasting time and paper."

"Let me judge the best use of time and paper." He brought the chair legs down with a *bang* that made me flinch. "Let's try again, shall we? This time, start at the top and run through everythin' step-by-step."

I discovered the true meaning of a hot seat as a bead of sweat trickled between my shoulder blades. I don't know how crooks can take interrogations on a regular basis. They can't be good for the heart or the nervous system.

Sheriff Wiggins waited patiently, silently. He didn't say a word; he didn't have to. The determined gleam in his onyx-hard eyes spoke volumes.

My mouth felt like a bucketful of sand. I moistened dry lips with the tip of my tongue, then took a deep breath. I started at the beginning but, out of loyalty to a friend, left out the part about the conversation I'd overheard. I ended my narrative recounting how all of us believed Lance wasn't really dead but only playacting.

While I talked, he jotted notes. I had a sneaky feeling he knew I'd committed a grievous sin of omission. Any second now I'd be given a hefty penance and instructed to sin no more.

Or charged with a felony.

After I finished, he gave me a long look. I was proud of myself for resisting the urge to confess my transgressions. I forced myself to calmly inquire, "Is the interrogation over, Sheriff?"

"Miz McCall," he drawled, "consider this meetin' an interview. I'm savin' the interrogation for later."

I got to my feet, picked up my purse, and gathered what was left of my composure. As I left the room, I gave the lemon bars, snug and pretty beneath a dusting of powdered sugar and plastic wrap, a lingering look. I'd half a mind to snatch them up and give them to someone more deserving — and nicer — than the mean ol' Sheriff Wiggins.

CHAPTER 14

My meeting with the sheriff had taken longer than I had anticipated. The man obviously had too much time on his hands since he was treating an accident like a real case. *Accident?* My mind balked at calling it murder, or even manslaughter. But dead is dead regardless of what it's called.

And what if Lance's death wasn't accidental?

I tried to stifle the pesky little voice inside my head. How had a bullet instead of a blank gotten into the gun? *If* it wasn't an accident, someone had to have put it there. But who? Surely Claudia hadn't meant it when she'd told Lance she'd find a way to get rid of him — one way or another. It was merely a figure of speech. People say those words all the time.

Don't they?

Other than Claudia, who'd want Lance dead? The dark-haired woman he argued with behind the Piggly Wiggly? And why had he been with Krystal? I was still mulling this over when I arrived home. I noticed a car parked in the Brubaker drive and wondered if yet another real estate agent was showing the house to a prospective client. It would be nice to have neighbors again. Most of the time I enjoy being the only house on a cul-de-sac, but sometimes I feel like the Lone Ranger. The lots on either side of me remain empty until their owners reach retirement age.

Many consider growing older a curse, but not the majority of the retirees I know. It's a blessing, a true blessing. Now mind you, no one wants the wrinkles and various and sundry aches and pains that come with aging, but there's a certain undeniable freedom in retirement. Time is yours to do as you please. You can spend your days on the golf course, tennis court, at a bridge table, or in a La-Z-Boy watching the Weather Channel. The choice is yours. While younger folk are scrabbling to earn a living, you can sit back and enjoy the fruits of your labors. Ask anyone I know. They'll tell you they love retirement.

A glance at the dashboard clock told me I was running late. I had barely enough time to throw my casserole together before Bill arrived. Maybe, just maybe, Krystal would want a dinner tray in her room. I'd try to convince her she needed all the rest she could muster before reporting for the first shift at the diner. With her out of the picture, Bill and I could share a cozy casserole for two. I could ply him with home cooking heavily spiced with my own unique brand of charm.

My pleasant bubble burst at the sight of Krystal in the kitchen. She glanced up guiltily, a box of soda crackers in one hand. "Mrs. McCall, I didn't hear you come in."

"Please call me Kate," I said. I put away my purse, shrugged out of my blazer, and then, after washing my hands at the sink, headed for the pots and pans.

"Hope you don't mind my going through your cupboards."

"Not at all. I told you to make yourself at home." I filled a large pan with water, added salt, and set it on to boil.

"It was kind of you to invite me to stay with you."

"It'll be nice to have company for a change." I switched on the oven, setting the dial at three hundred fifty degrees. Next, I opened the refrigerator and pulled celery and onion from the vegetable bin. I chopped, diced, and stirred. Will wonders never cease? Here I thought I'd lost the ability to multitask.

"I can't tell you how much I appreciate your offer." Krystal replaced the crackers on a pantry shelf. "You don't know the first thing about me."

"Well," I said brightly, not one to ignore the sound of opportunity knocking, "why don't we get better acquainted while I'm fixing dinner."

"Sure," she replied, taking a seat at the kitchen table.

I took out a Pyrex dish and set it on the counter. "Why not start by telling me your last name?"

"It's Gold. Krystal Gold."

Krystal Gold . . . hmm. Her name conjured visions of sparkle and glitter — and lots of it. Bling, as it's called. "A pretty name," I murmured, trying to sound noncommittal.

"Thanks. My real last name was Weindorfer, but I hated it. I changed it legally soon as I got out of high school. Kids were always making fun of me."

"Yes, kids can be cruel, but they can be a lot of fun, too." I reached for the can opener and opened the cream of mushroom soup. "When my children left for college, I volunteered at a grade school. I especially enjoyed

142

the kindergartners. That is, when they weren't sticking crayons in their noses or beans in their ears."

"I like kids, too." Krystal's voice turned dreamy. "I always wanted a big family."

I stole a glance at my houseguest. She was a pretty, young woman who appeared to be in her mid-twenties, though her actions made her seem younger. She was much too pale, though, and, except for her generous bra size, reed slender. I wondered if she was anorexic or bulimic. Dr. Phil had a show on the subject once. His guest had been so thin, her shoulder blades jutted out like a pair of wings. That would never be a problem where I was concerned — not since the invention of Peanut M&M's.

"At the diner, May mentioned you were headed for Myrtle Beach. Do you have friends or relatives there?" I asked as I dumped a package of noodles into the water, which was now bubbling merrily.

"No, we're not close, but I heard Myrtle Beach gets a lot of tourists. I thought it might be easy to find a job there."

"What kind of job?"

"Oh, I don't know." Krystal wound a strand of long dark hair around her index finger. "I thought I'd look around once I got there. See what's available. I've been traveling all over the country, working at this and that. If all else fails, I can usually find a job waiting tables."

Most people love to talk about themselves. Once started they can't seem to stop — but not Krystal. In spite of my many questions, she remained a mystery. Maybe *The Complete Idiot's Guide to Private Investigating* will give me some insight into the art of interview and interrogation. Sheriff Wiggins, I'm certain, had it down to a science but didn't seem the sort to share technique. When all else fails, he probably resorted to more drastic measures. I wouldn't be surprised if he kept a pair of thumbscrews in his back pocket as added persuasion.

I scanned the countertop for the final ingredient for my pièce de résistance. Where was the tuna? I could've sworn I'd left it there along with the soup and noodles I'd taken out earlier. I'm sure it had been there, nice as could be, before I left to meet the sheriff. There had to be a logical explanation. Were my eyes playing tricks? Had I hallucinated Charlie the Tuna's picture on a blue can? Maybe I'd absentmindedly returned the can to the pantry. Frantic, I pawed through shelves filled with cans, jars, and boxes. Soup, beans, and pie filling. I shoved aside cake mixes and packaged rice.

I discovered a mix for lemon poppy seed scones I had purchased long ago and given up for lost.

"Something wrong, Kate?"

I wanted to scream but didn't want to frighten Krystal. This was a disaster of the worst kind. How does one make tuna noodle casserole without the star ingredient? I needed tuna. I needed it now!

"The tuna fish. I-It's gone." I felt as if I were losing it. I took a deep breath to quiet my burgeoning hysteria. I wasn't usually this easily upset. Maybe it was a delayed reaction to seeing a man killed. Maybe it was seeing my hopes of a cozy evening with Bill the Tool Man dashed. Or perhaps — plain and simple — I was going bonkers.

Krystal rose abruptly and left the kitchen. I heard the door leading onto the deck open, then close. She returned a moment later carrying a small cereal bowl. "I'm sorry, Kate. There's nothing left. It's all gone."

Save for one tiny telltale scrap of tuna, the dish had been licked clean. I stared at it in dismay. "What? Who . . . ?"

"He was so scrawny. I felt sorry for him."

"He . . . ?" I struggled to wrap my mind around the problem before I unraveled completely. Had a beggar in dire need of tuna shown up on my doorstep? And the sixty-four-thousand-dollar question: What to do about Bill's dinner? A tuna noodle casserole minus the tuna equals a noodle casserole. Oh, yum!

I shot a glance at the clock. Bill was due any second. No time to run to the Piggly Wiggly. Immediately my mind went to Plan B, only to discover I didn't have a Plan B. I didn't have a Plan C either. Drat! I hate when that happens.

Out of the corner of my eye, I saw Bill's pickup turn into my drive. My panic ratcheted up a notch — or three. It wasn't bad enough there was no dinner; I didn't have time to primp. I needed to run a brush through my hair, freshen my lipstick, spritz on pricey designer perfume guaranteed to make me a femme fatale.

As if on cue, the doorbell pealed. Frantic, I raced to the pantry, grabbed a bottle of vanilla extract from the shelf, and dabbed some behind each ear. Krystal gazed at my antics in wide-eyed fascination.

"Kate, you're scaring me. Are you all right?"

"I'm fine, I'm fine." I added an extra dab of vanilla to the valley between my breasts. I saw this trick recently on one of those morning talk shows. An expert on something or other claimed men found the scent of vanilla irresistible. As an added bonus, it saves buying pricey perfume.

"Then you're not angry with me?"

The bell rang again.

"There isn't time," I called over my shoulder as I hurried toward the foyer. "Angry will have to wait 'til later."

I flung open the door. "Bill!"

I must have sounded surprised — or out of breath or both — because he looked at me quizzically. "Kate, you all right? You were expecting me, weren't you?"

"Of course, of course." My laugh was a nervous fluttery sound. I stepped aside to let him enter. "Come in, come in." I kept repeating myself but couldn't seem to stop. My speech pattern mimicked echoes down a canyon.

"I know how much you like Riesling," he said, handing me a bottle of my favorite white wine.

He looked . . . great! He wore a navy Windbreaker over a blue chambray shirt, which emphasized the color of his eyes, and freshly pressed Dockers. The man didn't need a tool belt to make my heart dance a samba.

Collecting my wits, I led him into the kitchen, where Krystal stood clutching the empty cereal bowl and looking anxious. I made the introductions and explained Bill had a friend willing to take a look at her Civic but he needed her car keys.

Bill shrugged out of his jacket. "Planned to make myself a grilled cheese sandwich for supper when you called. Couldn't turn down your offer of tuna noodle casserole."

At the word *tuna,* Krystal burst into tears.

Bill's eyes widened in alarm. "Whoa! What did I do?"

I took the bowl from Krystal's hands and offered her a tissue from the box on the counter. "There's been a last-minute change in tonight's menu."

"I'm s-sorry, Kate," Krystal blubbered. "He looked like he hadn't eaten in days."

"Krystal, you're not making any sense. Who hadn't eaten in days?"

"The c-cat. The orange cat." She sniffed noisily. "I saw him prowling around your backyard. He looked half starved, so I fed him the tuna."

Suddenly all the pieces fell into place. The cat I had assumed as feral was always on the lookout for food. "Tang," I said by way of an explanation. "That's the cat's name. He's been coming around for handouts for months, but seems to be people-shy."

Bill frowned. "Tang? Like the orange-flavored drink the astronauts used in the space program?"

I nodded. "The one and the same."

"The space program?" Krystal sniffed.

"If memory serves, NASA first used it during the Gemini missions."

Bill was a font of information. I wondered if he ever considered being a contestant on *Jeopardy!*. If there were a *Law & Order* or *CSI* category, I might consider it myself.

"Gemini?" Krystal brightened, wiping away the last of her tears. "I'm a Gemini. My birthday's June thirteenth."

"The space missions I'm referring to took place in the mid-sixties," Bill explained patiently.

"Oh," Krystal said. "That was way before my time. I wasn't even born yet."

Bill and I exchanged smiles, then shook our heads. Ah, the innocence of youth.

"Well," I said briskly, "no sense crying over spilled milk, as the saying goes. Grilled cheese sandwiches sound like the winner. Think I might have some tomato soup to go along with them. And," I added with a smile, "we have lemon bars for dessert."

"I'm s-sorry, Kate." Krystal broke into a fresh bout of weeping. "I ate them."

I stared at her in disbelief. "All of them?"

She bobbed her head, sniffling and snuffling. "Once I started, I couldn't seem to stop. I've been craving lemon ever since I found out I'm pregnant."

CHAPTER 15

The sight of cheese sandwiches grilling in a pan sent Krystal flying out of the kitchen. I heard a muffled, "Sorry, morning sickness." Then a bedroom door slammed.

Bill watched her sudden departure with a befuddled expression. "Morning sickness, this time of day?"

I nodded and turned toward the stove. "Good thing Krystal's not working the evening shift."

"From the expression on your face just now, I'd venture this is the first you've heard of the woman's pregnancy."

"It's my own fault," I said, giving the tomato soup a stir. "I should have guessed she was pregnant the second I spotted her with a box of soda crackers."

"You've taken on more than you bargained for, haven't you? How much do you know about her?"

I shrugged. "Not much. Her real name

was Krystal Weindorfer. She changed it to Krystal Gold after she got out of high school. Said she's originally from Iowa. That's about it. Oh, yes, one more thing. She's a sucker for scrawny orange cats with a yen for tuna."

"And she craves anything lemon," Bill added.

Both of us chuckled at the reminder of our almost-dessert. It felt good to laugh — nearly like the old, pre-Michigan days.

Over soup and sandwiches, we talked about this and that, impersonal things, keeping the conversation light until our plates and bowls were empty.

"What do you think will happen to Claudia?" I broached the subject we'd avoided thus far.

"It doesn't look good," Bill responded. "Any way you cut it, she was the one holding the smoking gun."

"Just the same, it makes me nervous to see the way Sheriff Wiggins is pursuing the case. Can't he understand that it was just a dreadful accident?" There I go again using the *A* word. I found it ever so much more palatable than murder and manslaughter. Or worse yet — homicide.

"I'm sure he'll consider that everyone backstage had access to the gun. It wouldn't have been all that difficult to slip a bullet into the chamber after Lance announced he was going to read the part of the villain."

We weren't talking the *A* word now. We were talking cold-blooded and calculated. Once again my mind balked at the notion. "Who would want Lance dead?"

Other than Claudia, I wanted to add but didn't. She didn't really want him dead as much as wanted him to leave his mitts off her life's savings. There was a big difference — at least to my way of thinking.

"Ledeaux didn't seem the sort to make friends easily; quite the opposite. He had a God-given talent for rubbing folks the wrong way."

Like the brunette I'd seen him with? Even Lance and the usually even-tempered Bill had had a minor altercation before rehearsal. How many others had Lance antagonized?

"What do you suppose the gunshot residue test and fingerprinting will prove?"

"Hard to say. Somehow I don't think the sheriff will wind up with much more information than he has now."

I rose from the table and refilled our coffee cups. "I only wish Claudia'd never heard of Internet dating. I don't know what possessed her to run off and marry a virtual stranger."

"Hope she had the good sense to have him sign a prenup."

"Monica said the same thing over breakfast the other day."

Bill stared into his cup, his expression glum. "My brother said prenups are the only way to go for people our age."

"They may be practical, but they don't seem very romantic. Marriage should be based on love and trust. If you can't trust the person you're about to marry, whom can you trust?"

Bill smiled that sweet, shy smile I loved to see. "I told my brother exactly the same thing."

Nice to know we were in total agreement on the subject of matrimony at least. But I refrained from saying this out loud. Lots of men get nervous at any mention of marriage. Some, I'm told, even break out in hives. What I didn't want to do was send my mild-mannered tool guy running for cover.

"And what did your brother have to say to that?" I asked.

Bill's smile vanished. "He said, 'No fool like an old fool.' Bob's convinced people our age should exercise caution and common sense before entering into a relationship with someone they barely know. He said if feelings are real, they'd still be there."

"Hmm. Interesting." I sipped my coffee while pretending to give the matter serious consideration. But a different notion plagued me. Was Bill's brother responsible for the distance between us since his return? Had Bill been brainwashed by brother Bob? How was that for a fine example of alliteration? Too bad I couldn't find humor in it.

I began gathering the dinner dishes. "How is your brother, by the way?" I asked, careful to keep my tone neutral "Has he fully recovered from his bypass surgery?"

"Bob called to tell me he signed up at a gym." Bill got up from the table and started loading the dishwasher. "Said he goes every day and walks two miles on the treadmill."

In some respects Bill and I are like an old married couple. We're as comfortable as an old pair of shoes, yet oftentimes there's a certain zing to our friendship/relationship. Right now, I was ready to add a dash of chili powder to the mix. Problem was, I was afraid too much spice might give Bill heartburn, figuratively speaking. I deliberately turned my thoughts from hot to cold.

"Unless Krystal raided the freezer, we should have enough ice cream for dessert. There's still some of that good hot fudge sauce you brought back from Michigan." For months, I'd listened to Bill rave about Sanders Milk Chocolate Hot Fudge Sauce, a Michigan delicacy. I'd found a jar on my doorstep along with a brief note after his return. How sweet, pardon the pun, I'd thought at the time. Later, I wondered why he preferred leaving it rather than giving it to me in person. Now I wondered whether Bob was to blame.

"I feel sorry for Janine now that the play is on hold," I said as I got ice cream dishes down from the cupboard.

Bill eased the door of the dishwasher closed. "How's that?"

"Janine's the new president of Pets in Need. If you recall, opening night proceeds of *Forever, My Darling* were going to benefit the shelter they planned to build. The group's really disappointed the funds won't be forthcoming."

"That's a shame," Bill commiserated. "Speaking of being newly elected, I forgot to mention I'm the president of the Rod and Gun Club. One of my first projects will be a seminar on gun safety."

A little like locking the barn door after the horse ran off, I wanted to tell him. No way will a gun safety class benefit Lance Ledeaux — or Claudia. I couldn't rid myself of the notion that time was running out for her to be a free woman.

I kept going over and over everything Bill had said the night before. The bullet didn't get there by itself. That fact was indisputable. If Claudia didn't place it there, someone else did. But who? Why? I'd tossed and turned half the night pondering these questions.

I drove into Brookdale and dropped Krystal off at the diner, reminding her I'd be back later to pick her up. I'm not by nature a morning person. The alarm on my body's clock doesn't buzz until at least eight; on rare rainy days, even later. Nothing I like better than to snuggle under the warm covers and listen to the patter of rain on the roof. I didn't know how many of these early mornings I could take. I only hoped Bill's friend wasn't just a good mechanic but a fast one.

Home again, I brewed a pot of high-test Colombian coffee. Once the caffeine started circulating through my veins, I picked up the phone and dialed Pam.

"It's up to the Babes to save Claudia," I said without preamble.

"Good morning to you, too," she returned cheerily. "What do you propose we do?"

"If I knew the answer, I wouldn't be asking for help." I grabbed the pot and topped off my cup. "Unless we do something, I'm afraid she's going to be charged with manslaughter."

"You'll come up with a plan, Kate. You always do."

"Thanks," I said dryly. I wished I shared her confidence. Right now my bag of tricks was running on empty.

"No problem. That's what BFFs are for." Pam sounded inordinately proud at her use of teen jargon. "How's your houseguest doing? You two bonding?"

I waited a beat, then dropped the bomb. "She's pregnant."

"She's what?"

"You heard me. Preggers, knocked up, got a bun in the oven, with child, in the family way." I recited my thesaurus.

"I get it, I get it! Well, that explains why she fainted. And why she's so well endowed."

"That and a boatload of silicone," I replied. "Krystal's what I'd call BBFBBM."

"BBwhat? Kate, have pity on me. I'm texting impaired."

I simply couldn't keep myself from grinning. If I hadn't been so preoccupied worrying over Claudia, I would have done my happy dance right there in the middle of the kitchen. Shows what surfing the Net can do to expand one's vocabulary. "BBFBBM," I informed her smugly, "stands for body by Fisher, brains by Mattel."

I heard Pam moan from blocks away. "Kate, you are sooo bad!"

"I know, but you love me anyway."

"By the way, how did your 'date' go with Bill last night?"

I never should have mentioned — however casually — that Bill was coming for dinner last night. "It wasn't a date, Pam. It was more of a fiasco."

I proceeded to tell her about Krystal's feeding a stray cat my last can of tuna, then polishing off the lemon bars I'd intended for dessert. While giving Pam my sob story, I happened to glance out the window. I nearly dropped the phone when I saw a dark-haired woman get out of an expensive-looking silver gray automobile across the street, pop the trunk, and take out a set of expensive-looking luggage. *Expensive* being the operative word. And not just any dark-haired woman, but one who looked vaguely familiar.

"Pam, I think someone's moving into the Brubaker house."

"You sound a little . . . distracted. Anything wrong?"

I leaned forward for a better look, my nose brushing the glass. "Unless my eyes are deceiving me, the woman looks like the one I told you about. The one I spotted with Lance behind the Piggly Wiggly."

"Promise you won't do anything foolish — such as confront her and accuse her of murder."

"Promise." Confrontation would never do. The situation called for subtlety. "Gotta run."

CHAPTER 16

Confrontation vs. subtlety. After some thought, I decided subtlety probably wasn't my strong suit. I tried to strike a balance and came up with a semisubtle plan for introducing myself to my new neighbor — and possible murder suspect. I appointed myself as a one-woman Welcome Wagon.

I hummed as I put chocolate-chip cookies, still warm from the oven, into a pretty flowered gift bag and added contrasting tissue. I'd even substituted macadamia nuts for the usual pecans. My neighbor ought to be impressed with my culinary skills, at least those in the cookie department. For a final touch, I tied the handles together with matching ribbon. After admiring my handiwork one last time, I picked up the bag and trotted across the street.

I rang the bell, prepared to don my friendliest smile. I was going to bond to Serenity Cove's newest resident like Gorilla Glue, a glue that advertises to work when others fail.

I waited, then waited some more. Was the lady of the house indisposed? Deaf? Antisocial? I was about ready to give up and try a different tactic when the door opened. A fog of cigarette smoke drifted out like pine pollen on a spring breeze.

"Don't know what you're selling, but I don't want none," came a voice so deep and raspy, it was hard to tell if its owner was male or female.

I discreetly placed my foot between the door and sill. "I'm not selling a thing." I smiled so sweetly, it might've induced a diabetic coma. "I just wanted to welcome you to the neighborhood."

After a moment's hesitation, the door opened wider, and I caught a good first look at my new neighbor. The woman was older than I initially thought, but then years of heavy smoking can cause premature aging. I know this because Monica lectured on the subject once during bunco. A network of fine lines fanned out from the corners of her eyes and striated her upper lip. In my opinion, her hair was way too dark to look natural. It put me in mind of aging male actors who dye their hair in a vain attempt to regain their youth. These men should take a tip from their female counterparts and go for the lighter, softer, kinder shades — not who-are-you-kidding black.

Enough said! Back to the subject at hand. My neighbor was also a little heavy-handed in the cosmetics department, especially when it came to eyeliner and mascara. In spite of the clumped lashes and black liner, her eyes, a pale watery green, were probably her best feature. She wore a red V-neck sweater with metallic stripes, snug black jeans, and gold hoop earrings the size of saucers.

I may have been giving her the once-over, but she was doing the same with me. It was probably a good thing neither of us could read minds. "Hi," I said. "I'm Kate McCall. I live across the street." I held up the bag of goodies. "I brought you a little something."

From the way she suspiciously eyed the gift, I wondered if she was the long-lost white sheep of the Wiggins family. Her look made me feel like one of those maligned door-to-door vacuum cleaner salesmen. I shifted from one foot to the other. I'd half a notion to return home and eat the cookies myself. "Chocolate-chip cookies are my specialty," I said in a last-ditch effort as Welcome Wagon hostess.

She took them reluctantly. "Thanks."

Just as she was starting to close the door, inspiration struck — or perhaps it was desperation in the guise of inspiration. "Do you play bunco?"

"Bunco? You mean the dice game?"

"Yeah, that's the one. It's been around for ages."

The woman shrugged diffidently. "Used to play a long time ago . . . when my daughter was little. Why do you want to know?"

"A group of us get together a couple times a month to play. Rosalie, the woman who used to live here, subbed occasionally. Since you're new to Serenity Cove Estates, I wondered whether you'd like to fill in sometime if we're short a player. Give you a chance to meet some of us."

"Name's Nadine, Nadine Peterson." The woman cracked a smile, an honest-to-goodness smile. "Just made a fresh pot of coffee. Care to join me?"

"Sure, I'd love to." I breathed a sigh of relief. My friendly overtures weren't a flop after all.

"Place is a mess. Wasn't expecting company," she said, leading me through the house.

I peeked into the living room as I trailed after her. Except for the absence of framed photos, nothing much had changed since my last visit months ago. I couldn't help but wonder if anyone had informed the new tenant that the previous occupant had been murdered.

Nadine motioned to countertops cluttered with bags and boxes. "Warned you the place was a disaster."

I picked a box off a kitchen chair and placed it on the floor. "Didn't know Earl had the house on the market."

"He doesn't, or at least not yet. I'm renting until I make up my mind whether I want to move here permanently." She began opening and closing cupboards.

"If you're looking for cups, the one on the right."

She turned to me with a frown.

"Rosalie, the old owner, and I used to be friends," I explained. "We'd get together for coffee every now and then."

"*Used* to be friends? You're not anymore?" She pulled two mugs down from a shelf.

This was proving a tad awkward. Hadn't anyone mentioned parts of Rosalie had been dispersed in and around Serenity Cove Estates? Since body parts don't mix well with coffee and cookies, I opted for the easy way out. "Ah, Rosalie died rather unexpectedly," I said.

It occurred to me that as far as the information highway went, I was giving out more than taking in. What I really wanted to learn was whether Nadine Peterson was the one I'd seen skulking around with Lance behind the Piggly Wiggly. Yet Polly was certain she'd seen Lance with Krystal. We couldn't both be right. Or could we? Nah, what were the odds of Lance being involved with two brunettes? Besides, brunettes weren't his type. I clearly remember Claudia's saying Lance was partial to redheads such as Marg Helgenberger on *CSI*. Polly must have been mistaken. The woman I'd seen him with drove a late-model silver sedan, not a beat-up Honda Civic, a car I'd come to associate with Nadine.

Time to get on with my investigation. Best to start with the easy questions and go from there. My recently arrived text, *The Complete Idiot's Guide to Private Investigating*, had advised that to get people to talk, first get them to like you; become their friend; be charming and witty.

"So, Nadine, what brings you to Serenity Cove Estates?" I asked in my most charming and witty manner. "Do you have friends here?"

Nadine set a jar of Cremora and packets of sweetener on the table along with two mugs of coffee. "Don't know a soul in this place," she confessed, sitting opposite me.

Don't know a soul? Not even Lance Ledeaux, actor and playwright? Was I mistaken and not Polly? Or was the woman an accomplished liar? Time would tell.

I took a cautious sip, careful not to burn my tongue. "There are dozens of retirement communities all over the South. How did you happen to settle on this one?"

Nadine dumped nondairy creamer into her cup, then added two packets of sweetener. I was beginning to wonder whether or not she was going to answer. She might think I was just plain nosy. Imagine!

"An acquaintance recommended this place," she answered at last in that raspy smoker's voice, "so I thought I should check it out. If I don't like it here, I'll head farther south, maybe Tampa or St. Pete."

I wondered whether that acquaintance could have been Lance. If so, judging from the little scene I'd witnessed, the reunion hadn't been a happy one. I took another sip of coffee and considered my next move. My guidebook had warned against breaking an established bond with the interviewee. Rather than chance that happening, I took a slight detour.

"As much as Serenity Cove Estates loves

gossip, I suppose you've heard about the director and star of our play getting shot during rehearsal."

She reached for a pack of Marlboros nearly hidden behind a sack of canned goods. "Mind if I smoke?" She didn't wait for an answer before pulling out a cigarette.

Actually I did mind, but detectives have to make sacrifices to solve their cases. I noticed Nadine's hand trembled, and I took this as a clue I was on to something.

She cursed under her breath when her Bic lighter failed after several flicks. Successful at last, she took a long drag, then blew a plume of smoke toward the ceiling. "Yeah," she muttered, "I heard people talking in the checkout line at the grocery store."

"Such a shame," I murmured sorrowfully. "He was quite a famous actor, you know."

"You don't say."

"You'd probably recognize him if you'd seen him. He's had bit parts in some movies and been on TV."

In my humble opinion, Nadine Peterson seemed visibly upset, but she was trying to hide it. I needed to know why. I'd be relentless if I had to. Sheriff Sumter Wiggins, beware; I'm giving notice.

She tapped ash into a saucer I recognized as part of Rosalie's good china. I tried not to cringe. "What did you say the guy's name was?" she asked.

"I didn't, but it's Lance. Lance Ledeaux. Ever heard of him?"

"Nope, can't say I have," she said, taking another deep drag on her cigarette.

I smothered a cough. "Lance played a corpse once on *CSI*. When he was shot, we all thought he was faking it — trying to impress us with his acting ability."

Smoke belched out of her mouth at her harsh bark of laughter. "How much 'acting ability' does it take to play a dead guy?"

"He was pretty convincing."

"Has the person who shot him been arrested?"

"My friend Claudia shot him, but it wasn't her fault," I explained, standing to leave. "No way Claudia would kill someone. It was an accident." I was still in denial and reluctant to admit that someone had deliberately put a live round into the chamber, knowing Claudia would fire the gun at Lance. "In due time, the facts will come to light and prove her innocent. And," I added, "if it wasn't an accident, all we have to do is find out who might have wanted Lance dead. Piece of cake, right?"

Even though I'd caught only a glimpse of her, I felt reasonably certain Nadine Peterson was the same woman I'd seen with Lance behind the Piggly Wiggly. Why would she deny knowing him? The question plagued me as I slowly walked home. I vowed to find the answer.

CHAPTER 17

That night was bunco. I hoped the evening's game would be a distraction. It'd been more than a week since Lance was shot. Instead of being reassuring, the extended radio silence from the sheriff's department was making me increasingly jittery.

The Babes' powers of persuasion had been taxed to the max. We'd coaxed, cajoled, and threatened, and in the end Claudia agreed to join us. She'd been in a funk ever since that fateful night — understandably, given the circumstances. But we were determined to do our darnedest to cheer her. At times like these, you needed to surround yourself with girlfriends.

My home was the designated site for the "intervention." I'd spent all afternoon preparing for the event. While going through my recipe file earlier that day, I'd come across an old tried but true recipe for whiskey sours. This had been our friend

Pete's specialty drink. He and my husband, Jim, had once worked together, and the two men had remained friends into retirement. It helped that Pete's wife, Elaine, and I also got along famously. I'd smiled as I concocted a batch and stuck them in the freezer. Pete's whiskey sours had the reputation for putting everyone in a happy mood.

Next, I'd pulled out the recipe Rosalie had once given me for her favorite appetizer — Asiago cheese toast. All that was left to do was pop it under the broiler until brown and bubbly.

I stood in the great room and looked around. Dice, pencils, and score sheets. Bell on the head table. Tiny bars of dark chocolate in diced-shaped dishes. We were ready to rock and roll.

The Babes arrived right on schedule. They arrived in twos and threes, laughing and chattering with an undertone of forced gaiety. Polly, resplendent in shocking pink and lime green, came in with Gloria. Following them were Diane and Janine, who were still discussing the recent selections of Novel Nuts, Serenity's book club. Monica and Connie Sue were next, accompanied by Claudia, looking drawn but determined. I welcomed her with a big hug, happy to see she had abandoned the black leather and figure-hugging sweaters for her more conservative style of dress. I'd know the real Claudia was back for good when her hair was no longer crayon red. The noise level climbed several more decibels as the rest filtered in.

I gave the drinks a whirl in the blender, then poured the slushy blend into glasses. "Help yourself, ladies," I said as if the Babes needed an invitation to imbibe. The cheese appetizers were snapped up in a jiff. I caught Connie Sue practically drooling over the chocolate truffles I'd set out.

"Oh sugar, you're killin' me," Connie Sue moaned. "Just killin' me."

Apparently unafraid of dying, Rita helped herself to a piece of foil-wrapped temptation. "I heard chocolate is good for you."

"Only dark chocolate," Monica informed us in that I'm-the-expert tone of voice she often adopts.

Janine nodded her agreement. "Dark chocolate contains antioxidants, the same kind found in green tea, red wine, and blueberries. I read where a study showed it lowered blood pressure."

"But not white chocolate or milk chocolate; only dark chocolate," Monica repeated, kind enough to remind us lest we were woolgathering and failed to hear her the first time.

Monica once worked as the office manager for an internal medicine group. Even though Janine is a card-carrying registered nurse, Monica fancies herself the last word on anything — and everything — medical. Unless it's a glaring case of misinformation, Janine, being a kind and gracious soul, humors her.

"A chocolate a day keeps the doctor away," Polly cheerfully misquoted. Reaching into the candy dish, she withdrew a small handful.

"Well, maybe one for medicinal purposes," Connie Sue said with a grin. An expression of pure bliss settled over her face as she savored the rich chocolate.

Taking my cue from Connie Sue, I offered the candy dish to Claudia. "Here, honey, take a couple. They'll make you feel better."

"Kate's right, you know," Monica said, jumping in, eager to impart another morsel of wisdom. She shoved a strand of brown hair behind one ear. "Chocolate — dark chocolate, that is — releases endorphins in the brain. That's why it lifts a person's mood."

"Bring on the chocolate. I sure could use my spirits lifted." Claudia's mouth twisted in a bitter smile. "Bad enough Lance is dead, but the sheriff's acting as if I killed him on purpose."

Hearing her say that, I made up a new rule right then and there. "Anyone who so much as mentions Sheriff Wiggins gets a whopping fifty points taken off their score. Ladies," I said in my best NASCAR imitation, "start your engines. Let's play bunco!"

Everyone scrambled to find a place at one of the three tables. I took a seat opposite Claudia at the kitchen table, which, by the way, I appointed head table. Claudia had remembered to bring the tiara she had won the last time the Babes gathered for bunco. Also at our table were Monica, who eyed the tiara with blatant envy, and Tara. Before ringing the bell to signal the start of the round, I refilled Claudia's glass. She might have a headache in the morning, but I was going to guarantee her a good night's sleep.

We rolled ones. It wasn't long before the whiskey sours kicked in and made their contribution to our little party. Amidst much giggling and laughter, we rolled twos, threes, fours, and fives. We outdid ourselves with jokes, witty repartee, and humorous anecdotes. We were ready for a spot on cable TV's Comedy Central.

Polly's face crinkled in confusion. "What

are we rolling?"

"Pay attention, Mother, or I'm cutting off the booze," Gloria chided. Mother and daughter had found themselves partners in the final round of the first set. "Sixes. We're on sixes."

"Hmph!" Polly sniffed. "I knew that. Just checking to see if you were paying attention."

Gloria wagged her head, a martyred expression on her face. "I suppose you're aware you just rolled a baby bunco."

"I did?" Polly stared in amazement at the trio of deuces she'd just thrown. "I mean *I did.* Good for me, another five points."

"Bunco!" Pam sang out.

Monica grinned like the Cheshire cat in heat. I'd have to be blind not to see she planned on taking the tiara home. The woman made no bones about her coveting the rhinestone-encrusted band. I'd be surprised if she didn't wear it to church.

Claudia and I advanced to table two. I paused long enough to top off her glass.

"Shame on you, Kate. You're going to make me tipsy."

"What're friends for? Besides" — I winked — "you have a designated driver tonight — Monica." Monica was a teetotaler except in times of severe stress. Then she ordered bourbon — straight up.

The second set began amidst a lot of good-natured bantering. We began shaking and tossing dice with more enthusiasm than finesse. This time Rita was my partner, with Claudia and Connie Sue completing the foursome. The dice made their way around the table with none of us having much luck. Ones seemed to have fallen off the planet.

"All right," Claudia announced. "Enough of this. Let's see if I remember any of the techniques I saw high rollers use in Vegas." Cupping the dice in both her hands, she rattled them, blew on them for luck, then let them fly. Behold, a baby bunco appeared.

"You go, girlfriend," Connie Sue said, cheering on her partner.

Rita and I glumly watched Claudia's winning streak. "Never been to Vegas," I mumbled. "Maybe I should go, learn a trick or two."

"You oughta." Claudia's run of luck over, she passed the dice to me. "Vegas is a happening place. Morning, noon, or night, walk into any of the casinos, and you'll hear the jingle of slot machines. It's music to the ears."

"Jack talked about going there for our twenty-fifth," Pam commented from her spot at the head table. "Neither of us are gamblers, but I'd like to see what all the fuss is about. Maybe take in a couple shows."

"Let my example serve as a warning," Claudia told her. "Don't bring anything home with you. Marrying Lance Ledeaux was the biggest mistake of my life. If I never hear the name Vegas again, it'll be too soon. Think Vegas and I think Lance. Don't know what came over me."

Connie Sue reached across and patted Claudia's hand. "There, there, sugar. Don't be so hard on yourself. You're not the first woman to fall for a pretty face. And you won't be the last."

"He was one handsome dude all right," Polly chimed from an adjacent table.

Claudia's expression clouded. For a moment, I thought she was about to cry, but to my surprise, she burst into laughter instead. The Babes and I looked at her worriedly, all of us probably wondering if she was about to have a meltdown.

"Yeah," Claudia said, regaining control, "he was good-looking, all right, but should've been after all the time and effort he put into it."

"He was tall," Polly said. "I prefer my men tall. Lance must've been at least six feet."

Claudia rolled a single one, then slid the dice to Rita. "Actually, Lance was only five feet ten. He wore lifts in his shoes."

"Oh," Polly murmured, obviously disappointed. "We rolling ones or twos?"

I recognized Gloria's sigh. "Ones, Mother. We're still rolling ones."

Monica scowled at Megan when she failed to score. "Well, Lance certainly had a youthful appearance. Claudia, you know I'd never say anything to hurt your feelings, but he looked years younger than you."

I cast a worried glance at Claudia. Along with the rest of the Babes, I had been trying valiantly to raise Claudia's spirits. Then along comes Monica, who practically accused her of robbing the cradle. But instead of upset, Claudia looked almost . . . amused.

"Lance claimed he was fifty-four, but I recently found out he was sixty." Claudia rolled a satisfying series of ones. "He confessed he'd had some cosmetic surgery done a couple years ago."

"He must've taken after Ronald Reagan," Polly commented.

"How's that?" Claudia asked absently.

"Except for the temples, Lance didn't have a single gray hair on his head. I know 'cause I notice these things."

Her run of luck over, Claudia surrendered

179

the dice and helped herself to a chocolate. "Sorry to burst your bubble, Polly, but he colored it."

"No, you don't say."

Claudia nodded. "Shortly after we were married, I found an empty box of Clairol for Men in the wastebasket."

Connie Sue's luck picked up where Claudia's left off. "I always admired Lance's California tan. Not even Brad Murphy, our golf pro, has one to compare."

I wondered if this round would ever end. It seemed to go on, and on, and on. How long would it take for those at the head table to rack up twenty-one points? At this rate, we'd be here 'til midnight. In the meantime, the Babes were dissecting a poor dead guy more thoroughly than the coroner.

"Lance's California tan?" Claudia hooted. "The man was deathly afraid to go out in the sun."

Janine's nursing background came to the fore. "Worried about skin cancer?"

"Uh-uh." Claudia picked up the dice and let them fly. "More like worried about wrinkles. Lance bought his tan in a can."

"Don't that beat all." Polly shook her dead sadly. "Fake tan, dyed hair, and lifts in his shoes. Tell me, Claudia, Lance Ledeaux, that his real name or as phony as the rest of him?"

"Bunco!" Monica shouted, and I breathed a sigh of relief that the round finally ended.

The clanging of the bunco bell almost drowned out the sound of another bell — the doorbell. Almost . . . but not quite.

CHAPTER 18

"I'm coming. I'm coming," I called as I hurried to answer the door.

The doorbell pealed repeatedly, each ring more insistent than the one before.

I saw the flash of red and blue through the sidelights even before I opened the door. My heartbeat revved into overdrive. Police? Fire? EMS? Had our bunco game grown so hot and steamy, it set the house ablaze?

I found Sheriff Wiggins on my doorstep. A quick glance at his face, and I knew it wasn't a social call. He wasn't dropping by to beg for more lemon bars. He looked official with a capital *O*. My guilty conscience kicked in. Was I about to be arrested for sins of omission?

"Sheriff . . . ?" I tried to keep the nervous wobble out of my voice, but don't think I succeeded. "What brings you here?"

"I've been informed Miz Ledeaux is here."

I peeked around him, no easy task with a

man the size of a moon crater, and saw he'd brought reinforcements. Deputy Preston stared straight ahead and didn't meet my gaze. I spotted a second deputy, one I'd seen during a previous encounter with law enforcement. Sad to say, I didn't know the man's name — or whether he could be bribed with baked goods.

I fidgeted with the pendant I was wearing. "We're right in the middle of bunco. Couldn't this wait?"

" 'Fraid not, ma'am. I have a warrant for her arrest."

I gaped at him. "Surely this is a mistake. Claudia wouldn't hurt a soul. She's the epitome of kindness. Lance's death was a horrible mistake."

"Step aside, Miz McCall, and let us be about our business." Strange that such a beautiful baritone could suddenly hit the wrong note.

While the fingers of my left hand twisted the slender silver chain at my neck, my right hand clutched the door handle until the knuckles gleamed white. "Lance and Claudia were newlyweds. What reason would she have to kill him?"

True, the cad was going through her money like water, but she'd have found a way to stop this without resorting to violence. Had the sheriff found out about Lance's spending? The Super Bowl bet? The Jaguar?

"Miz McCall," he drawled, "unless you want to be charged with —"

"Obstruction of justice?"

He frowned so deeply, his brows pulled together in a unibrow over the bridge of his nose. "I was about to say harborin' a fugitive. Now kindly step aside."

I think he just made up the harboring a fugitive part, but he didn't look in the mood for a friendly debate. Wordlessly, I did as he asked and allowed him and his men to enter.

Reluctantly I led the sheriff and his deputies through the foyer. The sheriff stopped so abruptly on the threshold of the great room that I was surprised he didn't leave skid marks on my tile. Preston and his fellow officer did likewise, their hands automatically resting on their holstered weapons.

The sound of a male voice, or maybe the fact I hadn't yet returned, had drawn the attention of the rest of the Babes. Alarmed, they stared at the sheriff and his men in morbid fascination.

The sheriff's cold-eyed stare zeroed in on the dice. "What's goin' on heah?"

I let out an impatient huff. "I told you — we're in the middle of bunco."

The man had a nasty habit of ignoring my explanations. Months ago I thought I'd made it clear that bunco was nothing more than a harmless dice game. Apparently he'd stuffed that bit of information into a file labeled RAMBLINGS OF AN OLD WOMAN.

"Well, well, did we interrupt some kind of illegal gamblin' operation?"

"Illegal gambling?" Monica gasped, her eyes wide in disbelief.

"Men," he ordered his deputies, "have yourselves a good look around. If you see any traces of unlawful gamin' and bettin', collect the evidence."

"Here," Polly said, offering Deputy Preston a trio of dice. "You want 'em, take 'em. Not having much luck tonight anyway."

Preston ignored Polly's outstretched hand. "Don't see any money, Sheriff."

I resented this invasion of my home and didn't care if my irritation showed. "Is this a raid, Sheriff?"

"Aren't you supposed to have a search warrant?" Diane spoke up.

"Diane's right, you know," Pam said, jumping into the fray. "We're not stupid; we watch TV."

Our indignation must've been contagious, because one by one the Babes rose to their feet, arms folded across their chests, no longer intimidated but outraged.

"What next?" Janine asked. "Arrest school kids for playing Monopoly during spring break?"

Tara nodded in total agreement. "What about Yahtzee?"

"Yahtzee's played with dice. Does that make it illegal?"

I stared in surprise to see sweet little Megan with her chin jutting defiantly. The child had definitely had her feathers ruffled.

"And then there's dominoes," Rita pointed out reasonably. "Are they going to be outlawed, too?"

The sheriff's jaw hardened until I could see the muscle jump and twitch. He was clearly outnumbered — and outmaneuvered by twelve angry women. "I didn't come tonight to interfere with your . . . recreation. I'll take your word that no money crosses hands. That this is no high-stakes game."

"The winner gets a tiara," Polly volunteered. "That considered 'high stakes'?"

Polly sounded innocent, guileless. Had it been me, I might've been tempted to inject a liberal dose of sarcasm into the question.

Sheriff Wiggins's laser-sharp eyes swept over each of us in turn before settling on Claudia. "Miz Ledeaux, you'll have to come with us. I'm placin' you under arrest for the murder of your husband, Mr. Lance Ledeaux."

All eyes turned to Claudia. She looked white faced and terrified.

"Preston, please escort Miz Ledeaux to the patrol car."

Preston stepped forward and took Claudia by the arm. Claudia wasn't about to go softly into that good night. She dug her heels into the Berber carpet and tried to jerk free. "I'm not going anywhere. I didn't murder Lance."

"Ma'am," Preston said, his voice low but firm, "if you don't come quietly, the sheriff's going to have me put you in handcuffs. You don't want that, do you, in front of all your nice lady friends?"

Claudia's gaze darted around frantically until she found me. "Kate," she pleaded, "call Badgeley. Tell him what's happened."

Needless to say, bunco ended early. Seeing Claudia hauled off in the sheriff's cruiser had a sobering effect on the Babes that not even a pitcher of whiskey sours could dispel. Fortunately, I was able to reach Badgeley Jack at home. He assured me he'd go at once to the sheriff's office. He told me to get a good night's rest — fat chance! — and call him in the morning for an update. I'd decided to go one better. I'd be waiting on the doorstep when his office opened.

Surprisingly, Krystal managed to sleep through the entire bunco game and ensuing brouhaha. I envied her. That kind of ability almost made me wish I were pregnant. Notice the word *almost*.

After driving Krystal to work at the Koffee Kup the next morning, I bided my time over coffee and a blueberry muffin. There was no sense driving all the way home, just to turn around again. Besides, muffins were a nice change from my usual bagel and cream cheese routine.

While savoring my second cup of coffee, I made a mental note to call Bill and have him put a bug in his friend's ear. Krystal needed her car — and sooner rather than later. The problem was she had no money. In a moment of uncontrollable generosity, I'd offered to pay for the repairs. I used to *lend* money, but no more. I've found loaning money is the best way of destroying a friendship or blighting a relationship. Now I *donate* money, no strings attached. If I get paid back, great. If not, so be it.

A glance at my watch told me it was nine o'clock and time to leave. I left Krystal, who'd waited on me, a hefty tip. Maybe she'd use her tip money to repay me. Maybe pigs will fly.

Badgeley Jack Davenport IV's office was located three blocks down, across from the courthouse. The cornerstone of the two-story brick building bore the date 1887. His name was neatly stenciled on the door in gold letters. While the exterior may have been unimpressive, the same didn't hold true for the interior. The minute I stepped foot inside, I felt as though I were in a Victorian parlor. A settee in ruby red velvet and several overstuffed chairs were grouped near a fireplace with a hand-painted tile surround. A gigantic Boston fern occupied the space usually reserved for logs. An Oriental rug in tones of ruby, sapphire, and emerald covered the hardwood floor. I don't know much about antiques, but I'd wager the elaborately carved mahogany end tables were genuine and not reproductions. Bad Jack, it seemed, was a man with expensive tastes.

A woman with lots and lots of yellow hair piled high and sprayed within an inch of its life sat behind an enormous mahogany desk. The large flat-screen computer monitor was the only modern concession.

She turned to greet me, her round face wreathed in a friendly smile. "Mornin'.

How y'all doin'?"

"Mornin'," I returned, unintentionally imitating her lazy drawl.

"Name's Aleatha Higginbotham. I'm BJ's personal assistant," she said with an irrepressible giggle. "Sounds much fancier that way than sayin' I'm his secretary, don't it now?"

I found myself instinctively warming to the woman. Ms. Higginbotham looked as soft and fluffy as one of those body pillows I'd seen on sale at Target — and just as comfy. She seemed to favor bright, splashy colors — pinks, purples, and reds — if her present outfit was any indication. Some might call her flowered polyester blouse gaudy, but I thought it suited her just fine.

"What can I do for you, hon?"

"I'm here to see Mr. Davenport. He's representing a good friend of mine," I added.

"I don't suppose that person happens to be Ms. Claudia Connors Ledeaux, would it now?"

"Why yes, how did you guess?"

"I like to tell folks I'm psychic, but don't think anyone believes me."

I wasn't sure quite how to respond, so I chose the easy route. "Is Mr. Davenport in?"

"He called to say he's running a mite late.

Shouldn't be long. Why don't you have a seat? Care for a soda? I'd be happy to put on some coffee."

"Ah, thank you, but no." I gingerly lowered myself onto the velvet settee. I bet even repeat offenders were careful not to crush the fabric.

"Had you pegged for a Yankee the minute you walked in. Almost offered you iced tea, but all's I got is sweet tea. Most folks from up north don't care for it. It's an acquired taste." She straightened a stack of mail on the edge of her desk, lining it up with military precision. "Sorry about your friend's trouble. But she's come to the right place. If anyone can help, it's Badgeley."

I couldn't help but notice she referred to her employer by his first name. "Have you worked for Mr. Davenport long?"

"Heavens, yes," she said with a laugh that set her ample bosom jiggling. "Ever since he got out of law school."

"So he's always had an office here in Brookdale?"

"Mercy, no. He had a thrivin' practice over in Birmingham. Sold it and moved to Brookdale after the missus died. I had nothin' keepin' me in Alabama, so I packed up and came along. Real happy here, too. Guess both of us are small-town folks at

191

heart. Where did you say you were from?"

"Toledo," I replied. What the heck, it wasn't exactly a state secret. Slick as ice, the woman had me answering a question that hadn't been asked. Maybe I should take notes.

"Toledo? That in Indiana?"

"Ohio."

"Right, Ohio. Never had cause to cross the Mason-Dixon Line. Like it fine here in the South. Did go to Vegas once, though. Isn't that where your friend hooked up with Mr. Ledeaux?"

Our conversation ended when Badgeley Jack charged through the front door. "Sorry I'm late, Miz McCall. I went by the jail to see my client, then stopped at the courthouse. Her arraignment's set for this afternoon at one."

CHAPTER 19

The Babes and I presented a united front at Claudia's arraignment, filling the entire first row of the courtroom. Diane, Tara, and Megan had managed to finagle time away from work. Diane agreed to stay an hour later at the library. Tara, brave soul, traded nap time for playtime with a coworker at the day care center. Megan arrived at the last minute in pink dental scrubs after bribing a friend to switch lunch hours. Out of the corner of my eye, I saw Bill slip into a seat at the rear. Eric Olsen, out of uniform in jeans and a polo shirt, slid in beside him in a show of support for a fellow actor. I noticed he gave Megan a friendly wink as she hurried past. Um, interesting . . . I wondered if more than friendship had blossomed between the pair.

Promptly at one o'clock, Judge Rochelle Blanchard entered and took her seat on the bench. She was an attractive woman I estimated in her mid-forties with skin the color of café au lait. Her tall figure made an impressive sight in the flowing black robe with its starched lace collar. The stern, unsmiling expression on her face had me wondering if she was related to Sheriff Sumter Wiggins.

Just then a side door of the courtroom opened. Claudia, accompanied by Badgeley Jack Davenport, stepped out and approached the bench. My heart wrenched at the sight of her. She looked drawn and pale after a night in jail. She still wore the same outfit she had at bunco, but the wool slacks and sweater were wrinkled and no longer looked fresh. Although she had run a brush through her hair and applied lipstick, no amount of makeup could conceal the dark circles under her eyes.

"I hate to see her like this," I whispered to Pam.

"Me, too," Pam said, giving my hand a squeeze.

"Suppose she knows we're here?" Gloria wondered, her voice hushed.

"She knows," Janine answered. "I saw her glance our way."

The judge banged her gavel, and we lapsed into silence. A slight man with thinning hair and stooped shoulders — the prosecutor, I assumed — joined Claudia and her attorney. The bailiff read the charge of involuntary manslaughter.

Polly leaned across her daughter to ask, "What's that mean?"

"Shh, Mother."

Polly's lower lip jutted out, clearly not happy at being shushed. Believe me, it isn't a pretty sight when a septuagenarian pouts like a two-year-old.

Judge Blanchard leveled a look at Claudia. "How does the defendant plead?"

"Not guilty, your honor," Claudia said, her voice quiet but firm.

"Attagirl, sugar," Connie Sue whispered.

I felt like shouting my approval as well. Maybe have Connie Sue Cheerleader rally the Babes. I could almost hear her yell, *Give me an* I!. *Give me an* N! until we spelled *innocent.* The world, the court — and Sheriff Wiggins in particular — needed to take note that Claudia was indeed innocent of the horrid charge against her. Our friend wasn't a murderer.

Badgeley Jack, dapper as usual in a candy-striped bow tie and navy blazer, addressed the judge. "Your honor, my client requests she be released on her own recognizance."

The county prosecutor fairly bristled at the request. Even the sparse hairs at the nape of his neck stood at attention. "Your honor, the state objects. The prosecution has just learned the defendant recently renewed her passport and is deemed a flight risk."

"The defendant will relinquish her passport and is further advised not to leave the county without permission of the court," said the judge. After consulting her calendar, Judge Blanchard set a trial date. She banged her gavel, concluding the proceedings.

We gathered round Claudia, liberal with hugs and words of encouragement. She smiled wanly, a store mannequin's vacant smile. She was a mere shadow of her old self. I recalled her saying that meeting Lance had been the sorriest day of her life. From her expression, I could see today also ranked high on her list of sorriest days.

"You need anything, anything at all," Monica said, "all you have to do is ask."

Rita patted her back. "We're here for you, honey."

Claudia swallowed noisily, her eyes suspiciously bright.

"Ladies," Bad Jack interrupted our little reunion, "if you'll kindly excuse us, Miz Claudia and I have some unfinished business. I'll personally escort this fine lady home after all the formalities have been arranged."

With his hand riding protectively at the small of her back, he steered Claudia out of the courtroom.

Bill stood waiting in the hallway when we emerged. I felt shaken and close to tears by everything that had just transpired. My dear friend was facing a trial and possible imprisonment. I desperately wanted to help, but I wasn't sure how. I hated feeling useless; powerless.

One look and Bill must've sensed I was in need of moral support. Putting his arms around my shoulders, he drew me aside. "There, there, Kate, don't worry. Things have a way of working out, you'll see. From all accounts, you found Claudia one of the finest lawyers in the state."

Sniffling, I burrowed my face into his shoulder, shamelessly exploiting the opportunity. I took a deep breath, inhaled the crisp, clean scent of soap and pine aftershave, and instantly began to feel better. "I know in my heart Claudia would never hurt anyone — much less kill them."

Bill alternately rubbed and patted in an awkward but endearing attempt to soothe. "The sheriff's a smart man. He'll sort things out."

I pulled away and stared up at him. "Do you really think so? Or are you just trying to make me feel better?"

A lengthy silence ensued. He avoided looking at me, his baby blues fixed on a point somewhere above my head.

"Bill . . . ?"

Finally he gave a sheepish smile. "Guilty as charged."

"Hush." I placed a fingertip against his lips. "Guilty isn't the word to use inside a courthouse."

Suddenly I felt some of my usual spunk return. The pity party where I reigned as guest of honor came to a screeching halt. I took a half step back and squared my shoulders. At times like these, friends needed friends. No one knew Claudia better than the Babes. If the sheriff couldn't be depended on to prove her blameless, it was up to us.

I smiled at Bill. "Thanks for lending me your shoulder. I'm feeling much better."

"Glad I could help." Bill returned the smile — the one that always made me a little weak in the knees.

"Some of the Babes are going to reconvene at the Cove Café for a strategy session. Care to join us?"

"Me? Alone with all those women?" Bill

appeared alarmed at the notion. He began retreating down the hall. "Maybe another time."

I smiled as I watched him leave. Bill had a bashful streak a mile wide. But that didn't make him a coward — far from it. When the chips were down, I'd seen him transform himself from shy suitor into a knight in shining armor. Granted, our friendship/relationship may have encountered a temporary setback, but with time and patience, I was certain he'd come around — even if it meant my turning into a brazen hussy.

The Babes and I drove back to Serenity Cove Estates and reconvened at the Cove Café. The lunch rush was over by the time we arrived. We pulled two tables together to form a makeshift conference table. My stomach growled noisily as I was about to sit down, reminding me I hadn't eaten anything since the blueberry muffin earlier in the day.

Seeing us gather, Vera MacGillicudy brought our usual drinks without our having to ask. Goes to show why she's the Babes' favorite. "Anything else, ladies?" she asked. "Y'all need menus?"

My stomach gurgled again, drawing the attention of Pam and Rita sitting on either side of me. I ignored Monica's disapproving glare and ordered a burger and fries. Before she had a chance to launch into a lecture on fat grams, Pam followed suit. Next, Gloria and Polly agreed to split a chicken quesadilla. Connie Sue ordered her usual fruit plate, and Janine a cup of beef barley soup. Only Rita and Monica insisted they weren't hungry.

Once Vera headed for the kitchen, we got down to business.

"Exactly what is 'involuntary manslaughter'?" Pam asked. "Kate, you met with Claudia's attorney this morning. Did he give you an explanation?"

"BJ said —"

"BJ?" Monica raised a dark brow in a passable imitation of Sheriff Wiggins.

"Badgeley Jack Davenport the Fourth, to be precise. He told me to call him BJ. He said that's what his friends call him."

"Hmph," Monica sniffed. "Seems the two of you are getting along rather well."

Ignoring her, I assumed my role as professor-at-large with a certain aplomb. "BJ said manslaughter is defined as the unlawful killing of another without malice."

"Where does the 'involuntary' come into play?" Janine squeezed lemon into her iced tea.

I did the same, then added a packet of sweetener. "The 'involuntary' has to do with criminal negligence."

"Which is what, Miss Smarty Pants?" Connie Sue drawled.

"According to BJ, criminal negligence is the reckless disregard of the safety of others." I was amazed at how much legal jargon I had absorbed in the relatively short period of time I'd spent with BJ Davenport. "He said the prosecution will contend Claudia is responsible for Lance's death because she showed reckless disregard for his safety by not checking the gun before firing it."

After a prolonged silence, Pam cleared her throat. "Did Mr. Davenport happen to mention what the sentence usually is for involuntary manslaughter?"

I took a sip of iced tea, marveling that it slid past a lump in my throat that felt the size of a watermelon. "No more than five years."

Rita toyed with the handle of her coffee cup. "Could be worse if the charge were murder. South Carolina has the death penalty."

I don't know about the rest of the Babes, but I suddenly lost my appetite. The thought of a burger and fries made my stomach twist into a knot.

"Was Diane able to contact either of Claudia's sons?" Gloria asked.

"Diane said they both wanted to come." Pam fiddled with the wrapper from her straw, first pleating, then smoothing it. "Claudia told them to stay put. She insists there's nothing they could do."

"Y'all," Connie Sue said, fluffing her perfect honey blond bob, "I think Claudia's too proud to let her babies see her like this."

"But what about when this comes to trial?" Gloria asked. "She'll need the support of her family."

"We'll cross that bridge when we come to it," I said with more conviction than I felt. "In the meantime, I want each and every one of you to think of a way to help Claudia through this."

I was only too happy when our food arrived and talk veered away from Claudia.

"How are things working out with your houseguest?" Polly asked, tucking into her quesadilla.

"Fine," I said, nibbling a fry though no longer really hungry. "She spends most of her time sleeping — that is, when she's not throwing up."

"Don't tell me Krystal's pregnant?" Monica looked shocked at the notion.

"Bingo!" Or, in this case, should I have

said *bunco?*

Connie Sue speared a chunk of melon. "What about the baby's daddy? He in the picture?"

"She hasn't said a word, and I haven't asked." I took a tentative bite of my burger. I glanced across the table and noticed Janine hadn't touched her soup. "You're awfully quiet, Janine. What's wrong?"

"Other than Claudia, you mean?" She gave a humorless laugh. "Don't mind me. I'm just a little preoccupied wondering what will become of the Humane Society's plans for a new shelter. I really hated to be the bearer of bad news when the play was canceled. The members were so disappointed."

Rita picked a couple of pretzels from the bowl of munchies Vera had brought. "I agree. It's a damn shame. The play was really starting to come together."

I idly stirred my tea. "What ever happened to the old adage, 'The show must go on'?"

Lunch forgotten, the women stared at me as if I'd suddenly sprouted wings.

Janine was the first to recover. "The show *could* go on!" she exclaimed, more animated than I'd seen her in days. "We could pull it off. I know we could."

"You bet!" Rita leaned forward, eager to

reclaim her job as stage manager. "How hard can it be?"

Now I was the one who stared. "I was kidding, ladies. I didn't expect to be taken seriously. We don't know the first thing about putting on a play. That was Lance's job, remember?"

Gloria ignored my outburst. "Who would we get to replace Lance? He wasn't only the star, but the director."

"I don't think Claudia's keen on returning to the stage." Polly added a dollop of sour cream to her last bite of quesadilla. "What if the sheriff hauls her off on opening night? We'll be in a worse fix than we are now."

"So we'll hold an audition," Pam said, warming to the notion. "We'll find a replacement for both leads. That shouldn't be too difficult."

I couldn't believe my ears. My BFF siding with the enemy? Wait 'til I got her alone. "Who'll direct?" I asked, hoping to sprinkle reality dust over this harebrained idea.

Connie Sue thoughtfully munched a grape. "The director ought to be someone already familiar with the play. That would make things a whole lot simpler."

Polly blotted her lips with a napkin. "I'm willing to give it a shot."

"But, Mother," Gloria protested, jumping in to make the save, "we need you in charge of costumes."

"Oh, yeah, I forgot. I already got me an important job."

We let out a collective sigh of relief. I squirted a blob of ketchup onto my plate, then dredged a fry through it. The notion of resuming production of *Forever, My Darling* seemed to be taking on a life of its own.

And I had only myself to blame.

"I've got the perfect solution," a little imp prompted me to say. "Who's better qualified than someone who was in charge of casting from the get-go? Someone familiar with both the script and the roles." Smiling sweetly, I raised my iced tea. "I nominate Janine for director."

"Here, here!" Connie Sue lifted her water glass high. "Y'all, let's toast Janine Russell, brand-new director of *Forever, My Darling.*"

Rita clinked her cup against Gloria's. "I vote we dedicate the play to Claudia Connors Ledeaux."

The show might go on, I vowed amidst all the chatter, but I intended to keep my eyes peeled for anyone with more than a passing interest in the prop table. And this time the gun would be the best money could buy — at the dollar store.

CHAPTER 20

Notices of the upcoming audition were plastered on bulletin boards from Serenity Cove Estates clear to Brookdale five miles down the road. No place was exempt: the Piggly Wiggly, the rec center, the Koffee Kup, and the pro shop at the golf course. We'd even chipped in for a small ad in the *Serenity Sentinel.* Date and time were set for the following night.

The role of director fit Janine more snugly than OJ's glove. She'd wasted no time appointing Bill and me as her assistants in recasting the two leads. Personally, I think it was revenge for nominating her as director. She also made it known she preferred her title changed to artistic director as opposed to plain old director. Well la-di-da, I said to myself. She could call herself anything she pleased as long as she got the show on the road.

Meanwhile, I kept busy with mundane

tasks. At least I could cross grocery shopping off my to-do list. I swear it had taken twice as long with people at every turn wanting to stop and talk. The topic of Lance's death — I still stubbornly refused to call it murder — had been hot, hot, hot in the frozen food aisle at the Pig. I was surprised the freezers hadn't sprung a leak with temperatures soaring skyward. What a mess that would've been with soggy vegetables and melting ice cream. Ugh! I grimaced at the thought.

I was lugging in the last of the groceries when Krystal, dressed casually in gray sweats, accosted me. "It's my day off," she complained. "I haven't even been able to take a nap. That blasted phone's been ringing nonstop ever since you left."

"Sorry, Krystal," I said, nudging the door closed with an elbow. "Probably folks wanting to ask about the audition."

"I guess." She started to help unload the grocery bags, then paused, holding up a can of pet food for my inspection. "What's this?"

Did the girl need glasses? Any fool could plainly see it was premium-brand cat food, the kind advertised on TV. I was sick and tired of sharing my tuna with an ungrateful feline. Besides, I didn't want to chance the possibility of another tuna-free casserole like on the night I'd invited Bill to dine. "I wasn't sure which one Tang would like, so I bought a selection: tuna select, choice of the chick, and veal-beef medley. I thought we could serve any leftovers creamed over toast points for dinner some night."

From the frown on her face, Krystal failed to see the humor in my little joke. "Tang doesn't like the fancy canned food," she said.

I stopped shoving vegetables into the bin. "Tang told you this?"

Krystal gave a head toss, sending her long dark hair flying over her shoulder. "He prefers regular tuna, not pet food — albacore is his favorite."

I rolled my eyes and resumed placing lettuce, carrots, and celery in the crisper. The silly cat wouldn't come within ten feet of me, but here he was, having heart-to-hearts with Krystal.

"I tried feeding him one of those fancy brands the other day, but he just turned up his nose and stalked off." Krystal continued to unload grocery items onto the counter.

"What happened to the old phrase, 'Beggars can't be choosers'?"

"Never heard it before. Certain things he likes; certain things he doesn't, just like people at the diner. Tang has certain expectations when it comes to food."

"You know this for a fact, or are you making it up as you go along?"

"You've never been around cats much, have you, Kate?"

"No, my husband was allergic." I stored the empty plastic grocery bags with the other items I recycle. It's the creed I live by. I'm a firm believer in the three Rs: reduce, reuse, recycle. Right about now, I was wishing I could recycle my houseguest to Myrtle Beach.

"Kate, I, ah . . ." Krystal struck a hand-on-hip pose reminiscent of vintage World War II posters I'd seen. Rita Hayworth and Lana Turner sprang to mind.

I stopped what I was doing and gave her my full attention. "Out with it, girl."

"I was wondering if it'd be OK if I tried out for a part in the play."

Well, Krystal's question certainly explained the posturing. The part of Roxanne, Claudia's former role, was that of femme fatale. My command of French is practically nonexistent, but even to my untrained ear, *fatale* sounds too much like fatal. And fatal reminds me of Lance sprawled *deader 'n a doornail,* as Bernie so eloquently phrased it.

"Well . . . ?"

Krystal's voice jerked me back to the present. "No, of course not," I said. "It's an open audition."

"Great," she replied, breaking into a smile. "I wondered if it was only for residents of Serenity Cove. Since technically I'm only a visitor and not a resident . . ."

"By all means come. You're welcome to try out for the part." I found a spot for the expensive — and unappreciated — pet food on a pantry shelf. "Besides, you won't be the only nonresident in the play. Eric Olsen, that nice young policeman from Brookdale, is playing the part of detective. Do you have acting experience?"

Krystal busied herself rearranging the stack of mail lying on the counter. "Ah, I was in the drama club in high school. And I had a small part in a road show of *Grease*."

"*Grease*?" I nearly knocked over a box of Cheerios. "As in John Travolta and Olivia Newton-John? The 'grease is the word' kind of *Grease*?"

"Yeah, that's the one." She shrugged. "I was Marty Maraschino."

"Wow!" I said, truly impressed. "With those credentials, maybe we don't even need an audition. You'll be a shoo-in."

"That wouldn't be fair. I don't want people saying I won the role just because

I'm staying with you."

"I suppose you're right." Who would have guessed Krystal would turn out to be a genuine actress in the guise of a pregnant waitress and resident cat lover? "I know my friend Monica is determined to read for the part."

"Monica? You mean Mrs. Pulaski?"

"The one and only." One Monica is quite enough, thank you very much.

"Then it's all set. Can I hitch a ride with you tomorrow night?"

"Sure." I was beginning to feel like a soccer mom ferrying Krystal back and forth. Maybe I should bribe Bill's buddy with a batch of cookies to work faster on her Honda. It was worth a try.

"Guess I'll go to my room and read over the script one more time." She started to leave but turned back. "I forgot to mention I turned off the ringer on the phone. And, while you're at it, you might want to check your answering machine. I think I heard someone leave a message."

"Right, thanks."

Groceries stored and kitchen tidy, I entered the room I tentatively refer to as the library. Its name had gone through a series of changes during the time I lived there — den, study, and finally, library. The word seems a trifle ostentatious for a room boasting a humble magazine rack. Once the play is over, I'm going to ask Bill to build some bookshelves. And while he's at it, I'll apply my feminine wiles. Poor guy will never know what hit him.

The little red light on the answering machine flashed impatiently. Pressing the button, I heard not the voice of an aspiring actor, but that of Tammy Lynn Snow.

Miz McCall, drawled the familiar voice, *I've been trying to track you down all afternoon. Sheriff wants you in his office first thing tomorrow morning. Nine o'clock sharp, he said.* The message clicked off.

I glanced at the clock. It was too late to call now to learn the reason for the summons; Tammy Lynn had probably left for the day. If nervous tension caused weight loss, I'd be skinny as a rail come morning.

I decided to bide my time at the Koffee Kup after giving Krystal a ride to work the following morning. There was no sense going home only to turn around for my meeting with the sheriff. I instructed her to keep my tank — I mean cup — topped off with high octane. None of that decaf for me. I needed every spare molecule of caffeine I could swallow.

"And, Krystal, bring a slice of lemon meringue pie to go along with the coffee."

She looked at me oddly. "Isn't it a little early in the day for pie?"

"Just bring it." So much for being skinny as a rail. Guess nervous tension can work in one of two ways. At this rate, I'd be round as a Teletubby before the appointed hour. I didn't care if all the other early birds were chowing down on eggs and grits; I needed fortification. And for me fortification came in the form of lemon pie heaped mile high with fluffy white meringue.

I glanced up as the door of the diner swung open and Bill sauntered through. My heart went into its familiar tap dance at the sight of him. Flap-brush-step. Flap-brush-step. My, oh, my. Our eyes met. He smiled; my heart cheered. I may be getting a little old for such a robust cardiovascular work-out, but I'll die happy.

He wove through the tables, working his way toward my booth. I racked my brain for witty repartee — or even mediocre repartee. "Hey, Bill," I said, and winced inwardly at the inane attempt.

"Hey, yourself."

Not sure whether I mentioned this, but here in the South, *hey* replaces its northern counterpart, *hi.* It's one of the few Southernisms I've adopted. I've been dying to sprinkle *y'all* into conversations with my children, but I haven't found a way to do it without sounding hokey. *Y'all* coming from a Yankee loses something in the translation.

"Mind if I join you?" Bill asked.

Mind? Was he kidding? "No, of course not," I said, trying to sound offhand. Bill slid into the booth opposite me. Krystal returned, coffeepot in one hand, pie in the other. "Hey, Mr. Lewis. What can I get you?" she said, beaming a bright smile at him.

Bill beamed right back. "I'll have what Kate's having."

"Pie versus grits?" I said when Krystal left after filling Bill's cup. "We're starting a trend."

"No contest." He sipped his coffee. "I once let a waitress bully me into trying grits. Damned if I didn't catch her watching to see if I ate them or not. Might as well have been eating wallpaper paste far as I was concerned."

"Many of the finer restaurants feature shrimp 'n grits on their menus. It's considered a delicacy."

"I've noticed. Maybe someday I'll give it a try — or not."

The subject of grits exhausted, we lapsed

into companionable silence.

"What brings you into town this early? Aren't you usually at Tai Chi about now?" Bill asked.

Tai Chi would certainly have been preferable to being skewered by Sheriff Wiggins. He'd put me through the paces faster than Marian, our Tai Chi instructor. A tiny part of me warmed at the knowledge Bill was aware of my habits. Another part, not quite so tiny, was reluctant to tell him about my summons to the sheriff's office. I didn't have the foggiest notion why the man wanted to see me, but it couldn't be good.

"Ah, I, er, have an appointment this morning," I managed to stammer. "What about you?"

"Me, too, have a meeting, that is."

Before I could decide to pursue or abandon the topic of meetings, Krystal returned with Bill's pie. She presented the perfectly centered slice of lemon meringue as regally as a cupcake to the queen. She flashed another bright smile at him, and, I swear, batted her eyelashes. "Here you go. Anything else I can get you?"

The green-eyed monster opened its mouth and took a bite. Was Bill frequenting the diner for more than pastries? Maybe to admire Krystal's Barbie-doll bosom? Jealousy? At my age? I quickly squashed the thought as unworthy.

"No, thanks, Krystal," he said.

She went off, but not before I noticed the wink she gave him. Sheesh! How was a card-carrying member of AARP supposed to compete with a woman half her age? And a pregnant one to boot.

Oblivious of any undercurrents, Bill dug into his pie. "So, tonight's the big night."

I stared at him blankly before it dawned on me. "Right," I said, relieved to have my mind functioning again. "The audition."

"Suppose we'll have a big turnout?"

I shoved my empty plate aside. "If my phone's ringing off the hook is any indication, we will. News about Lance has drawn a lot of attention. Gotten folks curious."

"I don't know the first thing about judging auditions. How do you propose we go about this?"

"I thought we'd take our cue from *American Idol*. You can be Simon."

Bill looked at me over his coffee cup. "Is he the good-looking, popular one?"

"That's the one. You have until seven p.m. to brush up on a British accent. Since I hate giving anyone bad news, I'm appointing myself Paula. I'll just tell everyone how great they look." I held up my hand to ward off any objections. "I know, I know. She's no longer on the show, but she was always my favorite."

"What about Janine? Who's she supposed to be?"

I shrugged nonchalantly. "She's going to be Randy Jackson."

Bill polished off the last of his pie. "Isn't Randy a man?"

"Yeah." I drained the last of my coffee. "And to complicate matters further, he's black. Janine's going to have to ad-lib."

I glanced at my watch. "Gotta run."

"Me, too." Bill dabbed his mouth with a napkin, then reached for his wallet, extracted some cash, and tossed it on the table. And I thought I was a generous tipper. "Guess I'll see you tonight."

"Guess so," I called over my shoulder as I headed out the door. Unless, that is, the sheriff threw me in the slammer for withholding evidence, aiding and abetting, or the old standby, obstruction of justice.

CHAPTER 21

It was silly to drive to the sheriff's office when I could have just as easily walked. Since I skipped Tai Chi, I could've used the exercise. I was afraid, however, that if I left my car parked near the diner, I might've been tempted to return for more fortification in the form of lemon meringue pie.

I happened to look into my rearview mirror and watch as Bill pulled into the parking space behind me. As I opened the car door, I spotted Monica and Rita approaching from the opposite direction. Rita waved when she saw me. Monica merely grimaced. It appeared we were all headed for the same destination. Did that mean we were all going to be charged with a laundry list of felonies? Could we choose our cell mates?

Bill, always the gentleman, held the door open as we filed in.

Bernie Mason looked up from a dog-eared issue of *Field & Stream* as we entered.

"What're you guys doin' here?"

Gus Smith was present, too, but he merely grunted.

Tammy Lynn, drab as usual, dressed head to toe in beige, rose from her desk and did a head count. "Sheriff asked me to show y'all down the hall to the interview room."

Nervous looks bounced back and forth between us like banked shots off a pool table.

Rita assumed the no-nonsense expression that probably worked well in her former position as branch manager of a bank in Cleveland. "I, for one, would like to know what this is all about," she demanded.

To her credit, Tammy Lynn didn't falter. She was no shrinking violet about to default on a loan. "Ma'am, the sheriff will explain everythin'. Kindly be patient."

"Patient?" Monica huffed. "I want to know why we're being treated like a bunch of criminals when we haven't done anything wrong."

"The sheriff will explain," Tammy Lynn repeated, holding open the door of the interview room.

I was surprised to step inside and find Claudia along with BJ Davenport seated side by side at the battered metal conference table. It was the Claudia of old —

almost. Gone was the fire-engine red hair and back was the softer, strawberry blond shade I'd always admired. But gone still were her sparkle and zest.

"Hey, Claudia," I said by way of greeting, taking the chair next to her.

She mustered a smile. "Hey, yourself."

We were freshmen assembled for the class I'd come to think of as Inquisition 101. I peered into the corners for telltale torture devices. No thumbscrews in plain sight. No stakes piled high with kindling. But I didn't trust wily Sheriff Wiggins. As for stakes and kindling, the ever-efficient Miss Tammy Lynn Snow probably kept a supply handy in the storeroom.

The door banged open. At least, it sounded like a bang because it had that kind of effect. We straightened in our seats, our spines erect, our nervous systems on full alert. The sheriff's entrance seemed to elicit that kind of reaction, even for the pure of heart. This trick was even more impressive than the one-eyebrow lift thingy he'd perfected.

"Mornin', y'all," said the Grand Inquisitor himself.

We seemed to be suffering from an epidemic of lockjaw. Even BJ held his tongue.

The sheriff dragged out the chair left

vacant at the head of the table and lowered his two-hundred-pound-plus frame. "Suppose y'all are wonderin' why I called y'all here. . . ."

My case of lockjaw subsided. Unable to stand the strained silence another second, I piped up, "Not counting you, Sheriff, we have eight people here. Just the right number for two tables of bunco. Anyone bring dice?"

I had hoped to inject a little humor, break the ice so to speak, but not even a coast guard cutter could have broken through tension this thick.

The sheriff shot me a look. If his eyes had been lasers, I'd have been ash. "Let's start over again — before the interruption," he drawled. "S'pose y'all are wantin' to know why I asked y'all here this mornin'." he repeated for the benefit of the deaf, feeble-minded, or terminally irreverent amongst us.

We nodded in agreement. Our movements were so coordinated, I wondered if the others would be game to form a synchronized swim team. Senior Olympics, here we come. Then the image of Bernie Mason in a swimsuit popped into mind, and I scrapped the notion.

"I won't waste your time or mine any

longer." Sheriff Wiggins slapped a manila envelope on the table and slowly withdrew a report. "Got the results back from the lab in Columbia. Y'all remember bein' tested for GSR and fingerprinted?"

BJ adjusted his bow tie, this time a polka-dot affair. "I assume since you called all of us here, the evidence incriminates more than just my client."

"Now wait just a cotton-pickin' minute." Bernie surged to his feet, his face an alarming shade of fuchsia. "I object to being lumped in the same category as the one who pulled the trigger and killed her husband —"

"Deader 'n a doornail," I muttered, louder than I intended.

Bernie gave me a fish-eyed stare. "I was about to say," he said, sounding miffed, "deader 'n a skunk."

"Well, excuse me all to pieces." *Take that, Bernie Mason.*

If Sumter Wiggins had had a gavel, he would have banged it. The glare he sent us served just as well. In another life, he'd have made a good nun. He tapped a forefinger the size of kielbasa on the pages in front of him. "This came in yesterday. I found it interestin', to say the least, that so many of you had managed to test positive. Some of you in both categories."

Next to me, Bill shifted in his seat. Monica studied her manicure while the others all looked as if they longed to be elsewhere — except for BJ. I noticed he had brought out a hand-tooled leather notebook and was busily taking notes on a yellow legal pad.

"Miz Ledeaux," the sheriff continued, "I can understand how you might test positive for both since it's a well-established fact that you fired the shot that killed the deceased — Mr. Lance Ledeaux."

BJ half rose. "I object."

"Give it a rest, Davenport." The sheriff motioned him down. "Save your theatrics for the courtroom. I'd like to review" — he picked up the report and began to read — "why fingerprints also belong to Bill Lewis, Bernie Mason, Gus Smith, Monica Pulaski, and Rita Larsen? I'm double-checking to make sure I have my facts straight."

I'm ashamed to admit I felt a little left out from this illustrious list. What was I doing here anyway? I thought of the Tai Chi class I was missing. This very minute I could be Grasping the Bird's Tail or slinking through Snake Creeps In.

"Care to explain once more — for the record — why your fingerprints happen to be on the murder weapon? Let's start with you, Mr. Lewis."

I gave Bill a sympathetic look. He was on the hot seat and, from the look on his face, wasn't too happy about it.

"Why wouldn't my prints be on it? It's my gun — I told you that before."

"And so you did." He made a show of noting this in his ubiquitous black book. "And what about you, Mr. Mason? How do you explain the fact your fingerprints are all over the barrel?"

"Since when is looking a crime?" Bernie picked at a ragged cuticle. "My brother-in-law's always bragging about his Smith and Wesson. Wanted to see what was such a big deal."

"Me, too," Gus muttered. "Just curious, is all."

The sheriff noted this, then turned his attention to Monica and Rita. "What about you ladies? You the curious types, too?"

"Of course my fingerprints are on the gun," Monica replied, sounding defensive and frightened at the same time. "It was part of my job."

A dark brow lifted. "And your job was . . ."

Monica raised her nose in the air. "I'm the prop princess."

"Mistress," I hissed. "Mistress, not princess." You'd think Monica would realize by now the task didn't come with a tiara.

The sheriff ignored my outburst as if it hadn't occurred. "What about you, Miz Larsen? Handlin' the gun part of your job as well?"

Rita looked discomfited — a rare occurrence. Normally it took a lot to rattle her. I compared her to the *Queen Mary* — big and stable, not likely to sink in a storm. "I, um, like to keep things neat. I may have picked up the gun after the shooting and put it with the rest of the props."

"May have . . . ?"

Rita gave a curt nod. "That's right. How was I supposed to know Lance was really dead and not just pretending?"

He gave her a hard, unblinking stare. "Guess that's a tricky call when someone has a bullet hole in their chest and stops breathin'."

"For crying out loud," I protested. "Lance was a professional corpse. He got paid good money to look dead. *CSI* has the best corpses on TV. You'd know that if you ever watched TV."

"I'll take that under advisement, ma'am," the sheriff replied, his tone droll. "Now let's get on to the next item up for business: gunshot residue."

"Keep me out of this." Bernie held up

both hands as though warding off an invisible enemy. "I'll admit, I looked at the gun, but no way could I have gunshot residue on my hands. I handled the gun *before* Ledeaux was shot, not after."

"Settle down, Mason," the sheriff growled. "Your hands tested negative, but the others . . ."

His coal black gaze crept around the table, resulting in a lot of squirming, a lot of shifting. Yup, I said to myself, he'd have made a good nun. If a person could make adults twitch, fifth graders wouldn't stand a prayer.

"What about you, Mr. Lewis? Care to explain?"

"How many times do I have to remind you, Sheriff, the gun was *mine?* I handed it to Ledeaux personally that very morning right after cleaning it."

The sheriff's scowl deepened. "I hear that right? You say you cleaned it?"

Bill nodded. "You heard me."

Although Sheriff Wiggins didn't look pleased at Bill's response, he jotted it all down. "Let's move on, shall we? Miz Larsen, I suppose you're goin' to claim you got residue on your hands in an effort to keep things neat and tidy."

Rita's face was stony. "More than likely that's how it happened."

The spotlight shifted to me. "And you, Miz McCall, how did you happen to come in contact with gunshot residue?"

"I have no idea," I said, surprised at finding my name on the list.

"Did you at any time handle the weapon?"

I replayed the events immediately following the shooting. "No," I said at last. "Not that I recall."

He drummed his fingers against the metal table. Tap, tap, tap. Slow, incessant, irritating to the max, the sound was like a leaky faucet at two a.m. "Are you telling me GSR — as they say in the trade — flew through the air and, by chance, happened to land on your hands?" Not waiting for a reply, he went on as though ruminating. "Another strange finding. Miz Ledeaux's hands were negative, almost like she washed them. Or wiped them clean."

Just like in the Sunday comics, a lightbulb went on inside my brain.

"Judgin' from your expression, I can see your memory is returnin'."

Coming back like a bad dream would be more like it. I debated what to say, but since we'd all seen Claudia pull the trigger, I decided there wasn't any harm in relating how I'd probably come into contact with GSR. Just hearing the acronym — GSR —

gave my confidence a boost and reminded me I wasn't a rank amateur when it came to crime solving.

"Once we realized Lance was really dead and not faking it, I went to comfort Claudia." I envisioned myself on the witness stand, calm, poised, relating my account before a packed courtroom in an intelligent, precise fashion while the jurors listened with rapt attention. *I'm ready for my close-up, Mr. DeMille.* "Claudia appeared to be in shock. When I took hold of her hands, they were cold as ice. We sat her in a chair. Then I went to get her some water. She was shaking so badly, the water spilled, and she wiped her hands on her slacks to dry them."

"Mmm."

That it? Mmm?

The sheriff made a production out of writing everything I'd said in that darn book of his. I'd love to get a peek at his notes. Then again, they might prove boring. *Miz McCall twiddled her thumbs. Mr. Lewis shrugged his shoulders. Miz Pulaski failed to make eye contact.* Etc., etc. You get my drift.

Rita stared pointedly at her Bulova. "Are we done yet, Sheriff?"

"You have somethin' more important waitin'?"

Mama always said you catch more flies

with sugar than you do with vinegar. This seemed a good time to take the old adage out for a stroll. I smiled sweetly. "You're a busy man, Sheriff Wiggins. My friends and I don't want to take up any more of your valuable time. We've answered your questions. Unless we're under arrest . . . ?"

"Temptin' as that may be . . ."

Bad Jack snapped his portfolio shut. "Since my client's already been charged with manslaughter, isn't this meeting a little superfluous, Sheriff?"

The sheriff remained unruffled. "I'm well aware, sir, we're not at a loss for witnesses who'll testify they saw Miz Ledeaux fire the fatal shot. That said, I don't want some slick city lawyer tellin' the jury my department failed to do its job properly. I'm a man who likes to dot my i's and cross my t's."

Claudia rose to her feet, her voice shrill. "How many times do I have to tell you I never intended to kill Lance? Why can't you believe it was all a terrible accident? That somehow a bullet left in the chamber went unnoticed?"

"Miz Claudia, please," BJ remonstrated.

Claudia jerked free of his attempt to catch her sleeve. "I planned to divorce the bastard. Not kill him."

The sheriff didn't blink, didn't miss a

beat. "So you admit to havin' marital problems with the deceased?"

I heard a collective intake of breath.

Claudia, my friend, what have you done?

BJ sprang to his feet. "My client admits no such thing. Even a blind man could see the dear woman's overwrought as a result of your constant badgerin'."

Claudia flung her head back and laughed. "I'm done mourning the son of a bitch. Should have known better than to marry a man as phony as his dyed hair and fake tan."

BJ turned to his client. "Unless you plan to find another attorney, Miz Ledeaux, I advise you not to say another word."

Claudia seemed about to object, but one look at her attorney and she wisely kept silent. Right before our very eyes, Badgeley Jack Davenport IV changed from affable to formidable. For the first time in our brief acquaintance, I could see how the man had earned the sobriquet *Bad Jack*. If I ever *accidentally* shot and killed a sleazy con man, he'd be first on my list of lawyers.

Bad Jack tucked his gold ballpoint into the inner pocket of his suit. "Finished, Sheriff?"

"For now." Sheriff Wiggins flipped his notebook shut but made no move to rise. He pinned us in our places with a hard, penetrating stare. "Accordin' to the evidence from the state crime lab, I could consider y'all suspects along with Miz Ledeaux. Y'all had means and opportunity. Only thing lackin' is motive. Once I find that, the case is pretty well sewed up."

Motive? Oh, boy! Claudia was up the proverbial river without a paddle. Up the river, in this case, being the state pen.

CHAPTER 22

I'd eaten my margherita pizza in blissful solitude. I'd invited Krystal to join me, but she wanted to read her scene a final time before the audition. She'd vanished into her room with the script in one hand, a sleeve of soda crackers in the other. I'd no sooner put the last of the dinner dishes in the dishwasher than the phone rang.

"Kate, it's for you," Krystal yelled from down the hall after picking up the extension. "Some woman wants to sell you something. Want me to tell her you're not home?"

The thought was tempting. Ever since I'd written a check to the college alumni association, they'd been pestering me for another on a daily basis. They'd zeroed in on the most inopportune times: dinnertime, nap time, bathroom time. Patience, I reminded myself. The caller was likely some hapless student trying to earn beer money.

"I'll take it." I sighed the sigh of the

martyred, ready to be polite but firm as I picked up the phone. "Hello."

"Mother, is that you?"

"Yes, dear, whom did you expect?" My daughter, Jennifer, lives in California. Not just California, mind you, but Brentwood, home to stars and celebs. She lives there with her husband and former nerd, Jason Jarrod. Jason discovered contacts and Armani shortly after certain powers that be discovered he could forge a contract more binding than Cheddar cheese in a nursing home. Jen and Jason, along with my two adorable granddaughters, Juliette and Jillian — the Four Jays as I call them — lead a charmed life. At least, they do if listening to Jennifer is any indication.

"You sound strange, Mother. Who answered the phone, one of your gambling buddies?"

I've tried, but without success, to explain bunco to my daughter. She equates a simple dice game with a den of iniquity involving high-stakes gambling. She fears I'll lose my retirement pension and end up on the street as a bag lady. "No, sweetheart. It was Krystal, my houseguest."

"I don't remember your having any friends named Krystal. Do I know her? What's her last name?"

Jen was firing more questions than I had the time — or inclination — to answer. "Krystal is someone I've recently met. She's staying with me temporarily until she gets back on her feet."

"Feet? What's wrong with her feet? Is the woman crippled?"

Even as a child, Jen had an overactive imagination. Her close proximity to Hollywood seems to have aggravated the condition.

"There's nothing wrong with Krystal's feet, dear. It was only a figure of speech." I lowered my voice, not wanting Krystal to overhear. "The young woman's been having a run of bad luck. I asked her to stay with me while her car is being repaired and until she earns enough money for a fresh start in Myrtle Beach."

"I can't believe you invited a perfect stranger into your home."

I chuckled. "Trust me, Jen, Krystal's far from 'perfect.' "

"You know what I mean, Mother. This woman could turn out to be a serial killer, preying on elderly women."

"I thought we agreed the term 'elderly' doesn't apply when you're talking about me," I reminded her sternly. Between Jen's referring to me by the *E* word and Steven's sending me literature on assisted living centers, a lesser person might actually begin to feel old. How that felt, I haven't a clue.

"Besides, Jen," I continued, "it's a well-known fact most serial killers are men." There, that tidbit was designed to make her feel better about my roommate.

"Sorry, that salient point slipped my mind."

"No need for sarcasm, Jennifer Louise." She knows I mean business whenever I resort to using her middle name. She absolutely hates the name Louise, which happened to belong to Jim's mother. I console her by telling her we could have named her Bertha after my mother. That usually stops further complaints.

Clear across a continent, I heard a sigh. "You worry me, Mother. Inviting a stranger into your home doesn't show sound judgment on your part."

"Everything's fine, dear. No need to worry." I glanced at the clock, which showed six fifteen. "I can't talk long, honey. Auditions are scheduled for seven."

"For that little show you and your friends are putting on? I thought auditions had finished a long time ago."

Did I hear a yawn in the background? Time to wake her up. "We need to replace both leads because Claudia shot Lance."

"Shot? As in shot dead?"

"Claudia's been a wreck even though she's out on bail." I smirked. Jennifer wasn't yawning now. Knowing my daughter's penchant to overreact, I'd purposely avoided mentioning the incident unless provoked. I hoped I hadn't gone and put my foot in my mouth, but it was too late now. "The whole thing was an unfortunate accident."

Do wishes really come true? Or were those simply song lyrics?

"Bill and I were just saying the other day . . ."

"Bill! Who is Bill?" Jen's voice rose. "Mother, are you seeing someone?"

Where my children are concerned, I'd kept Bill under wraps so to speak — along with Lance's untimely demise. After all, I'm a grown woman. I don't need to report my love life to my children. Take my son, for example. Ask Steven about his dating life, and I get the deep freeze. He's entitled to his privacy — and I'm entitled to mine. Quid pro quo. The eternal question: Why do some things work in theory only?

"Bill Lewis happens to be a friend of mine. A good friend," I added.

"A boyfriend!" Jennifer wailed. "Mother, you have a boyfriend? How could you let another man take Daddy's place?"

"No one will ever take your father's place, sweetie," I soothed. "Bill is simply a *friend.*"

"Y-you need to protect yourself."

Was she thinking protection as in *protection?* I couldn't believe we were having this conversation.

"I assume you're not foolish enough to think of remarrying," Jen continued. "If that even crosses your mind, I'll have Jason draw up a prenup. His are absolutely the best. No one can touch them. Don't make the same mistake as a lot of women your age and rush into things. Remember, Mother, no fool like an old fool."

This old fool had heard enough. "Sorry, dear, gotta run. Don't want to be late."

"B-but, Mother . . ."

I disconnected.

"Don't be nervous," I told Krystal as we pulled into the lot at the rec center.

"I'll be fine, Kate. No need to worry."

Since Krystal didn't seem to be suffering from a confidence crisis, I did as she suggested and ceased playing mother hen. I couldn't help but notice the large number of cars already there. Did they belong to late-in-the-day exercise fanatics? Or to a plethora of aspiring actors? My questions were answered the minute I stepped inside.

"Have to make more copies of the script," Rita said, rushing past us in the hall outside the auditorium. "We ran out."

I swung open the double doors and found a couple dozen people laughing and chatting. A few held scripts but, I surmised, most had come out of curiosity. No one — and I repeat, no one — in Serenity Cove Estates wants to be the last to hear a juicy bit of gossip. We pride ourselves on being well informed.

I spotted Monica pacing in front of the prop table. Her lips moved as she read from the pages clutched in one hand. Intent on the script, she seemed unaware of the activity surrounding her. She was obviously out to challenge Krystal for Claudia's role in the play. Too bad she didn't know 'Grease was the word,' *Grease* in this case being synonymous with Krystal.

The stage was no longer festooned with yellow crime scene tape, which our legion of bystanders probably found disappointing. I wondered if any had searched the boards for bloodstains. If so, some tech-savvy soul would probably post them on YouTube. Amazing how computer-literate some folks are — folks who grew up watching *Howdy Doody* and the *Ed Sullivan Show* on old black-and-white TVs. Guess it goes to prove you *can* teach old dogs new tricks. Not that I'm admitting to "old," mind you.

"Break a leg," I told Krystal as I hurried to join Bill and Janine, the other two members of *Auditions 'R Us* who were seated behind a utility table set up at the foot of the stage. "Sorry, Janine," I said. "I'm going to have to ask you to move."

She frowned at me. "What *are* you talking about?"

"Tonight I'm Paula," I explained. "Everyone knows Paula always sits on Simon's right."

"Who's Simon?"

"I'm Simon," Bill said in a British accent so atrocious it had me rolling my eyes.

With a shake of her head, Janine switched places. "Don't tell me. Let me guess. If you're Paula and Bill is Simon, I must be . . ."

"Randy."

"Isn't there a pretty brunette? And what about the new one?"

"I thought we'd keep with the original three judges."

"OK, OK, I get it. Paula, Simon, and Randy have seniority."

I settled into the chair Janine vacated and rummaged through my purse for a notebook and pen.

Janine leaned closer. "I wonder about you, Kate. First you fixate on all those crime and punishment shows on TV. Now it's *American Idol*. Surely so much television can't be good for a person. Maybe you should find another interest."

"Such as?" I could sense Bill following our conversation with interest.

"Take genealogy as an example. Many people enjoy learning more about their ancestors. I've heard there're some great software programs out there."

"I'll take the matter under advisement," I said, mimicking Sheriff Wiggins's words from earlier that day.

Genealogy vs. *Idol*? I'm not sure how finding out your great-grandfather was born in a country that no longer exists measures up against young hopefuls competing to become the nation's new singing sensation. I took Janine's advice with a grain of salt. I know she meant well.

"Time to get down to business," I said. "Janine, your part's easy. Just keep using the expressions 'yo dawg' and 'Hey, check it out, dude.' "

"What about me?" Bill asked.

"Just roll your eyes and shake your head after I give my opinion. Easy as pie, right?"

Janine brought out a notepad and prepared to take notes. "After I check it out, dude, what exactly do you do?"

I batted my eyelashes and simpered, "I tell everyone how nice they look. I want everyone to like me."

Bill gave me a nudge and whispered, "Remind me again why I let you talk me into this."

Rita, in her official capacity as stage manager, hustled over to our table. "Here," she said, placing a sign-up sheet in front of us. "This is a list of the people auditioning. I thought it might be easier if we paired them up. You know . . . male and female. Claudia and Lance? Roxanne and Troy?"

I skimmed the list and recognized most of the names. Krystal's, it seemed, had been an add-on.

"Showtime!" Rita clapped her hands to get everyone's attention. "All of you take a seat until your name is called." She consulted a copy of the list. "Monica, you'll read with Ed Beckley."

Considering the debacle of her earlier audition, I confess to being surprised Monica was giving this another shot. I guess she aspired to greater heights than being the prop princess. I had to hand it to her, though; she had grit. But no matter how

241

hard you tried, grit wasn't spelled t-a-l-e-n-t.

Monica and Ed ran through the scene. They had their lines down pat, but infused as much emotion as someone reading the phone book. Next up were Trixie, a gal I knew from golf clinics, and Jerry Buckner, another Serenity Cove resident. Trixie was already complaining that rehearsals would take time away from golf. In spite of her whining, she gave a commendable performance as Roxanne. Jerry, on the other hand, was just this side of terrible.

"Well," Bill whispered, "what do you think?"

"Yo, dude!" Janine growled, getting into the swing of things. "For me that was a little pitchy."

Bill's lips twitched as he tried to hide a smile. "And you, Kate, er, Paula?"

Smiling demurely, I propped my chin on my folded hands. "Dare to follow the path of your dream."

Bill frowned. "I don't understand a word of what you said."

I smiled vacuously and gave his shoulder a playful jab. "Precisely."

We — Paula, Simon, and Randy — rocked on through a series of readings. At last, Rita called Krystal front and center. I was shocked, no better word for it, when I heard Gus Smith's name called as her partner.

Just as I'd anticipated, Krystal blew away the competition with her rendition of Roxanne. She literally breathed new life into Lance's insipid dialogue and made the show come alive. Gus, however, caught me totally unaware. The guy was as opposite as a guy could be from Lance Ledeaux. Where Lance was handsome, Gus was, well, plain. Lance commanded attention; Gus blended into the woodwork. But onstage, Gus underwent a metamorphosis. His voice deepened, his paunch melted, he stood taller. He turned into a credible Troy.

When auditions were over, the decision was unanimous. Krystal and Gus were the reincarnated version of Claudia and Lance pretending to be Roxanne and Troy.

Rita thanked everyone for coming for tryouts. "It's a wrap."

But it wasn't a wrap for me — far from it. I kept thinking about Krystal's previous experience onstage. Could acting have been her link with Lance? And just how well had they known each other? How odd that her arrival coincided with Lance's departure.

Curious and curiouser.

CHAPTER 23

It was like old times. Almost.

Claudia and I lounged in the comfy, chintz-covered wicker chairs in her four-seasons room overlooking the fifteenth fairway, enjoying a cup of hot chocolate — not just your run-of-the-mill hot chocolate, but Godiva's finest. There's nothing like hot chocolate on a chilly afternoon to cure what ails you.

I glanced over at Claudia, curled like a giant tabby in a corner of the settee. She reminded me of Tang, that dad-blame cat Krystal was determined to tame. I have to admit that the girl was making progress coaxing him inside, using my albacore tuna as bait. The silly animal was as picky about people as he was about his diet. He showed a distinct preference for Krystal while pointedly ignoring me.

"I wish you had kicked me in the shin at the sheriff's office," Claudia murmured.

"The Claudia of old would have kicked back."

"BJ warned me to keep my big mouth shut. But did I listen? Instead, I spouted off about what a jerk Lance turned out to be. I might as well wear a big letter *M* on my chest for 'motive.' "

"Everyone knows you'd never hurt a flea."

"Everyone but Sheriff Wiggins." Claudia stared out the window. "He's bound and determined to send me to prison — or worse."

Worse, I knew, meant the death penalty. I shivered, cold in spite of my turtleneck. It would mean the sheriff would have to upgrade the charge from manslaughter to first-degree homicide. But first he needed to build a stronger case.

For a while neither of us spoke. Instead, we sipped our hot chocolate, which had grown lukewarm, and avoided looking at each other.

"I haven't told this to a soul, Kate," Claudia admitted, "but Lance and I were having serious problems."

"Problems?" I repeated putting on an innocent act. I wasn't sure I wanted to hear this, but what kind of girlfriend would I be if I didn't listen? In some instances knowledge may be power, but in this case knowledge might be incriminating.

"It wasn't bad enough Lance turned out to be a phony, but he was slowly killing me financially."

Killing? I shuddered inwardly at her poor choice of words.

"At the rate he was going, it wouldn't take long. The bank called to inform me Lance withdrew thirty thousand dollars. When I confronted him, he claimed it was for a surefire bet on the Super Bowl."

"Wow!" I blew out a breath. "Thirty thousand? That's a huge chunk of change."

Claudia nodded, her expression glum. "You can say that again. The icing on the cake was getting a call from the manager of a car dealership regarding an order for a Jaguar."

"Jaguar, hmm." I toed off my loafers, stretched my legs out on the ottoman, and wiggled my stocking feet. "I thought Lance loved his vintage Camaro."

"He claimed a Camaro no longer fit his image, whatever the hell that meant." Her lips twisted into a bitter smile. "His hopes were set on being *discovered* by some hot-shot in Atlanta with Hollywood ties. He was convinced *Forever, My Darling* would be snatched up and optioned for a screenplay — starring none other than Lance Ledeaux, of course."

"Of course," I murmured.

"It irked Lance to be called a 'has-been,' or 'second banana.' He yearned to be a leading man. Said he was tired of people remembering the face, but never the name."

I sipped my no-longer-hot hot chocolate. "Yeah, it must've been rough on his ego."

"His ego knew no bounds." Claudia nodded thoughtfully. "He was happy only when in the limelight — or gambling."

"You mentioned the Super Bowl. Was he into sports gambling?"

"You name it; he bet on it. Vegas was his version of heaven on earth." She set her cup down on the glass-topped table. "That's why I was surprised when all of a sudden he wanted to leave Vegas and come here."

"Whatever the reason, all of us were glad you came home."

I stared out the wall of windows overlooking the fairway. The green, green grass of summer had changed into the brittle beige of winter. The afternoon had turned overcast with the high only in the low fifties. Only a few hardy duffers, bundled in fleece jackets and hats with earflaps, braved the course. I have to admit I haven't played much golf since four of us Babes made a grisly find on the eighth hole some months back. Maybe this spring . . .

"I've always loved this spot," Claudia said, looking around at the profusion of greenery that rimmed the room, the same Boston ferns and various houseplants I manage to murder on a regular basis. Suddenly she lowered her head into her hands and burst into tears. "Kate, I don't know what I'm going to do if I'm sent to prison and have all this taken away."

I went over, put my arms around her, and patted her back. "There, there, Claudia, everything's going to be all right. You'll see."

When her sobbing finally subsided, I handed her a box of tissues.

"I didn't deliberately kill Lance. I could never kill anyone." Sniffling, she blotted her tears. "I've thought about that night over and over again. There's only one explanation, one person to blame."

"Who's that, sweetie?"

"Bill Lewis."

"Bill . . . ?" I echoed, stunned by the accusation.

"Think about it, Kate. Bill didn't like Lance. Remember how the two argued just before Lance was shot? You can't deny Bill knows his handguns. Polly told me he's the newly elected president of the Rod and Gun Club. And," she concluded, "it was his

Smith and Wesson."

After leaving, I drove around aimlessly. Claudia certainly couldn't have meant my Bill Lewis. Not my sweet, shy hunk of a handyman with the killer blue eyes. Yet she seemed convinced he was responsible for Lance's death — either accidentally or accidentally on purpose. Was Bill equally convinced the chamber was empty when he'd loaned Lance his gun?

And if Bill wasn't responsible, who was?

I wouldn't be able to rest until I knew the answer. Before I lost my nerve or changed my mind, I decided to pay Bill a visit. I spotted his pickup in the drive and parked behind it. I felt a little nervous as I traipsed to the front door and rang the bell.

Though I'd been there before, I wasn't in the habit of dropping by unannounced. Did this make me a shameless, man-chasing trollop? Back in the day — my day — it was taboo for a woman to even phone a man. A lady waited for the gentleman to call her. She might grow old and wrinkled in the process, but she never, ever, phoned him. Times may have changed, but I'm still on the low end of the learning curve.

No one seemed to be home. I rang the bell a final time and was just about to leave when the front door opened. And there he stood, my own personal version of Mr. February. A pair of safety goggles dangled around his neck; a tool belt hung low on his narrow hips. A gray waffle-weave Henley peeked from a plaid flannel shirt, and a spattering of sawdust covered his faded jeans. Suddenly I felt transported back to fourth grade and my first schoolgirl crush on Joey Trapani. I still have the Valentine he gave me at recess tucked away somewhere.

"Kate!"

Bill actually sounded happy to see me. I took this as a good omen. "Maybe I shouldn't have come. I can see I'm interrupting your work."

"Nonsense. Feel free to interrupt anytime." He held the door wide. "Come in, come in."

Still feeling a bit nervous, I trailed after him through the foyer. I glanced around, unobtrusively I hoped, but didn't see any changes since his return from Michigan. Simple and uncluttered. Neat as a pin. Some might even call his style of decorating Spartan. A card table and four folding chairs made up his dining room set. A leather sofa, recliner, and flat-screen TV were the only furnishings in the great room. It was a home in dire need of a woman's touch. I bit my tongue to keep from volunteering. Down, shameless hussy, down!

"How about I put on a pot of coffee?"

"Sounds perfect."

"Great. May I take your coat?"

"I'll just keep it here," I replied. Shrugging out of my lightweight jacket, I draped it over the back of a kitchen bar stool. "Looks like you're in the middle of another of your woodworking projects."

"I'm making a gun rack." He tugged off his safety glasses and tossed them on the counter. "The guys in the Rod and Gun Club asked me to make one as a sample for them."

Making a gun rack? Swell. A perfect segue. "Do you own a lot of guns?" I asked with the studied casualness worthy of a seasoned detective — at least my version of a seasoned detective. I'm no Lennie Briscoe from *Law & Order,* but I'm learning.

Bill moved about the kitchen, his movements efficient and economical. He filled the carafe with water, then carefully measured coffee. "I have a rifle for hunting and a couple handguns I use for target shooting."

"Including the one you loaned Lance?"

"Yeah, I've got a concealed weapons permit. Took a class the sheriff's depart-

251

ment offered." He took a partially empty bag of Oreos from the cupboard and heaped them on a plate, which he set in front of me.

Now, some men might ply women with alcohol, but they should take a page from Bill's book. I say, ply them with chocolate, gentlemen. They'll be putty in your hands. First hot chocolate at Claudia's, now Oreos with Bill; the chocolate gods were smiling on me. I must have been a good girl to rate this kind of treatment.

"Bill," I said, nibbling a cookie, "there's something I need to ask."

"Shoot."

Shoot as in bang-bang? Another segue I couldn't ignore. "Since you brought up the subject of shooting, is it possible you might've left a bullet in the gun you gave Lance?"

He turned, looking as unhappy as I'd ever seen him, a half-filled mug in his hand. Oh dear. Was I about to hear a confession? If so, what next? Turn him in to the sheriff? Wave as he was hauled away in a squad car?

"I can't tell you how many times I've asked myself the same question," he said at last.

The cookie in my mouth turned tasteless. "Is there even a remote possibility?"

"I've gone over this a thousand times, Kate." Resuming his role of host, he finished filling a mug for me, then poured another for himself. "As I told the sheriff, I cleaned the gun that morning before handing it over to Ledeaux. If there was a bullet in the chamber, there's no way I could have missed it."

"You're positive?"

"Very positive." He sat down beside me at the breakfast bar. "I've been around guns since I was a kid. No way I'd be that care-less. Face it, Kate. This was no accident. Someone wanted Lance dead."

"But who?"

Ever since the shooting, I'd had trouble wrapping my mind around the notion that Lance had been murdered. The word *accident* seemed safer, less frightening. As I said before, denial is a wonderful thing; best defense mechanism God ever created. But time had come to take my head out of the sand and face facts. Bill was absolutely certain he hadn't left a bullet in the cham-ber. And the only place Claudia would've killed Lance was in a divorce court.

"Time to get down to business." I reached for the large purse I always intend to trade in for a smaller one. At times like these, though, it's good to have everything at your fingertips — things such as latex gloves, an LED flashlight, and my very own little black book, which bore an uncanny resemblance to the sheriff's. I dragged out the notebook and rummaged around for a pen. "Let's make a list."

"What kind of list?"

"Work with me, Bill." I flipped open to an empty page. "We need to write down all possible suspects. Then we'll eliminate them one by one."

"How do you propose we do that?"

I sighed. Clearly Bill needed guidance — my guidance, that is. I'd be more than happy to take him under my wing and teach him the ropes of being a PI. "Remember what Sheriff Wiggins said about the Big Three?"

Bill frowned. "General Motors, Ford, and Chrysler?"

I sighed. Figures coming from someone who lived in Michigan most of his life. "The Big Three in detective work are motive, means, and opportunity. Everyone backstage had means and opportunity. All we need to do is find out who, other than Claudia, had a reason to want Lance dead. A walk in the park for two pros like us, right?"

"If you say so," Bill agreed reluctantly, but

didn't look convinced.

I proceeded to write down the names of everyone who had been present at rehearsal the night Lance was shot. "Let's start by crossing both of us off the list since neither of us is guilty. I'll scratch Claudia off the list, too, since we believe she's innocent."

Bill pointed at the next name on the list of possible suspects. "Monica?"

I shook my head. "Monica would never shoot anyone."

"Why's that?"

"She has a weak stomach and can't stand the sight of blood." I drew a line through her name. "If she ever decided to kill someone, she'd use poison."

Bill's eyes danced with amusement. "Has anyone ever told you that you have a devious mind?"

I refused to be sidetracked by a pair of baby blues. "Rita would never kill anyone either." Hers was another name to cross off.

"She have a weak stomach, too?"

"Rita's a gardener. She likes to plant things and watch them grow. I once saw her refuse to throw out an African violet infested with mealy bugs. That's not the type of person who'd cold-bloodedly kill a human being."

"Guess not." Bill took a sip of coffee.

"That leaves only Bernie and Gus on your list. Since Gus met Lance for the first time when I introduced them, what motive could he possibly have?"

I crossed Gus from my ever-shortening list. I stared at the plate of Oreos. Wasn't chocolate supposed to be good for you? Dark chocolate, Monica had preached, not white chocolate, not milk chocolate. Yep, Oreos looked dark to me. I helped myself to another cookie. "That leaves Bernie Mason as the prime suspect."

We sat for a moment in silence, contemplating the possibility.

Heaving a sigh, I suddenly knew what I had to do. Slowly, and with some regret, I drew a line through the name of our lone suspect. "Bernie has the backbone of an amoeba. He'd never get up the nerve to murder someone."

I flipped a new page over in my notebook. "Let's look at this a different way," I said, bowed but unbroken. I then proceeded to tell Bill about Polly seeing Lance looking chummy with a dark-haired woman she swore was Krystal.

"But Krystal's new in town. What motive could she possibly have?"

"I confess it's a long shot. The only possible connection I can see is that both she and Lance had previous acting experience."

"You're overlooking the fact she wasn't at the rec center that night."

I didn't want to hear the voice of reason. I wanted to solve the case, clear Claudia, and get on with my life. Next I told Bill about seeing Lance arguing with a dark-haired woman behind the Piggly Wiggly — a woman driving a luxury car identical to that of my new neighbor, Nadine Peterson.

"Since this Peterson woman wasn't at the scene of the crime either, even if she had motive, she still lacks means and opportunity."

Bill was proving a star pupil in the Kate McCall School of Private Investigation — a school about to go defunct without a single suspect.

CHAPTER 24

I idly riffled through the stack of yesterday's mail still waiting to be opened. The house seemed quiet with Krystal at work. Funny how quickly one grows accustomed to having another person around — and how unusually quiet it becomes with them gone. Until now, I thought I'd adjusted nicely to Jim's death. Granted, I get lonely at times, mostly evenings and weekends. Evenings the two of us used to gab over dinner, then watch TV or read the paper. Weekends meant get-togethers with friends; maybe taking in dinner and a movie — couple activities.

For a short time, Bill helped relieve the emptiness. I'd invite him over for a home-cooked meal. Afterward we'd pop corn and maybe watch a video. Hold hands on the sofa. Kiss good night. It'd been nice while it lasted — I missed the closeness. While we were slowly regaining lost ground, our relationship still wasn't back to where it had been before his brother's heart attack.

I was about to set the mail aside when an ad from an online dating service, Love Line, Inc., caught my eye. Had such an innocent scrap of paper started Claudia's downward spiral? Had it seduced her with sweet illusions of romance, excitement, and male companionship? Then again, what's so wrong with romance, excitement, and male companionship? I could stand a little of those myself. I was torn between the temptation to rip open the envelope or toss it in the trash. Common sense prevailed. I threw it away.

A business envelope bearing a Nashville postmark and a logo of a judge's gavel captured my attention next. *Down with Deadbeats* was written in large block letters in the upper-left corner. Just below, written in a smaller font, *Tennessee's Premier Detective Agency.*

"Hmm," I muttered aloud. "Interesting."

All right, busted! I confess that on occasion I do talk to myself. And on rarer occasions, I even talk back. I rationalize this by saying sometimes it's the only way to have an intelligent conversation.

Down with Deadbeats was about to follow the path of Love Line, Inc. when a second glance revealed the letter wasn't addressed to me but to my new neighbor, Nadine Peterson. My fingers itched to pry the flap open and find out why Ms. Peterson needed the services of Tennessee's premier detectives. All I had to do was steam the envelope open with a teakettle. It didn't require rocket science. Through the years, I'd watched the same trick done a dozen times on TV. Then my conscience kicked in, reminding me mail tampering was against the law, and spoiled my fun.

Heaving a sigh of regret, I slipped on a sweater and headed across the street. I intended to be neighborly even if it killed me. For a nanosecond, I debated my next step. I could easily slip the envelope into the mailbox at the end of her drive. Or I could deliver it in person. I opted for the latter.

As on my last — my one and only — visit, Nadine Peterson was slow to answer the door. A lesser person would have given up, but not I. My persistence paid off when Nadine finally appeared, a smoldering cigarette dangling from her fingertips.

"Kate, isn't it?" she asked in her deep, throaty voice.

I held out the envelope. "This was delivered to my mailbox by mistake. I thought it might be important."

She gave it a quick glance. "Sure, thanks."

I wondered how many times her voice was mistaken for that of a man. If eye shadow alone were any indicator, there'd be no question about her gender. She wore enough eye makeup to supply an entire class of eighth-grade girls.

From her expression, I could tell she was about to close the door in my face. "I, ah, couldn't help but notice the postmark. You from Nashville?"

"Yeah, I guess you might say that."

I tossed out another gambit. "Nashville's a great city."

At least it had looked great when Jim and I sailed through at seventy miles an hour on our way to Graceland. I've been a big Elvis fan since I was a kid. Jim took me there some years back for my birthday. We even spent the night at the nearby Heartbreak Hotel. He drew the line, however, at listening to Elvis nonstop all the way home. Some men just don't have an ear for the classics.

Nadine took a drag from her cigarette and blew out a plume of smoke. "Nashville's OK, I guess."

Getting this woman to impart information was harder than pulling random chin hairs. Her evasiveness only served to whet my curiosity. Down with Deadbeats? Deadbeat fathers? Boyfriends? Husbands? I racked my brain trying to remember what *The Complete Idiot's Guide to Private Investigating* had to say about recalcitrant witnesses. I reminded myself to review that chapter before exam time.

I dug deep into my bag of small talk. "Nice weather we're having. On the cool side, but nice. Daffodils will be blooming before long."

She flicked ash on the doorstep. "I'm not into flowers."

I dug deeper. "How do you like it here so far?"

"Fine."

"Are you meeting people?"

"Some."

This would never do. I was glad I wasn't being graded on technique. Maybe I should come right out and ask if she knew Lance Ledeaux — and why they argued. Nadine, I was fairly certain, *was* the woman I saw with Lance behind the Pig — same car, same hair. Too bad I hadn't gotten a better look at the face.

I made one last attempt to forge some sort of bond. I smiled with the genuine warmth of a toaster oven. "Maybe we can get together for lunch sometime."

"Give me a call." She stuck the cigarette in the corner of her mouth and closed the door, leaving me standing on the front step.

I could take a hint. The interview was over.

I heard the phone ring even before I pushed open the door. I rushed to answer it before the machine picked up. "Hello," I said, sounding a bit breathless after my mad dash.

"Miz McCall . . . ?"

Dang! Should have let the machine get it. Instantly I realized my mistake upon recognizing the Voice of Doom, also known as Tammy Lynn Snow. Was it too late to disguise my voice? Adopt a Spanish accent? *Hola, señora?* Grow up, Kate, I chided myself. Put on your big-girl panties and deal with it.

"Hey, Tammy Lynn. How're things?"

"Sheriff Wiggins wants to see you here in his office," the girl said without preamble.

I groaned. I simply couldn't help it. Why wasn't my caller telling me I'd won the South Carolina lottery? Or requesting a liver transplant?

"I, ah, I'm kind of busy right now." Liar, liar! I touched my nose to see if it had grown any. Pinocchio, Pinocchio, wherefore art thou Pinocchio?

"Sheriff said he'd be happy to send

Deputy Preston if you needed a lift."

Send a deputy? Well, that kicked my heart into overdrive. There must be some pretty serious stuff on the agenda. I opted for one more whopper. I crossed my fingers and hoped I'd be able to recognize myself next time I looked in the mirror. "Ah, I have a previous engagement."

"He was very specific when he told me not to take any excuses. Can you be here by three o'clock?"

"Fine," I snapped, and instantly regretted it. There was no need to take out my frustration on Tammy Lynn. "Sorry, Tammy Lynn. Tell the sheriff I'll be there."

After I hung up, I stood for a moment, a hand over my heart to still its racing. Question after question popped into my head. Why did the sheriff want to see me? Was this another group meeting? Or was I going to fly solo? And if I was convicted of obstruction of justice, could Claudia and I request to be cell mates?

One thing I did know, however. I needed some sound legal advice between now and three o'clock. I dialed BJ Davenport's office and explained my predicament to Aleatha Higginbotham. My desperation must've communicated itself across the line, because Aleatha, bless her heart, promised to squeeze me into BJ's schedule.

Somewhat relieved, I called Bill, Rita, and Monica. None of them had received a summons from Tammy Lynn. I had a bad feeling about this. It looked like I was going to be the sole guest.

"I heard jail food is very unhealthy," Monica advised. "Deep-fried and loaded with fat. Be sure to ask for a jumpsuit one size too big in case you gain weight,"

Monica was only trying to be helpful, right?

"Hey, Miz Kate," Aleatha greeted me with a smile. "Don't you look nice this afternoon."

"Thanks, Aleatha." Maybe I should have studied at the Higginbotham School of Fashion. My dress code bore a closer resemblance to Tammy Lynn Snow's. Unlike Aleatha's wildly flowered blue and green ensemble, I was wearing a beige twinset and brown flannel pants. Figured I'd go with neutrals since I might be wearing hard-to-miss orange soon enough.

"Can I get you a glass of tea or a soda?"

"No, thanks," I said. "I don't want to risk drowning the butterflies in my stomach."

"No need to fret with BJ helping. He said to send you right in."

BJ looked up when I entered and came out from behind a massive antique desk. "Miz Kate," he said, welcoming me with the warmth reserved for an old friend, "you're lookin' pretty as a picture this afternoon. Have a seat."

I gave him a wobbly smile as I complied. "Sheriff Wiggins called. He wants to see me."

He lowered himself onto the edge of the desk. I noticed he was wearing his signature bow tie. Today's pick was navy blue imprinted with tiny green palmettos, South Carolina's state tree. Snazzy!

"Don't let Wiggins get your panties in a twist," he counseled. "Now tell me, how can I help you?"

I set my purse in my lap, folded my hands primly, then took a deep breath. "Tell me everything I need to know about obstruction of justice. And when you're done, kindly explain withholding information. Bottom line: Can I be arrested?"

A vertical frown formed between his brows. "What kind of information are you withholding?"

I looked down; I looked up. I looked anywhere but directly at him. "Um, I, ah, happened to overhear Claudia and Lance argue the night he was shot."

"Mmm, I see. Just what were they arguin' about?"

"Money."

"And you're afraid to tell the sheriff."

"I'm more afraid of incriminating Claudia."

BJ got up from his perch and prowled the room, hands behind his back.

I fiddled nervously with the strap of my purse. "He suspects I've committed a sin of omission."

"I'd advise you to come clean. Don't embellish anythin'. Just tell him what you heard. Arguments between husbands and wives are commonplace. Show me a husband and wife who don't argue, and I'll show you a husband and wife who don't speak to each other."

"But I heard Claudia say 'over my dead body.' "

He grunted. "Merely a figure of speech. Folks say it all the time."

"But most husbands don't turn up dead half an hour later."

"Good point, but don't remind the sheriff of that sorry fact."

"There's more," I said miserably. "She threatened to get him out of her life — 'one way or another.' "

"Surely Miz Claudia didn't mean that in

the literal sense. I'll make a case it was a harmless statement made under duress. I'll stress Miz Ledeaux is a savvy business woman who'd use the legal system — not a Smith and Wesson — to get rid of the bastard. Sorry for the vulgarity, ma'am," he apologized, "but that best describes the deceased."

I let out a sigh of relief. Maybe my information wasn't so damning after all. People used figures of speech all the time, didn't they? Especially under duress. What greater stress could there be than realizing the man you'd just married was out to rob you blind? Claudia's remarks were perfectly justified.

"Would you like me to accompany you to the sheriff's office?" He flicked his wrist to look at his watch. "I have an appointment in about ten minutes, but I'd be happy to cancel."

I could tell from where I sat it was a Rolex — the real deal and probably worth at least a thousand dollars. Seeing it made me feel better. He must be very good at his job to be able to afford such an expensive piece of jewelry. Talking to him made me feel marginally better. "That won't be necessary," I told him, "but I'll program your number into speed dial — just in case."

BJ came over to me, and taking both my

hands in his, said, "Miz Claudia is fortunate to have a friend like you. Don't you worry none. I'll do right by her."

My newly acquired calm, however, vanished the instant I entered the sheriff's office.

Glancing up from her desk, Tammy Lynn shoved her overly large glasses higher on the bridge of her nose. "Afternoon, Miz McCall. Sheriff said to send you straight to the interrogation room down the hall. He's waitin'."

I gave myself a pep talk as I proceeded down the hallway. I had nothing to fear but fear itself. I don't remember who said it first, but it seemed to fit the occasion. I'd *always* answered the sheriff's questions truthfully. I hadn't lied. Might have left out a few teensy details was all. If he'd asked me whether I'd heard Claudia scream that she'd get Lance out of her life — "one way or another" — I'd have replied, yes, matter of fact I did hear that. It wasn't my fault the sheriff didn't ask the right questions.

I found the sheriff seated in his favorite creaky chair. "Have a seat, Miz McCall," he said without looking up from the folder in front of him.

I gingerly sat in the lone chair opposite him, placed my purse beside me on the worn-tile floor, and folded my hands primly on the table. "You wanted to see me, Sheriff?"

"Seems like you and I have some unfinished business." He glanced up and skewered me like a beef kabob with that sharp gaze of his. He looked around. "What, no gifts, no presents, this time? My, my, what's the world comin' to?"

He was mocking my gift-bringing habit. In New Orleans, I believe there's a term for such generosity: *lagniappe,* meaning a small gift for nothing. Truth was, I'd debated bringing him a little something, but decided against it at the last minute.

"Knowing how your mind works, Sheriff, I was afraid even a tiny gift might be misconstrued as a bribe."

"You're absolutely right, ma'am. This isn't a social call. You might even call it an official interrogation."

Oh dear, I was in for it now. We'd gone from interview to interrogation. Time for me to come clean and beg forgiveness. Bless me, Sheriff, for I have sinned. . . .

CHAPTER 25

Sheriff Wiggins consulted his notes. "I had a nice chat with Miz Marietta Perkins, who works the desk at the rec center in Serenity Cove Estates. Miz Perkins happened to be on the job the night of Mr. Lance Ledeaux's untimely demise."

Marietta Perkins, huh. That little snitch. Wait 'til I tell the Babes about her loose lips. See if we chip in for a nice gift come next Christmas.

"Miz Perkins said you arrived at the auditorium that night shortly after Mr. and Missus Ledeaux."

"And if I did?"

He ignored my question. "Miz Perkins also claims she heard loud arguin' comin' from that direction and, bein' a conscientious person an' all, went to investigate. Said she started to open the door, and she saw you standin' there. She was about to say somethin' but returned to answer the phone at the front desk. Her memory is quite clear on the subject. She's the sort who pays attention to detail."

Attention to detail, my foot. Marietta Perkins was what Granny would've called a Nosy Parker and what Mama would've called a busybody. In either case, she was a woman who stuck her nose where it didn't belong.

"What I want to know is this," the sheriff continued. "Did the argument between Mr. and Missus Ledeaux have to do with money?"

Before I could answer, he held up a hand — a hand large enough to serve as a Stop sign. All it needed was some red and white paint. "Let me share another item of interest. I have it on good authority Mr. Ledeaux placed a rather large bet on the Super Bowl — a bet, by the way, he'd have lost. Ten thousand is a heap of money."

"*Ten* thousand?"

Something in my tone must have alerted him. His brows knit in a frown. "Lot of folks argue over lesser amounts."

I mentally replayed my earlier conversation with Claudia. The amount she'd mentioned was considerably more than ten thousand, though I have to agree with the sheriff on one point: Ten thousand *is* a heap of money.

"I'll admit I did hear them talk about a Super Bowl bet. Lance, it seems, had a gambling problem, but you know that already, so why am I here?"

"Any other financial problems you're aware of?"

I shrugged my shoulders. "Lance had expensive tastes and a limited budget. My friend, Mrs. Ledeaux, told him she'd had enough of his spending."

"Was that all she said?"

"Ah, not exactly." I shifted in my seat, trying to get comfortable. Criminals probably confessed just so they could find a softer chair.

The sheriff leaned back, folding his arms over a line-backer-sized chest. "S'pose you define 'not exactly.' "

I stared down at my folded hands. I could use a manicure, I noted. I could use a good stiff drink even more. How far would I get if I made a run for it? I recalled BJ's advice: *Come clean and don't embellish.* I hauled in a deep breath and let it rip. "I heard Claudia tell Lance she'd find a way to get him out of her life. I think she planned to divorce the low-down, nest egg–sucking snake."

"She mention divorce?"

"Not in so many words." I took one look

at that lifted brow and those hard-as-drill-bit eyes and knew I was going to sing like a canary. "She might have said something along the lines of, 'I'll do whatever it takes.' "

He made a note of this.

I felt like pond scum. No need for thumb-screws. Just call me Tweety Bird. "I suppose you know about the Jag?" I asked in a small voice.

"As in Jaguar . . . the expensive automobile?"

I nodded miserably. "Lance ordered one from a dealer in Augusta."

The sheriff let out a low whistle. "Man sure had good taste."

Mea culpa. Mea culpa. Through my most grievous fault. Forgive me, Claudia, I have caved. At this point in the interrogation hardened felons, repeat offenders, even psychopaths, probably broke down and confessed to stealing crayons from the five-and-dime as youngsters. Sheriff Wiggins, alias the Grand Inquisitor, had that kind of effect once he shifted into "official" mode.

"That's it. Am I free to leave?"

"It would've saved us both time and effort if you'd told me all this at the beginnin'," he drawled lazily. "Wouldn't have had to call you back, but now you know the difference between an interview and an interrogation."

I stood, slinging my purse over my shoulder. "Just because Lance was a freeloader doesn't mean Claudia killed him. You admitted yourself that he was a gambler. Anyone could have put a bullet in that gun."

"Who'd know Ledeaux would step into the role of villain that particular night and insist they use props?"

"It could've been anyone at rehearsal. Everyone heard Lance announce he was going to take Bernie's place after our break. It was his idea that Claudia use the gun to make the scene more realistic."

"Who else wanted him dead?" He tapped his pen against the table and regarded me thoughtfully.

"Lance wouldn't have won a congeniality award if he was the only contestant. Why, that very afternoon, I saw him having what appeared to be an argument with a dark-haired woman behind the Piggly Wiggly. I think the woman happens to be my new neighbor, Nadine Peterson. And my friend Polly saw Lance chummy with a dark-haired woman she swears is my houseguest, Krystal Gold. So you see, Sheriff, there are plenty of persons of interest."

I strode toward the door, pleased with

myself for having fired an answering salvo. One problem lingered, however. I paused, my hand on the knob. "Are you certain your source had his facts straight when he told you Lance bet ten thousand on the Super Bowl?"

The sheriff stopped jotting notes and looked up. "Yeah, why?"

"If you check bank records, you'll find Lance made a withdrawal for *thirty* thousand, not ten."

He shuffled through a pile of papers until he found the one he wanted. He ran his finger over the page until he found the entry he searched for. "Says here, ten grand to the bookie; another ten grand found on the body."

"I'm no math whiz, but ten and ten add up to twenty. That leaves another ten thousand unaccounted for." I hitched my purse higher. "Follow the money, Sheriff. Follow the money."

His eyes narrowed suspiciously. "You still watchin' those cop shows on TV?"

"Never miss *Law & Order.* That bit of advice courtesy of Cyrus Lupo, homicide division." I smiled for the first time since entering. "Good detective, but the man needs a shave."

As I left the office, I gave a fleeting glance

out of habit to the Most Wanted posters tacked near the door. I'm always on the lookout for a familiar face. A woman living alone can't be too careful.

It was rather nice having the house to myself for a change — not that Krystal was a nuisance; just the opposite. She kept pretty much holed up in her room along with Tang, that darn orange cat forever following her. The two seemed to have formed a connection of some sort over my albacore tuna. Tonight Janine had picked Krystal up after dinner and the two headed for rehearsal. Apparently my services weren't required. Janine said she wanted to concentrate on the scenes involving Krystal's and Gus's characters and bring them up to speed. She wanted them to get *into the space,* whatever that meant.

I decided to make the most of my solitude. I settled on the sofa with a dish of rocky road ice cream in one hand, *The Complete Idiot's Guide to Private Investigating* in the other. I hoped to glean a shred or two of wisdom from the book. Sheriff Wiggins clearly needed all the help he could get — whether he admitted it or not. At times the man couldn't see past the end of his nose. He was so set on Claudia's being guilty, he wasn't even trying to apprehend the real culprit. Fortunately, he had the help of the Babes.

Leafing through the book, I wondered if perhaps the situation warranted an emergency bunco session. Maybe if all of us put our heads together we could find out who really killed Lance. With all the hullabaloo about the play and rehearsals, bunco had been shoved to a back burner. We needed to bring it forward and crank up the heat.

The phone rang just as I finished scraping the last spoonful of ice cream from the bottom of the bowl. After the day I'd had, I really wasn't in the mood for conversation, but I quickly changed my mind when I heard the caller's voice.

"Steven!"

"Hi, Mom."

Jim always liked to boast that our son inherited his brains and my looks. I'd have been happier if he'd inherited an urge to call his poor widowed mother more often. Steven's calls are sporadic at best. I know, I know. He's busy. But I ask you, how many times do I have to remind the boy of how long I was in labor?

"Great to hear your voice, honey. Where are you this time?" Steven has an important job buying do-dads and gizmos for a well-known chain based in New York City. His work takes him all over the globe — to places only a few can locate without the help of Google.

"I'm still at the office," he said. "I was about to meet some friends for a drink, but I wanted to call first."

"Any special reason for the call, dear?" Hope springs eternal for the mother of a son who's still single at thirtysomething. I keep wishing he'd meet a nice girl, someone like Tara, perhaps, settle down, raise a family. So far he's married to his job. Occasionally I hear references to friends — friends named Sam or Joe. I'd rather hear about friends named Kimberly or Ashley. But what's a mother to do?

"I'll get right to the point, Mom. I talked to Jen last week."

I mentally tried to recall the gist of my conversation with my daughter. No red flags waved in the breeze. I was home free. "It's nice to know you and your sister keep in touch."

"Jen's worried about you, and so am I."

"Whatever for? I'm perfectly fine." Or at least I thought I was before picking up the phone. Now I was starting to have doubts.

"Jen told me you were involved with some man out for your money, your pension."

I blinked. Man, what man? Did Lance have an evil twin? "Steven, what on earth are you talking about?"

"Jen said you're seeing some gigolo by the name of Bill Lewis. She asked me to check up on him. See if he was on the up-and-up."

I couldn't believe my ears. Bill, a gigolo? If I weren't so angry, I would have laughed. "Steven James McCall, shame on you!"

Using my son's middle name never had the same effect on him as it had on our daughter, but it had been worth a try. Maybe instead of James it should've been Louise.

"Jen and I are only looking out for your best interests, Mom. One can't be too careful these days. There are a lot of guys looking for a free ride."

I thought of Lance and kept my mouth shut.

"So," Steven said, "I did what any concerned son would do. I did a background check."

"You what! Please, tell me you did no such thing."

"It's no big deal, Mom. You don't have to thank me."

"Thank? *Spank* would be more like it."

"No need to get upset. It's not good for

your blood pressure."

"You had no right to pry into my personal affairs." Oops! Wrong choice of words. I *wasn't* having an affair. "I meant my personal *business.*"

"You're being emotional. Background checks are commonplace these days."

I drew a deep, calming breath. And then another. "Steven, dear, with an attitude such as yours, it's no wonder you can't find a wife. Where's your spirit of romance? What about love and trust?"

"The gang's waiting for me, Mom. I don't have time for a lecture. Getting back to the subject —"

"By all means," I cut in. "Let's get back to your snooping into my privacy."

"You'll be pleased to know this Bill Lewis is who he says he is. His credit rating is good. Other than a mortgage, he has no outstanding debts. He was married only once. His wife, Margaret, is deceased. He has one child, a son living in Ohio. Records show no lawsuits or criminal record. He has never filed for bankruptcy, and there are no liens against his property. Seems like he lived most of his life in Battle Creek, Michigan, which, by the way, is where they make breakfast cereal. And one last thing — he isn't listed on either the terrorist watch list or as a sex offender."

"Well," I said when he finally ran out of breath, "that's certainly very comforting, but much more than I needed to know." Whatever happened to the concept of invasion of privacy?

"If you want, Jen or I could fly out, look this guy over, give you our opinion."

"Absolutely not!" I clutched the phone 'til my knuckles shone white. "Bill happens to be a friend — a very good friend. How would you feel if I started doing background checks on your friends Sam or Joe?"

"This is different," he answered after a lengthy pause. "You're a senior citizen."

"Age has nothing to do with it. I'm not senile."

"Of course not, Mom. I didn't mean to suggest you were."

I detected a hint of condescension in his voice, but before I could take him to task, he mumbled something about having to run, and then he disconnected.

I was still fuming later when I heard Krystal's key turn in the front door. The sound was followed by an ear-piercing shriek. Instantly I ran to see what was wrong.

"Krystal . . . ?"

She stood on the threshold, her eyes wide in horror, staring down at the doormat.

Pointing a shaking finger, she managed to gasp, "It's . . . it's . . ."

I followed the direction in which she pointed. A container the size of a shoe box rested on my welcome mat. I forced myself to pick it up when instincts dictated I squeal like a sissy. A dead bird lay inside, its poor little head bent at a forty-five-degree angle. I stared at it in morbid fascination. I couldn't seem to help it.

"It's just a dead bird," I said, stating the obvious. "Tang must've left it there. I'm told cats are notorious for doing such things — bringing gifts and offerings of affection."

Krystal gazed at me as though I had taken leave of my senses. "I never heard of a cat putting his offerings in a gift box. All Tang lacked was a ribbon and a bow."

The girl had a point. I took a closer look. There was something else strange about this picture. It wasn't just any bird — a wren or finch — but a canary. A dead canary.

Visions of mobsters in vintage black-and-white films — Cagney, Raft, and Robinson — danced in my head. Didn't they use dead canaries as warnings to folks who talked too much? Was the real murderer starting to get worried? I continued to stare at the dead canary. It was an omen, I decided.

But definitely not a good one.

CHAPTER 26

"Have you heard the news?"

Pam was the first to arrive for bunco. The others would be along shortly. Actually, it was Janine's turn to host bunco, but she asked me to trade since being artistic director was taking up so much of her spare time.

"What news?" The cork came loose with a satisfying *pop!* Tonight I was serving a nice pinot grigio — the Babes' white wine du jour. We'd already sampled our way through a wide variety of chardonnays and Rieslings. I set the wine aside and started to dole out the sweets.

"Claudia" — Pam paused for maximum effect — "has been rearrested."

Now it was my turn to pause, Peanut M&M's in one hand, dice-shaped candy dish in the other. "What do you mean — 'rearrested'?"

Pam perched on a stool at the breakfast bar. "Jack, my Jack, happened to be driving by her place after golf committee. He saw a deputy lead her away in handcuffs."

"Oh my God!" I moaned. "This is terrible."

M&M's spilled all over the counter as I threw the bag down and rushed for the phone. I dialed Claudia's "bad" attorney, but my call went to voice mail, so I had to be content with leaving a message. I felt sick to my stomach at the thought of Claudia's being arrested a second time.

"This is my fault for being a stool pigeon," I wailed.

"Don't blame yourself, Kate."

Pam picked up the scattered M&M's and returned them to the dish. I couldn't bear to look at them. The candies might as well have MOTIVE and MEANS printed on them.

"If I hadn't sung like a canary, none of this would be happening." Needing to lighten my guilty conscience, I confessed to Pam, my BFF, that I'd spilled my guts to the sheriff during a brutal interrogation.

Pam scooted off the stool and gave me a hug. "Nonsense. You're giving yourself entirely too much credit. Sooner or later, facts were bound to surface. It's hardly classified information Lance Ledeaux was an unemployed actor who'd been spending money like crazy ever since he married

Claudia."

"It's the last of the Big Three," I muttered disconsolately.

"Ford, GM, and Chrysler?"

Yet another person from Michigan. I mustered a smile. "No, silly, the Big Three as in motive, means, and opportunity. Lance's extravagant spending goes to supply motive. She already had means and opportunity."

News Claudia had been taken into custody made my pre-bunco agenda even more imperative; more urgent. For this reason I'd lied — an itsy-bitsy white lie — and told Nadine our game started at seven thirty instead of seven. The Babes and I needed time to discuss Claudia's case and form a plan of action. Since Nadine was unofficially a "person of interest," she wasn't privy to our little discussion.

"Anyone home?" Polly sang out. Not waiting for an invitation, she strolled into the kitchen, resplendent in her version of grunge chic in a tie-dyed shirt and jeans — not just any jeans, mind you, but ones that came premade torn and frayed; the kind no self-respecting wife would allow her husband outside to mow the lawn in for fear of what the neighbors might think; the kind of jeans that cost mega-bucks in upscale department stores.

"Mother's been shopping," Gloria explained lest we'd been struck blind by Polly's dazzling array of colors. Gloria, as though trying to counteract her mother's flamboyancy, was dressed conservatively in gray slacks and a sweater. The forest of gold chains around her neck supplied the only hint of color.

Monica and Connie Sue were next to arrive, followed in short order by the rest of the Babes. From the noisy greetings and number of hugs, a casual observer would have thought we hadn't seen one another in an age.

"Where's Megan?" Tara asked Pam after disengaging herself from Polly's enthusiastic welcome.

"She's running lines with Eric for their big scene together."

"Whom did you get to sub?" Rita, the ever practical, asked.

I set out the fruit and cheese tray I'd prepared. "Krystal agreed to fill in as long as I promised to keep the cupboard stocked with tuna for that darn cat that's been hanging around. Some might consider that bribery."

Diane poured herself a glass of wine. "It's

nice you have a pet, Kate."

I fought the urge to roll my eyes. "I'd hardly call that mangy orange fur ball a pet. Nuisance is a better word for it."

"Why's that?" Janine asked, sampling a strawberry.

"Well, for one thing, Tang has a generous and giving nature. A little too generous and giving for my taste."

"I think that's sweet," Connie Sue drawled, then looked around to see if others agreed. "Don't y'all think that's sweet?"

"I'm talking dead-critters kind of 'sweet.' Tang likes to deposit gifts on my doorstep. Things like mice, a squirrel's tail, and, once, a dead skunk. Thank goodness it wasn't a live one, or you would've heard my scream clear to Georgia."

"Eeuww!" Connie Sue shuddered dramatically.

"His last present," I continued, "happened to be a dead bird."

I refused to elaborate on the fact that said offering had arrived all but gift wrapped — or that it wasn't a run-of-the-mill wren or mockingbird, but a canary.

Monica filled a glass with ice, then added diet soda. "Recent studies show that those of us who own pets are usually healthier and happier than those who don't."

What would the Babes do without Monica to keep us informed? Name a subject and she could quote a "recent study." At times I wonder if I should forego my beloved *Law & Order* and *CSI* and read more so I, too, could quote recent studies. But before I opt for drastic measures, sanity always returns.

Connie Sue daintily sipped pinot grigio. "Thacker is allergic to cats. He says dogs make better pets. He says they're a font of unconditional love."

Connie Sue was as fond of quoting her husband as Monica was fond of quoting recent studies. We jokingly refer to him as St. Thacker of Macon. "Well, Connie Sue, that's another of Tang's drawbacks. He's never heard the term 'unconditional love.' He avoids me like the plague while cozying up to Krystal. The darn stray doesn't realize it's me, not Krystal, who's the font of unconditional albacore."

Diane looked around. "Speaking of Krystal, where is she?"

"I handed her my car keys and sent her into town for more tuna. I told her to take her time."

"I thought we were supposed to play bunco," Monica complained. "Where is Claudia, by the way?"

"Claudia begged off, so I asked my new neighbor, Nadine Peterson, to sub." And much to my surprise, Nadine had accepted the invitation. The woman wasn't the friendliest person on the planet, but I'd show her I'd learned a thing or two about Southern hospitality. I glanced at my watch and knew it was time to speak my piece.

"Listen up, ladies." I held up both hands, signaling for the Babes' undivided attention. "Truth is, I wanted to talk with you about Claudia before Krystal and Nadine arrive."

"What's wrong? Is she sick?"

Pam looked my way, then cleared her throat. "She's been arrested a second time."

"How?"

"Why?"

"What happened?"

I raised my voice and spoke over the shock, the outrage, the concern. "We can only assume the charges against her have been changed from manslaughter to murder. I have a call in to BJ, but I'm still waiting for him to get back to me. I'm afraid, ladies, if we don't step up and do something, Claudia's going to prison for murdering Lance. We can't let that happen."

"What can we do?" Gloria asked, her forehead knit with concern.

"I think we all agree that Claudia would never knowingly shoot anyone, much less kill them."

The Babes nodded. I took this as a sign of encouragement and continued my call to arms. "I think it's also safe to assume that none of us present that night put a bullet in Bill's gun."

More nods. Perhaps we should change our name to the Bobble-Head Babes.

Rita folded her arms over her impressive bosom and cocked her head. "Who'd want to kill the no-good worm?"

"I saw Lance acting real chummy with a woman who looks like Krystal," Polly volunteered.

"And I saw Lance behind the Piggly Wiggly arguing with a woman who bears a striking resemblance to Nadine Peterson," I added. "I thought we'd start by trying to find out all we can about Krystal Gold and Nadine Peterson and their possible connection to Lance."

"But they weren't even there the night Lance was shot," Janine protested.

I was afraid someone would point out the glaring error in my logic. Darn! I hate when that happens. But I refused to let a little thing like logic stand in my way. "Think outside the box, ladies. Think outside the box. Once we find motive, means and opportunity can't be far behind. Then all we need to do is connect the dots. How hard can it be?"

I could tell from their expressions they weren't easily swayed by my rhetoric. "Where is your spirit of adventure? Your sense of camaraderie for a fallen Babe?" I challenged. I envisioned myself as Napoleon rallying his troops, but conveniently ignored his dismal defeat at Waterloo. "We need to rise to the occasion, ladies, not let minor details stand in the way of victory."

Rita scowled down at me from her lofty height. "Anyone backstage could have placed a bullet in that gun. Shouldn't we check out everyone, including Bill, Bernie, and that new guy, what's his name — Gus?"

"Bill swears there wasn't a live round in the chamber when he gave the gun to Lance, so we can cross him off our list. Gus didn't meet Lance until he started work on the set, but I'll ask Bill to keep his eyes and ears open just in case. As for Bernie, the only thing he's capable of killing is crabgrass."

"OK," Diane said, casting a worried look toward the door. "Krystal and Nadine are due to arrive any minute. How do you suggest we go about this?"

I smiled and reached for the dice.

CHAPTER 27

Though I rarely win the tiara, I turned out to be high roller on *Who Wants to Be a Detective.* The grand prize? I won the honor of exercising my dubious investigative skills on Nadine Peterson.

"All right, ladies, let's roll again."

And so we did. The dice made the circuit. Points tallied, Polly was the undisputed runner-up. Her assignment? Getting the skinny on Krystal Gold.

She grinned ear to ear, clearly up for the task. "Always wanted to be Columbo. This'll give me a chance to wear the trench coat I brought along from Chicago. Good thing it's got a zip-out lining, or I'd roast down here."

"That's not fair," Connie Sue said with a pout. "You get to have all the fun. I want to help y'all, too. What if I chat up Marietta Perkins at the rec center? She was workin' that night. That witch doesn't miss a trick."

"Good idea," I said. "Marietta probably even knows what color your toenails are painted."

"I'm pretty good around computers. Why don't I see what else I can turn up about Lance?" Diane offered. "Maybe it'll give us a clue as to who might want him dead."

I high-fived Diane. "The Babes rock!"

Tara plucked grapes from the tray I'd set out. "You might start with a background check," she suggested. "It's amazing how much information's out there."

"Ain't that the truth?" I muttered under my breath. Thanks to Steven, I knew more than I needed to about background checks. Maybe Lance would turn out to be a terrorist. A pervert. Or a deadbeat. Maybe all three.

Deadbeat? As in Down with Deadbeats? I made a mental note. The first item on my agenda would be to find out precisely what kind of cases Tennessee's Premier Detective Agency specialized in.

The doorbell pealed just then, bringing the meeting of Bunco Babe Crime Solvers to a close. I hurried to greet my neighbor — and designated "person of interest."

"Nadine!" I exclaimed, adopting a tone worthy of Miss Congeniality. "So glad you could make it."

Nadine took a last drag from her cigarette, then flicked the butt into a pot of pansies on the front step. "Saw all the cars. Thought I had the time wrong."

"The girls and I had a little unfinished business to attend to. Didn't want to bore you with it." I held the door wide and stepped aside. "Come in."

I led her through the foyer and into the kitchen where the Babes were gathered like turkey buzzards awaiting road-kill.

"Care for a glass of wine, Nadine?" I asked after introductions were completed. "I've got a nice pinot grigio, or if you prefer a red, I'll open a merlot."

"Got a beer?"

"Beer? Let me take a look." My smile never faltered. I was beginning to worry my facial muscles might stay that way. Now, I've never been much of a beer drinker, but I like to keep some on hand just in case — just in case of what I'm not exactly sure. Maybe someday Bill will drop by, all hot and thirsty, after a hard day at the Rod and Gun Club. He'll strip off his shirt, revealing a hard, toned bod, and . . .

Then, I usually wake up.

I hoped none of the Babes noticed I was flushed — a minor power surge, as I like to call them. I pulled a beer from behind the skim milk. "Um," I said, clearing my throat, "let me get you a glass."

"Don't need one." Taking it from me, Nadine twisted off the cap and chugged the brew straight from the bottle.

Krystal, her dark hair pulled back and fastened with a banana clip, breezed in. "Sorry I'm late, everyone," she said, sounding out of breath. "As long as I had wheels, I stopped by the diner to see if May had finished next week's schedule."

"Now that everyone's here, let's get started." Tara headed toward the card table I'd set up in the great room. "Some of you get to sleep late, but I have to get up early to stay ahead of a bunch of four-year-olds at the day care center."

"Sugar lamb," Connie Sue crooned, "some of us have earned the right to sleep 'til noon if that's what our little hearts desire."

"Chalk it up as another perk of retirement," Gloria said agreeably, topping off her wine. "Right up there alongside of Medicare and Social Security."

"Six Saturdays followed by a Sunday," Janine quipped.

Rita patted Tara's back. "Retirement is a reward, honey, not a punishment."

Polly hooked her arm through Krystal's.

297

"Kate said you've never played bunco, dear. Let me show you the ropes." I didn't miss the wink she sent my way.

Smiling, I followed Polly's shining example. *"Come into my parlor,"* said the spider *to the fly.* "C'mon, Nadine. You can be my partner at the head table."

Connie Sue and Diane joined us. I could tell from the gleam in her eye that Connie Sue was committed to the Free Claudia Campaign. And I knew Diane would uphold her end as well. Nadine was toast.

I rang the bell. "Let the games begin."

I didn't have to wait long before Connie Sue made the first move.

"So, Nadine," Connie Sue, former Miss Peach Princess, purred so sweetly that visions of magnolias danced in my head. "Tell us a little about yourself. I'm just dyin' to know more about you."

"Ain't much to tell."

Connie Sue wasn't easily put off. "I don't believe that for a minute, sugar. Why don't you start by tellin' us where you're from?"

"Tennessee." Nadine picked up the dice and promptly rolled a trio of sixes — a baby bunco. When she failed to score on her next toss, she slid the dice to Diane.

Tennessee? Um, that was odd. It occurred to me — belatedly — that for someone raised in the South, Nadine didn't have much of an accent. If I had my little black book next to me, I'd make a note of this. But I suspect that would've been too obvious. Discretion was key. Maybe Nadine was the one in need of a background check. If I weren't so miffed at Steven, I'd ask his advice on various Web sites.

Diane picked up the conversational ball and tried an end run. "You still have family there?"

"Yeah." Nadine selected a chocolate from the dish — dark chocolate, of course, to forestall another of Monica's lectures — and peeled the foil. "A daughter."

"A daughter," Connie Sue cooed. "How nice. Children are such a blessin', aren't they?"

Nadine shrugged. "I guess."

Our skill at bunco matched our skill at drawing out useful information. Unfortunately, thumbscrews weren't an option. Diane racked up an impressive two points before passing the dice to me. My luck was nonexistent, so I slid them to Connie Sue, who fared no better.

"You ladies are pathetic," Nadine said in her raspy smoker's voice. "Let me show you how it's done." Giving the dice a careless toss, she flicked her wrist, and let them tumble. Three ones appeared as if by magic.

"Bunco!" I yelled, banging the bell to signal the end of the round.

Nadine held up the empty beer bottle. "Don't s'pose you have another?"

"Sure thing," I said, scrambling to comply. Maybe alcohol would loosen the woman's tongue since all else failed. I didn't feel the teensiest twinge of guilt as I brought out another cold one. A quick survey of the fridge showed I had four more waiting in the wings. If need be, I'd duck out for a beer run.

"I need a potty break." Krystal streaked for the nearest bathroom.

"Good time for a cigarette." Nadine headed for the door, already digging through her pocket for a lighter and a pack of smokes.

Janine rolled her eyes. Tara groaned. At this rate, it was going to be a long night. "Everyone agree to one set tonight instead of the usual two?" I asked hopefully. I didn't hear any complaints.

The women returned, Krystal looking less pained and Nadine reeking of cigarette smoke, and we shifted places. Since Nadine and I were winners at the head table, we stayed where we were and Polly and Krystal joined us.

"Ready?" Not waiting for an answer, I clanged the bell — probably more forcefully than necessary.

"Since you're new at bunco, Krystal, I'll keep score," I offered. "The first team to reach twenty-one points rings the bell and calls bunco."

"Gotcha."

We took turns shaking and tossing, but the head table, except for Nadine, seemed to be jinxed.

Failing to score — again — Polly shoved the dice in my direction. "Some folks are lucky; some aren't."

Krystal heaved a heartfelt sigh. "Wish I could be lucky where men are concerned. I always seem to attract losers."

"Me, too," Nadine grunted. "The love-'em-and-leave-'em kind."

"Ditto," Krystal concurred. "Men are stupid creatures."

Nadine snorted, a sound that started out as a laugh but ended as a cough.

Men are stupid creatures? Where had that come from? Polly and I exchanged furtive glances. Were we on to something — finally? Was Nadine talking about stupid creatures in general? Or one in particular? If so, by any chance could his name be Lance Ledeaux?

Her turn once again, Nadine scooped up the dice and did her toss-flick-tumble routine. Lo and behold! A trio of twos appeared.

"Bunco! Bunco!" Polly called out, halting play.

"Wow!" I said, truly impressed. "With that kind of luck, you ought to buy a lottery ticket."

"Been there, done that."

"Ever win?" Behind her trifocals, Polly's faded blue eyes sparkled with curiosity.

"Yeah. Won big a couple months back." Nadine polished off the last of her beer and smothered a burp. "Say, do I have time for a cigarette?"

Between all the cigarette breaks and potty stops, bunco finished later than usual. Diane stifled a yawn as she was leaving. "Sure glad the library opens late tomorrow."

I waved from the porch as the last of my guests pulled away. Nadine, the tiara perched at a rakish angle on her head, assured me she could make it across the street under her own steam in spite of the six beers she'd consumed. I had to hand it to her. The woman could hold her booze.

Switching off the porch light, I went inside. As I placed the last wineglasses in the dishwasher, I experienced a growing sense of frustration. Instead of the rousing success I'd hoped for, the evening had been a dud. We were still no closer to finding out who wanted Lance Ledeaux dead. All we had learned was that both women sub-scribed to the men-are-stupid-creatures theory of evolution. And that Nadine Peter-son had hit it big in the lottery.

Just where did those tidbits leave us?

Exactly nowhere.

CHAPTER 28

Call me an optimist, but I dialed Claudia's number on the off chance she'd pick up. I know, I know, Pam's hubby had seen her carted off in a squad car. Still, I couldn't help but hope it had been a case of mistaken identity. Claudia's phone rang and rang before switching to voice mail. I was worried sick about her. The warning bells inside my head had reached *Titanic* proportions. Disaster, disaster, disaster! Sinking, sinking!

I was proving to be a menace to myself. After putting a load of unwashed clothes in the dryer and the orange juice in the cupboard, I gave up trying to be productive. My pacing had practically worn a path in the ceramic tile. I fairly fizzed with nervous energy but couldn't seem to concentrate. It was already ten fifteen and there hadn't been a single word from BJ. He hadn't bothered to return my call last night even though I asked him to regardless of the hour. I'd called his office promptly at nine and spoken with Aleatha. She was sweet as pie, but not very helpful. In fact, she was so downright sweet, I didn't realize how unhelpful she was until after disconnecting. Tricks like that probably make for a great secretary.

I darted another look at the clock. Were the hands even moving? Maybe we'd had a power outage — one of those glitches that last a split second but necessitate resetting every darn clock and appliance in the entire house. Narrowing my eyes, I squinted at the big hand. Darn, I saw it move a smidge.

The phone rang, finally, and I made a mad dash to answer, fumbling the handset in my haste.

"Kate? That you?" It was Bill. "You sound out of breath. Everything all right?"

I sank down at the kitchen table. "I'm fine, Bill. I was just expecting a call from Claudia's attorney."

"Bad Jack, eh. What's up?"

I felt like wringing my hands, which is a little hard to do when holding a phone, so I opted for a sigh instead. "On his way home from the golf committee last night, Pam's husband saw Claudia being led off in handcuffs."

Bill let out a low whistle. "Sorry to hear

that. Anything I can do to help?"

"Not at the moment, but thanks for offering." I knew I could count on Bill. He'd supply a shoulder to lean on, an ear to listen, or lend a handkerchief if need be. Sturdy, dependable, sensible. A true friend. That pretty well summed up Bill Lewis. Of course, he'd never replace Pam as my BFF, but then Pam didn't inspire the same fluttery feeling in my tummy as Bill did.

"I wanted to let you know my buddy just dropped off Krystal's car. It's purring like a kitten."

Mention of a kitten had me glancing around, half expecting to spot Tang lurking nearby and eavesdropping on my conversation. Of late, I'd seen Krystal coax him into the house. Sneaky little bugger, that cat. One look at me, he'd vanish under Krystal's bed never to be seen again, at least not by me. *My tuna, my house,* I wanted to scream at the silly critter. I added "ungrateful" to my list of grievances.

"I know you don't want to miss BJ's call, so I won't keep you. I'll be happy to drop the car off tonight, provided someone gives me a lift home."

"No problem," sayeth Kate McCall, mistress of understatement. "Krystal has rehearsal, but I'd be happy to give you a ride.

She'll be thrilled to get her car back." And so would I. This meant no more getting up early to drive her to the diner. Selfish, I know, but to me retirement means no more alarm clocks. Even when I was an early riser, I wasn't an early riser. I'm just not hardwired that way.

"Let me know when you hear something about Claudia. And, Kate . . ." He paused. "Don't let yourself get too upset. It can't be good for you. See you later."

Aw shucks, Bill sounded worried. I smiled a little at hearing that. It's been a while since a man fussed over me — not since Jim — and I rather liked the notion. I'd been tempted — almost — to invite him for dinner, to lure him into my man trap with beef stew or chicken pot pie, but I stopped myself in the nick of time. I didn't want to seem like a pushy broad. There's nothing more pathetic, to my way of thinking, than a woman who sets her cap for an attractive single man and will stop at nothing to gain his affection. My thoughts circled back to Claudia. Is that what she'd done with Lance? If so, look where her machinations had landed her — free room and board at the county jail.

Another glance at the clock confirmed the electricity was still coursing through wires, conduits, and whatever, although the hands plodded along with painful slowness. Weary of waiting for the phone to ring, I grabbed a light jacket and my purse and headed out the door.

Fifteen minutes later I found myself in BJ Davenport's office. Aleatha stopped pecking away at her keyboard, and her round dumpling of a face creased into a smile. "Hey, Miz Kate."

"Morning, Aleatha. Is BJ in by any chance? I need to talk to him."

"He walked in not more 'n a minute ago." Maybe I was coming down with a case of acute paranoia, but Aleatha's smile didn't seem to beam quite as brightly as before. "Sorry, hon, but he doesn't want to be disturbed. He's busy workin' on a case. You know how it is."

Maybe I did; maybe I didn't, but I did know I wasn't in the mood to be put off. Aleatha sounded as though she'd taken a page from Tammy Lynn Snow's manual, *How to Protect Your Boss from Nosy Women.* BJ didn't want to be disturbed? I'd show her disturbed if it meant calling in reinforcements. And by reinforcements I was referring to the Babes — armed and dangerous and full of attitude.

I planted my feet firmly in front of her

desk and folded my arms over my chest. "I'm not leaving until I speak with him."

Aleatha looked at me long and hard, then chuckled. "Like I always say, girlfriends are like bras. They're there to give support." She pointed a fuchsia-painted nail at a closed door. "He's in his office, but if he asks, tell 'im I was away from my desk. Say I must've been on a potty break."

"Gotcha." Turning on my heel, I charged into BJ's office like a locomotive gathering speed.

He never looked up from the papers strewn across his desk. "Dammit, woman! Didn't I warn you —"

"We need to talk — now."

This got his attention. It got mine, too, since I'm usually the candidate most in need of an assertiveness-training seminar. "I demand to know what's going on with Claudia."

BJ's ever-present bow tie, a wild affair in bright yellow and orange, was askew, the top button of his shirt undone, and his sleeves rolled to the elbows. He hurriedly ran a hand over his snowy mane and almost tipped over his coffee mug in the process. "Miz Kate," he apologized, "please excuse my attire. Aleatha failed to inform me of your presence."

"Aleatha's in the john," I stated baldly. "I want some answers, BJ."

He tossed down his pen and shoved aside the legal pad. From the resigned expression on his pink, wrinkle-free face, I could tell he knew I wasn't going to budge until I got some answers. "Forgive me, dear lady, where are my manners? Please make yourself comfortable."

I perched like a sparrow on a clothesline at the edge of the comfy-looking client chair he indicated. "The Babes and I are the closest thing Claudia has to family here in South Carolina. And families stick together . . . no matter what."

"True, true. Can't argue with that logic." He folded his hands over his rotund belly and stared at me across the cluttered desktop. " 'Fraid the news isn't good, Miz Kate; not good at all."

My stomach twisted into a knot big enough to hold an ocean liner in port. "Just how bad is it?"

He pursed his lips, studying me for a long moment, sizing me up no doubt to see if I was a fragile flower or a steel magnolia. "The charge against Miz Claudia has been changed."

"Changed to what?" I heard a fragile-flower quaver in my voice.

"Murder. First degree."

His words held me spellbound, unable to move, almost unable to think. I needed a moment to process that Claudia stood accused of murder in the first degree.

Eventually I became aware of BJ regarding me strangely. He had a should-I-ring-for-the-smelling-salts look on his face. I stiffened my spine and sat up straighter. I'd become a steel magnolia or die trying. "What happens now?"

"Apparently Sheriff Wiggins convinced the prosecutor that Claudia had a strong motive to kill her husband."

"First degree?" I echoed. "Isn't that premeditated?" Cell by cell, the synapses in my brain started firing again. I shuffled through my mental filing system of old *Law & Order* episodes, wishing I'd taken notes instead of simply watching. Maybe I should learn Microsoft Excel and design a spreadsheet. I'd enter such items as criminal charges, clues, and evidence. I'd be so organized, the FBI would beg to study my method.

BJ continued, his cool gray eyes never wavering from my face. "The fact Bill Lewis and Monica Pulaski both swear the chamber of the Smith and Wesson was empty at the beginning of rehearsal that night means someone — the killer — deliberately and with malice aforethought brought the bullet to the scene and placed it in the weapon. Hence, premeditation."

I felt heartsick.

"Miz Claudia was rearraigned this morning before Judge Blanchard and a bond hearing was held."

"So she's out on bail?"

He shook his head. "Sorry to say that's not exactly the way things went. Judge Blanchard happens to be, pardon the expression, a hard-ass. Miz Claudia's bond was revoked. She'll be a guest of the county until she comes up for trial."

Claudia in jail? This ship was definitely going down, all hands lost at sea. "Why didn't you call me?" I cried, my voice sharp with anger. "My friends — the Babes — and I would have been there to offer moral support, if nothing else."

"I tried to convince her y'all would want to be there, but Miz Claudia was adamant. She made me promise not to call any of you. Said she didn't want y'all to see her sent to jail. Sorry, Miz Kate, but I was obligated to honor my client's request."

"Of course," I murmured. "Can I visit her?"

■ ■ ■ ■

Glancing around, I understood why Brookdale County Jail wasn't listed as a tourist attraction. I'd never been inside the county jail before — or, for that matter, any other kind of jail. I'd hoped to keep my record unsullied. Before being allowed into the visitors' room, I'd been patted down, wanded for weapons, and had my purse searched for contraband by a prison guard who bore a striking resemblance to Jabba the Hutt.

All dingy green cinder block and worn brown linoleum, the place, in my humble estimation, was in dire need of a serious makeover. Air freshener would also have been a boon. It reeked of stale — stale sweat; stale hope. A waist-high partition and sheet of grimy Plexiglas separated the visitors from the inmates. I took a seat on a hard-backed wooden chair and prepared to wait.

Eventually a door buzzed open on the opposite side. I barely recognized the woman who emerged in the rumpled orange jumpsuit. It broke my heart to see Claudia this way, bereft of makeup, her hair combed but not curled, and with dark circles under her eyes. She was followed into the room by an armed guard, a fortysomething female whose ample figure strained the seams of her beige and brown uniform. The guard took up a post just inside the door in case Claudia wanted to make a break for it.

"Hey," I said, mustering a smile.

"Hey, yourself," she answered. "I almost told the guard to send you away."

"Well, I'm glad you didn't." I started to rest my hands on the counter between us, but jerked them away when I encountered something sticky. Cooties? I folded my hands in my lap instead. "I want you to know your friends haven't deserted you. Don't think for a minute any of us believes you're guilty."

"God, Kate, how did I ever get into this mess?" Claudia closed her eyes briefly, then shook her head. "What will my sons think?"

"Surely they need to be told what's going on. Want me to call them?"

"Not yet. I'd like to wait a while longer." She drew a shaky breath and tried to smile. "Maybe the miracle I'm praying for will happen, and I'll wake up from this horrible nightmare."

"You've got the best trial attorney around. Surely that must be some comfort."

"Of course, it is. BJ's been wonderful."

She glanced over her shoulder at the guard who looked to be asleep with eyes wide-open, then dropped her voice. "The prosecutor convinced Judge Blanchard that the sheriff has a strong case against me. Things don't look good."

I tugged on my lower lip, debating how much — or how little — to say. Go for it, Kate, I counseled. Things can't get much worse. "Claudia, hear me out. I've given the matter a great deal of thought, and I agree with Sheriff Wiggins on one point. The bullet didn't get into the chamber all by itself. Someone had to have put it there."

"But who?"

"Bill swears the gun wasn't loaded when he gave it to Lance, and I believe him. Monica said she checked it herself exactly the way he showed her, but saw only blanks in the cartridge."

"I swear on my mother's grave, Kate, it wasn't me."

"I know, honey, but think hard. Do you know of anyone who might have wanted Lance dead? Any enemies he might've had?"

Her forehead crinkled in concentration. "None that I know of."

Ignoring the stickiness, I tapped my fingers impatiently against the worn wooden counter. "You mentioned Lance was fond of gambling. That he placed a good-sized bet on the Super Bowl. You also once said you left Vegas sooner than planned. Could that be because of any gambling debts he might've had?"

Claudia seemed to consider this, then shook her head sadly. "I wondered about that myself, but I don't think so. I checked my bank statements pretty carefully, but didn't come across any large withdrawals, except for the thirty grand I told you about. I think Lance just wanted to remove himself from temptation. Besides," she continued, "he'd just finished *Forever, My Darling* and was eager to get it into production. He was convinced Serenity Cove Estates' close proximity to Atlanta would be a big plus — the perfect place to stage his masterpiece."

"The sheriff mentioned they'd found another ten grand on Lance's body. Even in my math-challenged mind, ten and ten add up to twenty. Do you have any idea where the other ten thousand could have gone?"

Claudia thought it over, then shook her head. "No, not a clue."

My line of questioning seemed to have reached a dead end. We sat, neither of us speaking, while I searched for another approach. None of my favorite TV detectives would've given up this easily, and neither would I. "Think back, if you will, to the night of the shooting." There, that sounded like an oft-scripted line. Regardless of what some people, such as Monica, try to tell you, a person can learn lots from watching TV. "Is there anything that stands out in your mind?"

Throwing back her head, Claudia closed her eyes. "I remember how loud the last shot sounded. So loud it made my ears ring."

Hmm. Now that she'd mentioned it, I'd noticed, too. With each utterance of *Take that* in the script's line, *Take that! And that and that!* the sound of gunfire had seemed to grow progressively louder until the final ear-shattering blast. A fitting conclusion, I'd thought at the time.

"Anything else?" I prompted.

Claudia opened her eyes, then rubbed her temples; whether she was deep in thought or fending off an impending migraine I couldn't tell. "There is one more thing. . . ."

At some point in our conversation, I should've brought out my little black notebook and taken copious notes. I could have kicked myself for the oversight. Details like that could cause me to flunk Private Investigating for Wannabe Detectives.

"The gun kicked as I fired the last shot. I

almost dropped it right then and there."

"That it?"

She nodded, looking exhausted — exhausted and old. "It all happened so quickly, but just for an instant I imagined surprise crossed Lance's face." Blinking back tears, she added, "I may have wanted him out of my life, Kate, but I didn't want him dead."

CHAPTER 29

"Coffee?"

"Decaf?"

"Does a cat have nine lives?" I winced at my choice of words. Cat, kitten, tuna, they all reminded me of the same orange feline.

Bill settled onto a stool at the breakfast bar. "If I drink regular coffee after six, I turn into a frequent flier on the old movie channel at all hours of the night. Must be a sign of getting old."

"Mmm . . . I love old movies. Mickey Rooney and Judy Garland." I filled two mugs with decaf and took the stool next to Bill.

"Bogart and Bacall."

"Hepburn and Tracy. They don't make 'em like that anymore."

True to his word, Bill had come by with Krystal's car. His mechanic friend had even washed and waxed the little Honda Civic until it gleamed. I hadn't said a word to

Krystal about her car's being returned. I wanted to surprise her.

Bill took a cautious sip of coffee. "How come Krystal's at rehearsal and you're not?"

"There's something to be said for having a bit part." I cradled the coffee mug in both hands, savoring its warmth. "Janine wanted to focus on act one. I have to hand it to Krystal. She never seems to mind all the time spent in rehearsals. She's a real pro. Did I tell you she had a part in the road company of *Grease* in Atlanta?"

"Atlanta?" Bill raised a brow. "Say, wasn't Lance there in a play of some sort when he and Claudia hooked up?"

"You're right, he was. You don't suppose . . . ?"

Bill considered the possibility, then shook his head. "Nah, too much of a coincidence. What are the chances?"

For an instant, I thought we might be on to something. Disappointment left a bitter taste in my mouth. "Atlanta is huge," I admitted grudgingly. "Lots of theatrical stuff going on in a place that size."

But just in case it wasn't happenstance, I made a mental note to swing by the library and ask Diane if she'd come across anything interesting when she Googled Lance. "Not to change the subject," I said, "but I visited

Claudia this afternoon."

Bill paused, peering at me over the rim of his half-raised coffee mug. "How's she holding up?"

I shrugged. "As well as can be expected, I guess, for someone with a first-degree murder charge hanging over their head. I know in my heart she's innocent, Bill. I'm not going to rest until I find out who's responsible."

"Considering Ledeaux's personality, you'd think there'd be a list of suspects as long as my arm."

"You'd think." I took a sip of coffee. "Sheriff Wiggins is determined to pin the blame on Claudia. And all because she happened to pull the trigger. Go figure."

"Some folks just can't see beyond the obvious." Bill drained his mug, then set it down. "Hate to rush off, Kate, but tonight's poker night at my place. Guys are coming at eight, so if you don't mind giving me a lift . . ."

"Sure." I hid my disappointment as best I could. "Let me grab my purse."

We didn't talk much on the short ride over. Bill's house was along the golf course, on Gardenia Court just off Oleander Avenue. I kept stealing looks his way, but he seemed unusually preoccupied and disinclined to talk. An uneasy feeling coiled in the pit of my stomach.

Was I about to get dumped?

A gazillion questions buzzed through my brain, temporarily stomping out worry over Claudia. Was this the point in our relationship where he would tell me he wasn't all that "into" me? Or we should start seeing other people? That things just weren't working out; his fault, of course, not mine? Suddenly I was a senior in high school all over again and Patrick Taylor was breaking up with me a week before prom. Then Patrick, the rat fink, turned around and invited Melanie Johnson, the tramp. I turned into Bill's drive and braked next to his Ford pickup.

Unbuckling his seat belt, he turned to face me, his expression serious. "Kate, there's something I have to tell you. I hope you won't hold it against me."

I braced myself for what was about to come. Bill had an affair with an old flame in Battle Creek. Maybe contracted an incurable disease. Or joined the Peace Corp and was moving to Zimbabwe.

"Shoot," I said, as in *Take that! And that and that!* I flinched at my choice of words. Good thing I wasn't holding a loaded Smith and Wesson.

"Something happened while I was away. Something I'm not proud of."

Here it comes, Kate, brace yourself, there's another woman. Probably a floozy who tempts men with home-cooked meals. I held my breath, prepared for the worst.

"I told my brother and my niece all about you."

I waited for the other shoe to thud on the floor. When nothing happened, I started to breathe again. "I don't understand. How was that a bad thing?"

He swallowed, looking miserable in the reflected glow of a coach light at the edge of the drive. Miserable but brave — a combination I found endearing. "My brother and niece are convinced you're a 'designing woman' out to get my life savings. Judy, my niece, called you a Jezebel."

Me . . . a designing woman? Jezebel? I'd never thought of myself in those terms. Now that I had, I have to admit the notion rather intrigued me. They made me sound like some sort of Medicare Mata Hari.

"The two of them badgered me until I promised to take things slow. They kept saying, 'No fool like an old fool.' "

Déjà vu all over again, as the philosopher Yogi Berra once said. I distinctly remembered my daughter, Jennifer, making the

323

exact same comment.

"But that's not the half of it," Bill confessed dejectedly. "My niece ran a background check on you on the Internet."

The mention of *background check* started a bubble of laughter down deep inside. A bubble that swelled and swelled until it couldn't be contained. Try as I might, it was bigger than both of us. It burst out, not as a coy giggle or a hearty chuckle, but as a full-bodied laugh. I laughed until tears rolled down my cheeks. All the while I was aware of Bill watching me with concern. The poor man was obviously worried I'd lost my marbles. Finally regaining a modicum of control, I dug through my purse for a crumpled Kleenex.

"Here." Smiling a little in spite of himself, Bill handed me a neatly folded white handkerchief.

"Thanks," I managed between bouts of giggles.

"Here all this time, I was afraid you were going to be mad — or disappointed. If I'da known it would make you laugh so hard, I would've told you weeks ago."

He listened with bemusement as I told him about Jennifer's unwarranted concern about *my* pension. How she referred to him as a gigolo.

"Who, me?" he exclaimed, his pretty blue eyes rounding in disbelief. "A gigolo?"

I nodded, then went on to admit that my son, Steven, had run a background check on him similar to the one his niece had run on me.

Bill's lips twitched in a smile. "Well, I'm relieved your family knows I'm not on the terrorist watch."

"Or a pervert," I added solemnly. "And I'm happy your brother and niece are aware I don't have a criminal record or liens against my property."

"No lawsuits . . ."

"No outstanding debts other than a mortgage."

Another giggle escaped; then we both laughed ourselves silly.

Bill sobered first, then reached for my hand. "Forgive me, Kate?"

At this point I'd have forgiven him anything. I hadn't felt this good in an age. "Whatever for?"

"Maybe the kids were right after all when they said there's no fool like an old fool." Raising my hand to his lips, he brushed a kiss across the knuckles, causing my heart to go into a skid. "I never should have listened to my brother."

"Why did you?" I asked when I'd recovered enough to speak.

He gave me that bashful smile I'd always found so appealing. "I've never been real smooth where the ladies are concerned. My brother, Bob, on the other hand, always had a way with women. I never should have let him influence me, but little by little he eroded my self-confidence. When I came home and saw how things had turned out for Claudia and Lance, two people who had rushed into things, I decided it might be best to heed Bob's advice. To take things slow. Get to know each other better."

"Do you still feel that way?" I asked quietly, glad it was dark enough so that Bill couldn't read my expression to see how much his answer mattered.

"I had one of those come-to-Jesus moments people talk about and realized I'd be an even bigger fool if I let you get away."

He scooted closer — no easy feat with a center console — and sealed the deal with a kiss that made my head spin.

Caught in the bright beam of headlights, we broke apart abruptly like teenagers caught necking on Lover's Lane.

Bill swore softly under his breath as he pulled away. "Almost forgot about poker night. That must be Gus. He's usually first to arrive. Are things OK between us?"

"More than OK." I went to switch on the ignition and realized I had never turned it off. There was more than just one motor running. "Well, if you don't mind dating a Jezebel, I have no trouble seeing a gigolo. I'm fixing a pot roast Sunday. Care to come for dinner?"

He climbed out of the car and grinned back at me. "See you Sunday."

I smiled all the way home.

CHAPTER 30

The following Monday, rehearsal started promptly, courtesy of the drill sergeant formerly known as Janine.

"All right, everyone," Janine called out. "Bring some energy! Bring some action!"

Who would've ever thought mild-mannered, laid-back Janine would turn into a tyrant? The artistic director title had gone to her head faster than Asti Spumante on New Year's Eve.

"How many more times do we have to rehearse this stupid scene?" Bernie whined.

" 'Til I'm satisfied," Janine snapped.

Usually, just out of general principle, I disagree with Bernie, but in this case I heartily concurred. We'd been rehearsing since six p.m., and even Krystal looked ready to fade. I said it before and I'll say it again. She's a real trouper. Not once had she used her pregnancy as an excuse to quit early, although I wouldn't have blamed her if she had. I wondered how people would react if I told them *I* was pregnant and wanted to call it a night. I'm not, of course, but it would be fun to see their reactions. I bet rumors would travel through Serenity Cove Estates faster than a California wildfire.

"One more time," Janine the slave driver instructed. "Stay in the world of the play."

I hadn't the foggiest idea what that meant, but I gave it my best shot. I was grateful the part of Myrna, the housekeeper, didn't require a lot of acting ability. Having been a housewife the better part of my life seemed adequate training for the role. I could shake a feather duster and run a vacuum with the best of them.

I watched from the wings as Eric and Megan went through their scene. Megan, too, seemed typecast as an ingénue. I ask you, just how hard can it be for a perky blue-eyed blonde to play a perky blue-eyed blonde? When I thought about it, Eric had an easy role as well. He transitioned from clever rookie cop in real life to clever detective in Lance's playwriting masterpiece. Megan, I noticed, seemed to have her lines down pat, but Eric needed a lot of help from Pam, who was acting as prompter.

"Sorry," he apologized for the nth time,

running his hand over his sandy blond military-style haircut. "I've been pulling extra shifts at the department in order to get time off for the rehearsals and performance."

"Take five, everyone," Janine said brusquely. "Afterward, we'll run through it again top to bottom."

Janine's announcement met a chorus of groans. "In case you've forgotten, tickets go on sale tomorrow. Time's running out."

Having said this, she beckoned Mort Thorndike, who had replaced Gus Smith for lighting and sound, aside to go over a list of suggestions. Eric and Megan huddled together in a far corner, but from their flirty smiles and giggles, I didn't think they were running lines. I made a mental note to ask Pam how she felt about her baby girl dating a policeman. The rest of the cast and crew dispersed in different directions, some heading toward the coffeemaker, others to the restroom. I didn't see any sign of Bill, so I wandered off in hopes of finding him. I must admit, Sunday's pot roast dinner had been a resounding success. I'm happy to report Jezebel and Gigolo have gotten their relationship/friendship back on track.

"BRB," I told Pam as I sailed out of the auditorium in hot pursuit of a certain blue-eyed devil. Pam looked puzzled, but gave me an absent wave as she made her way to her daughter's side. BRB stands for "Be right back" in texting jargon. I probably should ease up a bit, but can't seem to resist using it now and then. Truth is, I find it a lot more fun than either Morse code or Gregg shorthand.

I hugged my cardigan tighter around me. Marietta Perkins liked to keep the rec center's thermostat set on shiver. Some speculated she got a kickback from the utility company. Many complained, but to no avail. When it came to dictators, she was right up there with Adolf Hitler and Idi Amin. Well, that might be a *slight* exaggeration, but you get my drift.

As I strolled down the hall, I peeked into the exercise rooms. Mats were rolled up and shoved against the wall in readiness for tomorrow's aerobics classes. Yoga, stretch and tone, and Tai Chi were usually conducted in the smaller of the two rooms. Having to drive Krystal to the diner early every day had put a significant crimp in my weekly routine. I was glad the Honda was once again up and running. I'd sorely missed attending Tai Chi on a semiregular basis. I missed the glare of Marian, our instructor, when I zigged instead of zagged.

I wasn't sure I still remembered how to Repulse the Monkey. My Chi was dammed up and refused to flow. With all the worry over Claudia, I'd lost my inner calm. Where, oh where, did my *dantien* go? Where, oh where, did it wander?

A man toting a duffel came out of the workout room, mumbled good night to Marietta at the front desk, and shoved through the exit, letting in a blast of cold air.

Brrr! Shivering, I stuck my hands into the pockets of my cardigan for warmth and felt something hard and smooth. I reached in and pulled out an earring — a large gold hoop. For a moment I stared at it, puzzled. Then it dawned on me. I'd picked it up from the floor of the restroom the night of the shooting, slipped it into my pocket, and promptly forgotten about it. Until now, that is.

I examined the hoop more carefully. On closer inspection, it appeared to be real gold, probably valuable. No doubt someone had been frantically searching for a missing earring, and the whole time it had been snug in my sweater pocket. There were still two minutes left of my five-minute break — time enough to turn this into lost and found.

"Yes . . . ?" An unsmiling Marietta peered

at me through retro cat's-eye glasses. Someone needed to tell her they made her look like a witch. But that person wasn't going to be me. My bravery had its limits.

I extended my hand, palm out. "I found this earring a couple weeks ago in the ladies' room."

"And you're just *now* turning it in?" Her pursed lips and dark scowl reminded me of Mother Superior's expression after catching my best friend and me smoking behind the gym in tenth grade.

"Ah, sorry, I forgot. It was the night of the shooting," I added in a feeble attempt to expiate my guilt.

"Hmph," she muttered. "Poor excuse."

I almost begged her not to call my mother. Parochial schools are fertile breeding grounds for guilty consciences. No offense is too big or too small to make you grovel and beg forgiveness.

She plucked the earring from my upturned palm, examined it, then nodded with satisfaction. "The owner of this earring had me turn the rec center upside down looking for it" — she gave me the evil eye — "and all the time it was in *your* pocket."

"Ah, I have to get back to rehearsal. Please tell her how sorry I am."

"Mrs. Peterson will no doubt be pleased

to have her earring returned," Marietta said, reaching for the phone. "As a matter of fact, I think I'll call her right now."

"Peterson? Nadine Peterson . . . ?"

"That's right. Do you know her?"

Before Marietta could stop me, I retrieved the earring. "Nadine lives just across the street from me. I'll return it in person."

"Just the same, I'll call to let her know you have her earring."

Sheesh! As if I'd be tempted to keep it. What did the woman think I'd do with a solitary gold hoop? I suppose one could always have another hole pierced in one's ear. Piercings — along with tattoos — seemed to be all the rage these days.

I started to walk away but turned back. "I don't suppose you recall when Mrs. Peterson lost her earring?"

"Of course I do," she sniffed, obviously offended by the question. "There's nothing wrong with *my* memory. I'm not subject to those 'senior moments' so many of you people complain about."

She might as well have come right out and called me the despised *E* word — elderly. "Well . . . ?" I prompted, doing my best to ignore the insult. "When did Nadine lose her precious earring?"

"She lost it the same night Mrs. Connors

— I mean Mrs. Ledeaux — shot Mr. Ledeaux."

"Are you sure?"

She gave me a look that would have wilted fresh flowers. "I'm positive. Mrs. Peterson was new here. She came in and demanded a guided tour of the facilities."

"Then you were with her the entire time?"

"People think I have nothing better to do than sit at the desk all night and twiddle my thumbs. That's simply not the case. Mrs. Peterson assumed I was a one-woman Welcome Wagon. Well, I'm not. I have phones to answer, people to check in and out, and next month's schedule of activities to update. I don't get paid enough to be a tour guide *and* babysitter."

"So you didn't stay with her?"

"Isn't that what I just said?" Marietta snapped. Once again I was reminded of Mother Superior. Had she left the convent and been reincarnated as an irritable assistant manager? "I told her to feel free to look around," she continued. "I'd be happy to answer any questions she might have."

"Did she have any questions?"

"No." The frown deepened. "Matter of fact, in all the commotion, I didn't see her leave. She came back the following afternoon, however, and made a big fuss over losing that damn earring. Claimed it was a gift from her daughter."

At that moment, a woman I recognized by face if not by name — blame it on a senior moment — approached the desk with a question for Marietta about the mixed bowling league. Pocketing the gold hoop, I decided to take my leave.

My brain was running at warp speed.

According to Marietta Perkins, Nadine had been present the night Lance was shot. Added to that, I was reasonably certain Nadine was the woman I'd seen arguing with Lance behind the Piggly Wiggly. And what about the envelope from Tennessee's Premier Detective Agency, Down with Deadbeats? Was Lance Ledeaux Nadine's personal deadbeat?

Did this make Nadine Peterson a person of interest? Or did it simply boil down to a case of circumstantial coincidence?

I was mulling this over when Janine's strident voice interrupted my pondering. "Kate McCall! You've kept all of us waiting. Where on earth have you been?"

Mother Superior vs. artistic director? It was a tough call.

Bill shot me a sympathetic look while Gus Smith scuffed a sneaker along the floorboards and seemed to share my embarrassment. The rest of the cast and crew were clearly annoyed by my tardiness.

Not that I was keeping score, but I seemed to be doing an awful lot of apologizing in a relatively short period of time. "Sorry," I mumbled.

"All right, everyone, get into the space."

We shuffled about until we found our marks on a stage littered with props on a half-finished set.

"Make it look natural," Janine directed. "Don't do the furniture dance."

Janine was at it again, talking in play-speak only she could understand. I picked up the feather duster Myrna needed in act two. I could hardly wait for rehearsal to be over and detective work to begin.

CHAPTER 31

I booked out of rehearsal the instant it was over. Janine would probably have a conniption that I hadn't stuck around for her customary cast meeting, but she'd just have to deal with it.

As soon as I got home, I tossed my coat over the back of a chair and headed straight for the computer. I drummed my fingers on the desktop as I waited for it to boot. I was on to something. I could feel it clear to my toes — a kind of tingly sensation. Some might associate this sort of symptom with the onset of neuropathy, but not me. I was getting closer to the truth. What would I do if — when — I found something? Run to the sheriff? Unless I had something solid to go on, he'd laugh me out the door. He already had Claudia tried and convicted for Lance's murder all because, even though there was no physical evidence she'd substituted a live round for a blank, six people witnessed her pulling the trigger. That, of course, and a couple other trivial details — details such as her rat-fink husband's stealing her blind.

Things like the Holy Trinity of law enforcement: motive, means, and opportunity.

As soon as the computer finished its warm-up exercises, I clicked Internet Explorer and did a Google search for detective agencies. In less than half a second, I was confronted with more than a million possibilities — truly mind-boggling. *Viva la technology!* We've come a long way, baby, since the days the puppet show *Kukla, Fran, and Ollie* on TV was a big deal each evening. Focus, Kate, focus, I reminded myself. You can trip down memory lane later, but right now you're on a mission.

I narrowed my search to Tennessee, and voilà, found what I was looking for. "My, my," I murmured as I clicked on their Web site. I'd hit the mother lode. Down with Deadbeats, it seemed, was an agency specializing in finding deadbeats of all creeds, shapes, and colors. Men who reneged on child support. Husbands who skipped out on alimony. Employers who defaulted on workmen's comp. Exes who took off, never to be seen again after racking up huge credit card debt. I was leaning back in my chair, debating my options, when I heard the front door slam shut.

Krystal popped her head into the study/library/den. "Janine said to tell you you're fined ten demerits for skipping out early."

I glanced at her over my shoulder. "And you can tell Janine . . . Never mind. I'll tell her myself next time I see her."

"I'm beat. Think I'll turn in."

"Night," I called after her. Poor girl; she looked ready to drop. I needed to remind Janine to lighten up on her rehearsal schedule. It wouldn't do to have the pregnant star miscarry on opening night.

Just as I was about to return to the computer, I caught a glimpse of a bushy orange tail disappearing down the hall leading to the guest room. If I ever had a pet, I vowed, it would be a lot friendlier than the scruffy feline that had attached itself to Krystal. I'd half a notion to switch from albacore to the store brand that came packed in oil. Tang would be sorry he wasn't nicer to me when he had the chance.

I felt wired. A cup of chamomile tea might be just the ticket to help me relax. Turning off the computer, I went into the kitchen and filled the kettle. While I waited for the water to boil, I stared out the window. Lights still burned in the Brubaker house across the way, the temporary abode of Nadine Peterson. I found myself wondering exactly how much money the woman had won in the lottery. Even though she never came right out with the amount, I had a feeling it was substantial. She drove an expensive car and gave the impression she could settle wherever she wanted, cost no object.

My hand automatically went to my cardigan pocket and the gold hoop. Now was as good a time as any to return it. A glance at the clock told me it was only half past nine; not too late for a quick visit. Before I had a chance to talk myself out of it, I turned off the teakettle, grabbed a jacket, and skedaddled out the door.

Nadine's porch light switched on, nearly blinding me in its glare. I imagined one spooky green eye heavily rimmed with kohl pressed against the peephole.

"Nadine," I called out, addressing the closed door. "I have something of yours."

The door opened, and a plume of cigarette smoke drifted through the crack.

"What've you got?" Nadine growled.

I gave the door a gentle nudge and wedged my foot into the sill for good measure. "Mind if I come in?"

"Sure, why not," she said, stepping aside.

"Want a beer?"

Normally I drink tea — chamomile — at this hour. Occasionally coffee — decaf naturally. But beer? Once or twice a year I'll admit that I enjoy a brew, usually in July or August on days when the humidity surpasses the temperature. But, what the hey, there's no rule against having a cold one in February. "Sure, why not?" I replied.

I followed her toward the kitchen. A heady blend of smoke and nicotine clung to her like cheap perfume. Pulling a couple of frosty bottles from the fridge, she handed me one. Since she didn't offer a glass, I took my cue from her, twisted off the cap, and downed a swig. Icy cold and slightly bitter, it was a poor substitute for chamomile tea.

Nadine motioned to a chair. "Take a load off."

I sat. I sipped. I waited.

Nadine pulled out the chair next to me and, stabbing out one cigarette, fired up another. "So," she said, after inhaling a lungful of carcinogens, "what brings you here at this hour?"

"This." Reaching into my sweater pocket, I produced the gold hoop earring and set it on the table between us.

"Well, I'll be damned." Sticking the cigarette in the corner of her mouth, she picked up the earring and studied it through a haze of smoke. "Never expected to set eyes on this again. Where'd you find it?"

"In the ladies' room at the rec center." I watched her reaction closely, my detection skills on red alert. "Actually, I found it the night Lance Ledeaux was killed."

After taking another deep drag, she took the cigarette from her mouth and knocked ash into a dish on the table. Rosalie Brubaker would literally turn over in her grave at seeing her china so abused. "I thought I lost it then. Matter of fact, came back the next day. Asked at the front desk, but no one'd turned it in."

I nearly choked on my beer at her easy admission. "S-so," I sputtered, "you were there that night?"

"Yeah, so what?"

"Did you kill Lance?" Sometimes I amaze myself. This was one of those times. Where was common sense? Had good judgment deserted me? I could very well be seated across a table from a cold-blooded killer — a killer who might have a chain saw in the cellar, a machete tucked under the table, a semiautomatic in a cereal box.

To my surprise — and relief — Nadine didn't take offense. Instead, she tossed back her dyed-black hair and laughed. It was a phlegmy smoker's laugh that ended in a paroxysm of coughing. "Believe me, hon, I've been tempted to kill the bastard a time or two. Always managed to restrain myself for the kid's sake."

At this revelation, I sat up straighter in my chair. "You two have a child together?"

"Yeah, Julie's a single mom studying to be a nurse. She's a good kid. Never gave me a minute's worry."

I was trying to process all this. "B-but," I stammered, "I saw the two of you arguing behind the Piggly Wiggly. You're getting mail from Down with Deadbeats. According to the Internet, one of their specialties is finding fathers who weasel out of child support."

"Lance repented." Nadine tipped back her beer, then swiped her mouth with the back of her hand. "In fact, he insisted on giving me ten grand and ordered me to leave town. He was royally pissed when I told him I'd send it to our daughter instead. He was even more pissed when I told him I decided to stick around awhile." A complacent smile played over her lips.

"Ten grand?"

Ten thousand for a Super Bowl bet, ten to bribe Nadine, another ten found on his person the night he was killed. There you have it, folks, Claudia's thirty-thousand-dollar withdrawal. But still the question remained: What did Lance intend to do with all that pocket change? Trade in his Ralph Lauren for Armani? I took the only option open to me. I took another swig of beer.

"Didn't need the bastard's money. Not no more. Not after winning big in the Tennessee lottery. Besides, Lance didn't owe it to me; he owed it to our daughter. I'm used to taking care of myself, but she's struggling to raise a kid on her own and finish school. I feel sorry for the girl. When it comes to men, Julie doesn't have any better sense picking men than her old lady."

Since Nadine was in a chatty mood, I decided to milk it for all it was worth. I took another swallow of beer, which, by the way, tasted better as the night wore on, and asked, "Just how did you meet Lance?"

"Day after graduating high school, I left Chicago for good. Made it as far as Gatlinburg, Tennessee, on the money I'd saved. Found a job waiting tables in a barbecue joint. That's where I met Lance." She absently flicked ash into Rosalie's dish. "Gatlinburg is a big tourist trap. He had a song and dance act at Smokey the Bear Jamboree. We hit it off right from the get-go. We planned on heading for Hollywood, making a fresh start. Once he heard I was pregnant, though, the no-good bum cleaned out our savings and took off without me."

"How awful," I commiserated. Lance apparently was a scumbag long before Claudia met up with him.

"Don't go feelin' sorry for me, hon. I managed fine without him, and I'm still doing OK. Like I told you before, I hit it big in the lottery. Enough to find a shrink and hire Tennessee's premier detective agency to track the bastard down." She rose and went to the fridge. "Ready for another?"

I shook my head, wanting to save the second of my two annual brews for a steamy day in August. "What were you going to do to Lance once you found him?"

She returned, beer in hand, and shook another cigarette from the pack on the table. "If you think I planned to kill him, you're dead wrong." She let out a harsh bark of laughter at her own joke. "Dead wrong, get it?"

I polished off the last of my beer and got to my feet. "Better be going."

"Sure you don't want to stay, have another?"

"Thanks, Nadine, but it's getting late, and I have a busy day tomorrow."

Nadine walked me to the door. "You know

what, Kate? Down with Deadbeats was worth every cent I paid 'em. Wish you could have seen the look on the bastard's face first time he saw me. He was so afraid I'd screw things up with that new wife of his, he practically peed his pants. What he didn't know is that I've probably got ten times her money. Isn't that a kicker?"

And it was.

I replayed our conversation as I slowly walked home. Something about her story didn't quite hold water. Why stick around after her confrontation with Lance? It just didn't make sense. What was the old saying? Something like, *Hell hath no fury like a woman scorned.* Had Nadine just pulled the wool over my eyes? Had she been out for revenge all along, but was now trying to cover it up?

And where did that leave Claudia?

Facing a minimum of thirty years to life, is where.

CHAPTER 32

As a soporific, beer won hands down over chamomile tea. I was sound asleep the second my head hit the pillow. Way off in the distance, I heard ringing. I turned onto my side, burrowed into the pillow, and tried to ignore the racket. Go away, urged my dead-to-the-world, sleep-numbed brain. Go away, leave me be.

The ringing persisted. I emerged from sleep as languidly as a scuba diver at the bottom of the ocean floating to the surface. Prying one eye open, I squinted at the glowing red numerals of the clock on the bedside stand.

Three a.m.?

Who could be calling at this hour? I willed my second eye open. The clock's numerals hadn't changed. And neither had the blasted ringing of the phone.

Phone . . . ?

My body reacted to the three a.m. call

with a blast of adrenaline. A phone call at this time of night is every mother's worst nightmare. The question *Do you know where your children are?* immediately flashes through your mind. Had something happened to Jennifer? Or to one of my granddaughters? Then there was Steven. New York City is a dangerous place; one only has to watch *Law & Order* to know this.

I groped for the phone, fighting the panic that threatened to engulf me. "Hello . . . ?"

"Don't stick your nose where it don't belong," a deep voice rasped.

"Who is this?"

"Consider yourself warned."

I was left clutching the phone while a dial tone buzzed in my ear. My hands shook as I replaced the handset. Wide-awake now, I pressed an imaginary REWIND button and mentally replayed the conversation. The voice had been obviously disguised to the point where I couldn't be certain if it'd been male or female. At first I thought it belonged to a man, but now I wasn't so sure. Nadine Peterson had a deep, husky voice such as the caller's. Had I asked too many questions? Been too nosy?

I was getting closer to the truth — and someone was worried.

At this time of night — or morning — the

house was so still, so quiet, you could hear the whir of the heat pump as it cycled on, and the *ka-chunk* of cubes dropping from the ice maker. I wasn't afraid — not exactly — but I was glad I wasn't alone. I had Krystal nearby; Krystal and that darn cat.

For a long while, I lay staring at the ceiling, wishing I had a nice cold beer to lull me back to sleep.

Ticket sales were scheduled to begin at ten o'clock sharp. After last night's — I mean this morning's — phone call, I felt bleary-eyed and sluggish. Over coffee and a bagel, I pondered what to do. I thought about reporting the call to Sheriff Wiggins, but changed my mind. What could he do except tell me to mind my own business? No, thank you. I'd already heard that sermon one time too many. And what if the call had been a wrong number? Surely I wasn't the only busybody in town.

I loaded my breakfast dishes into the dishwasher and went to get showered and dressed. Not even my hair cooperated; one side wanted to curl and the other mutinied. I finally gave up. That's when I noticed there was a spot on my blouse. I hurried to find another, but the one I picked didn't match my slacks, so I had to change them, too.

About this time, I realized I'd have to exchange black loafers for a pair of brown. This meant my purse didn't match my shoes — a big fashion faux pas. With all the changing and switching, there was no time left to excavate my favorite necklace from the morass of costume jewelry in a drawer, so I clipped on a bracelet instead and — whew! — was good to go.

Diane and Connie Sue were waiting for me in one of the meeting rooms adjacent to the auditorium, which had been designated for ticket sales. I arrived ten minutes late, disheveled and out of sorts. Parking had been practically impossible. I had to content myself with a spot at the far end of the lot in a space reserved for staff. Next, I had to weave my way through a throng of people sporting travel mugs of coffee and morning newspapers. Thankfully no one paid much attention to a frazzled, frumpy blonde having a bad hair day.

Connie Sue, not a single strand of hair awry and looking like a model from a Talbots ad, eyed me up and down. "Honey lamb," she drawled, "who put you through the wringer?"

"Don't even go there." I knew I sounded churlish but didn't care. I plunked myself down behind the table in the only remaining chair and shoved my purse under the table where no one could see that it didn't match my shoes. "As soon as the last dad-blamed ticket's sold, I'm heading out for the Piggly Wiggly and stocking up on Bud Light."

Connie Sue raised a perfectly shaped eyebrow but wisely kept silent.

Diane slid a stack of preprinted yellow tickets over to me. "Your job is easy. All you have to do is ask how many tickets each person wants, mark it on this sheet, then turn them over to Connie Sue for seat assignments. I'll collect the money. Think you can handle that?"

"Piece of cake," I replied sourly.

"This oughta perk you up." Diane leaned closer, her hazel eyes alight with anticipation. "Wait'll you hear what I found out."

I felt my crankiness begin to dissipate. "Out with it, girlfriend. We don't have all day. The hordes are about to descend."

"Well," she said, her mouth curving into a wicked smile as she lowered her voice, "I've been surfing the Net, trying to find out more about Lance Ledeaux."

I glanced at the closed door, expecting it to burst open any second and be inundated with eager ticket buyers.

"Hurry up, Diane," Connie Sue wailed.

352

"I've got news, too."

"OK, OK," Diane said. "Remember Krystal's telling us she'd played Marty Maraschino in a revival of *Grease* in Atlanta? What she failed to mention is that Lance Ledeaux was in that very same production." Diane dropped her voice even lower. "Lance was — get ready — the Teen Angel." Arms crossed, she leaned back, obviously relishing the effect of her little bombshell.

Recovering first, Connie Sue splayed a hand over her heart. "Teen Angel?" she squealed. "No way! Surely you're joshin'!"

"Krystal and Lance in the same play? Are you sure?"

Diane smiled smugly. "Positive."

I looked from Diane to Connie Sue, then back again. "You know what this means, don't you? That means they knew each other, were friends."

Grinning widely, Connie Sue gave me a playful nudge. "Maybe more than friends."

It took a second for the full import of her insinuation to sink in. I'm also a little slow on occasion getting punch lines to certain jokes, but that doesn't make me a bad person, does it? "You aren't suggesting . . ."

"Don't be naive, sugar," Connie Sue chided. "Think about it. Lance could very well be the daddy of Krystal's baby. That would explain why she tracked him down. Maybe when he refused to fess up, she decided to teach him a lesson. Hormones do crazy things when you're preggers."

A rap on the door abruptly halted conversation. Nancy Walker poked her head in the door. "You ladies going to sell tickets or not? The natives are getting restless. Much longer, and I'm going to have to send for crowd control."

"Sorry, Nancy," I apologized. "Can you fend 'em off another couple minutes?"

"Tell 'em we're in the middle of an important meetin'. We'll be finished shortly," Connie Sue added.

"Five minutes," Nancy agreed with a grin. "More 'n that, I'm not responsible."

"Now for my news." Connie Sue wore a sly, cat-with-a-canary expression on her beauty queen face. "Y'all never guess what I found out when I ran into Marietta Perkins at the nail salon."

"C'mon, Connie Sue," Diane wheedled. "The suspense is killing us."

"Oh, all right, y'all talked me into it," Connie Sue acquiesced prettily. "The two of us got to talkin' about the night Lance was killed. Marietta, as y'all know, might be short on personality, but she's long on memory. She remembers a couple newcomers at the rec center that night askin' about the facilities. One happened to be none other than Nadine Peterson. The second person she swears was Krystal Gold. Afterward she got real busy at the desk. Claims she doesn't recall seein' either one leave. Couldn't swear if it was before or after the shootin'."

Wow! This wasn't just big. It was huge. Gigantic. Marietta with her fabulous memory placed not one but two persons of interest at the scene of the crime.

A banging on the door warned us our fortress was about to be stormed by a mob of irate customers. A chorus of angry voices added to the din.

"Open up. I've been waiting almost two hours."

"Yeah?" another voice chimed. "I drove all the way from Augusta."

"Big deal! I came from Aiken."

"That's a wrap," I announced an hour later.

Forever, My Darling was a sell-out. From all appearances, we had a surefire hit on our hands. There had been a few disgruntled customers, but for the most part, people seemed excited at the prospect of viewing a play where a man was actually killed. There was nothing like bloodshed to get the juices flowing. Nero probably observed that same human foible the first time he fed Christians to a bunch of hungry lions.

"It's been fun, y'all," Connie Sue said, gathering her things. "Hate to rush off like this, but don't want to be late for my massage."

Diane finished totaling cash and checks and put the proceeds in a locked box. "I'll deposit this and give Janine the receipt. Good thing I'm working noon to closing at the library. If I hurry, I might even have time to grab a quick lunch."

That made me the last of the ticket sellers. I'd just slung the strap of my purse over my shoulder when Bill popped by. "I was hoping to catch you. Can I interest you in lunch? The Cove Café is running a special."

Suddenly I was ravenous. "Sounds great. Give me a sec to freshen up."

Bill grinned. "You look fresh enough to me, but take your time."

Nothing like a compliment from an attractive man to make a girl's heart go pitter-patter, I thought as I dashed into the ladies' room. I freshened my makeup and ran a brush through my hair, hoping Bill would find my lopsided curls charming and not unruly.

When I returned, Bill was waiting right

where I'd left him. "Since the course isn't busy today, I borrowed a golf cart for the ride over."

My red and white chariot awaited. We easily could have walked the distance, but it was more fun to ride along one of the many cart paths that wind through Serenity Cove like spools of silver gray ribbon. I took a moment to admire the winter scenery, a far cry from winters in my native Ohio. The skies above were a clear, Carolina blue. February's temperatures were cool enough for a light jacket, but too warm for a coat. Sunlight speared through the boughs of towering loblolly pines, and red birds flitted about. Pansies, violas, and ornamental cabbage–filled pots set here and there, adding bright splashes of color. Today was Disney in living, breathing Technicolor. All that was missing was the refrain from "Bibiddi-Bobbidi-Boo." Sitting next to my very own prince charming in a jaunty red golf cart, I had to admit life was good. I could almost forget about Claudia's plight, the early-morning phone call, and the fact that a killer roamed free — almost.

At the Cove Café, we were greeted by a smiling Vera MacGillicudy and directed to a table. The special Bill referred to turned out to be a hot roast beef sandwich complete with mashed potatoes and coleslaw. A manly kind of lunch. I ordered a chicken salad sandwich instead with a side of fruit. After all, a girl has to watch her figure. At least she does if there's a man around to watch the girl who's watching her figure.

"Glad we aired things out the other night."

"Me, too," I agreed.

Vera returned with our drink orders, unsweet tea with lemon for me, coffee for Bill. After giving me a conspiratorial wink, she left us to talk.

I added sweetener to my tea. "How was poker night?"

Bill grimaced. "Terrible. I got hosed."

"Hosed? You lost?"

Bill looked sheepish. "A bundle. At least it seems that way for someone as conservative as I am. Turned out Gus Smith is quite a poker player. The guys finally got him to admit he used to spend vacations in Vegas. Let me tell you, the man sure knows his way around a deck of cards. Darned if any of us could tell when he was bluffing."

I would have liked to hear more, but just then my cell phone jingled. "Sorry," I murmured, rummaging through my purse, hoping I'd find it before it stopped ringing.

I recognized Polly's name on the display as I flipped open the cover. "Hey, Polly, I just sat down to have lunch with Bill. Can this wait?"

"No way, Jose," she chirped. "What I got to say is a matter of life and death. Get your butt back to the rec center RN."

"Registered nurse?"

"No, silly," she giggled, sounding more like a teen than a septuagenarian. "RN stands for 'right now.' You're not the only one into texting."

CHAPTER 33

A matter of life and death?

I bounced up, apologizing profusely and babbling incoherently about a rain check. Bill, bless his heart, looked both confused and disappointed by my sudden change of heart.

I found Polly waiting for me outside the entrance of the rec center. The Disney theme, so it appeared, still prevailed, although judging from Polly's garb, we had just departed Fantasyland and were heading for Animal Kingdom. She wore a tan zip-front hoodie lined in leopard fleece. A leopard print ball cap and matching ballet slippers completed her ensemble.

"What took you so long?" she demanded. Not giving me a chance to respond, she grabbed my arm and hustled me inside. "Wait'll you see what I found."

"This had better be good," I grumbled, thinking of the nice lunch I might've been enjoying with my favorite guy.

Polly cast a James Bond–worthy furtive glance over her shoulder. "I think I might've cracked the case."

I followed her down the hallway, past the meeting and exercise rooms, and into the darkened auditorium. She led me up the steps of the stage, then behind the curtains to the dressing rooms. There were two — one for men, another for women. I'd been told they'd been kept locked since the night of the shooting.

Polly flicked a switch in the one labeled LADIES. Instantly, fluorescent light flooded the room. Once my eyes readjusted, I noticed a long counter running along a mir-rored wall. On the opposite wall were hooks for clothes and plenty of electrical outlets. Other than a couple chairs and a bare floor, I didn't notice anything out of the ordinary.

"I turned down a chicken salad sandwich for this . . . ?"

Polly pointed an arthritic finger at one of the chairs. "Look."

So I did. As far as I could see, it was an ordinary chair, the type usually found in beauty shops; nothing special.

"Look harder," Polly instructed.

My forehead puckered into a frown. At this rate, I'd have to ask Connie Sue's advice on wrinkle creams. Polly was starting to worry me. She'd always been sharp as a tack as the cliché goes, but now she was seeing things that weren't there. "Polly, honey," I said, gentle as gentle could be, "there's nothing here."

Reaching out, she plucked a long dark hair from the chair's black vinyl. Clearly relishing the role of Sherlock Holmes to my bumbling Watson, she held the strand up for my inspection. "Ta-da!" she exclaimed. "Exhibit Number One."

All right, all right, I gave her points for good vision, but I was still worried. In my experience, people don't normally get excited over finding a single strand of hair.

Unless, that is, they're crime scene investigators . . .

Shades of *Crime Scene Investigation* (or just *CSI* to aficionados) . . . Had she latched on to something? Maybe a genuine clue?

Polly's wide grin gave me my answer. "I came here to take a look around, see what we'd need for opening night. Since the dressing rooms were still locked, I got the key from Nancy at the front desk. She said they've been locked tighter 'n a drum ever since Lance got killed. And there's more." She smirked.

"Don't stop now," I warned in my most

menacing tone.

"Nancy said the chairs are brand-new. They were delivered in the late afternoon on the day of the shooting. She remembers 'cause she had to stay late since Marietta had a flat tire."

Almost reverently I took the strand from Polly's hand. "You think someone with long dark hair might have been here in the dressing room the night Lance was killed?"

Polly's enthusiastic nod sent her permed curls bobbing. "I confess I'm disappointed in you, Kate. You're a little slow on the uptake. Hate to think what you're gonna be like when you hit my age."

"I may be slow, but eventually I make the connection," I said, feeling a trifle defensive.

"The only two people I know with hair like this are Nadine Peterson and Krystal Gold. Suppose one of them is our killer?"

"It could turn out that the hair belongs to one of the delivery people," I said halfheartedly. My time in Sheriff Wiggins's esteemed company was turning me into a skeptic.

"Thought about that, too, so I checked. Nancy remembered one man was black and buff; the other white, skinny, and bald. She claims the bald one reminded her of her son, and she started telling me all about male-patterned baldness."

Granted, a single strand of hair admittedly was flimsy evidence, but still worth investigating. Now, I'm no Miss Marple or Jessica Fletcher, but to me it suggested that someone other than cast and crew might have been in the dressing room the night of the shooting — someone who kept their presence secret; someone with long dark hair.

I pawed through my purse for a container of sorts. I wished I had Tools of the Trade with me, the handy-dandy box where I stored every sort of item I could think of to help in my investigations. I keep it stocked with Ziplocs in a variety of sizes, lots of latex gloves, a high-powered flashlight, tweezers, measuring tape — the usual crime tech's paraphernalia. Not having my toolbox, however, I settled for discarding my purse-sized tissues and using their plastic covering as a makeshift evidence bag.

"All right, Polly," I said after the strand was safely stashed. "Here's what we'll do. We need a hair sample from each woman to compare with the one you just found."

"You're on. I'll flip you for it." Polly dug into her handbag, also a leopard print, and produced a lint-covered penny. "Heads, it's Nadine; tails, it's Krystal. I'll take heads."

She tossed the penny, and we stared as it settled on the floor. "Looks like I get Nadine. I've already got a plan cooked up. Wanna hear it?"

"Whoa." I held up a hand like a traffic cop. "What I don't know, I don't have to testify about in a court of law."

Polly clucked her tongue. "Don't be such a wuss, Kate. Where's your sense of adventure? This could be fun."

When I returned home, the message light on the answering machine blinked feverishly. I hit PLAY and heard my daughter's voice.

Hi, Mom. It's me, Jen. Wanted to see how you were doing. Hope you're not bored.

I ran through a mental checklist. A pregnant houseguest. A starving cat. A friend who shot her husband. Nope! Definitely not bored.

Jen's question was followed by a slight pause; then she continued. *Are you still seeing that man, Bill What's-his-name? Just wondering. Call me.*

For once I was happy I'd missed her call. I wasn't in the mood to have her grill me about my friendship with Bill. I'm a grown woman, a mature adult. I certainly don't need to justify a relationship with a man I find attractive. And I didn't need her to caution me on the vices of gambling — namely bunco. I made a mental note to call her back later — maybe I'd pick a time when she'd be sitting down at the dinner table and couldn't talk.

"You're a wuss, Kate McCall," I chastised myself, reprising Polly's estimation of me, but I didn't care. Being a wuss wasn't necessarily a bad thing, was it?

First thing on my to-do list was get a sample of Krystal's hair for comparison with the one Polly'd found in the dressing room. Luckily, I had a great magnifying glass in Tools of the Trade. My homemade crime scene investigation kit had come in handy solving Rosalie Brubaker's murder last fall, but I hadn't had any reason to take it off the shelf in investigating Lance's death. His case required more of my investigative skills rather than my forensic expertise — until now, that is.

Thanks to Bill's buddy, Krystal's car was in good running order once again. This meant she was free to come and go as she pleased and not depend on me for rides. While working at the Koffee Kup, she'd formed friendships with several coworkers. This afternoon, she'd gone with a couple of them to the mall in Augusta. Krystal wanted to look at maternity clothes; not that she needed them yet, but she wanted to check out the styles. Her timing couldn't have been more perfect. I practically rubbed my hands together in gleeful anticipation of sleuthing.

Ask any of my former houseguests and they'll attest to my being an ideal hostess. I'd never dream of interfering with a guest's privacy. After all, every person deserves their own space, and I respect that. This in mind, I picked up a stack of freshly laundered towels and headed for Krystal's room.

And since I was already there, I decided I might as well look around.

I dutifully replaced the soiled towels with the fresh ones. I'd have to be blind as a bat not to notice the tubes of lip gloss, pots of blush, and wands of mascara strewn across the surface of the vanity.

Hitting PAUSE on sleuth mode, I strained my ears for any telltale sounds that might indicate Krystal's return. The house was still. Thorough being my middle name, I tiptoed to the window and peeked through the blinds. There was no sign of Krystal's car in the drive. If this were a movie, music would start to swell at this point, heightening the audience's sense of suspense. I suppose I could have hummed a few bars, but I contented myself instead with tentatively sliding open the top drawer of the vanity.

I sucked in a breath. I'd struck pay dirt with the first shovel load. The entire drawer fairly exploded in a bonanza of hairbrushes, banana clips, headbands, and ponytail holders. My eyes rested on one elastic ponytail holder in particular that happened to be entwined with several long brunet strands of hair. Reaching for it, I accidentally knocked several of the brightly colored bands to the floor. As I replaced them, I noticed something dark and shiny shoved to the back of the drawer. I stared, fascinated, then slowly pulled the drawer out as far as it would go.

A dainty little handgun was nestled amongst the barrettes and headbands.

Next to it lay a box of bullets. They weren't just any bullets, mind you, but, according to the bold black print on the box, the 9mm sort — the same caliber that killed Lance. I could feel my heart loudly knock against my ribs. I removed the box from the drawer, although it almost seemed to come of its own volition. As carefully as a bomb technician defusing a device that went tick-tock, I slid off the cover. . . .

The box was half empty.

CHAPTER 34

Polly frowned at me from her spot on the sofa. "Since when are you an expert on guns?"

"I'm not."

"Then what makes you so sure the bullets are nine millimeter?"

I smiled, feeling smug. "Because that's what it said on the label."

"Ohh . . . Good detective work."

Polly took another sip of her margarita. She was already on her second, and I'll confess, I was a little concerned. If our suspect didn't show up soon, we'd both be schnockered and in no shape to collect evidence. "Don't forget our plan once Nadine gets here," I warned. "Sure you're up for this?"

"Do cats have whiskers?"

Not only did they have whiskers, but I had firsthand knowledge of their voracious appetite for tuna. I don't know if all cats were programmed that way, but Tang certainly was. That confounded feline also had a predilection for the strange and unusual in the gift-giving department. Just yesterday I'd found a dead mouse on my doorstep when I went to bring in the paper. Then there was the matter of the dead canary, its poor little head all twisted, but I can't lay the blame on Tang. He hasn't mastered the nicety of gift boxes.

Polly helped herself to some of the bar mix I'd set out. "Next thing you know, you'll be joining the Rod and Gun Club."

"Stranger things have happened." I helped myself to bar mix as well. In honor of Plan A, as I'd come to think of it, I'd brought out a gourmet concoction of mini pretzels, salted nuts, and garlic chips I'd been saving for bunco, along with a requisite case of Bud Light.

"Sure Nadine's coming?"

I shifted on the sofa and plumped a pillow. "She didn't say for sure. Said she'd think about it."

"You mean I'm risking my liver, and she might be a no-show?"

"She'll show," I said without much conviction. My mind busily worked on Plan B, which also hinged on an ample supply of beer.

I was nearly ready to concede defeat when I heard a knock at the side door. I jumped up to answer before my guest changed her mind. "Nadine . . . ," I cried with the enthusiasm usually reserved for BFFs. I slipped my arm through hers and drew her inside. "So glad you could join us for happy hour. We were afraid you'd changed your mind."

"Ah, well, I got a little bored sitting around. *Dr. Phil* was a rerun."

Thank you, *Dr. Phil,* I said silently. Aloud I said, "Polly and I were just talking about you."

She peered at me suspiciously. "Yeah, what about?"

"We'd like the chance to get to know you better." I led her toward the great room where my partner in crime eagerly awaited.

"Almost did change my mind." Nadine shrugged off her black leather jacket and slung it over a chair. "Never turn down a beer, but it don't taste the same without a cigarette along with it."

Right then and there, I knew the supreme sacrifice was called for. Even though it pained me, I broke one of my cardinal rules: no smoking in the house. Up until now, my home had remained a smoke-free environment, essentially a virgin to the tar and nicotine twins. But I was willing to lay down my principles for the life of a friend. This should win me the Purple Heart for bravery above and beyond the call of duty. "Go ahead," I said with a smile that felt wooden. "Smoke if you want."

Nadine looked at me oddly, then shrugged. "As long as you don't mind . . ."

I handed her off to Polly. "Pardon me a sec. I'll be right back with an ashtray and a beer. Want a glass?"

"Hell, no. Straight out of the bottle is best."

Polly patted the cushion next to her. "Sit here. Take a load off."

I scurried off to the kitchen. So far so good, I thought as I rummaged through a cupboard for an ashtray. I knew I had one of those darn things somewhere for the occasional smoker to use on the porch or out on the deck. I finally found one shoved way to the back of a cupboard behind the soup bowls. When I returned to the great room, I noticed Polly had topped off both our margaritas. Good thing I'd picked up extra mix. I only hoped my supply of tequila would hold out.

I took up a position on Nadine's other side so that Polly and I flanked her on the sofa. "Here," I said, setting down the ashtray and handing her an ice-cold brew. I slid the bowl of pretzel mix closer. I was operating under the theory that with the woman's fondness for beer, she might have also developed a liking for bar food. "Help yourself."

"So, Nadine," Polly said, smiling the sweet grandmotherly smile she limits to infants and toddlers, "tell me more about striking it rich in the lottery. Never met an honest-to-goodness big-time winner before. Just between us girls, what's it like?"

"Crazy, I tell you. Just plain crazy." Nadine chugged her beer. "Reporters hound you day and night, always sticking a mike in your face and asking dumb questions. Things like what're you gonna do with five million bucks? Duh! Any idiot knows the answer. Spend it, that's what."

"You don't say," Polly murmured. "Gotta be tough."

"Damn right, it's tough. Folks you went to grade school with and haven't heard from since suddenly remember you're their best friend. Then there're the vultures, strangers, who start pestering. Invest in this, they say; invest in that. Go to hell, I tell 'em. I might not have a fancy education, but I'm no dummy."

Careful not to spill a drop, Polly raised

her glass and clinked it against Nadine's bottle. "You go, girlfriend."

I fought the temptation to roll my eyes. Next they'd be singing "Kumbaya" in two-part harmony.

"Lance would've shit a brick if he knew how much I was worth. He thought he could wave a measly ten grand in my face and I'd disappear. Well, it didn't work that way." Nadine's spooky green eyes held a fiendish glow of satisfaction. "Boy, was he pissed when I told 'im I intended to stick around for a while."

The instant Nadine slid a cigarette from her ever-present pack and flicked her Bic, I knew we were off to a running start. I sat back, prepared to enjoy the show. I didn't have long to wait.

Polly kept the conversational ball afloat. "Kate mentioned you and Ledeaux had a kid together."

"Yeah, a girl, Julie. She's studying to be a nurse."

Nadine polished off her beer and burped. I raced to get her another.

"If she's anything like her mother, I bet she'll make a good one, too," Polly remarked as I returned.

"Damn right she will. That girl's not the least bit squeamish. Strong as an ox, too." I tried not to cringe as Nadine aimed a stream of smoke at my pristine ceiling.

Nadine was well into her third beer when I gave Polly the high sign we'd agreed upon earlier. Time had come to get this little show of ours on the road. And we needed to do it before Polly drank herself into oblivion. Her small frame was no competition against Nadine's when it came to alcohol consumption. I'm afraid I wasn't faring much better. I felt a slight buzz as I got up to refill the bar mix. I'd no doubt, Nadine, on the other hand, could drink a stevedore under the table.

Setting the munchies on the coffee table, I *accidentally* bumped Nadine's pack of smokes and knocked them to the carpet where they scattered. Originally, I'd planned to spill bar mix, but this worked even better. There was nothing more precious to Nadine than her cigarettes — unless it was Bud Light. "Oh dear," I exclaimed in my best amateur-actress voice. "How clumsy of me."

"Here," Polly chimed, right on cue. "Let me help."

Nadine had beaten us to the punch and was already bent over picking up cigarettes. Our three heads butted together as we worked diligently. Just then Polly's charm bracelet *accidentally* tangled in Nadine's long, dark mane. Giving her wrist a sharp jerk, she broke free.

"Ouch!" Nadine squealed, holding her head and glaring at Polly. "Watch it. You're gonna give me a bald spot."

"Sorry," Polly said, attempting to sound contrite. "Guess I need to lay off the margaritas."

I could barely keep the smirk from my face when Polly glanced at me when Nadine wasn't looking. I wanted to high-five her so badly, I could scarcely contain myself.

After her fourth beer and countless cigarettes, Nadine finally decreed an end to happy hour. I made a mental note to call Gloria and have her fetch Polly, who had made a valiant attempt to match Nadine drink for drink. Polly definitely needed a designated driver, and I knew better than to think it should be me.

Polly hiccupped. "That went well, don't you think?"

I eyed her unnaturally bright eyes and flushed cheeks. "Sure you want to help with this?"

"Of course," she replied indignantly. "I was ready to risk my lungs and liver for the sake of our little experiment. I aim to see it through."

"Then, my dear Sherlock, let's proceed."

She swayed a little when she rose to her feet, and I put a hand out to steady her. "I think we should reverse roles. You'd better let me be Sherlock."

"Whatever you say." She hiccupped again.

Gloria was going to read me the riot act when she saw what condition her mother was in. I could hardly blame her. But Polly wasn't an easy person to control. That sounded lame, even to my ears, but it was the best I could come up with, given the circumstances. I steered my cohort in crime into the dining room and nudged her into a chair.

Earlier I'd decided the dining room was the best location for our little *experiment,* as Polly aptly phrased it. It also eliminated the possibility of Nadine's glancing in this direction from across the street and seeing our heads together. Using tweezers from Tools of the Trade, I carefully transferred the hair we'd found in the dressing room onto a sheet of white computer paper and labeled it EXHIBIT ONE. Next to it, I placed the hair sample I'd found twisted around Krystal's ponytail elastic, labeling it with her name and EXHIBIT TWO. Last, but by no means least, came Nadine's hair that had been *accidentally* caught in Polly's charm bracelet; this I labeled EXHIBIT THREE. I knew it was important to handle each strand with care. I'm pretty sure it had to do with hair follicles and DNA, but after a couple margaritas I wouldn't swear to it.

"Hey, Kate, you really know your stuff. You could be one of those SCI types like on TV."

SCI? Somehow that didn't sound right, but I didn't quite know why. I'd figure it out later. Basking in Polly's admiration, I was tempted to pull on latex gloves. That might be a nice touch, but it was probably overkill. Next I took out my fancy schmancy bright yellow LED flashlight, which had cost an arm and a leg, along with a magnifying glass. If people kept showing up dead around Serenity Cove, it might be time to invest in one of those jeweler's loupes. I'd think about it once my head cleared. I gave Polly a sidelong glance and saw that she was watching my every move with rapt, if bleary-eyed, attention. Using the Marg Helgenberger, aka Catherine Willows, single-fisted technique, I methodically scanned all three hair samples.

Polly leaned so close, I could smell the tequila on her breath. "Holy crap!"

We'd landed in the macaroni, an expression Jim's Italian coworker was fond of saying. We'd gotten lucky. The answer as to whom the hair belonged was plainly visible to the naked eye. There appeared to be a distinct color variation between the strands we'd obtained from Krystal and Nadine. Exhibit Two, Krystal's, showed dark with underlying red highlights. Nadine's, Exhibit Three, was dark as mud with no highlights whatsoever. It was also gray near the root because its owner, Nadine, needed a touch-up. The answer was blatantly obvious even to a pair of half-inebriated detectives.

Polly and I stared at each other. For a long moment neither of us spoke. Finally I broke the silence. "The hair you found matches Krystal's. That means she was backstage the afternoon — or maybe the evening — Lance was shot."

Polly hiccupped yet again. "Don't that beat all."

CHAPTER 35

That still left the matter of the gun I'd found in Krystal's drawer — and the opened box of 9mm shells. Krystal Gold topped my list of suspects. She had means; she had opportunity. All she lacked was motive.

My nerves strung tight, I jumped a foot, and I'm certain that's only a slight exaggeration, when the phone rang. It was the Suspect. Krystal, very thoughtfully for a person of interest, was calling to tell me not to worry; she'd be home late. She and her friends had decided to take in a chick flick and have a bite to eat before returning from their shopping trip in Augusta.

"No problem, dear," I told her. The girl might be a cold-blooded killer, but she was a considerate houseguest. "Have fun."

I emptied a can of floral air freshener to rid the house of lingering cigarette fumes. Once I had the place smelling like a funeral parlor, I went about straightening the house.

I plumped pillows, put dirty glasses in the dishwasher, wiped down countertops, all the while pondering my options. It was after six; too late to call the sheriff. Knowing him as I did, I thought he probably had Tammy Lynn screen his calls from meddling junior-grade detectives. Did a box of bullets and a strand of hair constitute evidence? The kind of evidence that would stand up in a court? The type that would make Sheriff Wiggins pat me on the back and say, *Attagirl.*

Maybe I should confront Krystal in the same way as I had Nadine. Come right out and ask, *Did you kill Lance Ledeaux?* Remind her that everything she said could and would be held against her in a court of law. Fortunately, Nadine hadn't shot me on the spot. I might not be as lucky the second time around. Krystal, after all, was armed and, for all intents and purposes, considered dangerous.

All this turmoil was wreaking havoc on the pleasant happy hour buzz I'd acquired. Tempted as I was to mix another margarita, I decided on coffee instead — the high-voltage, French roast kind, chock-full of caffeine. I needed to think clearly, not through a haze tempered by alcohol. So much for my no-caffeine-after-six-o'clock rule. Rules were made to be broken, right?

As I measured and ground beans, I kept wondering what my television mentors would do in this situation. I visualized my favorite rerun detectives, Lennie Briscoe and Ed Green, taking my evidence to the erudite DA, Jack McCoy. Jack would likely kick them to the curb, telling them not to darken his doorstep until they had enough to make a case. Then, their trusty no-nonsense lieutenant, Anita Van Buren, would order them back out on the street. I doubted Sheriff Sumter Wiggins would be as diplomatic.

I placed a filter into the basket of the coffeemaker and poured in water. What I really needed, though, was someone to act as a sounding board. Of course, the Babes came to mind. I knew I could phone any one of them — except Polly, whom Gloria had threatened to put to bed the instant they returned home — and they'd run right over. But it was dinnertime. I hated to interrupt that precious ritual where husbands replay their golf games, hole by hole, chip for chip, putt for putt, for their wife's entertainment, so I did the next best thing. I called Bill.

Once again the phone rang and rang. And once again, I hoped he wasn't in his woodworking shop where he couldn't hear the phone over the whine of power tools. I was ready to hang up when he answered.

"Bill, I need you," I blurted the instant I heard his voice.

"Um . . ."

"Like now. I need you now."

"Sure thing," he replied, sounding confused but game.

I realized then how I must have sounded — crazed, desperate, loony tunes. I struggled to correct the impression. "I didn't mean that quite the way it sounded. What I should have said is that I need to talk to you."

"Sure thing," he repeated, and this time I liked to imagine I caught a faint whiff of disappointment in his tone.

There would be time enough to mull that over later. Right now I had a gun. I had bullets. "I need someone solid and sensible to hear me out. You're elected." Then to my utter mortification, I hiccupped, a damning reminder of my semi-inebriated state.

There was a slight pause on the other end of the line; then Bill cleared his throat. "Kate, have you had dinner yet?"

Had I eaten? "Um, I don't think so. Does bar mix count?"

"I'll stop by the gas station on my way over and pick up a pizza. See you in fifteen minutes."

I released my death grip on the phone and disconnected. Bill was on the way, my white knight riding to the rescue. Not that I believed women needed knights and rescuing and such. I consider myself a liberated woman. I can bring home the bacon *and* fry it up in a pan. I am woman; hear me roar! If I close my eyes, I can almost hear Helen Reddy's seventies' battle cry. Still . . .

I hummed to myself as I set out place mats, plates, napkins, and silverware in anticipation of Bill's arrival. Now, some might think gas station pizza a bit odd. Before moving to the South, I'd have been one of them. Since then, I've discovered some gas stations even serve up tasty fried chicken and catfish. Oh, yes, another local oddity: The best rib eye steaks are found at the fish market. An elderly black gentleman, and I do not use the term "elderly" lightly, shuffles out of a back room and cuts them to order. My Jim used to love putting those babies on the grill and watching them sizzle.

Since coffee, even French roast, didn't seem appropriate with pizza, I filled glasses with ice and Diet Coke. If I couldn't get my much-needed caffeine boost one way, I'd try another. There were always the late-night oldies on the movie channel if I was too wired to sleep. I'd worry about that later.

Bill arrived right on schedule bearing pizza, hot, steamy, and spicy. Taking it from him, I motioned him to a seat at the kitchen table. "This looks great. Glad you thought of it." I slid slices of pizza onto plates and sat next to him.

"Care to tell me what's going on?" Bill asked as he took his first bite.

"It's Krystal," I said, daintily nibbling my slice. "I think she might be our killer."

"Whoa! What . . . ?" Bill sputtered around a mouthful of cheese and pepperoni.

For a moment, I feared I might have to perform the Heimlich maneuver, but he recovered quite nicely. "You heard me," I replied calmly. I took a larger bite this time, knowing food would hasten the absorption of alcohol in my system. "I suspect Krystal might be the one who murdered Lance. I need you to listen and tell me if I'm crazy."

And over gas station pizza dripping with mozzarella, he did just that.

There's nothing more appealing — or sexier — than a man who truly listens. I mean one who unselfishly gives you his undivided attention; one who listens as though his life depends on what you're telling him. It's just one of the many qualities I find so attractive in Bill. Neither of my children excels in the fine art of listening.

No matter how hard I try, I can't convince Jennifer that bunco isn't going to jeopardize my life savings. If Steven would ever give me his full attention for more than thirty seconds, maybe I could persuade him I'm not ready to be shipped off to one of those fancy assisted living facilities just yet. I'm happy and healthy right where I am, thank you very much.

"Well," Bill said, wiping his fingers on a napkin, "I can see why you're concerned. I agree that we don't have enough to bring to the sheriff. If he didn't believe he had a strong case against Claudia, he'd never have taken it to the prosecutor."

"But what about the gun? The bullets?"

"Anyone off the street can walk into a sporting goods store and purchase bullets. And even if the hair you found does belong to Krystal" — he held up a hand to forestall my argument — "there's no proof she substituted a real bullet for a blank. What's more, the fact they were in *Grease* together doesn't mean they're more than acquaintances."

I cleared the dishes, unhappy my theory had sprung more holes than a colander. "But," I protested, "Polly swears she saw the two of them together — canoodling."

"Canoodling, huh?" Bill mulled that over

as he dumped the empty pizza box in the trash. "It still doesn't give Krystal a reason to want Lance dead. Besides, a defense attorney might question the eyesight of a seventy-something woman who wears trifocals."

He had a point. Polly had been postponing cataract surgery for months, claiming only old people got cataracts. Old, I guess, is a matter of perspective. I tried a different route. "What if Lance *is* the father of Krystal's baby? If so, it would explain why she followed him to Serenity Cove."

"That puts a whole different spin on the matter."

I leaned against the counter, the dish towel in my hand forgotten. "Lance withdrew thirty thousand dollars from Claudia's account. The sheriff told me ten thousand of it went to a bookie for a Super Bowl bet. Nadine said he gave her ten thousand as a bribe to leave town. Police found another ten thousand on him when he was killed."

Bill let out a low whistle. "Men, even big spenders like Lance, don't carry around that much pocket change."

I raised a brow. "He might if he was being blackmailed."

Bill took up a post next to me at the counter, arms folded, ankles crossed. "Sure would hate to call in the authorities, what with Krystal being pregnant and all, if this turns out to be nothing."

I sighed. The last thing I wanted to do was to upset an expectant mother. I wanted only the best for Krystal and her unborn child, yet . . . "We still need to address the matter of the gun in her drawer."

"Honesty is always the best policy, Kate. Just come out and tell her you found it. Hear what she has to say."

I mulled over his advice. "What if we bend the truth a little? I could say she left her vanity drawer open and when I went to shut it, I noticed the gun."

Bill nodded, then asked, "Have you thought about what you might say if she asks why you were in her room in the first place?"

"Well, first I'd act highly offended that she might think I was snooping. Then," I said, warming to the role of indignant innkeeper, "I'd make her feel even guiltier by acting hurt. I'd end by informing her I was only being a conscientious hostess bringing her fresh towels."

The corner of Bill's mouth quirked in amusement. "Don't you mean conscientious *detective?*"

"Bingo!" I grinned. "Come on. Let me

show you the gun."

I led the way to the guest room and showed him what I'd found.

Bill removed the gun from its hiding place and held it almost reverently. "Sweet," he said in admiration. "A Sig Sauer. Can't be more than five and a half inches in all. Must weigh less than a pound. Perfect weapon for a lady."

Sweet? Perfect? It didn't look either of those to me. But it did look deadly, like a water moccasin, coiled and ready to kill an innocent bystander deader 'n a doornail.

After checking to make sure there were no bullets in the chamber, Bill slid the magazine out and pocketed it. "This way, if Krystal doesn't like the direction the conversation is heading, at least she can't shoot us."

"Thanks," I said dryly. "That makes me feel much better."

Over coffee — decaf this time — and chocolate-chunk cookies, we agreed on the script we'd follow when Krystal returned. I silently congratulated myself on calling Bill in as a consultant on the case. I felt immeasurably better knowing I wouldn't be alone when I demanded some answers from Krystal.

"By the way," I said, "while I was out today, my daughter called and left a message on the answering machine. She wondered if I was still seeing 'that man,' as she refers to you."

"My brother, Bob, called today, too. Wanted to know if I was still seeing 'that woman.' "

I studied Bill over the rim of my coffee mug. "And what did you tell him?"

Bill's eyes met mine, steady and direct. "I told him 'that woman' is the best thing that's happened to me since Margaret died. Told him not only was I seeing you, but I intended to keep right on seeing you. I should've known better than to listen to Bob in the first place."

I couldn't help but smile as I reached across the table for his hand. The sparkle in his pretty Paul Newman baby blues told me all I needed to know about the way he felt.

CHAPTER 36

Bill and I retired to the great room, but we were still holding hands when Krystal burst in carrying an assortment of shopping bags from various stores at the mall.

"Hey, you two," she greeted us. "You look all nice and cozy. Hope I'm not interrupting anything."

"Krystal," I said, bracing for the inevitable confrontation, "set your things down. We need to talk."

"Uh-oh." She laughed. "Am I in trouble? Mom used to use that exact tone whenever I tried to sneak in after curfew."

When neither of us returned her smile, her eyes slid from me to Bill. "Sure." She dropped down alongside me on the sofa. "What's up?"

Bill gave me a nod of encouragement.

I moistened my suddenly dry lips and took the plunge. "It just so happened as I was bringing you fresh towels that I noticed a vanity drawer ajar. When I went to close it, I noticed this."

Hearing his cue, Bill produced the Sig Sauer and the box of bullets from beneath a pile of throw pillows.

Krystal stared at them for a long moment, then seemed to collect herself. "So, what's the big deal? I have a concealed weapons permit. The gun's perfectly legal."

What was she going to tell me next? That she won the role of Annie Oakley in a revival and needed the gun for target practice? "The shells are nine millimeter — the same caliber used to kill Lance Ledeaux."

I couldn't be positive, but I thought she paled at the mention of his name even though her expression remained impassive.

"Why kill someone I didn't know?"

Aha! Now we were making progress. I'd caught her in a bonafide fib. "I don't believe you," I told her calmly. "Polly saw the two of you together, acting very . . . friendly."

"Polly?" Krystal scoffed. "The woman's half blind. The eye doctor told her months ago she needed cataract surgery, but she refused. She made me promise not to tell Gloria."

"Polly confided all this to you, a virtual stranger?"

Krystal shrugged with elaborate casualness. "She let it slip one day at the diner when she was having trouble reading the menu."

"I wonder if Gloria is aware of this," I murmured half to myself.

"I doubt it. Maybe you should give her a call." With this, Krystal jumped to her feet and started gathering her purchases.

"Not so fast." Bill stopped her, his voice quiet but firm. "Kate and I aren't finished."

Krystal plopped back down on the sofa. "I'm tired," she whined. "Is this going to take long?"

"You lied when you said you didn't know Lance." I watched her expression closely. "Diane did some research online. She discovered you and Lance both had parts recently in a revival of *Grease* in Atlanta."

Krystal pursed her lips. "What if we did?" she asked, sounding more like a petulant teen than a woman with her biological clock ticking — clearly a case of arrested development. "All right, all right, I confess. I was Marty Maraschino. Lance was the Teen Angel. At first I thought he was a little old for the part, but he had the right look. It's not against the law to be friends."

Friends, my foot! In for a penny, in for a pound, as my daddy used to say. I drew a deep breath and went for the jugular. "How do you explain being in the dressing room the night Lance was killed?"

My question was met with stunned silence. I felt Bill's gaze on me, but I couldn't afford to lose ground at this point in my interrogation. Keep your eye on the prize, Kate. Don't get sidetracked. "Trust me, Krystal, it's much easier answering me than it will be answering Sheriff Wiggins. He makes grown felons cry for their mamas."

"What makes you so sure I was there when Lance was shot?"

Hmm, she was trying to bluff her way out of it. But I was prepared for such a contingency. I pulled the ace from my sleeve. "We have proof."

"Proof . . . ?"

I wasn't about to elaborate on the single dark hair found by a woman with cataracts and identified by a crime-and-punishment junkie. Come to think of it, it was nothing short of miraculous that Polly with her faulty eyesight had spotted the strand in the first place. Talk about Divine Intervention.

All of a sudden, Krystal's resistance melted like a Popsicle at a Fourth of July picnic. "OK, I admit Lance and I knew each other."

"And . . ."

"And we agreed to meet after rehearsal

the night he was killed. He told me to wait for him in the dressing room."

Bill rested one arm along the curve of the sofa. "So the two of you were having an affair."

Krystal let out a contemptuous snort. "Past tense. We *had* an affair. It ended the day he took off in a rented RV with a rich old woman he met on the Internet."

An old woman with money! She had Claudia pegged — except, of course, for the *old* part. Poor Claudia; she never saw the disaster barreling toward her.

"If you weren't having an affair, why the clandestine meeting?" Bill asked.

Krystal shifted, trying to find a more comfortable position. From the pained look on her face, I doubt she succeeded. "I don't know why this is any of your business," she snapped.

Suddenly she wasn't the only one who was angry. "Listen up, young lady. My dear friend is charged with first-degree murder. She might very well spend the rest of her life in jail for something she didn't do."

Picking up a throw pillow, Krystal wrapped her arms around it. Her lower lip jutted in a pout. "I don't know why you're being so mean to me."

"We're not trying to be mean, Krystal.

We're your friends," Bill said soothingly, assuming the role of good cop to complement my bad-cop role. "We're only trying to get to the bottom of this. Why don't you start by telling us everything you know about Lance Ledeaux?"

She made a pretty picture, I had to admit, sitting on my sofa, dark hair spilling over one shoulder, eyes big and forlorn. Only a hint of a baby bump marred her otherwise knock-'em-dead figure. Again I thought, BBFBBM, body by Fisher, brains by Mattel.

Krystal heaved the sigh of a saint about to be burned at the stake. "Oh, all right."

"You can start," I said briskly, "by telling us how you knew Lance was here in Serenity Cove Estates."

"I ran into a mutual friend in Atlanta. Brent told me he'd heard from Lance, said he was living in — of all places — a retirement community in South Carolina. Brent claimed Lance'd invited him to come over when his play debuted. That was soooo like Lance," she sneered. "He thought he was God's gift to theater. No one in their right mind would not only write the damn play, but produce, direct, and star. Talk about ego! The man had no limits. Anyhow, I thought I'd drop by on my way to Myrtle

Beach, renew acquaintances." She smoothed her skirt. "I heard they were casting roles in one of those fancy productions they put on for tourists. I planned to work there until I started showing and had to quit."

"Go on," I urged. "What happened after you found him?"

"At first, I acted all nice and sweet. Told him how I was down to my last twenty bucks and needed a loan to tide me over."

"Then what happened?" I prompted.

"He refused."

"And . . ."

She shrugged. "And then I had another idea. I told him I was pregnant. He freaked. Next thing I knew, he was offering me money . . . ten grand . . . to leave town and get an abortion. He was supposed to give me the ten G's that night, but . . ."

"He was shot during rehearsal." Bill completed the sentence.

She blinked furiously as though trying to hold back tears. I didn't even see a glimmer of moisture. Apparently when it came to Lance Ledeaux, the emotional well had run dry.

"I'd planned all along to leave town, but I'd never get an abortion. I want this baby, but with Lance dead, I was flat broke. My car broke down. I was desperate. Luckily I found a job at the diner. You know the rest, Kate." She looked at me for confirmation.

Strangely enough I believed her hard-luck story. This wasn't the first time Lance had deserted a woman carrying his child. Good thing for Claudia, she'd been well past menopause — or maybe that wasn't such a good thing. It seemed the rat bastard only deserted pregnant women. With no child in the offing, the no-good scumbag might've hung around forever. I shuddered at the thought.

Bill cleared his throat, the sound snapping me back to the present. "How is it you have a gun and bullets in your drawer? The same caliber that someone substituted for blanks?"

"I dated a cop for a year or so. We used to go target shooting. He gave me the gun for a birthday present." Krystal absently toyed with the binding on the throw pillow where it had come loose. "Ted claimed he worried about me leaving the theater late at night. This way, he said, I could protect myself. And for your information" — she aimed a smug look at me — "a lot of handguns are nine millimeter."

I aimed a look right back. "Did you kill Lance?"

Her eyes widened in shock. "Is that what

this is all about?"

Duh! As I just mentioned, BBFBBM.

"Of course not!" she protested. "How could you even think such a thing?"

"Since you were backstage, you would've overheard Lance's announcement that the scene was going to be rehearsed with props. And . . . that he planned to switch roles with Bernie. It would have taken less than a minute for someone with knowledge of handguns to substitute a live round."

Bill nodded in agreement. "Everyone was busy doing their own thing. No one would've noticed."

Hearing this, Krystal promptly burst into tears. I had no doubt they were real. I also didn't doubt for a second they were meant for her and not for poor dead Lance.

Bill looked at a loss for what to do next. While he dug in his pocket for a handkerchief, I grabbed a handful of tissues from the box on the coffee table and shoved them at her.

"Are you going to tell the sheriff?" She attempted to dam the tears with a crumpled Kleenex. "He might think I came here to blackmail Lance. I know that's a crime, maybe even a serious one."

Blackmail serious? Gee, do you think? I patted her on the back. "Go to bed, Krystal. It's been a long day, and you have to be at work early."

"H-h-how am I supposed to sleep, knowing the two of you hold my fate in the palm of your h-hand?" she blubbered.

Yikes! What melodrama. Krystal induced flashbacks of damsels in distress being tied to the railroad tracks by a mustachioed villain. But I wasn't moved. Krystal was a player, manipulating the situation to her advantage — quite an accomplished little actress. She's the type who'll always land on her own two feet. "Take Tang with you," I told her. "I spotted him prowling around the deck a little while ago."

Bill and I watched as Krystal, sniffling theatrically, collected her shopping bags and headed toward the guest room.

Bill turned to me when the door clicked shut. "Well . . . ? What do you think? Is she telling the truth or not?"

I rested my head back against the sofa. Krystal wasn't the only one tired. It had been a long day for me, too. "I believe Krystal's naive, even devious, but I don't think she's a murderer. If so, why didn't she leave town after Lance was shot?"

Bill chuckled softly. "The fact that her car broke down might have something to do with it?"

I smiled wryly. "Leave it to you to find a gaping hole in my logic." My logic, or lack thereof, seemed to have sprung a lot of leaks these days. Maybe it was time to hang up my detective shingle.

"Glad to be of service."

I tried again to make sense of the night's revelations. "Krystal's pregnant, and Lance possibly is her baby's daddy. Call me sentimental, but I don't think she'd kill the father of her unborn child. Blackmail probably, murder no. And" — I sat up straighter — "if she intended to kill him, she'd have done it *after* he gave her the ten grand — not before."

Bill gave me a smile warm with approval . . . and affection? "Has anyone ever told you, my dear Kate, that you'd make a fine detective?"

"Certainly not Sheriff Wiggins," I said with a tired laugh. "That man might've told me many things, but that definitely didn't make his top ten."

CHAPTER 37

The previous night's dress rehearsal had been a disaster of epic proportion. Think *Titanic*; think *Hindenburg*; think Katrina. Think opening night and sell-out crowd. Translated, think laughingstock. There's good news and bad news about appearing before an auditorium filled with friends and acquaintances, folks you run into in the doctor's office, library, post office, and the Piggly Wiggly. The good news is they'll laugh at the jokes and applaud until their hands sting. The bad news is they'll never let you forget if you make a fool of yourself.

Why had rehearsal been so terrible? Take Gloria, for instance, who was playing the secretary. She kept suffering "senior moments" and exiting stage left instead of stage right and stage right instead of stage left. For my *big* scene, I accidentally brandished a poker instead of a feather duster and nearly gave Gus a concussion. He was very gracious, considering the amount of blood-shed. He insisted he didn't need stitches, but I'm not so sure. And last, but by no means least, Bernie kept missing his cues and muffing his lines while his buddy, Mort, snickered backstage. Bernie lost his cool, not that he has much to begin with, and threatened to punch Mort's lights out. Bill had to physically interject himself between the pair to keep them from coming to blows. Things finally settled down after Eric Olsen reached for his handcuffs and threatened to arrest the two of them.

Krystal Gold, the former Miss Marty Maraschino, was the only one to remain unruffled. She assured us a bad dress rehearsal was a good sign, but I don't think anyone believed her. Good or bad, the show had to go on.

Tonight *Forever, My Darling* would play to a packed house.

Seeing as I was out of bagels, I dropped a couple slices of cinnamon bread in the toaster and shoved down the lever. I suppose I should have felt excited — or nervous. But truthfully I felt . . . depressed. Two viable suspects, and we were still no closer to finding out who wanted Lance dead. I'd tried really hard to persuade myself that Nadine or Krystal could be our perp. But my gut feeling was that while both had fallen prey to Lance's faux charm, I didn't believe either of them capable of murder. Of revenge maybe, even blackmail, but not murder in the first degree. And where did that leave me?

Empty-handed without a single person of interest in sight.

No wonder I was feeling a little down, a bit discouraged. At this point, many people would resort to antidepressants. But I was made of sterner stuff.

When the toast popped up, I slathered it with butter. Typically I use low-fat substitutes, but seeing as how I was depressed, I opted for the real deal. If I didn't watch it, I'd be hauling out rocky road ice cream for breakfast. I poured a second cup of coffee, then went out to collect the morning newspaper — and let out a shriek that could be heard clear across the street.

I'd nearly stepped on a snake. I hate snakes. I loathe and despise snakes. Snakes terrify me. What was the rhyme Rita once told me about how to distinguish poisonous ones from nonpoisonous? It had something to do with colors touching. Red and black or yellow and red? This was one heck of a time to have a senior moment.

As I inched backward, I realized the snake

was either dead or sound asleep. Another observation struck me just then. The snake lay perfectly centered on my welcome mat, coiled as neatly as Great-grandma Elsie's bun; too neatly to be one of Tang's tokens of affection. It was almost as if someone had deliberately placed it there. A shiver raced down my spine. Could this be another warning for me to mind my own business? I shot a final look at the snake. It hadn't budged.

Shuddering, I slammed the door and twisted the dead bolt. If the snake was indeed alive and woke up from its nap on my doorstep, it could slither away. In the event it was dead, I'd worry about disposing of it later — much later.

Between bites of toast and gulps of coffee, I answered the phone, which rang incessantly. Polly asked if I had a mink stole for Krystal to wear in the final scene. Connie Sue was rounding up every bit of blue eyeliner she could get her hands on. Who uses blue? I wondered irritably. Didn't blue eyeliner go out with disco? Pam invited me to go with her and Megan for pedicures. Pedicures were the last thing on my mind. I decided to visit Claudia instead. She could use some cheering up, and maybe in the process, I could cheer myself up as well.

■ ■ ■ ■

The Plexiglas separating us looked as impenetrable as kryptonite. Claudia, if anything, looked even worse than the last time I'd seen her. When this misunderstanding was resolved once and for all, I was going to urge her to book a week at a spa. She desperately was in need of a little pampering — manicure, pedicure, massage, aromatherapy, hydrotherapy, the works.

"Hey," she said, greeting me with a wan smile.

"Hey, yourself."

"You didn't have to come. I know tonight's the big night."

"Thought you might like some company." I mustered a smile of my own. "Besides, it was either visit you or hang around and watch Janine implode."

"That bad, huh?"

"Actually, it's worse, so I came here to get away from all that depressing stuff."

She flung out a hand to encompass the dingy gray-green walls and dung brown floor. "Well, if this place doesn't cheer you up, nothing will."

Claudia's feeble attempt at humor was almost my undoing. We lapsed into an uncomfortable silence. I blamed it on the ambiance. The visitors' room of the county jail was a far cry from the cozy seating arrangement in Claudia's four-season room. No cushy wicker chairs; no droopy ferns — just a droopy prison guard posted inside the door.

Unable to withstand the silence any longer, I resorted to the old standby, "You're looking good." Liar, liar, pants on fire. If anything, Claudia looked used up. Translated, that meant lookin' tired, lookin' old, as if all the spark had been snuffed out.

"Has Judge Blanchard set a trial date yet?" I stuck my hands inside my jacket pockets to avoid contact with the sticky, germy countertop.

"BJ expects her to do that next week or so."

I nodded, unsure if I should rejoice or burst into tears at the news.

She tucked a strawberry-blond-gray-at-the-roots strand behind one ear. "Both my boys insist on coming next week. I tried to talk them out of it, but . . ."

"I'm sure they're worried sick over you. They'll rest easier after meeting your attorney and knowing you're in good hands."

"Bubba had a lawyer friend run a background check on BJ. Wanted to find out how high up the ladder he finished on the bar exams."

Background check? I winced, but Claudia didn't seem to notice.

"Bubba," she continued, "concluded anyone with the nickname Bad Jack gets it for a damn good reason."

Bubba, the Babes and I discovered some months back, is her son, Charles, a vascular surgeon in Chicago. Her other son, whom she refers to as Butch, is an engineer in Seattle. I'm not sure if I've ever heard his given name.

"God, Kate" — she put her head in her hands — "what are my boys going to think seeing their mother behind bars?"

All I wanted to do at that moment was put my arms around her and console her. If anyone was ever in dire need of a hug, it was Claudia. I cast a look in the guard's direction. No help there. He didn't look the type to dispense lollipops to curly-haired toddlers, much less hugs to women charged with murder one.

I tried to distract her by relating everything I'd learned about Nadine Peterson and Krystal Gold. She shook her head when I asked if Lance had ever mentioned either woman.

Our time together wound to a close. I left

with a promise to return soon.

"Tell everyone I said to break a leg," she called over her shoulder.

"And if someone actually did, I'd never forgive myself," I called back.

I left the jail, but I wasn't ready to return home and field calls from the disgruntled — and frazzled — cast and crew of *Forever, My Darling.* I had the niggling feeling there was something I'd overlooked, something still buried. Nadine and Krystal were living proof of Lance's torrid past. Maybe there was more dirt just waiting for the right shovel to come along. Please, Lord, I prayed, make me thy shovel.

I hadn't paid a recent social call on my favorite law-enforcement nemesis. Maybe time had come to rectify the oversight. We could share. And if that failed, due to his shortcomings in the sharing department — not mine — I could always fall back on the old standbys of begging and groveling.

Since my impending visit to the sheriff was more social than official, it called for a hostess gift of some sort. My mother would be so proud I'd carried out the tradition she'd instilled. Sheriff Wiggins was a difficult man to shop for. To complicate matters further, he didn't seem to enjoy presents the way most folks did. That man had a suspicious nature, viewing each little gift as a possible bribe. I knew from past experience he didn't have a sweet tooth, so that ruled out baked goods. The ivy plant I'd once given him had proven a disaster. It had leaked all over his desk, soaking a pile of papers before Tammy Lynn sopped up the mess with a wad of paper towels.

I solved my dilemma with a quick stop at the dollar store. When I first moved to the South, I wouldn't be caught dead shopping in one of these. Now the clerks know me by name. I've added dollar stores to my list of favorites right up there alongside Wal-Mart and Lowe's. All the basics of life can be found in a dollar store for a pittance of the price you'd pay elsewhere. When you're a widow on a fixed income, that's a blessing indeed. There you have it, folks, an unsolicited testimonial from a former disbeliever.

I pawed through a bin of Christmas items marked seventy-five percent off. A Santa windsock, a Frosty the Snowman candle, a pink-haired angel on roller skates. Just as I was diving into the bin headfirst for a snow globe minus its base, I heard a familiar voice.

"Miz McCall, thought that was you."

I straightened to find May Randolph, proprietor of the Koffee Kup, giving me a broad smile. I waved a wicker basket trimmed with a frayed red ribbon at her. "Never know what you might find here."

"You can say that again. By the way, shouldn't you be home getting ready for the big night?" Not waiting for a reply, she continued. "Krystal took off at noon today in order to run through her lines again. Can't wait to see her up on that stage. I was lucky to get one of the last tickets. They sold like hotcakes."

"My friend Janine was thrilled because proceeds benefit Pets in Need, the local Humane Society." I stepped aside to allow a stock boy to pass with a cart loaded with Easter decorations. I absently wondered how Sheriff Wiggins would like a stuffed bunny — no danger of a stuffed bunny springing a leak.

May sorted through the bargain bin, selecting, then discarding various items. "That money oughta put them well on the road toward that new shelter they want to build. Took my grandson out to see the animals at the pens last time he visited. He refused to leave until I said he could have one of those puppies someone abandoned alongside the highway. Let me tell you, my daughter was none too pleased, but she came around after she saw the little bugger.

Cutest thing you ever saw with his floppy ears and big brown eyes." May rejected an antlerless reindeer. "You must be an animal lover, too. Krystal said y'all have a cat."

"Actually, the cat is more Krystal's pet than mine." I felt like such a loser confessing this. I couldn't even befriend a silly stray. Given its choice, the darn cat had picked Krystal over me, the provider of albacore.

"Well, have a good one. Knock 'em dead." She waggled her fingers in what passed for a friendly wave, then wheeled her cart — er, buggy as they're called in the South — down the aisle and rounded a corner.

Between breaking a leg and knocking 'em dead, we were in for a busy night.

I was all set to leave the dollar store empty-handed, when I spotted the perfect gift for a surly sheriff: a words of wisdom desk calendar. It didn't matter that this was already February. There was still ten months' worth of pithy advice. I flipped to a random page and read: *Life ain't no dress rehearsal.*

"You got that right, sista," I muttered aloud, heading for the checkout.

CHAPTER 38

"Hey, Miz McCall."

Unlike the dollar store, where my arrival is greeted with enthusiasm, at the sheriff's office it was another story. I could describe the expression on Tammy Lynn's face only as . . . guarded.

"Is the sheriff in, dear?" I asked, ignoring the fact I was persona non grata. "I promise not to take up much of his time."

Tammy Lynn shoved her glasses higher on the bridge of her nose. "He's real busy, ma'am," she drawled. "You know how he gets when he's disturbed."

"I came prepared to take my chances." That was a polite way of saying I was prepared to brave the lion in his den. "Please tell him I'm here, and I have all afternoon if necessary."

I took a seat in the far corner and tried to look inconspicuous as I shamelessly eavesdropped on the whispered conversation volleyed back and forth between Tammy Lynn and her boss. When Tammy Lynn caught me, she dropped her voice to a whisper. "Sheriff Wiggins will be with you shortly," Tammy Lynn said, her manner prim as a school marm's, then turned her attention back to the computer screen.

To kill time, I riffled through a stack of dog-eared reading material piled haphazardly on a faux walnut table. Magazines such as *All About Beer, Combat Handguns,* and *Truck Trend* had replaced issues of *Southern Living, Better Homes & Gardens,* and *Martha Stewart Living,* which I'd personally delivered. But the real winner, if I were to judge, was one called *Tactical Weapons* — truly motivational reading for felons in training. *Oh, the places you'll go,* if I may quote the late Dr. Seuss.

I idly leafed through *All About Beer* and scanned an article on hops growing in the Pacific Northwest. Bored with fermentation info, I tried to engage Tammy Lynn in conversation. "So, Tammy Lynn, are you coming to our play tonight?"

"I'm fixin' to," she gushed, suddenly animated. "I wouldn't miss it for anythin'. My brother said Eric's been practicin' day and night."

I noted mention of Eric Olsen's name

brought roses to her cheeks. Unfortunately, Eric seemed rather smitten by the perky Megan Warner.

Further talk of either Eric or *Forever, My Darling* was cut short by the angry buzz of the intercom. Tammy Lynn jumped at the sound; her pretty but plain face bore a deer-in-the-headlights expression that quickly changed to apologetic. "Ah, Sheriff Wiggins will see you now."

I gathered my purse and the cute little gift bag, also purchased at the dollar store, took a deep breath, and started down the hall. Along the way, I gave myself a pep talk: I am a mature adult; I will not get flustered; I will not prattle like an idiot.

I forgot all three the instant I encountered Sheriff Sumter Wiggins.

"Miz McCall," he growled in that velvety baritone of his, "what brings you heah?"

"I appreciate your taking the time to see me," I said with a smile. "Brought you a little something."

His handsome dark face didn't crinkle with even a hint of a smile in return. "We've been over this before, Miz McCall. I don't want you bringin' me stuff. Folks might get the wrong impression."

"Nonsense." I waved my hand dismissively. "Who'd get upset over my giving you a cheap little something from the dollar store?"

"You do a lot of your gift shoppin' at the dollar store?"

Without waiting for an invitation, I sat down in the chair across the desk. "It's words of wisdom."

He did that one-eyebrow lift that I often tried to imitate but with less effect. "You insinuatin' I need help in the wisdom department?"

I forged ahead. "The first page I saw when I opened it read, 'Life ain't no dress rehearsal.' Think of how profound that is — not to mention topical."

He looked blank.

"Dress rehearsal . . . get it? Tonight's the play."

"The play, of course. It must've slipped my mind. I beg your pardon, ma'am. My social secretary failed to remind me of the grand occasion."

"No need for sarcasm, Sheriff."

He canted his head to one side, and studied me like a worm under a microscope. I could almost see the gears inside his head turning. I fought the urge to fidget.

"Did you by any chance recall more of the conversation you overheard between Mr. and Missus Ledeaux the night he was

416

murdered?" he finally asked.

"You're not thinking outside the box," I charged. There was something about that phrase that appealed to me. "You've got the wrong person. Claudia's innocent."

Leaning back in his chair, he locked his fingers together over his narrow waist. "That so?"

"Yes, that's so," I said with more spunk than sense. "You're afraid to color outside the lines, to take a chance you might be mistaken."

"Miz McCall, I realize Miz Ledeaux is your friend, and I commend your loyalty, but it's my sworn duty to follow where the evidence leads."

Since he hadn't tossed me out of his office yet, I decided this meeting was going remarkably well. Not trusting my run of luck, I plunged ahead. "Lance was a liar, a cheat, and a deadbeat dad with a penchant for gambling. If you'd thoroughly checked his background, you'd know there are lots — probably dozens — of people who wanted him dead."

"Dozens?" He shook his head sadly. "I must be pretty incompetent to be over-lookin' dozens of suspects."

"Oh, dear," I gasped, realizing how I must've sounded. "I didn't mean . . . I'm sorry if . . ."

Oops! This conversation had taken a decided turn for the worse. First, I acknowledged buying him cheap gifts. Next, I suggested he was lacking in the wisdom department. Then, to top it off, I questioned his competency. Good thing the man wasn't the sensitive sort.

"Knowin' how you like to play Nancy Drew, tell me everythin' you found out about the dozens of folks lined up to off Mr. Ledeaux."

That was all the encouragement I needed to launch into an account of what I'd learned about Nadine and Krystal and their relationship with Lance. "But," I concluded, "I don't think either of them killed him. I was just using them as an example of people who *might* want to harm Mr. Ledeaux."

He dropped the casual pose, leaning forward, his huge hands folded on the desk in front of him. "I admire your efforts on behalf of your friend, but it's not up to me to decide whether or not she's guilty of murder. That'll be up to a jury of her peers. Now, if there's nothin' else . . ."

I started to rise, when a thought occurred to me. Maybe I needed to heed my own advice and think outside the box; color outside the lines, so to speak. Whoever killed

Lance had been clever and cunning — a real pro, not a rank amateur.

All this time, I'd conveniently overlooked — or ignored — the fact that there might be a real pro, an honest-to-goodness criminal, in our midst. The time had come to shift the focus of my investigation. If there truly was a cold-blooded murderer in Serenity Cove — and I shuddered at the thought — then I knew where to begin my search.

"Actually, there is one more thing," I said.

Those pitch-black eyes of his rolled heavenward. I thought I heard a groan, but it might have been his chair squeaking.

"It occurred to me that any person living in Serenity Cove Estates or in the vicinity could be the guilty party. All the residents have access to the rec center. It would have been a simple matter to slip in or out. Marietta Perkins admitted to Connie Sue Brody that the place was so busy that night, she had a hard time keeping track of comings and goings."

The sheriff sighed, a sound that started at the soles of his polished size-thirteen oxfords and worked its way up through six feet two inches of muscle and attitude. "I'm sure, Miz McCall, you'll get to the point sooner or later. I'd prefer sooner if it's all the same to you."

I clutched the strap of my shoulder bag like a lifeline — which was exactly what I was trying to cling to in a last-ditch effort to save Claudia. "I wondered if you'd be kind enough, Sheriff, to allow me to look through your old Most Wanted posters. I know it's a long shot, but you can never tell what might turn up."

When he looked undecided, I dangled a carrot. "Besides, that will keep me out of your hair for hours, possibly days or even weeks."

"Sure thing," he said, brightening at the prospect. "I'll have Tammy Lynn set you up in the interrogation room."

Good as his word, the sheriff followed through on his offer. Minutes later I found myself ensconced in the drab and dreary windowless room where I'd been warned about sins of omission.

"Here you go, ma'am." Tammy Lynn plunked an arm-load of dusty binders on the table in front of me.

I eyed the heap with grim determination. I'd no idea how daunting the task would be. It'd keep me busy all right, clear into the next millennium.

"Holler if you need anythin' else," Tammy Lynn said as she departed.

Heaving a sigh that rivaled the sheriff's, I

got down to business. Felons, as I've previously noted, came in all sizes, shapes, and colors. I was happy to discover that the FBI had very thoughtfully had age enhancement done on some but not all of the fugitives. Makeovers are always a hit — even when done at the government's behest. Bald or thinning gray hair, medium build, average height. The social security crowd of felons, I discovered, would seamlessly blend into any retirement community in the country.

My eyes lingered on one photo in particular that looked vaguely familiar, but for the life of me I couldn't think why. Blame it on one of those danged senior moments. It was the caption underneath the picture, however, that really caught my attention. *Loves to leave a calling card, often in the form of a dead animal.* Were dead canaries or snakes considered dead animals? I wondered.

Frowning, I drummed my fingertips against the tabletop and played Place the Face, but without success. I read, then reread the man's bio. Guido, or whatever name he went by, was the reputed right-hand man of Bennie "the Thumb" Sisserone, a big-time Vegas mobster. According to the information on the poster, Guido was wanted for his role in connection with organized crime. Racketeering and extortion might have been mentioned, but played second fiddle to fifteen counts of murder. He was definitely not the type you'd want as a next-door neighbor.

I sneezed as I flipped through yet another binder and wished for the umpteenth time I'd taken an allergy pill. But at least, I consoled myself, I was doing something constructive.

I lost track of time until Tammy Lynn poked her head in the door. "Can I get you anythin', Miz McCall, before I leave for the day?"

"Leave for the day?" A glance at my watch had me slamming binders shut. "I didn't realize the time. Janine will kill me if I'm late."

"Here, let me help."

Between the two of us, we collected all the binders and stacked them on storeroom shelves. "I'll be back Monday to go through the rest," I told her.

"No problem. Just help yourself. If the interrogation room is in use, I'll clear off part of my desk for you."

"Thanks, honey. You've been a big help."

Tammy Lynn gave me a tentative smile. "Ah, ma'am, when you see Eric tonight, tell him Tammy Lynn Snow said, 'Break a leg.' "

I smiled back. "I'll do just that."

CHAPTER 39

Monica accosted me the instant I stepped foot inside the rec center. "You're late," she scolded. "Janine wanted us here fifteen minutes ago."

"Sorry," I mumbled, making a beeline for the auditorium with Monica nipping at my heels.

"Honestly, Kate, I don't know where your head is sometimes. What could be more important than being on time?"

Pam and Diane stopped setting up a ticket table long enough to wave. "Knock 'em dead," Pam called after me.

I was relieved when Monica scurried off to bust someone else for a minor infraction. As I ran up the stage steps, I spied Bill, looking good with a tool belt slung low on his narrow hips. He was busily making last-minute adjustments to a set he'd built to resemble a drawing room. He must've been inspired by a visit to the Biltmore Estate in

Asheville, because it looked like the real deal. He's got talent, that man.

He gave me a thumbs-up as I passed. "Break a leg."

Connie Sue spotted me as soon as I entered the dressing room. "C'mon, sugar. Let me put some color on those cheeks. You're lookin' a mite peaked." Looping her arm through mine, she guided me toward the mirror, nudged me into a chair, and went to work.

There was enough makeup spread along the counter to stock a department store: wands of lipstick and mascara, pots of blush and eye shadow, brushes, big and little, fat and skinny, foundation in a variety of shades. Then there were hair products, spray, rollers, blow-dryers, curling irons, and flat irons. Connie Sue seemed perfectly at ease amidst all the paraphernalia; her comfort level probably came from her days as a reigning beauty queen.

Polly darted about, adding accessories to various costumes, a scarf here, a brooch there. "Here," she said, presenting me with what at first glance appeared to be a dead skunk.

"Eeuww! What is that?"

"A wig, silly. Found it at the dollar store." Not waiting for a response, she nudged

Connie Sue aside and proceeded to tug the dang thing over my scalp. "This'll go perfect with the orthopedic shoes and support hose."

"Perfect," I muttered in disgust.

"Wait 'til you see what else I found for you." She dangled a contraption before my eyes that might have been used in the Middle Ages to torture heretics.

"What am I supposed to do with it?" I asked, dreading the answer.

"It's a corset," Connie Sue explained. "Meemaw had one just like it that she let us kids use to play dress-up. It'll give your character a nice erect posture."

"You'll look like an authentic housekeeper once I'm finished with you," Polly chortled with glee. "Don't know when I've had this much fun. Probably not since before Gloria made me stop dressing up for Halloween."

While I squirmed into ugly surgical stockings, I cast envious glances at Gloria, who played the secretary to Gus's character, Troy. Except for wearing makeup, which, by the way, looked quite flattering on her, she was dressed in her usual drab polyester pantsuit and a long strand of pearls. Lucky girl, no orthopedic shoes, no support hose, no wig — and no danged corset. I didn't expect Myrna to wear fishnet stockings and a miniskirt, but surely Polly could have found a compromise.

As soon as I was properly outfitted and made-up, I left the chaos in the dressing room to find a quiet spot backstage. It took only a split second to realize a quiet place didn't exist. I blundered right into the middle of an argument between Bert and Ernie. Oops, I meant to say Mort and Bernie. I always confuse the pair with the *Sesame Street* duo.

"You moron, you never listen to me," Bernie shouted. "I'm warning you: Do it that way and you'll blow a fuse."

Mort got right in Bernie's face. "I blow a fuse, all right, every time I hear your bellyaching."

"Only an idiot would take on a job when they don't know beans about what they're doing."

"Butt out." Mort's face was an alarming shade of red. "I know exactly what I'm doing."

Bernie gestured wildly toward a tangle of cords lying in a heap. "Any fool can see you've got too many electrical cords for a single outlet to handle."

"If you don't like the way I'm doing things, do it yourself," Mort sneered. "I quit."

"Gentlemen, please." Rita, looking every bit the stage manager with her headset, caught hold of Mort's arm before he could stalk off. "We need both of you if there's any hope of pulling this off tonight. I'm asking you to put aside your differences and do your job."

I marveled at Rita's composure. She remained unflappable in a sea of chaos; steady as the Rock of Gibraltar. It took a lot to rattle that woman.

"Bernie," she said, draping her arm over his shoulder, "I'd like you to go into the dressing room and help Gus get ready for act one. He needs help with his tie." Now, Rita is a plus-sized gal, standing eye level with Bernie and outweighing him by a lot. She could probably go ten rounds with him without breaking a sweat. I knew that and, from his sheepish expression, Bernie knew it, too.

After Bernie trotted off, Rita turned to Mort. "In spite of what Bernie said, Mort, you're doing a great job with the lights. Why don't you check with Bill and see if he has an extra power strip that might help the fuse situation."

"Sure thing, Rita. A power strip might do the trick."

"And, Mort," Rita called after him, "don't

forget to wear your headset so we can communicate throughout the show if we have to."

The headsets, I'm proud to say, had been Bill's idea. He found just what we needed at Radio Shack. I thought it made our little amateur production look very professional. Lance Ledeaux would've been proud.

From the rising noise level, I could tell the auditorium was starting to fill. When I peeked between a crack in the curtains, my stomach did a flip-flop. Tara and a friend from the day care center, programs in hand, ushered a steady stream of people down the aisle. If Claudia were here, she'd get a kick out of this. The pre-Lance Claudia, that is, not the post-Lance version.

I noticed Nadine Peterson near the front, looking in dire need of a smoke. From a distance she looked quite attractive with her dark hair, bright lipstick, and eerie green eyes. Tammy Lynn Snow, accompanied by a young man bearing a close family resemblance, took their seats in the next row. The young man was most likely her brother and Eric Olsen's friend, I thought.

Polly tugged at my sleeve. "Wait 'til you see Gus. I convinced him to wear a hairpiece. It occurred to me that anyone named Troy ought to have a full head of hair."

"And he went along with the idea?"

She grinned wickedly. "Well, I used a little cajolery. Told him how handsome he looked. Insisted it took ten or fifteen years off his age. Gotta check on Krystal and Megan one last time before the curtain goes up. Break a leg!" she said as she scurried off.

"All right, everyone." Janine, looking arty dressed head to toe in black, motioned us into a huddle. "This is it, the big night. Knock 'em dead."

Rita spoke into her headset to Mort, and the houselights dimmed. The acrobat I seemed to have swallowed executed a series of somersaults and backflips in my stomach. Feather duster in hand, I stepped onto the stage.

By the time we got to act three, I was actually beginning to relax and enjoy myself. So far so good; in spite of numerous invocations, none of us had broken a leg — or even sprained an ankle. I wished my kids were present to witness my glorious stage debut, though I doubted they'd recognize their own mother in the getup I wore. I scarcely recognized myself. I looked more like the Mama character Vicki Lawrence once played in the old Carol Burnett skits than Kate McCall, amateur sleuth. I never thought at my age I'd be bitten by the acting bug. Perhaps I should give up my fantasy of becoming a crime scene investigator and make a career out of playing middle-aged, frumpy housekeepers. After all, life ain't no dress rehearsal.

Both Krystal as Roxanne and Gus as Troy were doing a bang-up job — a couple of pros. I felt nerves flutter anew as the shooting scene drew near. I should have been used to this. It happened every time we got to the part where Claudia shoots Lance. It didn't require much imagination to envision Lance's inert body lying center stage, a bloodred boutonniere on his yellow oxford cloth shirt.

Drawing a deep breath, I entered, announced the arrival of the villain, ably played by Bernie Mason, then exited stage right to watch the rest of the scene unfold. I braced myself for the part where Krystal/ Roxanne tells Bernie's character, *Take that! And that, and that!*

As the tension mounted, I shifted my weight from one foot to the other. Glancing across the stage, I chanced to find Gus Smith watching me, a strange expression on his face. Our eyes happened to meet and a weird thing happened. Maybe it was the brightly striped red and yellow tie he wore that triggered my memory; I'll never know.

But whatever it was, I suddenly remembered the rhyme about the snake.

Red touch black, friend of Jack. Red touching yellow, kill a fellow.

Gus Smith was the snake — a poisonous one at that. I was staring into the face of Guido, "the Killer Pimp," one of the FBI's most wanted. My mind flashed back to the volumes of mug shots I'd stared at for the better part of the afternoon. I now knew why one of the faces had looked so familiar. Even though the man in the photo hadn't been smiling, his lips had been slightly parted — parted just enough to reveal a gap between the top two incisors. It was the exact same gap I was seeing now.

CHAPTER 40

Guido . . . ? I mouthed.

The final piece of the Rubik's Cube clicked into place. Strange as it may sound, viewing the man from a distance brought everything into sharper focus. Admittedly, the stage makeup and hairpiece helped. The time I'd spent examining Most Wanted posters at the sheriff's office and the post office paid off in aces. I was staring at an honest-to-goodness hit man. I was face-to-face with Guido, "the Killer Pimp."

Claudia had admitted Lance had a gambling problem. They'd had to leave Vegas early. What if Lance had gotten in over his head with Bennie, "the Thumb"? What if Bennie had wanted to make an example of Lance and ordered a hit? This made perfect sense. I'd read enough mysteries, seen enough movies, to make the connection.

But the sixty-four-thousand-dollar question remained: Did Guido suspect I was on to him?

I swallowed hard. The man hadn't avoided capture all these years by being stupid. His slitty-eyed, hard-mouthed stare was making me uneasy. I took that look as a yes. He was on to me big-time. I thought of the three a.m. phone call, the canary that used to sing, the snake on my doorstep. Next time he might not be so subtle. I was suddenly terrified. Even surrounded by others, I was no match against a certified killer. My mouth went dry; my heartbeat revved. Was EMS standing by with a defibrillator?

"Psst." Rita poked me in the ribs. "Kate, wake up. You're on."

I gazed at her blankly. "On? On what?"

Janine prodded me toward the stage and whispered, "Was that a shot . . . ?"

A shot? It took me a moment to comprehend what she was saying. It gradually occurred to me she was feeding me my line.

I wandered onto the stage. That's the only way to describe my entrance, considering the stupor I was in. "Was that a shot . . . ?" I mumbled and felt daggers from Rita and Janine in the wings.

Krystal saw me falter, and being the pro she was, picked up the slack. I'm sure more lines followed, but for the life of me I couldn't remember them, so I took the only option open to me — I improvised. "I think I'll bake some cookies," I declared in my best theatrical persona.

From the surprised expressions of my fellow cast members, I sensed cookies had nothing whatsoever to do with the scene. Krystal shot me a dirty look, then valiantly forged onward toward the conclusion. Gloria, Gus/Guido/Troy's secretary, made a premature entrance, no doubt confused by the script change. "W-was that a shot I just heard?" she stammered.

In the wings, I glimpsed Rita's stricken expression as *Forever, My Darling* began to unravel. Janine and Monica looked equally appalled.

At this point Gus/Guido entered and, true to the script, uttered his lines of dialogue proclaiming to an overjoyed Krystal/Roxanne that he hadn't been killed, but only wounded.

"I'll empty the dishwasher," I announced, projecting my voice like Janine had instructed.

Again the glitch, the awkward pause, as the entire cast struggled to incorporate my odd behavior into the context of the play. Only Gus Smith and I seemed to be on the same page — a page invisible to everyone but us.

"You stepped on my lines," Krystal hissed angrily as I exited stage right.

The second I was offstage I ran to find Bill. I found him standing next to Mort at the light board. A jumble of electrical cords covered the floor like vines in an Amazon rain forest. Normally, I have a proclivity for men in tool belts — especially ones with pretty blue eyes — but tonight I ignored my libido. I had other things on the agenda.

Bill looked up when he saw me, his eyes full of concern.

I yanked him aside, not wanting Mort to overhear. "G-Gus," I said, unable to keep the quaver from my voice. "Gus murdered Lance."

He drew me back even farther. "That's a pretty serious charge," he said in a hushed voice. "What makes you so sure?"

"I saw his picture in the sheriff's office — on a Most Wanted poster." My words tumbled over one another in their haste to be said. "He's Guido, 'the Killer Pimp,' hit man for crime boss Bennie 'the Thumb' Sisserone."

"You're certain he's the same man?"

"Yes . . . no, maybe." I wrung my hands, something I'd never done before in my entire life, but there's a time and place for everything. "With the hairpiece, he looks exactly like the guy I saw in the mug shot. He's one and the same, right down to the gap between his front teeth."

Bill raked a hand through his hair. "Jeez, Kate, even if he is this Guido person, why would he kill Lance?"

I latched on to his shirt front with both hands and shook him. "Work with me, Bill! Work with me! I don't have time for lengthy explanations. Guido is on to me. The play is in the last scene before the final curtain. The minute it's over, he's going to split, and we'll never see him again. Claudia will be up a creek without a paddle. We can't let that happen."

Or he could try to silence me for good.

"What do you want me to do?"

I glanced about frantically. There's never a sheriff around when you need one. Then I remembered Eric Olsen. He might not be a flinty-eyed sheriff, but he was law enforcement. Any port in a storm, right? "Eric, where's Eric?"

Bill peered over his shoulder. "Right now he's onstage."

I groaned inwardly. No help from that quarter. This was Eric's big moment, where he confronts Krystal/Roxanne about shooting the villainous Bernie. I made an executive decision. "Call the sheriff. Tell him what I just told you and for him to get out here RN."

"RN?" Bill was clearly perplexed.

"Right now!" I fairly exploded. Sheesh! Were Polly and I the only ones into texting?

I heard a rumble of applause signaling the end of the play. I saw Rita in the wings, pulling the ropes to close the curtain.

"Places, everyone," Janine sang out. "Curtain call."

"Kate, I don't know what's gotten into you," Monica berated me. Grasping my arm, she herded me toward the curtain to take a bow along with the other cast members. Not that I deserved one, but . . .

I caught Gus watching me, and I read his mind like a book. *He knows that I know all right, and he isn't happy about it.*

Janine jabbed me between the shoulder blades. "Take your bow, Kate."

Gloria and I went onstage to take our bows. Even my half-baked performance drew a rousing cheer. Next came Eric and Megan, hand in hand, followed by Bernie. Last, but by no means least, came Krystal and Gus, who drew a standing ovation. There was nothing like a packed house of mostly friends and relatives to boost the morale.

The cast joined hands for a final bow, then stepped back as the curtain closed a final time. Backstage was Ringling Brothers come to town. I tried to spot Bill amidst the confusion and felt a sharp prick in my lower rib cage.

Startled, I turned to find Gus at my side, a phony smile plastered on his face. He slid an arm around my waist. "Keep moving," he growled. "One peep out of you and this knife will wind up in your left ventricle."

I decided it prudent not to argue. The FBI had declared him armed and dangerous, skilled with a knife. This wasn't the time to test the accuracy of their information.

"You can't kill me with all these people around," I said with false bravado. "You'll never get away with it."

He chuckled as if he found my words amusing. Granted, my protest wasn't particularly original, but it's hard to be witty with a knife-wielding hit man holding you captive.

"Keep moving," he said in a low voice as we wound our way through the throng of well-wishers. "When they find your body, everyone will think it's an accident. I'm good when it comes to staging accidents —

some call me a virtuoso."

I saw Bill in a corner, his back partially turned, speaking urgently into his cell phone. From the scowl on his face, I assumed he wasn't having an easy time convincing the sheriff to get his butt out here. And where was Eric? Weren't guns and handcuffs standard police equipment?

As if by magic, Eric came into my line of sight. He stood not far from us, his arm draped over Megan's shoulder, talking and laughing with Tammy Lynn and the young man I took to be her brother.

Guido followed the direction of my glance. "Unless you want to see someone else hurt, don't think of calling for help."

I sucked in a sharp breath at another spurt of pain in my rib cage. For the first time tonight, I was grateful for the boned corset Polly had forced me to wear as part of my costume. Would metal stays deflect the blade of a knife? I hoped I wouldn't learn the answer to that question.

At that precise moment, the lights went out.

"Dammit, Mort," Bernie swore loudly. "How many times do I have to tell you not to overload a circuit?"

"Aw, stuff a sock in it, Mason," came the angry retort.

I used the diversion to break free, twisting sharply to the right, relieved to no longer feel a knife jammed against my ribs. "Help!" I screamed. "Grab Gus. Someone stop him. He killed Lance."

My words galvanized a flurry of activity. I heard banging and crashing coming from every direction. I groped about for a weapon and opted for the only thing at my disposal. "Careful!" I hollered at the top of my lungs. "He's got a knife."

My warning was accompanied by a bone-jarring thud as something heavy hit the floor not far from me, followed by a cry of pain and an expletive I don't care to repeat.

The lights flickered and, just as suddenly as they'd gone out, came back on.

An amazing sight greeted cast and crew. I straddled Guido, "the Killer Pimp," who lay sprawled headlong on the floor, brandishing an orthopedic shoe over his head like a mallet. Gloria stood beside us, her long necklace at the ready like a lasso. Connie Sue and Janine were both on cell phones, ostensibly alerting the authorities. Bill came forward, pointing Eric's gun directly at Guido.

"You can get up now, Kate. I've got him covered."

I slowly levered myself off Gus/Guido. Now that the adrenaline rush had subsided,

I was feeling a bit shaky. Just then a low moan caught my attention. I glanced over to see Eric Olsen, holding his leg and rocking back and forth in agony, caught in a tangle of electrical cords. Tammy Lynn Snow was at his side.

"I told you, you'd trip someone with all these cords lying around," Bernie berated his buddy, Mort. "But do you ever listen . . ."

Satisfied with how the evening had gone, I tuned out their bickering. Not only did we break a leg, but we knocked 'em dead.

CHAPTER 41

"Yoo-hoo, everyone! I'm baaack!" Claudia burst into the room, wearing a grin a mile wide.

Life just didn't get any better, I thought as I gazed around at my friends. The Babes were gathered at Monica's for our bimonthly bunco game. Just that very morning, Badgeley Jack Davenport IV called to inform me that all charges against Claudia had been dropped. BJ, bless his heart, knew how worried we all were about Claudia. Orange was definitely *not* her color. And as we all know, jumpsuits went out of vogue years ago.

The esteemed sheriff, Sumter Wiggins, had also called to confirm the news. Apparently the investigation into Lance Ledeaux's death had been reopened with the capture of Gus Smith, aka Guido, "the Killer Pimp," a frequent flier on the FBI's elite list of crooks and felons. Through FBI contacts —

I'm thinking snitches and bookies and such — it had been discovered Lance was in debt up to his waxed eyebrows to Bennie "the Thumb," a situation the Thumb didn't take lightly. After all, a mobster has nothing without his reputation. Bennie decreed Lance was going to be an example for those who welshed on their debts. It was pay up or else. Gus/Guido was hired to supply the *or else.*

The question remained: Why hadn't Lance repaid Bennie? The Babes and I concurred Lance was a gambler through and through. Some thought Lance bet on Bennie's being unable to catch up with him. I thought Lance craved one more toss of the dice that would result in a big payoff on Super Bowl Sunday. Whatever his reason, he took a chance — and rolled snake eyes.

Sheriff Wiggins confessed the case was practically a slam dunk since the state crime lab in Columbia discovered on the shell casing a partial print that was identified as Gus/Guido's. This hadn't been part of the original investigation, he explained, sounding a tad defensive, since a half-dozen people had witnessed Claudia pull the trigger.

Still another question puzzled me: Why didn't Gus leave Serenity Cove after killing

Lance? Why hang around? Bill had supplied the most plausible explanation. He said Gus had recently joined the ranks of retirees and had been looking for a place to settle down; a place where he could blend in. What better choice for a middle-aged man of average build, slight paunch, and thinning hair to blend into than a retirement community where three-fourths of the male population fit the same description; a place where a golf handicap mattered more than whether you'd been a CEO, ditch digger, or hit man. Who knows? Maybe Gus had unfinished business in Serenity Cove or perhaps he just wanted to bask in anonymity. After all, he thought he was safe here and far too clever for the FBI to ever find. Far be it from me to guess what goes on in the mind of a hit man.

Poor Bill, I thought, smiling to myself. He'd gotten this stricken look on his face when I'd finally gotten around to telling him about my late-night phone call warning me to back off. He shouldered all the blame for letting it slip to Gus during poker that I was hell-bent on finding the real killer. Bill promised to make amends this weekend by taking me out for dinner.

A loud *plop* brought me back to the present with a start. I turned to see Monica

444

holding a foaming bottle of champagne. "This calls for a celebration!" she announced.

"Don't suppose you got a beer?" Nadine shot the refrigerator a hopeful look.

Nadine was subbing one last time before taking off for Tampa. She was filling in for Tara, whose husband, Mark, was home on leave. Rita had sprung for a getaway for the couple at an exclusive B and B in Charleston.

Monica filled flutes with fizzing champagne, then went to the fridge and pulled out a can of Michelob. "Here you go," she said. I didn't miss the covetous glance she gave the tiara perched atop Nadine's head as she handed her the beer.

"I don't think you two have been formally introduced," I said, including both Nadine and Claudia with my statement. "Allow me the honors. Nadine Peterson, meet Claudia Connors Ledeaux. Claudia, meet Nadine. I believe you ladies have a lot in common."

Nadine popped the top of her Michelob and held the can high. "To Lance Ledeaux, the rat bastard."

Claudia raised her champagne flute. "To Lance Ledeaux, scumbag. May the rat-bastard scumbag rest in peace."

"Hear, hear," the Babes echoed.

"Tonight, y'all, down with dieting," Connie Sue proclaimed. "No countin' calories, no talk of fat grams."

"I'll drink to that." Polly, looking bright as a newly minted penny in copper-colored sweats with HOT BABE emblazoned across the front, chinked her glass against Diane's.

"Mother," Gloria said with a sigh, "you'll drink to anything."

I helped myself to a stuffed mushroom and practically drooled. "Mmm." Monica had outdone herself, but I'd always suspected she was a Martha Stewart wannabe.

Diane pointed to a tray of bacon-wrapped chicken nuggets. "If those are good, these are to die for."

Connie Sue sampled one of the chicken nuggets, then rolled her eyes heavenward. "Honey chile, you're goin' to have to cough up the recipe. Thacker's gonna love these babies."

"How's Eric doing, honey?" Janine, out of artistic director mode and back to former nurse, asked Megan. "That broken leg of his healing nicely?"

"He's getting around OK on crutches. Doctor said he'll be on desk duty another month yet."

The bangle bracelets on Gloria's wrist jingled as she reached for a cocktail napkin imprinted with dice. "I bet you've been a big help. The two of you seemed to hit it off."

"Truth is I haven't seen much of Eric since the play," Megan admitted. "Seems like Tammy Lynn Snow's taking real good care of him."

Polly patted her arm. "Don't you worry your pretty little head, dear. There're a lot more fish in the sea. Believe me, I know."

Pam nibbled a stuffed mushroom. "Megan isn't worried, Polly. She and Eric were just good friends. Now maybe she'll have more time to concentrate on her online classes."

"Oh, Mother." Megan rolled her eyes in a gesture similar to one Gloria often uses.

"Well, I'm glad this whole mess with Lance is settled once and for all." Claudia fluffed her new, sassy strawberry blond do. I noticed her nails were freshly manicured and, more important, the sparkle was back in her eyes. "I learned my lesson, but good."

"And that was?" I prompted.

"What happens in Vegas stays in Vegas."

"Amen," we chorused. To my ears, no Baptist choir on Sunday morning ever sounded as sweet.

"Attention, everyone!" I held up my hands for silence. "Besides Claudia's clean slate, we've something else to celebrate." I waited for quiet, then turned to Janine. "The sheriff informed me the FBI offered a fifty-thousand-dollar reward for information leading directly to the arrest of Gus Smith, alias Guido, 'the Killer Pimp,' alias August Smithson, alias A. G. Hanson, etc., etc. Since cast and crew of *Forever, My Darling* were instrumental in his capture, we're entitled to the reward."

"Fifty thousand?" Janine's eyes widened at the amount.

"That's right. I'm happy to report that all of us got together this afternoon and voted to donate the entire sum to Pets in Need for a new animal shelter. After all, if it weren't for you, there never would have been a production — and we might never have found the real killer."

"Or apprehended a dangerous fugitive," added my BFF, Pam.

Janine blinked back tears. "I don't know what to say. . . ."

"I do," Monica interjected before we all got teary eyed. "Ladies, let's play bunco."

We drifted off to find our places. I ended up sharing a table with Claudia, Nadine, and Polly.

"Say, Claudia, I've been wondering," Polly said with elaborate casualness, "Lance Ledeaux? That his real name?"

"Nope." Nadine burped.

We looked at her quizzically.

"His real name was Melvin. Melvin Peterson."

I frowned. "Peterson? But that's —

"Yup, same as mine."

"B-but, but . . . ," Claudia sputtered.

Nadine took a swig of beer. "The two of us never legally divorced. That's the real reason I wanted to track him down. Wanted to finalize the divorce we started years ago so he couldn't get his cotton-pickin' hands on my lottery winnings."

"Well, don't that beat all," Polly murmured.

"My shrink told me I needed closure," Nadine continued. "Guess he was right 'cause the only thing I felt for the bastard after meeting up with him again was pity. Still had his good looks, still had that smarmy charm. Still the same no-good bum. Even after years in Tinseltown, the guy never figured out his kind of talent was a dime a dozen."

Claudia deemed it time for a change of topic. "So, Kate, what's your houseguest up to these days now that the play and rehearsals are over?"

I unwrapped a chocolate truffle — dark chocolate, of course. "Krystal left a note saying the real father of her baby, her true 'soul mate' as she calls him, is out of jail, and they're getting back together. She apologized for any trouble she might have caused but claimed she didn't know what else to do. Apparently, she took up with Lance right after her boyfriend was sent to prison. When she learned Lance had married a wealthy older woman, namely Claudia, she decided to use that to her advantage and make some easy money." I popped the candy into my mouth. "She left this morning and took that darn cat with her."

Monica rang the bell, signaling the start of play.

I plucked an orange cat hair off my woolen slacks. Maybe my next pet will be a dog, I thought as I picked up the dice and let them roll.

ABOUT THE AUTHOR

Gail Oust, a multipublished romance author and former health care professional, recently relocated to South Carolina with her husband of many years. The Bunco Babes mysteries are her first venture into murder and mayhem. Visit her Web site www.gailoust.com.